The
Black Knight

*Also by Connie Mason
in Large Print:*

Lionheart
The Outlaws: Jess
The Outlaws: Rafe
The Outlaws: Sam
The Dragon Lord
The Rogue and the Hellion
To Love a Stranger
To Tame a Renegade
To Tempt a Rogue

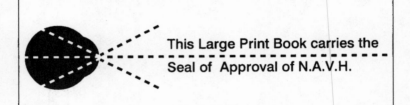

The
Black Knight

Connie Mason

Thorndike Press • Waterville, Maine

ISBN 0-7862-5162-X (lg. print : hc : alk. paper)

To Joe, Matt, James,
Alex, Arron, Nick, and Mason.
May my seven grandsons grow
up to be knights in shining armor.

Prologue

A lad aspires to knighthood.

Wales, 1336

The tall, imposing knight gazed at the strapping ten-year-old lad through cold gray eyes that held little compassion. "Do you know who I am, boy?"

The boy squinted up at the strange knight but did not flinch beneath that flinty, humorless gaze. "Nay, sir."

"Did your mother tell you naught about your father?"

"She said that he is English and did not want her. He married her and then abandoned her. I hate him!" the lad said with fierce vehemence. "Though I have never set eyes upon him, I shall always hate him."

"Hmmm," the tall knight said, stroking his beardless jaw. "Keep that hatred, boy. Nurture it. You will need it to draw upon in the years to come. The world has little use for bastards."

The boy drew himself up proudly, thrust out his square chin in a show of belligerence and declared, "I am no bastard, sir! Granny Nola said my father and mother were married by a priest in the village church, and she does not lie."

"You will have a hard time proving that, boy," the knight said harshly. " 'Tis best to lose those fanciful notions if you are to survive."

"Why do you care?" the lad challenged. "Who are you?"

"I understand your mother named you Drake," the knight said, ignoring the lad's questions. "She chose well. It means dragon. 'Tis a good name. You will do well to remember the meaning and live up to the promise."

Drake glanced over his shoulder at the shack he shared with Granny Nola and saw her standing in the doorway, anxiously wringing her hands. She looked frightened. Did the English knight mean them harm?

The knight continued to stare at Drake, as if trying to decide something of great import.

"What are you staring at?" Drake demanded boldly. "Who are you and what do you want with me and Granny?"

"I am Basil of Eyre, your father."

8

"Nay!" Drake denied, backing away. "Go away! I do not need you! I hate you!"

Basil clamped a hand on Drake's rigid shoulder. "There is a lot of anger in you, lad, but that is not a bad thing. You are going to have to fight every step of the way if you are to get along in life. Do you understand what I am saying?"

Drake shook his head.

"You will learn," Basil said. "How did your mother die?"

"Why do you care?"

Basil cuffed him on the head. "Do not speak thus to me. How did Leta die?"

"Fever took her. We were all ill, but only Mama died. She was the weakest."

Basil's face softened for a brief moment. "A pity," he muttered. Then his expression returned to its harsh lines. "Do you know why I am here?"

"Nay, and I do not care. Leave me and Granny alone. We do not need you."

"Methinks Lord Nyle will soon teach you manners. I was visiting Nyle of Chirk when I met your mother, you know. I was but a lad of eighteen and loved to hunt. Nyle's land marches along the border and we crossed into Wales to hunt boar. I came upon Leta picking berries in the woods. But that is neither here nor there," he said dismissively. "You are to pack your belongings and come with me."

Drake's chin wobbled despite his bravado. "And leave Granny? Nay, I will go nowhere with you. I do not care who you are."

"You *will* leave," Basil insisted.

"How did you find out about Mama? Who told you she died?"

"Years ago I asked Nyle of Chirk to keep me informed of your welfare. His spies reported to him regularly. They informed him of your mother's death, and Nyle sent word to me."

Drake's silver eyes, so like his father's, shimmered with unrelenting hatred. "Why? You never wanted us."

" 'Tis complicated," Basil explained. "My father had already betrothed me to Elise of Leister and would not allow me to break the betrothal. I have a wife, and a son a few months younger than you. 'Tis all you need to know. Go now and pack your belongings."

"Where are you taking me?"

"To Castle Chirk. Waldo, my son and heir, is fostered with Nyle of Chirk. In a few years he will become a knight, and you will be trained to become his squire."

Drake gave his head a vigorous shake. "Nay, I want to be a knight!"

"Bastards do not become knights."

"I *will* be a knight," Drake declared with the kind of determination rare in a ten-year-old boy.

"Retain that tenacity, boy; you are going to need it."

Chapter One

Love gives a knight courage.

Castle Chirk, 1343

Raven of Chirk cornered him in an alcove off the great hall. She had asked him to meet her after vespers to discuss something of great import. Seventeen-year-old Drake No Name, as he was cruelly dubbed by his half brother, Waldo, was ill prepared for Raven's startling request.

"Kiss me, Drake."

Drake gave Raven a teasing smile and easily held Nyle's irrepressible twelve-year-old daughter at bay.

"You know I cannot. You are betrothed to Aric of Flint," Drake reminded her. "Boldness does not become you, Raven."

"I will not wed Aric!" Raven declared with all the vehemence she could muster. "I want to marry you. Do you not like me even a little, Drake?"

"Aye, Raven, but you know 'tis your sister I love. Daria is everything to me."

12

"Daria is promised to Waldo," Raven declared.

Drake lowered his voice. "Can you keep a secret?" Raven nodded, her green eyes wide with curiosity.

"Daria and I are going to run away together," he confided.

"Nay! You cannot," Raven cried, aghast. "Daria is but toying with you. She would never marry a man with neither land nor wealth to his name. She is but fourteen, and fickle. She does not love you as I do."

An angry glow darkened Drake's silver eyes. "You are but twelve, and wildly imaginative if you hope to marry me."

She stamped her foot. "I am not imaginative! Daria is not the one for you."

"What right do you have to tell me who is the one for me?"

"Father would never allow it. You are naught but a squire in training. Waldo will earn his spurs soon and is heir to an earldom."

"You need not remind me that I am a bastard," Drake said angrily. "Waldo has reminded me of my low birth and position every day since I arrived at Chirk. We may have the same father, but that is all we have in common. At least Daria doesn't see me in that light."

"I urge you to think carefully before you do anything rash," Raven advised. "Daria is in love with love. She might consider running off with you, but to her it will be naught but a great adventure. Trust me when I say she will be relieved when Father finds her and brings her home. You will be the one he punishes."

At seventeen, Drake was his own man, had been since he had arrived at Castle Chirk. He had few friends among the other lads in training to become squires. And those slated for knighthood had no time for Drake No Name. He was taunted mercilessly by Waldo, Duff of Chirk, Lord Nyle's son, and their friends, and had learned at an early age to defend himself against bullies.

At the age of fifteen Drake had fallen hopelessly in love with Daria of Chirk, and had every reason to believe she returned his affections.

"You are wrong about Daria, Raven," Drake replied with asperity. "She loves me. Waldo can find another heiress to wed."

Raven sighed unhappily. Drake was the one wrong about Daria. She might let Drake steal kisses, and even encourage him to believe she would elope with him, but she would never, ever marry against her fa-

14

ther's wishes. Raven, on the other hand, would defy the devil himself to earn Drake's love. Raven knew her sister well. Drake was a handsome lad. Daria enjoyed Drake's attention but she would never marry him. She was slated to become a countess one day and would do naught to damage the betrothal between herself and Waldo. Why could Drake not see that?

Just then Waldo and Duff poked their heads into the alcove where Raven and Drake were conversing.

"What are you two doing in here?" Duff asked suspiciously. "Are you trying to seduce my sister, Drake No Name?"

"Sir Bastard is always aiming for something he cannot have," Waldo said with a sneer.

Unlike Drake, who closely resembled his father, Waldo looked nothing like Basil. He was large for his sixteen years, with the kind of bulk that would turn to fat in later years. He was blond where Drake was dark, and his eyes were pale blue instead of mesmerizing silver. He was not unhandsome, but there was something inside him that was ugly. Drake had borne the brunt of Waldo's hatred from the day they first met seven years before.

"I was the one who asked Drake to meet

me here," Raven freely admitted. "We were merely talking. Drake is my friend."

"Next time, talk where you are in plain view," Duff advised. "If Father even suspected that Drake was trying to seduce his daughter, he would banish Drake from Castle Chirk, or worse."

"I told you —"

Drake pushed Raven aside. "I do not seduce children, nor do I need you to defend me, Raven. I am perfectly capable of fighting my own battles."

Waldo stepped forward, his florid face more flushed than usual. It was obvious he had imbibed too freely of the ale served at the evening meal.

Waldo shoved his face forward until he was nose-to-nose with Drake. "Heed me well, Sir Bastard," he said, assaulting Drake with the offensive stench of sour ale. "You are naught but a squire in training. Speaking disrespectfully to your betters will earn Lord Nyle's wrath. You are a bastard; never forget it."

Drake's expression turned stony, giving mute testimony to the bitterness buried deep within him. "You will not let me forget," he bit out. "Heed me well, Waldo of Eyre — someday Drake No Name will have a name and prove his worth."

"As a squire?" Duff challenged.

"As a knight," Drake said with conviction.

"I believe him," Raven said in Drake's defense.

"Go to bed, sister," Duff ordered. "You are an impertinent wench and it does not become you. What would Aric of Flint say if he knew you were flirting behind his back?"

Duff, only son of Nyle of Chirk, was a square youth with a sturdy body and small mind. He was a follower, not a leader. Despite being three years older than Waldo, Duff followed Waldo's lead like a puppet on a string. When he saw how much Waldo despised his half brother, he was quick to treat Drake in the same despicable manner as Waldo.

Nyle of Chirk was gone most of the time, fighting King Edward's wars, and when he was home he did nothing to stop Waldo and Duff from verbally and physically abusing Drake. In fact, he never even noticed. It was Nyle's two lovely daughters who favored Drake with their attention.

At seventeen, Drake was a well-proportioned young man, blessed with a handsome face, a muscular though somewhat lanky build, and mesmerizing silver eyes. He had left puberty behind early and had caught the eye of every likely maiden who crossed his path. But Drake cared only for Daria, the woman he planned to wed. Raven was comely enough, though she lacked Daria's ethereal beauty, but she was far too bold and outspoken for Drake's tastes. In Drake's opinion, Daria would be wasted on Waldo.

Raven sent Duff a quelling glance. "I do not care what Father says; I will not marry Aric." Then she flounced off, her long chestnut hair bouncing against her rump, despite the veil and circlet meant to keep it restrained.

"I do not envy Aric," Waldo said, though his eyes belied his words as he stared after Raven with barely concealed lust. "Taming Raven will be no easy task."

"You made a wise choice with Daria," Duff said approvingly. "She is sweet and docile."

"Still," Waldo mused as he watched Raven walk away, "a little spirit in a woman is not a bad thing. Were Raven mine, she would buckle under authority soon enough. Taming her would give me a great deal of pleasure."

"You are but sixteen," Drake scoffed. "What do you know about taming a woman? Or pleasuring one?"

"More than you, Sir Bastard."

Drake's mouth thinned. He hated that name. Waldo had dubbed him Sir Bastard the day he arrived at Castle Chirk and boldly announced that one day he would become a knight. Of course Waldo had laughed at him, and from that day forward Waldo and Duff called him Sir Bastard or Drake No Name.

"Have you naught to say, Sir Bastard? Have you ever had a woman? Or does the code of honor you follow prevent you from enjoying a woman's body?"

"I will be pure for my wife when I marry," Drake replied, thinking of Daria and how much he enjoyed kissing her. But that was all he had allowed himself.

"Only fools adhere to so strict a code of honor," Waldo chided. "Women are to be enjoyed. Some priests teach that they have no souls. They say that if a woman refuses to submit to a man's will, she should be beaten into submission. I may be sixteen but I have learned to enjoy women in the way God meant them to be enjoyed. When they displease me, I know how to make them repentant. Do you not agree, Duff?"

Duff swallowed visibly. "Well, aye, but I would not wish to see either of my sisters mistreated."

"I will kill the man who hurts Daria," Drake threatened, staring steadfastly into Waldo's pale eyes.

Waldo laughed but took a step backward nevertheless. "So 'tis Daria you lust after," he said. "Leave my betrothed alone, Sir Bastard. 'Tis I who will take her maidenhead on our wedding night. Remember that."

"There is much I will remember," Drake bit out.

"Come, Duff, there are two comely maidens awaiting us in the village. Perhaps we can find a haystack to tumble them in."

Drake watched them leave, his eyes narrowed in hatred. He could not allow Daria to wed Waldo. Waldo did not abide by the chivalric code. He dishonored all women. As a child Waldo had been a bully, but as he left childhood behind his viciousness became more pronounced. Drake might not be a knight, but he adhered to the chivalric code, and he doubted Waldo would ever be a knight in the true sense of the word.

A true knight honored women.

A week later Drake saw Daria enter the mews alone and followed, eager for a private word with her. Drake had been riding

20

at quintain all day and was hot and tired, but when he saw where Daria was headed, he quickly followed.

He spoke her name quietly.

Daria turned, smiling when she saw Drake. "I saw you at the quintain and hoped you would follow," she said coyly as she stretched up to plant a sweet kiss on his lips. "I came to check on my favorite falcon. He was injured by a hawk yesterday."

Drake cared not about the falcon. He wanted to pull Daria into his arms and press her length against him, but he held himself in check. Though his seventeen-year-old body ached to experience love, no one but Daria would do, and he refused to dishonor her. "Your father returned today," he said.

"Aye. Plans are afoot to marry me to Waldo soon. I am nearly fifteen and Waldo is pressing Father to name a date."

"Is that what you want?"

She shrugged and lowered her eyes. "I must obey Father's wishes."

Drake grasped her narrow shoulders. "Nay, you cannot marry Waldo. You do not know what he is like."

Daria's hazel eyes sparkled with mischief, something Drake would have noticed had he not been so besotted.

"There is naught I can do," Daria said helplessly.

Drake pulled her closer, though he was careful not to let her touch the hardened place on his body that plagued him mercilessly. "We can elope," he said earnestly. "We have already discussed it. After we are wed, I will protect you with my life." When he saw her eyes widen, he added, "Do not look so shocked; many before us have fled their families to wed."

"I know, but . . . well, I never thought you were serious about eloping."

"I love you, Daria. Surely you know that by now. You are fourteen, nearly fifteen, old enough to marry, and I am seventeen, old enough to protect you."

"Hark, I hear something," Daria warned, turning toward the door.

" 'Tis naught," Drake said dismissively. "Heed me, my love. Meet me tonight at the postern gate. I will take two horses from the stables to carry us away. Bring naught but a change of clothing."

"Elope," Daria said, suddenly skittish. "But I did not mean . . . That is . . . Are you sure 'tis the right thing to do?"

"Do you love me, Daria?"

"Oh, aye, how can I not? You are handsome and brave, and so chivalrous."

"Then meet me at the postern gate after matins. Do not keep me waiting." Then he kissed her hard and strode away.

Daria stared after him, her brow wrinkled in consternation. The flirtation with Drake had been fun and slightly naughty, but Daria had always known she was meant to be a countess. Waldo might not be her idea of a perfect husband, but he possessed everything she wanted in life. Though Drake was handsome and brave and chivalrous, he was bastard born and had neither property nor wealth to his name. Still, it *would* be an adventure to elope with Drake, she thought dreamily. She knew her father and Waldo would find her, but what fun she would have before buckling down to marriage.

Of course, Daria would not give up to her virginity to Drake, for that belonged to her husband. And she knew Drake would not touch her if she did not wish it. Smiling to herself, she left the mews, her romantic heart fluttering wildly.

Raven waited until Daria had returned to the keep before stepping out from behind a keg where she had hidden herself. Loyalty to her sister and knowledge of Daria's fanciful nature warred within her.

In her heart she knew Daria was not right for Drake. Daria would never marry Drake and give up her chances of becoming a countess. Should she tell her father what Drake and Daria planned? she wondered. Or would it be better to pretend she hadn't overheard the conversation in the mews. At length she decided to confront Daria with what she knew.

"You eavesdropped!" Daria accused when Raven told her exactly what she thought of her plan to elope with Drake.

"Nay, I . . ." Raven gnawed the soft underside of her lip, aware that she could not lie to Daria. "Oh, very well, I admit I followed Drake to the mews."

"You want him for yourself," Daria charged.

"It would not matter if I did. Drake wants only you."

Daria preened for Raven's benefit. "He said he loves me."

"I cannot believe you are actually going to elope. 'Tis not like you, Daria. Methinks you are toying with Drake."

"So what if I am? If Drake had a title and lands, I would elope with him in a trice. He is better-looking than Waldo and has a much nicer disposition. But alas,

Drake No Name has little to commend him besides his pleasing face and body."

"So you are not going to elope," Raven said with relief. "Have you told Drake yet?"

"Nay, I will tell him tonight when I meet him at the postern gate. Mayhap Waldo will treat me in a more knightly fashion when he learns I intend to elope with Drake."

Raven's green eyes narrowed. "How will Waldo find out?"

"He will know," Daria confided.

"But . . . how?"

"I have things to do," Daria said dismissively. "We will speak of this later."

Infuriated by her sister's lack of feeling for Drake, Raven decided to seek him out and tell him that Daria had no intention of eloping with him. She managed to have a private word with him when she followed him outside after the evening meal.

"Drake," she called softly.

Drake stopped, peered through the darkness, and saw Raven lurking in the shadow of the keep. "Raven, is that you?"

"Aye. A word with you, please, Drake."

"Very well, but make it quick. I have preparations to make."

"That is what I wish to discuss. I know

you are planning to elope with Daria to-night. You are making a grave mistake, Drake. Daria has no intention of eloping with you."

Drake's youthful face hardened and his silver eyes took on an ominous sheen, giving a hint of the darkness inside him waiting to be unleashed.

"Do not try to dissuade me, Raven. Lying does not become you."

" 'Tis true, I tell you. Daria is using you to make Waldo jealous. Do not meet her tonight. I have a terrible feeling about the outcome."

"Go away, Raven. Your concern is mis-placed."

"I will tell Father!" Raven blurted out.

Drake took a threatening step in her di-rection and Raven shuddered. She'd never seen this side of Drake. His fists were clenched at his sides and his chin jutted out pugnaciously. His expression was hard, implacable. All his enmity was directed at her, and for the first time since she'd known him, she was frightened.

Without waiting to see what he intended, she turned and fled. This was a Drake Raven did not know. Did he not realize she would never betray him? She merely wanted to warn him, to let him know he courted danger. She loved her sister dearly, but she knew Daria's sights were set much higher than a landless bastard. She might enjoy her flirtation with Drake, but it was Waldo she intended to marry. Despite Drake's harsh words to her, Raven fully intended to hide herself by the postern gate tonight and do what she could to stop this folly.

Drake paced impatiently before the vine-covered postern gate. Daria was late. The horses he'd taken from the stables were safely hobbled in a wooded area beyond the outer walls; he had taken the utmost precautions to conceal their departure. He heard a voice and his senses sharpened. He whirled and suddenly she was standing beside him. Impulsively he pulled her into his arms and kissed her.

"I feared you had changed your mind," he whispered. "Are you ready? Where is your bundle?"

Daria darted a furtive glance behind her. "I . . . well, I . . . forgot."

"Never mind. I have been lucky at jousting and managed to save a few coins. We can purchase what you need later." He grasped her hand. "Come, 'tis time to leave."

Suddenly the sound of pounding feet echoed through the darkness. Drake whirled, stunned to see men advancing toward them with rushlight torches. Reacting spontaneously, he grasped Daria's hand and tried to pull her through the gate. Then someone ordered him to halt. Lord Nyle.

Moments later he was surrounded by Nyle, Waldo, Duff, and several men-at-arms. From the corner of his eye he saw Raven pop up from the shadows and he knew exactly what had happened. Raven had told her father.

Raw, searing hatred welled up inside him. Betrayed by a jealous woman. Nay, by a vindictive child who thought she was a woman. It was a lesson well learned. One he would never forget — nor forgive. Until his dying day he would remember that Raven of Chirk had betrayed him. He watched dispassionately as Waldo tore Daria, his one true love, from his arms and thrust her toward her brother.

"You have betrayed my trust, Drake No Name," Lord Nyle charged. "I could have you slain for dishonoring my daughter, or at the very least flogged. But because of the friendship I bear your father, I will be lenient."

"He does not deserve leniency," Waldo cried.

Drake saw Raven edging closer to him and he sent her a hostile look. He felt grim satisfaction when he saw her flinch. If he could get his hands on her she would do more than flinch, he thought bleakly. It would bring him great pleasure to see her stretched out on a rack before him, begging for mercy he would refuse.

Dragging his thoughts away from the traitorous Raven, he concentrated on Lord Nyle's words.

"As punishment, you will be banished from Chirk. You are seventeen, neither a knight nor a squire. Finding your own way in life without my patronage will not be easy, but I cannot forgive you for making free with my daughter. Daria is betrothed to Waldo of Eyre, if he will still have her."

Drake's tall, lanky frame stiffened with pride. "I did not make free with your daughter, Lord Nyle. We did naught but exchange a chaste kiss or two. I would never dishonor her."

"Well said, Drake, but 'tis of no consequence. You are no longer welcome in my home or on my lands. Go now, before I change my mind and have you thrown into the dungeon for the duration of your life."

"Know you that I will still have Daria," Waldo taunted Drake. "She was never yours to claim. 'Tis my bed she will occupy, my children she will bear. Carry that thought with you, Sir Bastard."

Having passed judgment, Lord Nyle grasped Daria's arm and dragged her away. Everyone else followed in his wake. This is the bleakest moment of my life, Drake thought as he stood alone in the darkness. Not only had he lost his home, but the love of his life. And all because of a jealous girl. Raven's betrayal had cost him everything.

As if reading his thoughts, Raven stepped from the shadows. "I did not betray you, Drake, honestly," she softly pleaded. "I cannot bear your hatred."

"You will bear it till the day you die," Drake vowed. "I will never forgive you, Raven of Chirk. Why did you do it? I thought we were friends."

"We were! We are! Pray listen to me, Drake. I would never hurt you. I love you."

His answer was a derisive snort. But he did not need to speak; his black look was more potent than words. He would not believe her no matter how emphatically she denied her guilt. He opened the gate and stepped through.

"Where are you going?"

"Does it matter?"

"Aye. Will I ever see you again?"

"Not if I can help it."

Then he was gone, melting into the darkness until not even his shadow was visible. Raven closed the gate, sobbing as only a twelve-year-old with a broken heart could sob.

Drake's mood lightened somewhat when he saw that the horses he had hidden in the woods were still hobbled where he had left them. One was the horse his father had given him and the other was a palfrey from Lord Nyle's stables. Drake felt no guilt over taking the prize mare. In fact, he felt quite pleased with himself for having had the foresight to choose so valuable an animal. Besides the horses, he had food to last several days, the coins he had earned jousting with the other squires, and his clothing. He would sell the spare horse and seek his fortune. Men had managed to survive on much less than he had.

If not for losing the woman he loved, Drake would consider himself lucky. He was young, healthy, and stronger than any of the other squires in training. He could survive on hatred alone, if he had to.

One day, he vowed, Drake No Name would have both name and lands. And mayhap he would emulate Waldo when it came to women. He would seek women simply for pleasure and naught else. Aye, 'tis what I will do, he vowed. He had learned his lesson well. Love hurt and he should avoid it at all costs. Never again would he allow himself to become vulnerable. Henceforth, he would follow his head instead of his heart, and avoid women like Raven of Chirk.

Chapter Two

A knight fights to acquire lands and title.

Castle Chirk, 1355

He rode across the outer bailey on his pure black destrier. Raven watched him from the window of her bedchamber. A bearer carried his banner, a red dragon emblazoned upon a field of black.

The Black Knight.

He was magnificent and frightening at the same time, Raven thought, leaning over the embrasure so she could see more of him. Clad in unrelieved black from his gleaming helm to the tip of his toes, he rode into the bailey at the head of a contingent of knights and men-at-arms in his service.

Jongleurs and harpers who visited Chirk to entertain the lord and his household spun glowing tales of the Black Knight's exploits. They told how he had saved the Black Prince's life and was knighted upon the battlefield by the king. They praised his courage, his strength, his amorous conquests. If he had a name, none remembered, for he had been called the Black Knight from the time he became the Black Prince's champion and appeared on the battlefield clad all in black like his prince.

Raven of Chirk was amply impressed by the Black Knight's stature and bearing. He sat his destrier proudly, even arrogantly, as he rode through the portcullis and into the inner bailey. Raven was startled when he lifted his head and stared directly at her window. She quickly stepped back, but not so far that she could not see him. Had he seen her? It mattered not. To the best of her knowledge, she had never met the legendary Black Knight.

Raven had heard so much about the mysterious Black Knight that she could not help being more than a little intrigued by the man. Today, however, was not a good time to admire strangers.

After the games ended, she was to be married to Lord Waldo, Earl of Eyre. She had but four short days left in which to escape this travesty of a marriage. Though she had cried and pleaded, Duff would not be swayed. Several years ago she had lost her mother and father to a virulent fever that had spread death and pestilence across the land. Had they lived, Raven knew they would not have forced her to wed Waldo, not after what had happened to her poor sister.

Dead at sixteen, married but a few months, Daria had died of a strange stomach ailment shortly after Lord Basil had been killed by poachers. But Raven could not relieve herself of the notion that Waldo had been responsible for Daria's untimely death. Then Duff, Waldo, and Aric had gone to France to fight with the king's army. Unfortunately Aric had been killed in battle at Crécy.

When Waldo returned from France, he asked Duff's permission to marry Raven. Duff gave his consent, but only if Waldo obtained a dispensation from the pope, for to wed one's sister-in-law was considered incest.

The dispensation arrived four long years later, and Duff had betrothed her to Waldo. During those four years Raven had seen little of Waldo, enjoying a peaceful time of virtual freedom, doing as she wished, whether it was riding the hills and moors on her favorite palfrey or making decisions that affected the inhabitants of the castle and village. Now her wedding day was at hand.

Raven descended the winding stone staircase to the hall and walked outside, crossing the inner bailey to the kitchen. As lady of the keep, it was her duty to check on food preparations for tonight's banquet, given especially to welcome the knights who had arrived to compete in the tournaments Duff planned as part of the wedding festivities. Knights from all corners of the kingdom had converged on Chirk to compete in the games and partake of the abundant food and drink offered by the lord of the castle. After the tournaments, they were all invited to celebrate the marriage of Raven of Chirk and Waldo of Eyre.

Raven would soon be a countess, a title she had never aspired to. She hated Waldo and wondered how she could submit her body willingly to a man she detested.

"Raven, wait!"

Raven stopped to allow her maid to catch up to her.

"Are you not excited? I cannot wait to see what the Black Knight looks like."

"I saw him when he rode in, Thelma," Raven confided. "He is just another man aspiring to greatness."

"Oh, but he *is* great," Thelma gushed. "They say he was knighted on the battlefield by King Edward himself for saving the life of the Black Prince. When he saved the prince a second time, the king gave him a title and an estate."

"So I have heard. He is now Earl of Windhurst. I heard his estate is a crumbling fortress built on a bleak cliff overlooking the southern coast many leagues away in Wessex. It has been unoccupied far longer than I have been alive. I doubt the impoverished knight can afford to repair the crumbling hulk, much less hire men to defend it."

"How do you know he is impoverished?" Thelma asked.

"I do not, really; 'tis just a guess."

"Oh, here comes Lord Waldo. He probably wishes a private word with you before the banquet tonight," Thelma said, scurrying off to join a group of servants at the well.

Raven's distaste was obvious as she waited for Waldo to reach her. He was a hulking bear of a man with a barrel chest and short, sturdy legs. He was not overly tall, or excessively fat, but his square frame exuded strength and authority.

"Did you wish to speak with me, my lord?"

"Aye," Waldo said. "There has been little time for us to talk since I returned to

Chirk for the tourney and wedding ceremony. Soon you will be mine, Raven of Chirk. I have waited a long time for you. I married Daria to please your father, and for her dowry, but 'tis you I wanted, you I desired. I was pleased when Aric of Flint died and freed you to marry me. I persuaded Duff not to betroth you to another during the years the pope considered my petition asking for permission to wed you. You have to admit I was more patient than most, Raven."

Raven stiffened. "You know this marriage is not to my liking. 'Tis not right. 'Tis incest to marry your dead wife's sister."

"I waited many years for a dispensation from the pope," Waldo said harshly. "You are well past the age when most girls marry, but I still find you desirable. I will not be denied, Raven of Chirk."

Raven flinched as he lifted a bright tendril of chestnut-colored hair from her shoulder and let it trail through his fingers. " 'Tis like living fire, just like you, Raven. Not pallid and lifeless like Daria. You would not lie beneath me like a log, with a long-suffering look on your face. Even if you do not like me, you will be more animated than Daria." He leered at her.

"Mayhap it is good that you do not like me. A little spirit in a woman is not a bad thing."

Raven bristled angrily. "How dare you speak of Daria in such an insulting manner! My sister is dead; she deserved better than you."

"Mayhap you would prefer a man like the Black Knight."

"Mayhap I would," Raven responded angrily. "Anyone would be better than you."

Waldo grinned. "Your fire, your spirit — 'tis what I like best about you, Raven. Taming you will give me great pleasure. As for the Black Knight, forget him. He devours women. 'Tis said he discards women quickly after he has taken his pleasure of them."

Raven's interest was immediately piqued. "How do you know?"

"We both fought at Crécy, though we never had occasion to meet. He was the Black Prince's champion and protected his back. Duff and I were merely knights fighting in the king's army. But tales of his prowess with the ladies are legendary throughout France and England."

"Have you ever seen him without his helm?"

"Nay, though I have known damsels who

have and vow he is quite handsome, in a dangerous sort of way." He gave her a narrow-eyed look. "Why do you ask? 'Tis not seemly for a bride to think of any man except her betrothed."

"All the servants are talking about the Black Knight, and I was curious. Has he no name?"

"None that I know of." His face hardened, making him almost ugly. "Forget about the Black Knight. Should he unseat all his opponents during the course of the tourney, he will still have to defeat me to win the purse Duff has promised to the champion. No one has ever unseated me," Waldo boasted. "The purse will be mine."

Raven said naught as she took her leave. But deep in her heart she prayed that the Black Knight thoroughly trounced Earl Waldo of Eyre.

The Black Knight had ridden confidently into the inner bailey until something made him glance up at the tower window. Then he'd seen a flash of rich chestnut hair and knew she was watching him. Beneath his black helm his face had hardened and his lips had curled in contempt.

Raven of Chirk.

Just the thought of her elicited painful

memories that years of war and competing in tournaments to earn his livelihood had failed to diminish. He had not known until he arrived that the tourney was part of the festivities celebrating the marriage of Raven of Chirk and Earl Waldo of Eyre, his half brother. Only the reportedly large purse Duff offered to the winner had drawn him back to Chirk, where memories of his lost love still pulled at the place where his heart once dwelled.

Raven of Chirk.

He hated her still, after all these years. Her betrayal had made him what he was today. He had changed overnight from a chivalrous youth who dreamed of becoming a knight and protecting his lady's honor to a hardened knight who had earned his reputation with his sword. After he had been banished from Chirk, the king must have seen promise in him, for he took Drake into his service as a squire. Drake's selfless act of bravery on behalf of the Black Prince had been incredibly foolish but well worth the reward.

Shortly after being knighted he had followed the prince's example and donned black armor. Thus the Black Knight came into existence. It was a far better name than Drake No Name, or Sir Bastard.

As the fighting in France grew increasingly fierce, the Black Knight distinguished himself time and again on the battlefield. Incredibly, he had saved the prince's life a second time and had been given an earldom. Windhurst and its extensive lands were his to claim. After the victory at Crécy, the Black Knight returned to England and earned further glory competing in tourneys and handily defeating every opponent pitted against him. He had earned wealth and prestige, but he intended the tourney at Chirk to be his last. With the promised purse, he would have enough money to restore and defend Windhurst.

Had Drake known that encountering Raven after all these years would arouse feelings he thought he had banished years ago, he would not have come. He knew Daria was dead. He had heard about her death shortly after it occurred and it had been a terrible blow. The life of a tender rose had been plucked before it had reached full bloom. Had not Raven betrayed him, Drake liked to believe that he and Daria would be happily married now, and that she would be alive today. He could not help thinking, though there was no tangible proof, that Waldo had somehow hastened Daria's death.

Something had died within Drake the day he learned of his beloved's death. Ambition had replaced unrequited love. Earning wealth and glory had become the code by which he lived. Ruthlessness and arrogance were his to claim. Where once he cherished womanhood, he now saw women as vessels of pleasure put on earth to ease men's lust. But one thing had not changed: his consuming hatred for Waldo of Eyre and Raven of Chirk.

The Black Knight tore his thoughts away from the past to greet Sir Melvin, Chirk's steward.

"Good morrow, sir. I am Sir Melvin, Lord Duff's steward. Welcome to Castle Chirk."

The Black Knight acknowledged Sir Melvin with a nod and waited for him to continue.

"The knights who have come to compete in the tournaments are camped beyond the walls with their servants and men-at-arms. Tents have been provided for your use and all are invited to dine in the great hall. Does that meet with your approval, my lord?"

"Your hospitality is greatly appreciated. My men and I will most happily share your table."

Formalities dispensed with, Sir Melvin turned away to greet another group of knights who had just entered the bailey. After the steward left, a knight in Drake's service rode up to join him. Sir John of Marlow pushed back his visor and looked at Drake askance. "Are we to set up camp beyond the gates, Drake?"

"Aye, John. Tents are being provided for us. Choose a likely site beside water, if possible. I will join you and the men directly. There is something I must do first."

A worried frown marred Sir John's handsome young features. "I know you do not like your half brother but do not, I beseech you, do anything foolish." Then he wheeled his destrier and left Drake to his morose thoughts.

Drake raised his visor and stared at the keep from which he had been banished twelve years before. Little had changed during the intervening years. He had not seen Waldo since he'd left and even now felt no compulsion to look upon his brother's face. The only reason he intended to seek out Waldo was to let him know the identity of the man who would unseat him in the tournament and win the purse.

Drake's destrier danced beneath him and

he soothed him with soft words. "Be easy, Zeus; tomorrow you will see plenty of action." He removed his helm and dismounted. A lad ran up to take the reins and Drake ruffled his hair. Everything was just as he remembered. People were everywhere — women with bundles under their arms; children herding pigs; carpenters haranguing their apprentices; servants, grooms, and squires going about their duties. Several men-at-arms taking their ease in front of the barracks eyed a comely maidservant drawing water from the well. A dozen buildings nestled against the curtain wall. Stables, smithy, shops for the castle craftsmen, barracks, pantries, and supply sheds. Drake saw Waldo wending his way around an ox cart laden with barrels of wine and lengthened his stride to intercept him.

Waldo gave Drake a passing glance, then took a second, more thorough look. Drake smiled grimly as he watched the color leach from Waldo's face. "God's blood! 'Tis *you!* I thought . . . we all thought you were dead."

Drake's eyes narrowed. "Why would you think that?"

"I . . . you . . ." Sweat popped out on Waldo's forehead. "We heard naught from you in years."

"Mayhap you never wanted to hear from me. As you can see," Drake said dryly, "I am very much alive."

Waldo made a slow perusal of Drake's distinctive black armor, coming to rest on the black helm he carried under his arm.

He staggered backward. "Nay! It cannot be! Not you! You cannot be the celebrated Black Knight, the man whose praises are sung throughout the kingdom. Why did I not know?"

"Perhaps because I did not want you to know."

"But how can it be? How did you accomplish such a feat?"

"Did you not listen to the jongleurs and storytellers?"

Waldo glared at him. "You left here with naught but the clothes on your back. And now you are . . ."

"An earl with lands of my own and knights in my service."

"Windhurst," Waldo said dismissively. " 'Tis naught but a pile of rocks perched atop a barren, windswept cliff."

"Nevertheless, 'tis mine, and so is the title."

"Why are you here? Daria is dead. You have no reason to return to Chirk."

Drake's silver eyes glinted dangerously.

46

"How did Daria die? You were married but a few short months."

" 'Tis water under the bridge, Sir Bastard," Waldo taunted. "Daria is dead and I am to wed Raven."

Drake took a menacing step forward. "What did you call me?"

"You will always be a bastard, no matter how many titles Edward bestows upon you."

"I am no longer a chivalrous lad with stars in my eyes," Drake warned. "My name and reputation have been hard won. I am the Black Knight, Earl of Windhurst by order of the king. If you ever call me Sir Bastard again, or Drake No Name, you will be sorry. I fear no man, Waldo of Eyre. Especially not you."

"Have you come to disrupt the wedding?"

Drake smiled without humor. "Nay. Raven is as treacherous as you are. I wish you joy of her. The two of you deserve one another. My reason for being here is quite simple. I intend to win the tourney and the purse."

Waldo's pale eyes narrowed. "Over my dead body."

Drake shrugged. "That can be arranged easily enough."

Waldo was more dismayed to see his older half brother alive than he let on. Waldo had done things, terrible things, to secure the earldom for himself, and he prayed Drake would never learn of them.

Raven had just left the kitchen when she saw the Black Knight talking to Waldo. He had removed his helm and had his back to her. She craned her neck to get a better look, but all she could see of him was thick black hair shorn to shoulder length, the favored fashion. More than a little curious about the mysterious Black Knight, she maneuvered around the wine cart to get a peek at his face.

A gasp was torn from her throat and she felt as if her lungs were on fire. She had seen that face a hundred, nay, a thousand times in her dreams. And each time his silver eyes spewed hatred at her.

Drake.

She could not begin to count the times she had wished for him to appear so she could explain to him that it had been Daria herself who had made sure her father knew about the elopement so he could stop it. Raven had learned that Daria had told her maid, fully aware that the girl would run straight to Lord Nyle with the tale.

Now he was here. Yet he was not the Drake she remembered from her youth. He was the Black Knight, the man renowned for his courage and strength, for his prowess with women, for his ruthless skill in combat.

The man who hated her.

She knew the moment Drake saw her, for he stiffened. Their gazes locked, held. The dancing silver eyes she remembered were now as cold and hard as the flagstones upon which she stood. She wanted to look away but couldn't. He held her suspended with the potent force of his enmity.

"Drake." Her voice trembled. "Are you truly the Black Knight?"

"Is that so difficult to believe?" Drake asked harshly.

"Aye . . . nay . . . I do not know. You have changed."

His mirthless laughter sent chills racing down her spine. "Aye, I am no longer the idealistic young dreamer you once knew. I have seen war and carnage, my lady, and that changes a man."

His steely gaze slid away to rest on Waldo, then returned to Raven with insulting intensity.

"I understand congratulations are in order. I am surprised you and Waldo were

allowed to marry. Incest is a serious of-
fense."

"I have waited years for a dispensation
from the pope," Waldo interjected. " 'Tis
long past time to claim my bride."

Drake stared at Raven as if he had never
seen her before. And in truth he had not,
not this Raven. The Raven he remembered
had been half woman, half child, with long,
gangly arms and legs and freckles on her
nose.

The woman standing before him had a
flawless complexion, creamy white with a
touch of sun upon her cheeks. She wore a
pale linen undertunic with tight long
sleeves beneath an emerald green satin
tunic trimmed in gold. A silk veil held in
place by a gold circlet failed to confine her
glorious chestnut hair. Her eyes, fringed by
thick, dark lashes, were as green as her
tunic and tilted up at the outer corners.
Her lips were rosy, and the bottom lip was
slightly fuller than the upper lip, giving her
a sultry look that hinted of passion. Drake
wondered if that passion had lain dormant
for Waldo to claim.

"Are you here to compete in the games?"
Raven asked Drake when the silence became unbearable.

"Aye. 'Tis what I do for a living. After the

war I was in sore need of sufficient coin to restore Windhurst, and the best way to obtain it was to compete in tournaments."

"The Black Knight's praises are sung far and wide," Raven said in a hushed voice. "You have become a legend, Drake."

Drake couldn't bring himself to smile at the woman who had betrayed him years ago. He might have forgiven her had Daria not died under mysterious circumstances. Daria was but a dim memory now, but Drake had never forgotten who had ultimately caused her death. Had not Raven alerted her father, he and Daria would have gotten safely away that night, and Waldo would never have gotten his hands on his fragile love.

"Legend or not, we will see who triumphs at the games," Waldo declared. He looked pointedly at Raven. "I am sure you have duties inside the keep."

Raven sent Waldo a scathing glance but did not openly defy him as she turned on her heel and flounced away.

"She will need taming," Waldo muttered, stung by her disrespectful manner. "Raven and I would have wed years ago but for that cursed dispensation from the pope. Duff would allow it no other way." His smile did not reach his eyes as he added, "There are ways of teaching a woman to obey her lord and master, and I know them all."

Drake stiffened; his mouth thinned into a white line. "Did you use those methods on Daria?"

For a moment Waldo looked confused. "Daria? She died many years ago. Daria was biddable enough until . . ."

Drake's silver gaze honed in on him with deadly accuracy. "Until . . ." he prodded.

Waldo must have realized he was on shaky ground, for he tried to shrug off his words. " 'Tis naught. I vow I cannot remember that far back. Our marriage was of such short duration we barely got to know one another. Did you know our father died shortly before Daria took ill? He was killed by poachers."

"So I heard."

Waldo's eyes shifted away from Drake's penetrating gaze. "Ah, I see Duff talking to Sir Melvin. I need to discuss arrangements for the tournament with our host."

Drake smiled grimly as he watched Waldo stride away. His half brother had changed little over the years, he thought. Though Waldo had fought at Crécy, they had not crossed paths.

Eager now to return to his men, Drake

whirled on his heel and strode away. People turned to watch him, some crossing themselves as he passed by. In his stark black armor he looked lethal and sinister, every bit as dangerous as his name implied.

As Drake rode over the drawbridge to the campsite Sir John had chosen, he had a niggling premonition that he should never have returned to Castle Chirk. He had not expected Raven to be so beautiful.

The banquet that night was the first of many held to celebrate the wedding that would follow the four days of tournaments. Raven sat at the high table between Waldo and Duff, withdrawn and unresponsive to the pageantry of the evening. Duff had hired jugglers, jongleurs, and acrobats to entertain during the lengthy meal, but they did not interest Raven. After encountering Drake in the bailey, she had thought of naught but the way his silver eyes had gone hard and flat when he had first seen her. It hurt to think that after all these years he still hated her for something in which she had had no part.

She glanced at Waldo from beneath a heavy fringe of lashes and wrinkled her nose in disgust. He was stuffing food in his mouth so fast that some of it escaped from between his lips and fell on his red velvet doublet. Waldo was not fat, but Raven could not help thinking his legs resembled lumpy sausages stuffed into his hose, and she shuddered at the thought of having to bear the weight of his heavy body on her wedding night. The thought of being intimate with Waldo was repugnant. She'd do anything, *anything* to escape this marriage.

Raven toyed at her food as dish after dish was paraded before her . . . brawn made from a pig's head and jelly, baked fish, roasted pork, venison, pheasants, many kinds of birds, an array of vegetables, pies and puddings. Her disgust with Waldo increased as he picked apart a lark and crammed it into his mouth.

The hall overflowed with knights and their squires and men-at-arms, and many extra tables had been set up to accommodate their great numbers. Raven made a slow perusal of the men partaking of the feast and frowned when she did not see Drake. She knew he had been invited, for everyone had been made welcome when they arrived and informed of the banquets to be held each night until the end of the tournament.

She wished Drake did not hate her so

much. Had they been on good terms, he might have been persuaded to help her. Then, from out of the blue, an idea popped into her head. It was outrageous, and hardly worthy of a second thought, but she had so few options. She could scarcely wait to find Drake alone and explain what had really happened all those years ago when he had tried to elope with Daria. If he believed her, mayhap she could convince him to help her escape this travesty of a marriage.

Suddenly Raven looked up from her trencher and there he was. The Black Knight. Clad somberly in black doublet and black hose, his appearance made such an impact upon those present that a hush fell over the hall as he found a seat among his men.

She gazed at his face and had the unaccountable urge to rub her finger across his full lips to see if they were as hard as they looked. His entire face was a contrast of sharp lines and angles. All the boyish fullness she remembered was gone, banished by skin stretched taut across prominent cheekbones. Her gaze slid downward over his body and the breath slammed from her throat.

There was not one bit of fat on his body.

He was all battle-honed muscles and rippling tendons and sculpted features. No other man in the entire hall could hold a candle to him.

Raven continued to watch Drake as he sat among his men and filled his trencher with food. Someone said something to him and a broad smile curved his lips. It was the first time Raven had seen him smile and the sight of it did strange things to her virgin body. Quickly she looked away, lest Waldo noticed her interest in the Black Knight.

"You are not eating," Waldo said, startling Raven from her reverie. "Does the food not please you?"

"I am not hungry," Raven said truthfully.

Waldo frowned. "You are too skinny. I do not like bony women." He leered at her. "You will fatten up when my babe is growing in your belly."

That thought made Raven lose what little was left of her appetite.

Drake was aware of Raven's scrutiny and tried unsuccessfully to ignore it. He was amazed that the scrawny, freckled, child he'd once known had turned into a beauty. She looked slim and elegant, but Drake knew instinctively that the body beneath the royal blue satin tunic she wore would be softly curved and pleasing.

Drake frowned and shook his head to clear it of disturbing thoughts. He cared naught about Raven of Chirk, no matter how lovely she was. Waldo was welcome to her.

"Why the frown, Drake?" Sir John asked. "Methinks you frown too much." He noted the direction of Drake's gaze and grinned. "Ah, 'tis the lovely Lady Raven? Did you not foster at Castle Chirk when you were young?"

"Aye. I trained with Lord Nyle's squires before he banished me."

"Aye, I remember," John said thoughtfully. "You said you fell in love with Daria of Chirk, but she was betrothed to your half brother. What happened to Daria? How is it that Lady Raven is to be married to Waldo?"

"Daria died mysteriously a few months after her marriage. Apparently Waldo petitioned the pope for a dispensation to wed Raven when her betrothed died at Crécy."

"Something in your voice tells me you do not like Lady Raven, my friend. Or is it that you like her too well?" John asked astutely.

"I like her not at all," Drake returned

fiercely. "She was a treacherous little bitch when I knew her, and as far as I am concerned, she and Waldo belong together."

Drake ate sparingly of the food and drank only a small amount of ale. He wanted a clear head when the games commenced on the morrow. While his men were being amused by the entertainers, he slipped away to return to camp.

Raven saw Drake leave the hall and was determined to follow. She hoped to catch up with him before he left the bailey so she could explain what had really happened all those years ago. They had been friends once; mayhap he would agree to help her.

Pleading a headache, Raven excused herself and left the hall. But instead of taking the stairs to her tower room, she used the servants' entrance and hurried around to intercept Drake.

Chapter Three

*Cruelty to an enemy is expected
from a knight.*

Raven caught up with Drake in the stables, where he had gone to retrieve his horse. She assumed he did not hear her soft footfall, for he gave no sign of it. She was nearly upon him when suddenly he crouched and turned, a blade appearing like magic in his hand.

Raven dragged in a startled breath. "Drake, 'tis I, Raven."

Drake relaxed, but not entirely. It was obvious he trusted no one in the fortress he had once called home.

His voice held a sneer when he asked, "What are you doing here, my lady?"

"I wish to speak with you."

"Does your betrothed know?"

She looked away. "I . . . nay."

"I cannot imagine what you have to say to me that I would be interested in hearing." He turned away.

She grasped his arm. "Drake, nay, I beg you, hear me out. 'Tis imperative that you

59

know the truth about what happened that night you intended to elope with Daria."

" 'Tis of no consequence, Lady Raven. Daria is long dead."

"We were friends once, Drake. I even fancied myself in love with you."

He laughed harshly. "You were but a child, and many years have passed since then. I am not the same naive youth you once knew."

"Think you I do not know that? One has but to look at you to know you have grown into an extraordinary man."

"Flattery, my lady? It becomes you not. What do you want of me?"

"I want you to believe me."

"Why does it matter so much?"

"If you believe I did not betray you and Daria, mayhap you would hear me out and grant my request."

Drake gave her a mirthless smile. "Aye, I understand now. You asked me to kiss you once and I refused." His voice took on a harshness that matched his expression. "Is it a kiss you want? I am a man with a man's needs. I will not refuse this time, Raven of Chirk."

She took an involuntary step backward, stunned by the ferocity of his words. "Nay, 'tis not . . ."

Her protest died in her throat as he reached for her, roughly dragging her against him. A torrent of heat shot through her and she leaned into him, bracing her hands against the broad expanse of his chest.

"Drake, I did not mean . . ."

"I know exactly what you want from me."

His lips burned against hers, hot, firm, yet not hard as she had supposed they would be. His kiss was hungry, relentless, eliciting a heated response from that secret place deep within her feminine center. When he placed a hand on her breast and squeezed, she sighed into his mouth.

Suddenly she wanted his arms to hold her, surround her, never let her go, but Drake pushed her away and gave her a mocking smile.

"Is that what you wanted, Lady Raven? Did you wish to compare my kisses with those of your betrothed?"

Raven drew back as if he had slapped her. "Nay, I need your help. I hoped, because of the friendship we once shared, that you might grant it."

Drake searched Raven's face. Her circlet and veil had fallen off when he had pulled her forcefully against him, and her chestnut tresses gleamed darkly in the moonlight. She had grown so beautiful, the sight of her took his breath away. But he forced himself to remember that beneath the tempting wrapping lurked a treacherous heart. He could not help wondering, however, why she sounded like a damsel in distress.

"How can I possibly help you?" he asked. "You have everything a woman could wish for. You are betrothed to a wealthy earl and will soon become a countess."

"You still do not understand, do you?"

"Nay. The hour grows late, Lady Raven. I must prepare myself for the tournament tomorrow."

She stopped him with a hand upon his arm. He felt a frisson of heat travel up his arm and lodge in every part of his body, particularly the lower part. The shock of it was not quite as unnerving as it had been when he had kissed her, but startling nevertheless.

"Please hear me out," Raven pleaded. "I cannot marry Waldo. I hate him. I believe him responsible for Daria's death, and . . . and I fear him."

Drake composed his features. If he had one inkling of proof that Waldo had been responsible for Daria's death, he would slay his half brother without a hint of remorse. "Why would he kill Daria?"

"I do not know; 'tis something I feel." She touched her heart. "Here."

"If you are so adamantly opposed to the wedding, why are you marrying him?"

"Duff and Waldo are friends. After Aric's death, Duff promised Waldo he would not betroth me to another until Waldo received permission from the pope for our marriage. It cost him a great deal to grease palms but the dispensation finally arrived. No amount of pleading on my part could convince Duff to betroth me to another, or to let me remain a maid."

Drake cocked a dark brow. "What is it you want from me, my lady?"

Raven cast a furtive glance toward the keep and moved deeper into the shadows. Curious, Drake followed.

"My mother's sister lives in Scotland. Her husband is an official in the Sottish king's court. All I ask is your escort to Scotland before the wedding ceremony takes place. I intend to throw myself on Aunt Eunice's mercy and beg her protection."

"I have no time to waste on squeamish damsels who fear marriage," Drake said gruffly.

"You do not like Waldo any better than I

do," Raven charged. "Have you never envied him for being your father's heir when you are the eldest son?"

Raven's words opened old wounds. Over the years, both Drake's mother and grandmother had insisted that Basil's marriage to Leta was legal and binding, that Drake had not been born out of wedlock. Granny Nola had sworn that proof existed, and when the time was right, Drake would have it. After Drake's father had died, it no longer seemed important to prove the legality of his birth. He had naught to prove to anyone. He was the Black Knight, a name earned through selfless acts of courage and skills honed in battle. He had no need of another name.

"Waldo is welcome to Eyre. I have Windhurst and a title bestowed upon me by the king."

"Please help me, Lord Drake," Raven pleaded. "I am desperate. I can be ready to leave whenever you say."

Her face was a pale oval, whiter than the moon illuminating it. Her eyes were wide and pleading, and he had to steel himself lest he feel pity for her plight. Drake knew Raven would not have an easy life married to his half brother. Though he and Waldo had fought on different fields of battle in

France, Drake had heard stories of Waldo's cruelty to his servants, to captives, and to women from the plundered cities. Waldo and his men-at-arms raped and pillaged at will, despite Edward's orders to the contrary. Drake would not trust Waldo with his pet dog.

But Drake had become a hard man, immune to pity. "Nay, I cannot help you. You are naught to me, Raven of Chirk. Our friendship ended the day you betrayed me. I trusted you with a secret and you ran straight to your father with it. Find another champion, my lady."

Raven gulped back a sharp retort, angry that Drake would not help her cause. "Is there naught I can do or say to change your mind?"

His silver gaze rested on her breasts, then slid downward, where it lingered on the place where her thighs met. For some unexplainable reason he wanted to insult her, to hurt her as she had once hurt him. He hoped his outrageous suggestion would send her fleeing. "Perhaps a tumble in the hay might change my mind."

Raven gasped. "What! You insult me, sir. You ask for that which I cannot give."

He gave her a mocking smile. " 'Tis what I counted on, my lady." Then he did something he should not have, something he would never have done had he not been uncharacteristically tempted by Raven of Chirk. He grasped her roughly and covered her mouth with his.

Her innocent response to their earlier kiss had intrigued him. Obviously Raven had never tasted passion before. That fleeting first kiss had been tame compared to what he really wanted to do to her. He wanted to probe her mouth with his tongue, to learn if it was as sweet as he suspected. He wanted to touch her virgin breasts and hear her sudden intake of breath when she felt the first stirring of arousal.

He ignored her strangled protest and deepened the kiss, thrusting his tongue into her mouth even as his hand sought a firm breast. But still it was not enough. He sucked on her tongue; her muted plea turned into a sigh as he found an erect nipple and teased it with his fingertips. It hardened against his palm and he smiled. Then he pressed a knee between her thighs, separating them so she could ride him.

Her sigh turned into a moan as she worked her softness against his knee, as if seeking something elusive. He knew exactly what she needed. He would have laid her down in the soft hay and taken her had not a voice calling out of the darkness interrupted them. His arms fell away and Raven would have fallen had he not reached out to steady her. He knew the moment she realized they were not alone, for he felt her tense and glance over her shoulder.

"Raven, where are you? Your maid said you did not return to your chamber."

"Waldo," she said in a hushed voice.

Drake said naught. His body stiffened, as Waldo made his way unerringly toward them. He carried a torch to light his way and had already spied them, so there was no escape.

Drake's hand tightened on the hilt of his sword when Waldo grasped Raven's arm and shoved her behind him.

"God's blood, woman! What are you doing out here with *him?* Have you no shame? I should beat you for this."

"I have done naught," Raven denied hotly. "The hall was so warm I decided to take some air before retiring."

"And you just happened to run into Sir Bastard," Waldo taunted.

Drake's sword was halfway out of its scabbard before he thought better of his impulse and shoved it back into place. Killing Waldo now would not win him the purse he sought. He would wait until they met in the lists to teach Waldo a lesson.

"Go to your chamber, Raven," Waldo bit out. "You will explain this to me on our wedding night. You have much to account for, my lady, but presently I have little time to take you to task. The tournaments start tomorrow at terce and I must conserve my energy."

Raven whirled and marched away, casting a single glance over her shoulder at Drake. Drake tried to ignore the desperation her expression conveyed as he returned his attention to Waldo.

"So, brother, you still covet what is mine," Waldo said with a sneer. "First Daria and now Raven. You cannot have her. I wanted her even before Father betrothed me to Daria. Raven has fire in her, as you surely have noticed, and I look forward to taming her. I have spent considerable time and money acquiring Raven," he continued. "Do anything to keep me from what is mine and you will live to regret it."

" 'Tis convenient, is it not, that Daria died so you could pursue Raven?"

"Aye, convenient," Waldo repeated but did not elaborate. " 'Tis legal, Drake. The pope himself gave me leave to wed Raven."

"You are welcome to her," Drake said. The words flowed easily from his mouth, though he was not certain he meant them. Raven had become an alluring woman. What man would not want her? She exuded sexuality and innocence at the same time. Or was she truly as innocent as she pretended? It annoyed him to think that Waldo had sparked passion within her. "Raven and I were merely discussing old times."

"Stay away from her, brother. You did not get Daria, nor can you have Raven. Her maidenhead belongs to me. Keep your interests confined to the tournament." His expression grew thoughtful, and then he gave Drake an ingratiating smile. "Mayhap I'll send you a flagon of Duff's private wine as consolation," he said in parting. "As a brotherly gesture, you understand."

Waldo's obsequious smile went unanswered. "I understand perfectly, brother." His penetrating gaze did not leave Waldo's back as his brother retraced his steps to the keep.

Suddenly Drake noticed something lying on the ground and stooped to pick it up. It was the gauzy veil that had covered Raven's bright hair. Apparently it had fallen when he had pulled her into his arms. Smiling to himself, he stuffed it inside his doublet.

Drake's squire was waiting up for him when he returned to camp. The lad sat on the cot, polishing Drake's black armor and helm by candlelight. He jumped up when Drake ducked inside the tent.

"Everything is in order, my lord. Your armor is polished and your weapons in good repair. Is there aught else you need?"

"Nay, Evan. You may seek your own bed now."

Evan ducked out the tent flap and ran into Sir John of Marlow's well-muscled chest. "Is Lord Drake in his tent, Evan?" John asked.

"Aye, Sir John, he just returned from the banquet."

John sent Evan on his way and entered the tent. Drake greeted him amiably. "I see you left the banquet still able to stand," he teased.

"Like you, I compete in the games tomorrow. Too much drink dulls the wits. Besides, the ale Lord Duff served was swill. He probably keeps the good stuff for himself."

Drake heard footsteps approaching and reached for his sword. "Who goes there?"

"Lord Waldo's man. My lord sends a

flagon of wine to aid your sleep."

"Did the man say wine? By all means bid him enter, Drake."

"Come," Drake called gruffly. Ordinarily Waldo was not a thoughtful man. Drake wondered what his brother was up to.

The man-at-arms, wearing Eyre colors of blue and gold, ducked into the tent and set the flagon down on the camp table.

"Lord Waldo sends wine with his compliments to the Black Knight," the man recited.

Drake eyed the wine with suspicion.

" 'Tis good French wine," the man was quick to add. "The best the castle has to offer."

"Ah." John sighed with none of Drake's reservations. "Good French wine is hard to come by. Break out the cups, my friend, and we shall toast to success tomorrow."

The man-at-arms started to back out of the tent when Drake stopped him with a harsh command.

"Wait! What is your name?"

"Gareth."

"Have you been in Waldo's service long, Gareth?"

"Aye, since before he became earl. I fought with him in France as a foot soldier."

"Waldo must trust you."

The fellow puffed out his chest. "With his life, my lord."

"Then you must drink with us."

John stared at Drake curiously. "Come now, Drake, why waste good French wine on this fellow when he obviously prefers ale?"

"That is so, master," Gareth said with alacrity. "Pray enjoy your wine."

"But I insist," Drake said.

"God's toenails, Drake, what has gotten into you?" John chided.

"There are cups in my war chest, John," Drake said. "Please bring one for each of us."

John obeyed, though he was obviously puzzled by Drake's insistence that the man drink with them. He found three pewter cups and set them on the table beside the flagon of wine. At Drake's nod, he poured wine into each of the cups. John held his cup to his nose and sniffed appreciatively.

"Ambrosia," he said, bringing the wine to his lips.

"Nay, John, do not drink . . . yet," Drake added as he brought his own cup to his nose and inhaled the heady aroma. "Gareth will drink first." He handed the cup to Waldo's man.

Drake watched Gareth closely, smiling with satisfaction when Gareth stared into the cup with horror.

"Drink up, man," Drake invited. "How often do you get to drink good French wine?"

"Are you daft, Drake?" John said.

"Drink, Gareth," Drake ordered harshly, stilling John's protest with a slash of his hand.

"Nay!" Gareth cried, spilling his wine on the ground. "I cannot." Whirling on his heel, he made a hasty exit.

John stared into his own cup, a perplexed expression on his handsome face. "What the devil!"

"Put the wine down, John," Drake said quietly. " 'Tis not fit to drink. 'Tis tainted."

John shuddered and carefully set the cup on the table. "God's blood, Drake, are you sure?"

"Nay, but you saw how Waldo's man acted when I asked him to drink first. You may test it if you like, but I would not recommend it."

"Nor would I," John said in a hushed voice. "I will take your word for it. What made you suspect?"

"Waldo does naught without a reason.

He has ever hated me. Sending the gift of wine is so unlike him, I immediately suspected trickery. Mayhap the wine would have made us too ill to compete tomorrow, but more likely it would have killed us."

John shuddered again. "Poison. Why does Waldo hate you? He is the earl, not you. You said there was never any question about Waldo being your father's heir, and that you are . . ."

"A bastard," Drake said, finishing where John left off. "Heed me well, John. One day I will prove that I am the rightful heir of Eyre. I have never doubted that proof exists. Granny Nola said that one day I would want to learn the truth, and that when I am ready, she would help me find it."

"Your granny is a wise woman," John said.

"Aye, she is also hale and hearty and her memory sharp. Besides myself, you and Sir Richard are the only men who know where to find her village in Wales. I trust no others. For a time I worried she might not be safe from Waldo, but no one but Lord Nyle and my father knew where she lived, and they are both dead."

"Your trust humbles me," John said. His gaze rested on the flagon. "What shall we do with the tainted wine?"

"Spill it on the ground behind the tent. Pour the wine from the cups into the flagon." Drake held the flagon while John poured the wine into it. John's hands shook so badly he splashed some of the wine on his hose. Then he followed Drake outside and watched as the thirsty ground soaked up the poisoned wine.

As soon as the flagon was empty, Drake awakened Evan, calling him out of the tent he shared with the other squires. The lad stumbled out of the tent, sleepy-eyed and yawning.

"How may I help you, my lord?"

He handed the empty flagon to the squire. "I have an errand for you, lad. Take this flagon to the keep and give it to Lord Waldo. Tell him it was delicious and extend my gratitude for his thoughtful gesture."

"Aye, my lord."

"Mind you, give it to no one but Lord Waldo," Drake said as the lad scampered off.

"You can count on me," Evan called over his shoulder.

John laughed softly. "Methinks brother Waldo will be surprised to see you looking hale and hearty in the lists tomorrow," John opined.

"So he will, John, so he will."

John took his leave. Drake returned to his tent, his mind whirling with all that had happened this night. Try as he might, he could not put Raven out of his mind. Her plea for help had been so desperate it had caught him off guard. So had her sweet kisses and startling burst of passion. She had stunned him with her heated response to what had begun as a mockery. Instead of showing his contempt for her he had found himself fighting his own body's incomprehensible need to throw her down in the hay, toss up her skirts, and fill her with himself.

God's blood! What was wrong with him? Raven of Chirk had become the kind of woman Drake had learned to avoid: treacherous and sexually stimulating at the same time. Women like Raven deserved men like Waldo. He could not forget that but for Raven, Daria would have married him. Though he would never know for sure what the future would have held if Daria not been torn from his arms, he did feel certain that she would still be alive today. But Raven had snitched to her father, and his future had taken a different course.

Sleep was hard won that night, and it

came at a price. Drake's dreams were filled with a green-eyed, chestnut-haired beauty.

Raven sat in the window embrasure, fully dressed and not yet ready to succumb to sleep. From her tower room window she could see beyond the turrets to where a large collection of tents were pitched in the fields outside the castle gates. She knew exactly where Drake and his followers were camped, for she had climbed to the parapets earlier and asked one of the guards to point out the Black Knight's encampment. She had identified Drake's tent immediately by the pennant flying from the tent pole: a red dragon emblazoned upon a field of black.

Raven sighed and turned away from the window. Being rebuffed by Drake had been the most humiliating experience of her life. She touched her lips, surprised by how swollen they still felt from his kisses. And her body. Sweet Virgin, never had her body felt so alive and vital. In all her twenty-four years she had never imagined how hard a man's body could be. Lord save her, but she could have gone on kissing Drake forever.

Lost in wicked musings, Raven was startled when Thelma burst into her chamber, followed closely by Waldo. "I told him you were sleeping, mistress, that it was not proper for him to enter your chamber without first asking your permission, but he would not listen."

"Get out!" Waldo bellowed.

Thelma sent Raven an apologetic look and scurried away.

"Close the door behind you," Waldo ordered curtly.

Raven girded herself for Waldo's anger. She had not long to wait.

"Your conduct is inappropriate, Raven," he berated. "I cannot condone wanton behavior in my wife."

"I am not yet your wife," Raven contended. "Besides, Drake and I were merely discussing old times."

"I am no fool, Raven. I know Drake kissed you. Look at you. Your lips are still swollen and your face flushed." He stalked her. Raven retreated until her back came in contact with the window embrasure. "I will not have it," he bit out, emphasizing each word.

"You accuse me falsely!" Raven retorted. "Think you I do not know you bedded one of the maids last night?"

" 'Tis a man's right to appease his lust. Mark me well, Raven of Chirk. Though I have waited years for you, should you become tiresome, I will satisfy my needs when and with whom I please. You will bear my heirs and run my home. I have been obsessed with you since you were naught but a bratty child with tangled red hair. But if and when I tire of you, I will seek other diversion."

"You make me ill, Waldo," Raven charged. "I do not wish to marry you, nor do I want to bear your children."

Waldo grasped the neck of her gown and dragged her against him. "Do not ever let me hear you say that again," he warned. "Once we are married I will teach you to obey. You were allowed too much freedom as a child. Most women your age have been married for years and have produced several children for their lords." He leered at her. "We will make up for lost time."

"Let go of me," Raven hissed as she tried to pry his hands from her.

"Nay, never. You are mine, Raven. God works in mysterious ways. Had God not wanted me to have you He would not have taken Daria and Aric of Flint. Your maidenhead belongs to me. I look forward with pleasure to bedding you on our wedding night."

As if to prove his words, he pumped his

loins against her in an obscene imitation of sex and ground his lips against hers in a parody of a kiss. All he succeeded in doing was hurting her, reinforcing her desire to escape this marriage. She must convince Drake to help her despite his earlier refusal.

Gathering her strength, Raven raised her knee to push Waldo away and hit a vulnerable spot. He howled in pain and lashed out with his fist. He struck her on the cheek, sending her spinning to the floor. She watched in surprise as he doubled over and clutched himself. Her small act of defiance had taught her something valuable tonight, a lesson she would not forget. If there was one place a man was vulnerable, it was that place he thought with instead of his brains.

The village priest said Mass for the jousters the following morning. The services were held in the open field, since neither the village church nor the castle chapel was large enough to hold so many. After the final blessing Drake returned to his tent to prepare for the first day of the tournament, which was slated to begin at terce.

In his tent, Drake armed himself with

the aid of his squire. His weapons consisted of a blunt lance and sword, since only blunt weapons were to be used by order of the king. He would carry a thick shield constructed to withstand the blows of such weapons, and special armor designed to reduce injury. His armor was black, as was his helm and pennant. Over his armor he wore a black tunic emblazoned with a dragon on the front. When the herald called for the jousters to make ready, Drake mounted his destrier, which was arrayed in black trappings trimmed in red, and rode to the lists to await his turn.

Drake glanced at the pavilion erected for spectators and saw Raven sitting in the front row amid her maids and visiting ladies. She wore a deep purple gown fitted at the waist and trimmed in ermine. The color should have clashed with her flame-shot hair, but instead made it appear more vibrant. She did not wear a hennin, a conical headdress with a trailing veil, choosing instead to cover her glorious hair with a filet cap of gold and a veil that covered most of her face.

Drake scowled as Waldo rode to the pavilion and lowered his lance toward Raven, expecting to be awarded his lady's favor. His scowl deepened when Raven pulled a tiny ribbon from her sleeve and tied it onto the end of the lance. Waldo gave her a mocking salute, wheeled his mount, and returned to the lists. Drake smiled grimly as he thought of the veil Raven had lost the night before in the stables. He touched the place where he had stuffed it inside his padded gambeson.

As Waldo wheeled his horse around, his gaze settled on Drake. Drake knew his brother had not expected to see him looking so well this morning. Waldo's face appeared bloodless, his expression one of disbelief. Drake gave him a mocking salute.

A moment later two mounted and armored knights entered the lists and took their places at opposite ends of the tilt, the wooden barrier erected in the lists to keep the horses from colliding. Drake watched with interest as the herald gave the signal to charge and each knight rode in a headlong gallop toward his opponent, lances aimed across their horses' necks. Passing left side to left side, they met in the middle.

The knight Drake favored, Sir William of Dorset, took a crushing blow, which broke his opponent's lance. Sir William's lance succeeded in unseating his opponent and he dismounted. Immediately a cry rose up from the spectators: "Fairly broken." Then both knights drew their blunted swords and continued the fight on foot. Sir William won handily, defeating his opponent with a skillful move that sent his opponent's sword flying. A loud chorus of approval rose up from the spectators.

And so it continued. Sir John was next, and Drake was pleased when his friend handily vanquished his opponent. Sir Richard, another of his knights, jousted next and won. Then it was Drake's turn.

Drake pulled down his faceplate and took his position at the tilt. When the herald gave the signal, both knights raced at full tilt toward one another. A sickening thud brought a gasp from the spectators as Drake's opponent was unhorsed and lay unmoving on the ground. When it appeared that he was in no condition to continue, his squires ran out and carried him off the field on his shield. The spectators were on their feet cheering.

Drake jousted three more times before a halt was called to the day's entertainment. Points were given for unhorsing an opponent, for striking his helmet, and for breaking a lance. At the end of the day the Black Knight and Waldo of Eyre had more points than any of the other jousters.

Clearly they were the contenders to defeat for the purse. And since only one winner could take the prize, it became abundantly clear that on the last day of the tournament the Black Knight and Waldo would be pitted against one another.

Chapter Four

*A knight should not kill simply
for the pleasure of it.*

The banquet that night was a boisterous affair. Those knights who had been unhorsed complained about the high ransom demanded by their opponents to regain their horses and arms, and the winners celebrated their victories. The rules specified that to the victor went horses, armor, weapons, property, and fines. Traveling from tourney to tourney, those knights-errant, who were gifted with the skill of battle became wealthy from the spoils, while losers returned home penniless.

Drake had earned more than glory participating in tourneys across the width and breadth of England. After the tournament he would have earned sufficient wealth to restore Windhurst, his ancient castle in the wilds of Wessex. The purse that went to the champion at the end of this tournament, which he fully intended to win, would enable him to hire mercenaries to defend his fortress once it had been restored.

A hush fell over the hall when Drake entered. An imposing figure clad in unrelieved black, he resembled a dark bird of prey amid a bevy of bright-colored peacocks. And no one was more vibrantly clad than Waldo. His rich green brocade doublet and yellow hose did nothing to enhance his stocky build and ruddy complexion.

Drake did not immediately seat himself, but instead strode to the high table, stopping along the way to receive congratulations from his fellow jousters. When he reached the dais, he gave his half-brother a mocking smile and a negligent bow.

"You were quite impressive today, Drake," Duff said by way of greeting. "You are naught like the boy Waldo and I . . ." His words fell off and he looked away, embarrassed.

"Referred to as Sir Bastard?" Drake challenged. "Hardly."

"You *were* incredible, Drake," Raven complimented softly.

"You are too kind, my lady," Drake said coolly. He dared not focus too much attention on Raven, though she looked disturbingly lovely tonight in scarlet velvet. He wanted no distractions to veer him from his purpose. He had thought too often about Raven these last two days for his peace of mind.

"You look hale and hearty after the grueling games today," Waldo said casually. Drake knew exactly what he was referring to.

"Aye, I was most fortunate. No opponent unhorsed me, nor did I receive a scratch or bruise. Save your compliments for someone who will appreciate them, *brother*. The wine you sent last night was delicious. Sir John and I thoroughly enjoyed it."

To his credit Waldo did not flinch, though it was obvious he had not expected Drake to mention the poisoned wine. "Since you found it so agreeable, mayhap I will send more tonight."

"Nay, do not bother," Drake said. His words carried a subtle warning, and apparently Waldo caught his drift, for his eyes did not quite meet Drake's. "I must remain clearheaded for the tourney," Drake added.

"I did not know you sent Drake wine, Waldo," Duff chided. "I hope you chose a robust French."

"The wine was a trifle bitter for my tastes," Drake said with sly innuendo.

Then he turned toward Raven, gave her a mocking bow, and sought a seat among his men.

"Bastard!" Waldo exclaimed the moment Drake turned his back.

"I find it difficult to believe you sent Drake wine, knowing how you feel about him," Raven remarked.

"Aye," Duff agreed. " 'Tis not like you, Waldo."

"Exactly," Raven said as a terrible thought seized her. Though she found it hard to credit, she could not discount it.

"You have to admit Drake No Name is a man to be reckoned with," Duff mused. "The Black Knight. Imagine that. 'Tis likely he will be declared champion and win the purse."

"Not if I have anything to say about it," Waldo bit out.

Suspicion raised its ugly head. Raven knew that Waldo did nothing unless it gained him something. Throwing caution to the wind, she said, "I know you, my lord. What was wrong with the wine you sent Drake?"

Waldo shot her a malevolent glare. "Naught was wrong with the wine. Did you not see my brother just now? He did not appear to be ailing."

Raven lowered her eyes to her trencher. Waldo had a look of guilt about him she did not trust. Her mouth was dry as dust, but rather than share Waldo's cup as was the custom, she called for her own cup and drank deeply. She heard a low growl of displeasure from Waldo but blatantly ignored him.

As the meal progressed, Raven found herself staring at Drake. He seemed to be enjoying the entertainment, she thought as the jugglers left and a bard walked to the center of the hall and tuned his lute. The bard had her rapt attention as he launched into a stirring rendition of the brave deeds attributed to the Black Knight. The more the bard sang the praises of the Black Knight, the darker Waldo's expression became. By the time the bard finished his song, which contained many verses, Waldo looked ready to explode.

As the men grew raucous and their talk vulgar, Raven excused herself. She wanted desperately to speak with Drake, to warn him about Waldo's evil machinations, but she knew not how or where to approach him. In the end, she decided that he must know Waldo well enough by now to suspect everything he did. But, oh, how she wanted to see Drake again. She would do anything to escape her upcoming wedding — even give herself to Drake if it meant he would help her. There was still time, she told herself. Tomorrow she intended to try again to enlist Drake's help. There had to be some way to escape this unwanted marriage.

If only the Black Knight was more like the Drake she once knew, Raven lamented. But the Black Knight was a hardened warrior with little compassion and even less charity. He had given his heart to Daria years ago and had learned to live without it. He had devoted his life to war, using his warrior skills to earn glory and wealth. And over the years he had never stopped hating Raven of Chirk.

Was there naught she could do to convince Drake to help her? Raven wondered. Apparently not this night, for when she crept down the spiral staircase from her tower room to see if he had left the hall, she saw him laughing and drinking with his knights. Sighing, she returned to her chamber and sought her bed.

The tournament recommenced the following day after Mass. The day dawned fine and warm, a good omen, Drake thought as he prepared for the day's jousting. Today he was the first to compete. On the first run against his opponent, neither was unhorsed, but Drake managed to strike off his opponent's helm. On the second run he unhorsed his opponent, but the man was able to continue the contest with swords. Drake quickly vanquished his opponent, winning the hapless jouster's horse, armor, and weapons. They added considerably to the growing number of trophies Drake intended to ransom back to their owners.

And so the day went. Tired but pleased with himself at the end of the day, Drake had won all of the contests in which he rode and was considerably richer.

Drake stayed but a short time at the banquet that night. Throughout the evening he found his gaze resting on Raven more often than he would have liked. Studying her from beneath hooded lids, he could not help noticing her sadness. She looked as if she wanted to be anyplace but sitting beside Waldo. When Waldo leaned toward her, she quickly leaned away. When he placed a particularly tender morsel of meat on her trencher, she shoved it aside. Drake almost laughed aloud when he saw Raven refuse to share Waldo's cup.

Whether he liked Raven or not, he had

to admire her. She was a stubborn wench. Too stubborn for her own good, he mused with sudden insight. If she continued to challenge Waldo, Drake feared Waldo would make her very sorry. Drake knew from experience that Waldo had a vile temper and would not allow his wife to defy him. A frisson of emotion smote Drake, but he quickly dismissed it. He could not afford an emotion that did not serve his purposes.

Drake decided to leave the banquet early that night, shortly after Raven made her exit. He had given his squire permission to make merry with the other squires, and his men appeared far from ready to leave, so he slipped unnoticed from the hall.

The single candle left burning inside his quarters sputtered out as a gust of air followed Drake inside the tent, but he did not bother to light another. He undressed to his bare skin and stretched out on his cot. He was bone weary and ached everywhere from being brutally battered during the jousting; tomorrow promised to be just as grueling. Within minutes he was sound asleep.

Minutes or hours could have passed when Drake awoke to the scent of danger. The hair on the back of his neck prickled, and he knew intuitively that he was not alone. The tent was completely dark. He deliberately slowed his breathing as he reached beneath his pillow for the hilt of his dagger. He sensed that someone was leaning over him, reaching for him, and he reacted with lethal agility.

He kicked aside the blanket, crouched low, and launched himself at the intruder. He would not put it past Waldo to send an assassin. The intruder fell beneath him; he heard a loud whoosh of breath. He brought the dagger forward but something stayed his hand. He went still, suddenly aware of the intruder's sex. He knew enough about women's bodies to recognize one when it was splayed beneath him. Soft breasts pressed against his chest, and womanly curves meshed pleasantly with his hardness. A low chuckle began in his diaphragm and rumbled past his lips.

" 'Tis just like Waldo to send a woman to do his dirty work," he whispered into her ear. "I must remember to thank him. It has been a long time since I have rutted between a woman's thighs."

The woman beneath him tried to speak but Drake quickly covered her mouth with one hand while searching her soft curves for a weapon with the other.

"What, no weapon? How were you supposed to kill me? Mayhap you intended to use my own weapon on me. Did you think I would become so lost in lust that I would not know what you were about?"

The woman gave a vigorous shake of her head and made noises deep in her throat, but Drake's relentless hold upon her mouth did not loosen.

Once again Drake's hand made a slow exploration of the woman's body beneath him. "You have a pleasing shape, lady. Are you Waldo's whore?"

The woman shook her head again and tried to bite Drake's hand, but he was wise to all the tricks she might employ. "This time I will accept Waldo's offering. Methinks you will be worth it, lady."

She squirmed beneath him as he hiked up her skirts and thrust his hand between her legs. "You smell good, lady," Drake said, burying his nose in her hair. "You please me well. Even though I cannot see you, your body tells me all I need to know."

Panic rose in Raven's breast as Drake hiked up her skirts and thrust his hand between her legs. He was naked. She could feel his maleness pressing intimately against her softness. She had crept from the keep tonight to plead one last time for Drake's help. Thinking him asleep, she had ducked into the darkened tent and only realized her mistake when he pounced on her without warning. She had known that surprising the Black Knight was not a good idea, one she was likely to regret.

But she had been desperate. The tourney tomorrow would be the last, and the day after that was her wedding day. She feared Drake would leave immediately after the tourney, so she had ventured out to his campsite tonight against her better judgment. And now it appeared as if she was about to be brutally ravished.

Raven tried to buck Drake off her as he dragged her legs apart and settled himself in the cradle of her thighs. She groaned, crushed by his muscular frame and unable to protest his vile treatment. He thought she was a whore sent by Waldo to do him harm. Somehow she had to convey her identity to him before he raped her.

Raven felt his male member brush against her woman's place and a scream rose in her throat. She tried to bite his hand again. This time God was with her, for she succeeded in sinking her teeth into the fleshy pad of his palm. His hand jerked away long enough for her to call out his name.

She felt Drake stiffen and raise himself up on his elbows. "Raven? God's blood! Was Waldo so desperate to be rid of me that he sent his betrothed to do me in?"

"Nay!" She tried to shove him away from her, but he was immovable.

"Why *are* you here?" he asked harshly.

"To plead for your help one last time. I cannot abide this marriage."

"Are you mad, lady? Waldo will beat you black and blue should he learn you visited my tent in the middle of the night."

"Are you going to tell him?" Raven challenged.

She had him there. He would not tell Waldo, and she knew it. Then his thoughts slid to a halt as Raven squirmed beneath him. A moan gathered low in his throat, threatening to strangle him. She felt amazingly good beneath him. He had but to flex his hips to enter her, and he was tempted to do exactly what his body demanded. Then his senses returned and he realized that taking Raven would mean committing himself to help her, which was not his intention at all. Reluctantly he levered himself off her and drew a blanket around his nakedness despite the darkness shielding him from her eyes.

"You had better go before I change my mind," he rasped. "And if by chance Waldo *did* send you, tell him it did not work."

He heard rather than felt Raven scramble to her feet. "I no longer know you, Drake. You are so entrenched in bitterness and bent on obtaining wealth that there is no room in your heart for compassion."

"I have no heart," Drake flung back. "Find some other knight to draw into your web of intrigue. Someone who still believes in the chivalric code. Once I am declared champion of the tournament, I will take the purse and begin rebuilding Windhurst. One day it will be as grand as it was before it fell into ruin."

"That is another thing I wished to speak to you about," Raven confided. "Waldo has trickery in mind. I wanted to warn you to take care. I know not what he intends next, but I am almost certain he tainted the wine he sent to you. Since you did not fall ill, I suppose you already suspected foul play."

"Aye, I know Waldo well, Raven. 'Tis not the first time he has made attempts upon my life. He hired an assassin to slay me shortly after I entered the king's service, before I distinguished myself in

France and became known as the Black Knight." His voice turned hard. "The man confessed before I ran him through. Strange, is it not?" he mused. "Why would Waldo want to do away with me? I pose no threat to him that I know of."

"I am not so sure you pose no threat to Waldo," Raven replied. "For some reason Waldo fears you. All was well when he thought you were dead. But when you appeared as the Black Knight, he felt threatened by you in a way I do not understand."

"One day, I vow, I will learn why Waldo wants me dead. Meanwhile, I must strengthen my holdings and prepare for the day I go forth to seek answers."

"You were my last hope," Raven said on a sob. "I am doomed."

He heard the muted sound of her retreating footsteps and had to steel himself against pulling her into his arms and soothing her fears. But he knew that involving himself in Raven's problems was not in his best interest. He owed her naught. She held neither his heart nor his fealty. All women must marry and give heirs to their husbands; why should Raven think she was different?

Still, the thought of Raven suffering Waldo's vile attentions did not sit well with him. The sooner he left this cursed castle, the better off he would be. Had he known he would be attending Raven and Waldo's wedding, he would not have come. He had assumed that Raven had long since married Aric of Flint, and that his brother was at Eyre, lording over his domain.

The sound of Raven's sobbing remained behind long after she slipped from the tent. He suffered an unaccountable sense of loss, as if he were more alone now than he had ever been in his life. He gave himself a shake to clear his head of disturbing thoughts that had no place in the life of the Black Knight and settled down to sleep.

Trumpets announced the final day of the tournaments. After attending morning Mass, Drake entered his tent to prepare himself for a strenuous day of jousting. Evan was waiting to dress him. First came his gambeson, then his shiny black armor. Last, Evan handed Drake his blunted lance and sword and fixed his helm upon his head. Drake had but one more thing to do before he donned his gauntlets. He removed Raven's veil from his war chest and tied it on his lance, where Waldo was sure to see it.

Drake entered the lists and waited on the

sidelines for his first contest. He knew the exact moment Waldo saw him, for his brother jerked in his saddle and spurred his destrier in Drake's direction. Drake smiled, aware that Waldo had recognized the veil.

"Which lady has honored you with her favor?" Waldo asked from between clenched teeth.

"Do you not recognize it?" Drake taunted, waving the veil before Waldo's face. "There is but one lady in the keep who owns anything so fine."

"Visitors have come from many leagues to attend the tourneys," Waldo answered. "Several ladies among them wear veils such as this one."

"So they do," Drake said dryly.

"Do you claim 'tis Raven's veil?" Waldo said in a hiss. "Where did you get it?"

"I did not say it was Raven's veil."

"She gave it to you."

"Nay, she did not."

Drake's cryptic answers seemed to enrage Waldo. His face turned so red, Drake feared he would explode. He almost regretted taunting Waldo in such a manner and prayed he had done no harm to Raven by displaying her veil. Making Raven the brunt of Waldo's anger was not his purpose, but he feared it was exactly what he had done.

"Only one of us can be declared champion, Sir Bastard," Waldo said jeeringly, "and the battle between us will not be fought with blunted weapons. When we meet, come with well-honed weapons and prepare for bloodshed." Wheeling his destrier, he rode away, leaving a stunned audience in his wake.

"Does he mean it, my lord?" Evan asked in a hushed voice. " 'Tis not seemly."

"Aye, seemly or not, Waldo meant it."

"He intends to kill you, Drake," Sir John said, voicing what the others feared to say.

"He will not kill me," Drake vowed. "Nor will I kill him. But I *will* win."

The jousting continued until it came down to two undefeated challengers: the Black Knight and Waldo of Eyre. A startled cry came from the spectators when they realized the swords and lances the two men carried were not blunted. The herald approached Waldo first, asking if he knew his weapons were not blunted. Drake saw Waldo nod. Then the herald approached Drake, asking the same question.

" 'Tis not my choice," Drake explained. "I am but complying with Waldo of Eyre's request. He wanted to fight with honed weapons and I follow his lead."

A buzz of excitement erupted from the spectators as Waldo and Drake took their places at either end of the tilt. Honed weapons were rarely used during tournaments, as they were mock battles and not meant to shed blood or take lives. The excitement grew as a hush fell over the crowd as they waited for the herald to give the signal.

When it came, a collective gasp broke the silence as the Black Knight and Waldo rode full tilt at one another. They met with jarring impact. Each lance found its mark but neither man was unhorsed. They rode to opposite ends of the tilt, whirled, paused a moment, then made a second run for one another. This time Drake's lance pierced Waldo's shield, striking his armor. Waldo's lance struck a glancing blow off Drake's helm as Waldo went flying from his horse.

Drake ignored the wild cheers piercing the air. He knew full well Waldo was nowhere near being defeated. Waldo gained his feet and withdrew his sword. Drake dismounted and threw Zeus's reins to Evan, who had run out on the jousting field to take charge of the destrier.

"Now we are on even footing, Sir Bastard," Waldo taunted as he circled Drake.

Drake brandished his own sword, waiting for Waldo to make the first move. "We will never be on even footing, Waldo," Drake said jeeringly. "I am the superior swordsman."

Waldo roared a garbled reply and struck out blindly. Drake easily deflected the blow with his shield. The battle became deadlier as Waldo charged again and again, his bullish strength making up for his lack of finesse. Drake deflected each blow, retaliating with well-placed blows of his own, driving Waldo back each time he charged forward.

The opponents circled each other warily, looking for an opening as they assessed one another's strengths and weaknesses. Their first heated encounter ended in a standoff. They had hacked away at one another with little effect.

"Bastard!" Waldo said in a hiss. "Eyre is mine. So is Raven. You will never have either of them."

Drake had no idea why Waldo taunted him with Eyre, unless he knew something Drake did not. Had Basil told Waldo the truth about Drake's birth? Did Waldo fear that Drake would try to wrest Eyre from him? His thoughts slid to a halt as Waldo attacked with renewed vigor. But Drake was up to the challenge.

The spectators went wild when Drake drew first blood. His sword had found a vulnerable spot in a seam where Waldo's breastplate joined the chain mail at his shoulder. But Waldo appeared undaunted by the superficial wound.

"Do you concede, Waldo of Eyre?" Drake asked. "I have drawn first blood."

"Nay!" Waldo shouted.

The battle continued. The din of clashing steel and the hollow ring of blows upon shields were lost amid the rousing cheers and catcalls of the enthusiastic on-lookers. This was a spectacle they had not anticipated. The thought of bloodshed both thrilled and appalled them at the same time.

White-faced, Raven watched the fierce battle being fought on the jousting field. When she saw that the weapons Drake and Waldo wielded were not blunted, she was seized with a sudden and unaccountable fear. She did not give a hoot what happened to Waldo: all her fear was for Drake, the Black Knight. She knew his reputation as a fierce warrior and an experienced swordsman was well deserved, but she also knew that Waldo was a canny fighter.

Though Drake had denied her request

for help, and held her accountable for something for which she was blameless, she did not hate him. As a child she had loved Drake, and she still felt emotionally bound to him. Unfortunately Drake had never returned her tender feelings.

Raven's silent musings skidded to a halt as the spectators leaped to their feet, cheering. She rose unsteadily, very much afraid of what she might see. Her breath escaped in a loud whoosh when she saw that Drake had drawn first blood. According to the rules, the battle could end there. Her heart nearly stopped when Waldo lunged at Drake, destroying her hopes of seeing an end to this vendetta anytime soon.

Raven knew precisely what had provoked Waldo's ire and could not imagine what had driven Drake to display her veil upon his lance. She knew full well that Drake had intended it as an insult, and that Waldo would feel compelled to retaliate. Had Drake known that his blatant insult would result in the use of real weapons instead of blunted ones? She doubted it.

Suddenly the mood of the crowd changed, as if everyone wanted to end this quickly, without further bloodshed. Raven watched with growing appreciation for

Drake's skill as he drove Waldo back, slashing relentlessly while successfully evading Waldo's counterattacks. Raven knew the battering each man took must be bone-crushing, but both appeared oblivious to the pain.

The pummeling continued, though it was obvious now that the Black Knight's skill far surpassed Waldo's and that Drake had been merely toying with Waldo before vanquishing him. Then, before the spectators knew exactly how it happened, Waldo's sword went flying through the air and Drake's sword was pressed against a vulnerable place on Waldo's throat, protected by neither helm nor breastplate.

The crowd was on its feet, declaring the Black Knight the champion. Then the herald stepped in to proclaim what the spectators already knew. The purse, the glory, and a chest full of gold and other property taken in ransom during the tourneys were the Black Knight's to claim. Some knights would return home penniless and defeated, but the Black Knight had accumulated fabulous wealth for his coffers.

Waldo was forgotten as men and women streamed out onto the jousting field to congratulate Drake, but Raven held back.

She did not wish to further provoke Waldo's anger. She left the pavilion in a rush. She needed time alone to think, to plan a way to escape this odious marriage. Everyone would be at the banquet tonight. The hall would be crowded and noisy. Perhaps she could slip away after the meal and make her own way to Scotland. She did not know if she would be successful, but she was willing to try. One thing she did know: if she was still here on the morrow, she would be forced to wed Waldo of Eyre.

Drake searched the pavilion for Raven and caught a glimpse of her as she hurried away. He did not expect her to congratulate him, not after he had ignored her plea for help, but for some unexplained reason he wanted her to acknowledge his skill and accomplishments on the jousting field. Extricating himself from well-wishers, Drake returned to his tent. He considered taking his prizes and leaving immediately, but something compelled him to stay for the wedding tomorrow.

Chapter Five

Claiming a foe's property is a knight's right.

The banquet that night was held in Drake's honor. As the champion, he was seated at the high table at Duff's right. Raven sat at her brother's left, and Waldo slouched beside Raven, his face dark and brooding. Visiting noblemen and their wives, who had been invited to sup with Drake at the high table, kept the conversation lively.

Drake made a concerted effort to ignore Raven, but despite his resolve, his gaze kept straying in her direction. He recalled how soft and pliable her body had felt beneath his, and how the fragrance of her woman's place had intrigued him when he thrust his hand between her thighs. He wished now that he had taken her there on the floor of his tent and sated his raging lust. Perhaps then he would have purged her from his mind and body.

Duff leaned over to speak to him and he reluctantly pulled his thoughts into less dangerous territory.

"The feast tonight is naught compared to the wedding feast tomorrow," Duff bragged. "Raven is my only sister now that Daria is dead, and Waldo my best friend. I have spared no expense. The day after they will travel to Eyre, and then I will be alone."

"Do you not fear for Raven's safety?" Drake asked with studied indifference. " 'Tis my understanding that Daria's death occurred under mysterious circumstances."

Duff, as fair as Drake was dark, scowled. " 'Tis naught but malicious gossip. Daria died from a stomach ailment. She was never very robust."

"If I recall, Daria's health was excellent," Drake contradicted.

" 'Twas a long time ago," Duff said with a shrug. "You wanted Daria, did you not? Aye, I remember now. You were going to elope with Daria, but Father found out and banished you from the castle. Count yourself lucky, Drake. You would have earned neither glory nor fame with Daria as your wife."

Drake's hands curled into fists. It appalled him to think that Duff thought so little of Daria, that he was giving Raven to the same man who might be responsible for Daria's death. He dared a glance at

Raven and met her unswerving gaze. Their eyes met and clung, hers filled with desperation, his with cool reproach. Then she lowered her gaze to her trencher. Drake felt an unfamiliar stirring within him and silently cursed himself for letting his guard down. He plied his knife and spoon with diligence as he tried to forget the fiery challenge of Raven's green eyes.

The long meal concluded and the entertainers were summoned. Raven rose from her chair and excused herself. Waldo leaped to his feet and spoke quietly to the squire standing behind his chair. The squire nodded and followed Raven from the hall. Both Drake and Duff looked askance at Waldo.

"I want to make certain my bride-to-be has a restful night, one without interference," Waldo explained. His gaze rested on Drake when he spoke. "I have instructed my squire to stand guard outside Raven's chamber until she emerges for the wedding."

Duff stared at Waldo a moment, then nodded. "'Tis most thoughtful of you, Waldo. It pleases me to know my sister will be in good hands. Raven can be a bit difficult at times, but she will come around."

"Aye," Waldo agreed. "She will indeed come around. I will see to it."

Drake's eyes narrowed as he considered the various methods Waldo might use to tame Raven, none of them particularly appetizing.

Raven paced her chamber in a rage. How dared Waldo place a guard at her door? How dared he treat her like a prisoner? They were not even married yet. How would he treat her when she was completely under his domination? Deciding to test Waldo's control, she boldly flung open the door. The squire came to instant attention.

"How may I help you, my lady?"

"Please step aside. I wish to leave," Raven said in her most authoritative voice.

"Sorry, my lady. Lord Waldo said you are not permitted to leave your chamber until Lord Duff arrives in the morning to escort you to the church. I am to admit no one but your maid."

Raven slammed the door in the young man's face, her anger explosive. Trapped. She was trapped in this chamber with no means of escape. No matter how much she abhorred the thought of becoming Waldo's wife, she had exhausted all her options.

Drake had been her last hope. She was doomed . . . doomed. Tomorrow the church bell might as well be tolling her death knell instead of announcing her wedding.

Drake was awake long before prime. He had not slept a wink the entire night. During the long, sleepless night he had searched his brain for an answer to Waldo's long-standing hatred for him and could discover no real reason for it. Nothing made sense.

Drake's mind turned to the wedding that would take place in a few hours. When the bell tolled sext, Duff would escort Raven to the church, where Waldo would be waiting to receive his bride. According to custom, the ceremony would take place on the church steps, conducted by the village priest. Afterward, both the invited guests and villagers would partake of the feast. The guests would gather in the hall while the villagers and castle servants would be served from long tables set up in the inner bailey.

Drake bathed in the stream behind his tent and dressed with care. True to the Black Knight's image, he chose a fitted black velvet tunic and black hose. Since

112

the occasion called for a dash of color, the wide sleeves of Drake's thigh-length tunic were lined in lime-yellow satin. Soft leather shoes with slightly pointed toes and silver buckles complemented his costume. As a final touch, Drake donned a hip-length cloak of purple velvet with an upstanding collar of vermilion cloth.

When the church bells tolled sext, he mounted Zeus and rode the short distance to the village church. He dismounted, handed his reins to his squire, who had trotted along beside him, and joined the crowd waiting outside the church for the bride to arrive.

Drake glanced at Waldo and a derisive smile twisted his lips. Gaudily dressed in a peacock satin tunic, wearing one green hose and one scarlet hose and a short cloak of scarlet velvet, he awaited his bride on the church steps with the priest. His face was flushed, as if he had imbibed long into the previous night, and his expression was one of gleeful anticipation.

A collective sigh rose up from the crowd as Raven came into sight. She rode upon the back of a snow white horse. Duff, who was dressed every bit as colorfully as the bridegroom, held the reins. Drake's gaze settled on Raven, robed in her wedding

113

finery, and the ability to speak left him. Her beauty rivaled the moon and the stars.

Her long-sleeved undergown was fashioned of gold tissue. Over it she wore a high-waisted gown of royal blue velvet, with a full skirt that covered the horse's rump like a shimmering blanket. Her high collar had a turnback of ermine, and her full sleeves were trimmed with a wide band of the same precious fur. Her headdress was fashioned of cream-colored net and trimmed with pearls. The trailing veil flowed loosely over her shoulders and down her back.

Drake's hot gaze did not stray overlong on her finery, but went unerringly to her face, and lingered. She looked tired, as if she had slept little the night before. As little as he, mayhap? Her eyes were shadowed and her mouth trembled; her gaze found his and clung to it. Then abruptly she looked away, as if aware that she could expect no help from the Black Knight.

Drake's eyes narrowed as she reached the church steps and Duff helped her to dismount. He winced when Waldo clutched her arm with more force than he thought necessary, dragging her up beside him.

The ceremony commenced. Drake watched with curious detachment as

Waldo and Raven were pronounced husband and wife. As the last words died away, the wrongness of the joining weighed so heavily upon him he had to turn away before he did something he would later regret. He wanted to tear Raven from Waldo's arms, though what he would do with her afterward, he had no idea. He tried to convince himself that Raven meant nothing to him, that he liked her no better now than he had before. Despite that, he considered her too good for Waldo. Yet it was Waldo who would undress her, Waldo who would hold her sweet, warm body in his arms. Waldo who would claim her virginity.

Dark, dangerous thoughts took root inside his brain, thoughts so outrageous he feared for his sanity. He did not want Waldo to be the first with Raven. Unfortunately there was little he could do about it. He had refused to help her escape this marriage and now it was too late. Or was it?

The feasting began immediately following the ceremony. Duff brought out the good French wine, and men and women drank freely of the potent beverage. The guests soon became rowdy. Vulgar jokes and crude advice concerning the wedding night and the deflowering were passed along to the high table, with little consideration for the delicate ears of the blushing bride. Drake held his tongue, drinking more wine than he should have. He wanted to get roaring drunk so he would not have to think about Waldo's heavy body claiming Raven's delicate beauty.

Little sobriety existed in the hall during the celebration, which lasted far into the night. Drake was deep into his cups but not too drunk to notice that Raven was being led off to the bridal chamber by her maid. Then Waldo said something vulgar concerning his virgin bride and what he intended to do to her. Drake knew Raven must have heard, for her steps faltered a moment before she squared her shoulders and continued. Something dark, cold, and threatening rose up inside Drake, nearly choking him. Someone had to pay for the injustices done to him and his mother by his father, his grandfather, and his brother.

Waldo had to pay.

Drake knew he should leave the celebration, but he continued to drink and brood and watch Waldo through slitted eyes. As the shadows lengthened, Duff and the guests began drifting away. Drake was more than a little surprised that Waldo had not yet joined his bride. Were he Raven's bridegroom, he would have been eager to consummate his vows. He glanced at Waldo. It did not take a seer to realize that Waldo, lolling at the table with his most trusted knights, was thoroughly drunk. His voice had grown raucous and the jokes bandied about the table were crude.

Sir John strode up to join Drake, noted the direction of his gaze, and said, " 'Tis time to leave. Forget Waldo. We leave this place considerably richer than we arrived."

"Look at him," Drake said disgustedly. "He lets his bride wait while he makes merry. He is so drunk he can hardly bestir himself from his chair." He gave a harsh laugh. "Methinks Waldo is in no condition to rise to the occasion when he does join his bride."

" 'Tis no concern of yours, Drake," John advised. "Let us be off."

Drake was halfway off the bench when he saw Waldo fold his arms on the table and lower his head onto them. "Look, John, Waldo has fallen asleep. His friends are deserting him to make their beds in the hall."

John sent him worried look. "What are you planning, Drake? I know that look well, my friend. Trouble brews, and it does not bode well for Waldo."

"How long do you think Waldo will sleep?" Drake asked as the same scandalous thought he had entertained earlier returned with renewed tenacity.

"You are drunk," Sir John exclaimed. "Your mind is not working clearly."

Drake smiled grimly. " 'Tis working well enough, my friend. Methinks Waldo does not deserve a wedding night. Mayhap I will take his place in Raven's bed."

John leaped to his feet, his face contorted with fear. "Are you mad? You have tempted fate many times in the past, but this surpasses anything you have ever done. Waldo will kill you. And what of the lady? Think you she will let you ravish her? The wine has gone to your head." He grasped Drake's arm. "Come away with me. 'Tis clear you are thinking with the head between your legs, not the one upon your shoulders."

"Nay, my friend, I am thinking clearly for the first time in days. Taking his virgin bride's maidenhead is the kind of revenge Waldo will understand."

"What if Waldo awakens while you are . . . er . . . relieving his bride of her virginity?"

"You will see that he does not awaken,"

Drake said as he rose and approached the dais. John followed close on his heels. Drake paused beside Waldo's chair, listened a moment to his snoring, and gave a snort of disgust. "If my brother awakens before I return, use the hilt of your sword to put him back to sleep. No one will know. His squires and men-at-arms have already sought their beds."

"I must be mad myself to abet this folly. How long must I wait here?"

Drake darted a glance toward the stairs leading to the wedding chamber and smiled. What he intended would not be rape. A subtle seduction was more what he had in mind. He wanted Raven to enjoy her deflowering.

"No less than two hours. Three, if you can manage to keep Waldo incapacitated that long."

John's blond eyebrows shot upward. "Three hours to deflower a maiden? You must be slipping, Drake. You have been known to accomplish the deed in less than half that time. What makes Raven so special?"

"I have known her since she was a small child. I do not hold any special fondness for her, but for friendship's sake, Raven's deflowering will not be rape."

The look John gave Drake was ripe with disapproval. " 'Tis not a good thing you do."

"Depends on how you look at it," Drake said, taking another long draft of wine to fortify his resolve. "Better me than Waldo. She may thank me for it."

Raven paced her chamber, loathing for her husband so sharp it was like a knife twisting in her gut. Tonight Waldo would come to her. He would expect her to be naked and waiting for him in bed. If she disobeyed or fought him, he could beat her or cause her serious harm. He would thrust her legs apart and tear into her, hurting her. And he had a legal right to do it as often as he liked. The thought of bearing Waldo's child made her want to retch. Yet for her own sake, she hoped she conceived this very night. Perhaps he would leave her alone after he got her with child.

The later the hour grew the more agitated Raven became. Earlier she had bathed in preparation for her deflowering. Then Thelma had taken her clothing from her and tucked her into bed. But Raven had risen the moment her maid left and donned a shift to cover her nakedness.

Then she began to pace and plan. The hour of compline came and went. It was nearing matins when she heard footsteps outside her door. She quickly doused the candle and waited in trepidation for her husband to ravage her, thus making their marriage legal in the eyes of the church.

The door opened and closed. She heard the key grate in the lock and she backed into the darkest corner between the nightstand and the bed. The soft rustle of clothing being shed brought a gasp from her lips. She knew he heard her, for she sensed rather than saw him looking in her direction. She clung to the wall, expecting him to reach for her and drag her to their marriage bed.

Dimly Raven wondered why he did not speak, or indicate what he expected of her, but her mind was too filled with lurid details of the marriage bed to think clearly. Then she heard footsteps stirring the rushes and knew with devastating certainty that in a very short time Waldo would rip her innocence from her. Something lurched inside her. Seized by fear and determination, she grasped the water pitcher sitting on the nightstand and stood ready to defend her virtue.

His face was shadowed as he appeared

in a slice of moonlight that spilled through the window. The breath caught in her throat. The light made a vivid slash across his body, defining every bulge and hollow of his well-honed warrior's body. He stood unmoving, hard and blatantly male. He stepped into the light and she saw his eyes — glittering silver slits against the strong lines of his face.

Drake! Not Waldo. Her mind spun crazily as her gaze wandered down the length of his body, her eyes widening when they came to rest on his manhood. He was full and hard, his sex jutting out from a tangled nest of dark hair. With difficulty she dragged her gaze back up to his face.

His name left her lips on a startled gasp. "I do not understand. Where is Waldo?"

"Come out where I can see you," Drake coaxed, slurring his words.

Her hold on the pitcher tightened. "You are drunk. Or mad. Or both. Waldo will kill you if he finds you here with me."

"Your *husband* is too besotted with wine to do you any good tonight, so I am here to take his place."

"You *are* mad. Unless . . ." She paused and stepped out into the slash of moonlight, where he could see her, her expression hopeful. "Have you come to take me away? To Scotland?"

Drake stared at Raven, his mouth suddenly as dry as dust. Her body glowed enticingly through the diaphanous material of her shift; the hills and hollows of her sweet flesh became a landscape of light and shadows. Her coral nipples poked impudently against her shift, and that dark, intriguing patch between her legs beckoned to him. He grinned and reluctantly returned his gaze to her face.

"Do I look as if I intend to take you away? Nay, lady, I but intend to rob your husband of his wedding night. If what I suspect is true, he has taken my birthright. 'Tis fitting that I take his wife's maidenhead in retaliation for all he has stolen from me."

"You would dishonor me?" Raven gasped, fully prepared to hurl the pitcher at him.

"Put the pitcher down, Raven. I intend to make love to you, not ravish you. 'Tis not you I dishonor, but your husband."

" 'Tis the same thing," Raven replied huffily.

"Are you still unhappy in your marriage? Or have you changed your mind?"

"Nay! I loathe Waldo, but that does not justify what you intend this night."

She hurled the pitcher. Drake caught it handily and carefully set it down on the floor. He reached her in two short strides, grasped her about the waist, and slammed her up against him. "What I intend this night will make you happy, I swear it."

"Bastard!" Raven hissed. "You do not want me for myself. You feel naught for me. I am but an instrument of your revenge. I will not allow it, Drake! Begone."

"Many have called me bastard," Drake replied through gritted teeth. "One day, I vow, I will prove my detractors wrong." He gave her a lopsided smile. "Think you I do not want you? You have but to look at me to see that I lust for you, Raven of Chirk."

Struggling within his arms, Raven cried, "You do not like me! You still blame me for betraying you and Daria despite my denial."

"Forget Daria," Drake said, lurching drunkenly. "I want to lay you on the floor and fill my hands with your bare breasts. I want to feel those long, pale legs wrapped around my hips when I bury myself deep inside you."

God's blood, he was drunker than he'd thought. It occurred to him that he would *have* to be drunk to do something so utterly dishonorable. But now that he was here, there was no turning back.

He gazed down upon her. Moonlight turned her eyes into seething pools of green fire. But it was her lips that intrigued Drake the most. Ripe and lush, they beckoned him, enticed him, lured him to taste of their sweetness. She must have realized his intent, for she opened her mouth to protest, but to Drake it was a blatant invitation. He brought his mouth down hard over hers.

A groan gathered in his throat when he realized she tasted as sweet as he'd imagined. He snagged a fist in her hair and deepened the kiss, thrusting his tongue into her mouth in subtle imitation of what he wanted to do to her below. He kissed her hungrily, fiercely, savagely slanting his mouth back and forth against hers.

She whimpered and somehow managed to drag her mouth away. "Drake, stop!"

"Nay, not now. You are far too tempting for a mere mortal to resist."

Raven knew exactly what Drake meant. Temptation worked both ways. Though she abhorred the reason behind Drake's seduction of her, her body had turned traitor the moment he kissed her. Could one hate and love at the same time? she wondered. His touch was pure fire. She was consumed by it. His hands were everywhere, roughly exploring her back, her waist, her hips, her buttocks, branding her, scalding her, claiming her.

Marshaling her strength, she pummeled his back when he swept her from her feet and carried her to her marriage bed, pinning her down with his hard body. He splayed his fingers through her hair, tilting her chin up with his thumbs as he blazed a path down her throat to her breasts, where he tongued a pert nipple through the material of her shift. His hands kneaded her breasts. Raven hissed a protest as he tore her shift from neck to hem and tossed it aside. Then his hands were on her bare skin, and though she fought against it, Raven felt a melting deep inside her. When he shoved her legs apart and settled between them, her senses returned and she fought desperately to dislodge him.

"Drake! Desist! You are drunk. You do not really want to do this."

"You are wrong, my lady. 'Tis precisely what I want."

She gazed into his determined eyes and knew she had lost. His rigid arousal rode against her, impressing her with the solid proof of his need. He was all heat and shocking hardness. She hissed out a breath when he grasped her hand and dragged it between them, curling it around his jutting manhood.

"Think you I do not want you? This is how much."

Raven's fingers closed reflexively around his staff. It pulsed with a life of its own, steel encased in silk. He was so big. Strength and virility throbbed within the palm of her hand as he let out a rasping cry. Would he hurt her? she wondered. She decided he would not, not as badly as Waldo, anyway. Frightened by the direction of her thoughts, she jerked her hand away.

Then his mouth closed over hers again, hungry, demanding a response, and receiving it despite Raven's reluctance to be drawn into his seduction. He kissed her until she thought she would swoon, until he had wrung a response from her. Apparently encouraged, he deepened his kiss. She sighed into his mouth when his fingertips teased the insides of her thighs. Then she felt an entirely new sensation as he slipped a thick finger inside her. Raven thought she felt him shudder but realized it was her own reaction she felt.

She moaned when his thumb slid over her, finding a sensitive spot he had stirred into aching need. He continued to kiss her as his stroking stoked the fire smoldering within her to a blazing inferno. She could not think, though somewhere in a remote corner of her brain she realized she should be fighting harder to resist. But all she could feel was liquid pleasure flowing through her . . . gathering and intensifying.

Despite the wickedness of the moment, Raven was experiencing passion for the first time in her life and reveling in it. Had she truly cared for her husband, she would have fought Drake tooth and nail, but she despised Waldo. She did not ponder the consequences, nor did she consider the severity of Waldo's punishment when he learned what had happened in her marriage bed tonight. Her senses exploded with the scent and taste of the man who was doing wickedly wonderful things to her.

With Drake's talented fingers arousing her and his kisses stealing her mind, Waldo no longer existed. This time she needed no coaxing as she reached between them and closed her fingers around his erection, stroking him to throbbing hardness.

"God's blood!" His rasping cry sounded as though it had been torn from the deepest part of him. "You try me sorely, lady." His eyes darkened to pools of molten silver. "Do you want me, Raven?"

" 'Tis not right," Raven replied after a lengthy pause. "We will both go to hell for this night's madness. But I cannot lie, Drake of Windhurst; I do want you. May God forgive me."

"You need no forgiveness," Drake said almost angrily. "You are blameless. An innocent, too inexperienced to stop me. Tell that to Waldo if he questions your lack of virginity."

Raven knew Waldo would react violently when he learned he had been cheated of her maidenhead, but she was too far gone with passion to think that far ahead. Later, after experiencing the pleasure Drake offered, she could hate him for dishonoring her. Naught mattered now, however, but experiencing more of the arousing things he was doing to her. She knew intuitively that bedding Waldo would give her no pleasure, and she desperately wanted to experience pleasure with Drake, if only for this one time.

Her thoughts slid to an abrupt halt when Drake touched her again between her legs. "You are wet and ready for me, sweeting." Then he slid his hands beneath her naked buttocks and positioned her for his entry. She felt him, smooth as velvet, hard and

129

hot, pressing against her entrance. She sucked in a shaky breath and waited for the pain.

"Relax," Drake whispered against her ear. " 'Twas never my intent to hurt you. There will be pain, but I will make it as easy for you as I know how."

Then he was inside her, stretching and filling her with his hardness. It hurt more than she had expected, and she cried out. Sensing her distress, he pulled almost out of her, then drove in again, tearing through her maidenhead in one clean thrust. Raven felt the sharp, rending pain and gave a muted shriek. Embedded deeply inside her now, Drake suddenly went still.

"I will not move until you tell me to," he rasped harshly. He raised his body up on his elbows and stared down at her. "I know it must feel strange to be totally possessed by a man."

She whimpered and suddenly Drake was stone-cold sober. Raven's cry of pain had instantly sobered him. Unfortunately it was too late to undo what had already been done. *God's blood!* He must have been mad to come here like this. As much as he hated Waldo, he would have never attempted so dishonorable a deed had he not been drunk.

"You are so big." Raven gasped as she moved experimentally beneath him. "The pain is not so bad now."

Drake's thoughts centered on the innocent woman beneath him. He had stolen her maidenhead and now he owed her something in return. Since he could not return her torn membrane, he felt compelled to give her pleasure.

He moved inside her slowly, deliberately, piercing her deeply, again and again, creating a rhythm that Raven was quick to imitate. She rose up to meet his thrusts, inviting him to thrust deeper, harder, faster. He was quick to comply, pounding into her as she threaded her fingers through his hair, holding his head and offering her lips.

Her blood heated and thickened as he kissed her lips, her throat, her breasts. She writhed mindlessly against him, offering more of herself as he sucked and licked her nipples. She heard him groaning and the sound sparked a responsive chord within her. She grasped at something just beyond her reach but had no idea what it was.

"You are nearly there," Drake rasped huskily. "I will not leave you, sweeting. Come. Come with me."

Raven started to ask where he wanted

her to go when something inside her broke loose. Suddenly she was awash in pleasure, spinning in a whirlpool of pure sensation. Instinctively her legs came around him, drawing him deeper into her center, each pounding thrust sending wave after wave of unspeakable delight coursing through her. She was still lost in the throes of ecstasy when he threw back his head, squeezed his eyes shut, bared his teeth in a feral growl, and released his seed. She felt the hot splash bathing her womb and let the pleasure of the moment carry her to oblivion.

An eon later she opened her eyes and saw Drake braced on his elbows, staring down at her with a strange look on his face. She pushed against him in an attempt to dislodge him. She heard him sigh as he pulled out of her body and moved away.

"I should not have done that," he said. Raven stared at him, appalled by his sudden flash of conscience. "I was drunk," he offered lamely. "All I can say in my defense is that Waldo provoked me." He grinned at her. "I cannot say I did not enjoy making love to you, Raven of Chirk."

Raven wanted to smack him, and would have if an insistent rapping upon her chamber door had not startled her.

"Drake. 'Tis time to leave. Waldo is stirring."

" 'Tis Sir John," Drake explained as he rose from the bed and hastily donned the clothing he had recently discarded.

"Be at ease, John; I am coming," he called through the door.

"Hurry, Drake," John urged. "I will meet you in the stables."

Drake turned back for one last look at Raven and felt an inexplicable stirring deep inside him. She lay supine amid the rumpled disorder of her marriage bed, a wanton creature with swollen lips and passion-glazed eyes. She looked as though she had been well loved and thoroughly sated. She also looked angry.

"Go!" she said angrily. "Waldo will kill you should he find you in my chamber."

"Will you care?" Drake asked.

"Nay! I hate you, Drake of Windhurst. Almost as much as I hate Waldo. You took away my innocence because of some deep-seated hatred for your brother."

"I took naught from you, my lady. Deny it all you want, Raven of Chirk, but you wanted me. You gave willingly. 'Tis Waldo I cheated, not you."

"The devil take you, Drake!" Raven

cursed. "You are well named, Black Knight, for your heart is as black as your trappings."

Drake offered no defense as he slipped out the door and closed it softly behind him.

Chapter Six

A knight protects those weaker than himself.

Raven rose unsteadily from the bed, wadded up the torn shift stained with the proof of her virginity, and kicked it beneath the bed. Her thoughts were in a turmoil as she struck a flame to the candle and poured water from the pitcher into a bowl. Despite everything that had happened, she still had the presence of mind to wash all traces of Drake's seed and her own blood from her thighs.

Her body still throbbed from Drake's loving, and despite her inclination to hate him for what he had done to her, she could not. Instinctively she knew Waldo would not have been as gentle with her as Drake had been. Waldo would have ripped into her, appeased his own lust, then chided her for complaining about his roughness.

Raven finished her ablutions and tossed the water and soiled washcloth out the window. Then she donned a clean shift and perched on the edge of the bed to think. Waldo would appear soon to consummate their marriage vows; he would expect to find a virgin. When he found no maidenhead, she feared he would kill her. It was not unheard-of for a husband to kill his wife for her lack of innocence. Dimly she wondered if he would be too drunk to realize her lack, then laughed at her own foolishness. Of course he would know.

That thought brought another. Had Drake been too drunk to consider the aftermath of his dastardly deed? Did he care that she would bear the brunt of Waldo's anger? Apparently not, for he had left with scant regard for her welfare. She had to rely upon herself now, decide her future. One thing was becoming increasingly clear: she could not, would not, let Waldo touch her. Not after Drake had shown her how pleasurable making love could be. Somehow she had to find a way to prevent Waldo from exercising his rights.

Raven's thoughts fled when she heard shuffling footsteps outside her door. Panic-stricken, she leaped to her feet just as the door opened and Waldo lurched inside. His gait was unsteady as he stumbled forward, his bleary gaze fixed upon her.

"Why are you not naked?" he roared. "Remove your shift and get into bed."

Raven stood her ground. "Nay."

Waldo's mouth dropped open. "You dare to say me nay?" he roared. Though his eyes were unfocused, his face was set in determined lines despite his obvious state of inebriation. "Do you deny my right to bed you?"

Raven's chin lifted. She had considered every possible course of action and had finally reached a decision scant seconds before Waldo burst into her chamber. She knew her life was at stake, but it would be worth it to gain freedom from Waldo.

"I do not want you in my bed, Waldo of Eyre."

His expression was almost comical. "You dare to defy me?"

"Aye. I dare anything to keep you away from me."

"Bitch!" he said with a snarl. "I will not be denied your maidenhead. I have waited too long for that pleasure. I married another when it was you I wanted. Your spirit, your fire, you are everything I have ever desired, not that pale sister of yours."

Raven braced herself against the bedpost, gathering courage. She had no idea how Waldo would react once she told him she was no longer a virgin, but he would find out ere this night was over. Taking a deep breath, she said, "You cannot take my innocence, my lord, for I no longer possess it. 'Twas freely given to another."

Raven watched in horror as Waldo's face turned from furious white to fiery red. Raven feared her rash tongue had been her undoing.

"Nay! You lie. Not even you would dare such defiance."

" 'Tis true, I tell you. Send for the midwife; she will confirm my lack of virginity."

He stalked her relentlessly, until she was backed up against the bed. She maneuvered around him but he followed, his face now a sickly shade of green.

His thundering voice was loud enough to awaken the dead. "With whom have you cuckolded me? I will have his name, wife. The bastard will die before the hour is out."

"You do not know him," Raven hedged.

No matter what, Drake's name would never leave her lips. As a child she had loved Drake. As a woman she still felt stirrings of long-suppressed emotion for him. *Before the cock crows,* Raven vowed, *Drake will discover that no one takes advantage of Raven of Chirk and gets away with it. Not even the illustrious Black Knight, the bravest of the brave.* Whether he liked it or not, she intended to confront Drake and demand that he make amends for what he had done to her.

Waldo was so close now she smelled the foulness of his wine-soaked breath. She gagged and turned away. Waldo grasped her chin between his thumb and forefinger in a hurtful grip and forced her to look at him.

"Name the coward you are protecting, Raven, ere I beat his name out of you."

"Did you beat my sister, Waldo?" Raven challenged. "Did you kill her when she displeased you?"

His beady eyes blazing with fury, he hauled his hand back and slapped her. The stunning blow sent Raven crashing to the floor. He bent to lift her for more of his abuse, but Raven, still in control of her senses despite her reeling head, rolled across the rushes to escape his heavy hand.

"I know who you fornicated with," Waldo bellowed, lumbering after her. " 'Twas my bastard brother! You fornicated with him beneath my very nose. I will kill him. Right after I kill you."

Raven searched frantically for a weapon. In his drunken rage, she feared Waldo would make good his threat. She rolled away again, and suddenly the pitcher she had flung at Drake earlier, the one he had caught and placed on the floor, lay within her grasp. Curling her hand around the handle, she held her breath as Waldo bent forward to drag her to her feet. Expelling a whoosh of air, she brought the earthenware pitcher down on Waldo's head, shattering it into a hundred pieces. His stunned gaze met her own elated one, and then he collapsed in a boneless heap on top of her.

Raven shoved him off her, leaped to her feet, and slowly backed away. When Waldo did not move, she skirted him and ran to her clothes chest. Dragging out the first gown she laid her hands on, she dressed quickly and pulled on her sturdiest shoes. When Waldo still did not move, she shook a pillow free from its casing and filled the pillowcase with all the clothing she could stuff into it. Then, despite the warm weather, she threw a dark, fur-lined cloak around her shoulders and edged toward the door.

As she passed Waldo's prone body, she wondered if she had killed him. She did not like him but she did not wish him dead. It would be a heavy burden to bear. Gathering her courage, she bent and placed a hand on his chest. The steady beat of his heart beneath her palm relieved her of all guilt. With grim purpose, she slipped out the door and noiselessly descended the spiral staircase.

She paused at the foot of the stairs and listened a moment to the snoring and snorting of the men sleeping in the hall. Torches placed in sconces around the hall provided sufficient light for Raven to ascertain that all was quiet. Rather than leave by the main entrance and risk discovery, she skirted the hall and exited through a door used by servants to bring food in from the kitchen.

No one was stirring in the inner bailey. Inebriated guests and men-at-arms were sprawled against the keep wall and curtain wall. Raven slipped around the snoring men and approached the stables. She breathed a sigh of relief when she found it deserted but for the horses.

With quiet efficiency, Raven saddled her favorite mare and led her from the stables. No one stopped her. The guard at the gate was slumped against his post, sleeping off the wedding ale. She did not mount her horse until she had passed through the barbican and crossed the drawbridge that had been lowered to allow the visiting jousters to return to their campsites outside the castle walls.

★ ★ ★

Sober now and in complete control of his mind, Drake found himself mercilessly plagued by his conscience. He had abused the chivalric oath he had taken and was deeply troubled by his dishonorable act. He had allowed his quest for vengeance to blur his judgment. What he had done to Raven was unconscionable. Furthermore, only a coward would have left Raven to face Waldo's rage alone. He was not proud of what he had done. The Black Knight had performed many scandalous deeds in his life, but never had he dishonored a lady.

Cold sweat popped out on his brow. What would Waldo do to Raven when he discovered she had no maidenhead? Cursing himself for a fool, Drake quickly changed from his wedding finery and roused his squire from his bed.

"Awaken the men," Drake ordered crisply when the sleepy-eyed lad appeared. "I want them ready to ride when I return."

" 'Tis still dark, my lord, and the men have imbibed freely at the wedding feast," Evan said.

"Rouse them anyway, Evan. We may be required to leave in haste."

Evan gave him a puzzled look. "Where do you go, my lord?"

"I left unfinished business behind in the keep," Drake bit out. "Go now."

Drake had decided to return to the keep to save Raven from Waldo's rage. He did not want to kill his brother if he did not have to. No matter what he did, though, he would doubtless be declared an outlaw by his king and country. But honor demanded that he offer Raven his protection. If that meant abducting her to keep her safe, so be it.

Drake recalled Raven's sweet response to his seduction and felt himself growing hard. Her body, everything about her, was perfection. He had not expected to take such enjoyment in her womanly charms. Not even experienced women had satisfied him as Raven had tonight. And how had he repaid her? By stealing her virginity and leaving her to suffer the consequences. Honor demanded that he make amends. The least he could do was to make it possible for her to flee to Scotland. He would offer Sir John as escort.

The thunder of pounding hooves caught Drake's straying attention and he reached for his sword. The moon hung high in the sky, bathing the ground in silvery shadows. Drake squinted through the darkness and nearly lost the ability to speak when he recognized both the horse and rider. Upon the back of a pure white mare sat a woman whose rich chestnut hair gleamed darkly in the moonlight.

Raven.

Drake's brow furrowed with concern as he waited for her to reach him. He had no idea what had taken place after he'd left her bedchamber, but his imagination conjured up several unpleasant scenarios. Not one of them pictured Raven riding into his camp well after the hour of matins.

Raven brought her mare to a halt and Drake reached up to lift her from the saddle.

"What happened? Where is Waldo?"

"Lying on the floor of the bridal chamber." She paused, squinting up at him. "He knows." Her voice was flat, devoid of all emotion.

"He knows?" Drake repeated dumbly.

"Aye, I told him I was not the innocent he expected and he flew into a rage."

"You told him? He did not find out for himself?" The thought that Waldo had bedded Raven after Drake had made love to her had caused him a wealth of anguish. Her words seemed to soothe the pain.

"I did not want him touching me."

"Was he sober enough to know what you

were telling him?"

"Aye." She touched her cheek. "He did not take it well, so I bashed him with the water pitcher. He was unconscious when I left. With luck, he will not stir until we are well away."

Drake's eyebrows rose sharply upward. "*We?* Are you including me, my lady?"

"Waldo knows 'twas you. He knew there could be no other and has vowed to kill you."

Drake searched her face. It was half-concealed by shadows and he could not see it clearly. "Did the bastard hurt you?"

Raven lifted her chin, giving Drake a clear view of her face. "Not enough to stop me from bashing him. He will kill me if he finds me."

Drake saw the darkening bruise on her cheek and rage seethed through him. He reached out and gently caressed the bruise. "Nay, he will not kill you, Raven of Chirk. I will not let him."

Her eyes darkened with unbridled fury. "Tell me no lies, Black Knight, for I will not believe them. You left me to face Waldo's wrath alone, and for that I will never forgive you. You knew he might slay me and yet you left me to face his fury alone. You owe me your escort to my aunt's home in Edinburgh."

"Believe what you will, Raven, but I intended to return to the keep to make amends for what I did to you. I was going to help you flee. Now that you are here, Sir John will escort you to Scotland."

"'Tis a bit late for your conscience to make an appearance, Drake of Windhurst," Raven said with rancor.

Evan's arrival forestalled Drake's answer. "The men are making ready to ride, my lord." He gave Raven a sidelong glance. "Will the lady accompany us?"

"Nay," Drake said. "Send Sir John to me posthaste."

Evan sprinted off to do Drake's bidding.

Raven fidgeted nervously, casting furtive glances over her shoulder. "Waldo will awaken soon, and I do not wish to be anywhere near when he does."

Men were moving about now, preparing for their departure. Drake guided Raven away from the commotion so he could speak privately to her.

"Sir John will give you escort to Scotland. 'Tis the best I can offer. Unfortunately I cannot offer my own services, for I am needed at Windhurst."

Sir John strode up to join them, saw Raven, and blinked in surprise. "Evan said you wished to speak with me."

"Aye, John. You know Lady Raven, I believe."

"Aye. Please excuse my bad manners, my lady. I am surprised to find you here at this late hour."

"There is scant time to lose, John," Drake said, jumping into the silence left by Raven's embarrassment. "Lady Raven has urgent need of an escort to Edinburgh. I offered your services."

John sent Drake a disapproving look. "I knew no good would come of this night," he said sourly.

Raven let out a wounded cry. The sound made Drake cringe, for he knew he was the cause of her distress.

"I am sorry, Raven. Sir John knows everything."

"E-everything?"

"Aye." He returned his attention to John, avoiding Raven's murderous glare. "What say you, John? Will you escort Lady Raven to Edinburgh?"

"You are not thinking clearly," John chided. "Am I right in assuming that Raven is fleeing from her husband?"

"You are right, of course," Drake concurred. "She must leave immediately, before Waldo rouses his men-at-arms. Should

147

Duff decide to join him, we will be sadly outnumbered."

"Am I also correct in assuming that Waldo knows what, er . . . happened in the lady's bridal chamber tonight?"

"Damn it, man, speak your piece."

John turned his attention to Raven. "Lady Raven, does Waldo suspect you might flee to Scotland?"

"Duff would know if Waldo does not. I sought permission to visit my aunt after Duff betrothed me to Waldo. He knew I disliked Waldo and would try to seek my aunt's protection. He denied my request and refused to let me leave the keep unaccompanied."

John nodded sagely, then returned his attention to Drake. "Edinburgh will be the first place Waldo will look for his wife. Think you he will let anyone keep him from Raven? Nay, Drake, Waldo has legal right to take his wife back into his custody."

Drake massaged his throbbing temples, wondering how in God's name he had allowed himself to take Raven's virginity. Honor now demanded that he make amends. He had hoped that sending her to Scotland with an escort would suffice, but instead his life was becoming more complicated by the minute.

"I wish to go to Edinburgh," Raven said firmly.

Drake sighed wearily. "John is right. Waldo will find you within a sennight, and when he claims you your punishment will be severe. Is that what you want?"

"Your concern is touching," Raven said with a touch of sarcasm. "Unfortunately it comes too late. Should my aunt and her husband be unable to protect me, you need not worry, for you will have done your part in getting me there."

Drake did not like the sound of that at all. Abruptly he came to a decision he feared he would live to regret. "You will not go to Scotland."

Raven set her mouth in stubborn lines. "I *will* go."

"You are my responsibility. You would not be in this predicament had I not acted unwisely. Had I not interfered, Waldo would have taken your maidenhead as was his right, and you would be his wife in every way."

Raven's expression grew mutinous. "Aye, and I would have hated every moment of it. Mayhap you did me a favor, Drake of Windhurst."

Drake chuckled mirthlessly. "And mayhap I did myself *no* favor."

He glanced at the bulging pillowcase tied to her saddle horn. "I see you came prepared. Good. We ride for Windhurst immediately."

"Windhurst! Nay. North to Scotland." She mounted her mare and tried to wheel her around, but Drake grasped the reins.

"Hurry the men along, John," Drake ordered crisply. "And send Sir Richard to me. I have a special assignment for him. Dawn is fast approaching and the servants will soon be stirring. We must be away before Waldo awakens and cries the alarm."

Distraught, Raven made a futile attempt to wrest the reins from Drake's hands. She did not want to go to Windhurst. Drake had made it clear that she was naught but an imposition, a burden he had not planned on. Why had he suddenly found a conscience, she wondered, when it had not bothered him while he was making love to her? He had stolen her innocence and left her to face the consequences alone. As a child she had loved the black-hearted devil, only then he was sweet and kind and honorable. She would have accompanied Drake to Windhurst, and gladly, had he not made it clear that she was naught but a penance he had to bear to atone for his sin.

Raven glanced toward the keep and saw

pinpoints of light moving through the darkness. "Torches." Her warning captured Drake's attention.

"God's blood! Waldo has awakened and called out the guards."

"To Windhurst!" Drake cried, spurring his mount.

Raven felt her mare jerk forward and realized that Drake still held her reins. Soon she was riding hard, away from Castle Chirk, away from Waldo, and toward a new life with a man who had used her as an object of revenge against his brother and now considered her a trial he must bear for his sins.

They rode south across the moors and plains throughout the remainder of the night and far into the morning. Raven was so hungry her stomach felt as if it were touching her backbone. They had just crossed a shallow creek when Drake finally called a halt to water and rest their horses, and to prepare the wild game his huntsmen had bagged during their march southward. Raven saw no signs indicating that they were being followed, and she breathed a sigh of relief. She did not relish another encounter with Waldo, for the next time she knew she would not escape unscathed.

Raven sought a shady place beneath a tree and sat down to rest. She closed her eyes for a moment and must have fallen asleep. She did not awaken until she felt someone shaking her. She opened her eyes and saw Drake leaning over her. He was holding a hunk of meat on a stick that smelled delicious.

"My hunters brought in several hares and a small deer. Are you hungry?"

"Famished." She accepted the meat and tore into it with gusto. "When will we reach Windhurst?"

"Not for several days. 'Tis a long way. Windhurst Castle sits on an arm of land in south Wessex that juts out into the sea. 'Tis near the village of Bideford."

"Have you ever seen your holdings?"

"Aye, some years ago. But I lacked the funds to renovate and fortify the castle until now, and saw no reason to go back. After years of competing in tourneys, I have earned enough wealth to repair Windhurst and fund my own army."

Raven chose her words carefully. "I will be in your way. Mayhap you should reconsider and send me to Scotland with Sir John."

He glanced away, and Raven thought he looked as if he had just eaten something sour. "I owe you my protection."

She gave him a disgruntled look. "I will not argue that point with you, but I asked for escort to Scotland, not to some remote castle that has lain in ruin longer than either you or I have lived."

His scowl deepened. "You will be safer with me."

"I cannot live with you forever, Drake. One day you will want to take a wife and I will be in your way. What then?"

"Do you wish to return to Waldo?"

"You know I cannot. I would live in a hovel before returning to Waldo." Suddenly an idea occurred to her, and her face brightened. "I will petition the pope for an annulment."

Drake brushed her words aside with a wave of his hand. "That could take years."

Her face fell as she considered her bleak future. Remaining with Drake would endanger his life, for she knew Waldo would not rest until he had her back in his control. Eventually Waldo would remember Windhurst and come with his army to storm the castle. And by Drake's own admission his fortress was ill prepared to withstand a siege.

"Is there nowhere else I can go to be safe? Mayhap Londontown," she mused.

" 'Tis said one can lose oneself in a town that size."

Drake seemed to consider her suggestion before discarding it out of hand. "Nay. You are gently raised and could not survive on your own in Londontown." He searched her upturned face, then let his gaze slide down the length of her body. "Mayhap I will keep you as my leman."

Raven bristled indignantly. "Does the Black Knight always get what he wants?"

His sexually charged smile sent a shiver down her spine. "Always. You asked for my protection, Raven, and I am extending it to you. I will become your protector and your lover. 'Tis not such a terrible fate, is it, sweeting?"

"You go beyond the bounds of madness," Raven charged. "If I recall correctly, you do not like me."

He dropped down beside her. "Mayhap I have changed my mind. You are a tempting morsel, Raven of Chirk."

Raven's chin rose defiantly. "I will not fornicate with you, Drake of Windhurst."

His next words were low and seductive, setting her heart to pounding erratically.

"Will you not? We shall see about that, my lady."

He cupped her chin in his large palm.

She gazed deeply into his silver eyes and recognized something that both frightened and thrilled her. With a jolt of something akin to shock she realized that this man possessed the power to consume her, body and soul, if she did not guard against him. She had every reason to hate him, yet she could not find it in her heart to do so. Had he not visited her chamber on her wedding night, she would now be chained to Waldo forever.

Raven knew Drake's seduction had not been an honorable act, that he had stolen her maidenhead because he hated her husband, but indirectly it had gained her freedom, precisely what she had been longing for.

Her thoughts would have continued had she not realized that Drake's lips were so close she could feel his breath fanning her cheeks. She realized then that he was going to kiss her. She pressed her back against the tree but there was no escape as he closed the space between them. A startled puff of air left her lungs as his lips descended over hers and his hands grasped her shoulders, pulling her hard against him. His mouth moved slowly, coaxingly over hers, licking the corners of her lips, then thrusting his tongue inside for deeper penetration.

Raven felt her world tilt and spin wildly out of control as his hands sought her breasts beneath her cloak and his talented fingers molded her nipples into aching buds. Just when her body turned traitor and she leaned into him, he abruptly withdrew and handed the plate back to her.

"Eat, Raven. You will need all your strength for the journey ahead." Then he was gone. Raven stared after him in consternation. Apparently he was fully prepared to use his seductive wiles to have her as his leman, and she made a silent vow to resist becoming another of the Black Knight's conquests.

Drake sat apart from his men, eating his food without really tasting it. The devil take Raven of Chirk, he thought morosely. She fed his passion as few women ever had. He wanted her. Now. He wanted to press her down into the hard ground, push up her skirts, and thrust himself inside her tight, sweet passage. He had been the first with her, and for some unexplained reason he wanted to be the last. He shook his head in bewilderment. The notion of wanting Raven was not a comfortable one, especially after bearing her ill will all these years. Who would have thought she would

156

grow into a raving beauty with a body that would tempt a saint? And the good Lord knew he was no saint.

"You seem preoccupied, Drake," Sir John said as he joined Drake. "Do you want company?"

Drake's greeting was anything but welcoming. "Suit yourself."

John eased down beside Drake. "What are you brooding about now, my friend?" He gave Drake a knowing look. "Is it the fair maiden who has you all adither?"

"I have stolen Waldo's bride, or have you forgotten?"

"Nay, I have not forgotten. I warned you 'twas folly but you would not listen. What happens now, Drake?"

Drake could not conceal the flare of remembered passion that kindled in his eyes. He recalled with pleasure every minuscule detail of Raven's deflowering, and the recollection left him wanting more.

"I owe Raven my protection."

"Are you determined, then, to take the lady to Windhurst?"

"I have no other choice."

Drake's scowl did not deter John. "There is still time to send her to Scotland. Mayhap I was wrong to suggest that the idea was not a good one. I fear Lady

Raven will prove more trouble than she is worth."

"I fear you are right, John, but I have no recourse."

"I know you, Drake. The men are making bets on how long it will be before the lady becomes your mistress. We all saw you kiss her. Methinks the lady is more of a distraction than you are willing to admit."

Drake's gloom fled before his smile. "I want Raven, John. I want her as my leman. And when, if ever, I decide to take a wife, I will still want her."

"That good, is she?"

Drake rose abruptly. "I will countenance no disparaging words about Raven. Inform the men they are to treat Lady Raven with the respect due to one of her station. That goes for you, too, John."

Drake's dark mood and curt warning did not appear to bother John. He rose gracefully and gave Drake a mocking bow. "Something tells me the lady will not yield as easily as you think. It will be interesting to see who wins this battle of wills. My money is on the lady."

Chapter Seven

A knight despises weakness in himself.

They made camp that night in a wooded area. Bowmen set out immediately to hunt for their evening meal while Evan built a fire. Raven edged close to the fire and pulled her cloak tightly around her. Though midsummer still held jurisdiction over the land, the dark forest held a chill reminiscent of those cold days to come between Lammas and Michaelmas.

Shifting uncomfortably beneath the curious glances of Drake's men-at-arms as they moved about the campsite, she searched for Drake and felt inexplicable panic when she failed to find him.

"Drake went out with the hunters."

Raven was surprised to see Sir John standing at her elbow. She flushed, embarrassed that John had read her mind so easily.

"Come," he said, grasping her elbow. "Evan placed a blanket on the ground for you to sit upon. You must be exhausted. It has been a long day."

John did not seem in a hurry to leave. He sat down beside her and stretched out his legs toward the fire.

"Have you known Drake long?" Raven asked curiously. She had countless questions about Drake's past. She wanted to know everything that had transpired from the time he'd left Chirk until now.

John was not the least bit reticent. "Aye. We fought together at Crécy in France. I am a landless knight, just as Drake was before he distinguished himself on the battlefield and was awarded Windhurst and an earldom. Doubtless you have heard how he saved the Black Prince's life. I feel privileged to have fought beside Drake. When the king rewarded him with land and a title, I swore fealty to him and have been with him ever since."

"And the men-at-arms?" Raven asked. "Have they all sworn fealty to Drake?"

"Aye. Though most serve him for wages, they are all loyal to the Black Knight, my lady. You have naught to fear from them."

Perhaps not from Drake's men, but she certainly had much to fear from the Black Knight himself, Raven thought. But that did not stop her from satisfying her curiosity. Tales of the Black Knight's courage were legendary, but it was his private life she was most curious about.

"Has Drake no wife?"

"He has had no time for a wife. But now that he is finally settling down at Windhurst, I suppose he must think about heirs and such."

"I have heard that women throw themselves at his feet."

"Aye, and he accepts their homage as his due and rewards them by walking upon their backs," John said, tongue in cheek.

Raven hid her smile behind her hand. "Tell me true, Sir John, does Drake have a leman? Or more than one, mayhap?"

"Drake has had many women, but presently claims no leman. Anything else you care to know, my lady?"

"Methinks you have told her enough," Drake said as he strode up to join them. They had been so engrossed in their conversation that they'd failed to hear him approach.

Sir John leaped to his feet. "Drake! Must you sneak up on one like that? Have the hunters returned?"

"Aye. Have you naught else to do but regale Lady Raven with my exploits?"

John's lips curved upward into a

mocking smile. "I was but satisfying the lady's curiosity."

Obviously Drake did not share John's mirth. "I hope that is all you are planning to satisfy."

Raven gasped in outrage. "Drake! Your arrogance is appalling."

Drake looked down at her sternly. "I am but protecting your virtue, my lady."

"A little late for that, is it not?" Raven said dryly.

"Excuse me," John said, giving Raven a courtly bow. "I must see to the men and horses." He hurried off, apparently happy to remove himself from their verbal sparring.

Drake, however, seemed in no hurry to leave. "If you have questions about my past, Lady Raven, I suggest you ask me."

"Is it so unseemly that I would wish to know more about my champion?"

"So long as you don't delve too deeply into my private affairs."

"Such as your women?"

His silver gaze searched her face. "They would not interest you."

Raven's curiosity still clamored for knowledge about the Black Knight's romantic conquests, but she gave a wave of dismissal and said, "You are right. Your exploits are of no interest to me."

Drake dropped down beside her. "You already know the important things about me. My father claimed I was bastard born. I lived with my mother and grandmother in a small village in Wales until my mother died. Then my father came for me and placed me in Lord Nyle's service. I fell in love with your sister but she was taken from me, as you are well aware. Now you know everything."

Not quite, Raven thought. There were still areas of mystery surrounding the Black Knight. Incredibly, she wanted to know the name of every woman he had bedded. That thought startled her, and she dropped her gaze to her lap.

"I prefer that you not question my friends about me behind my back," he added.

Raven's nod of acquiescence seemed to satisfy him, for he rose and excused himself. A short time later Evan arrived with a generous portion of roasted hare on a stick and a cup of ale. Raven ate with good appetite, licking her fingers and sighing happily after she had devoured every bite. Though the fare was a far cry from the elegant meals served at Castle Chirk, it tasted better than anything she had ever eaten.

Raven glanced across the campfire where

Drake was sitting with Sir John, and quickly looked away in embarrassment when he turned his head toward her and met her gaze. A moment later he rose and walked over to join her.

"Would you like a bath, Lady Raven?" he asked, offering her his hand.

Raven's small hand was swallowed by his as he pulled her to her feet. "A bath sounds wonderful. Is that possible?"

"Aye. There is a brook a short distance from the camp. I sampled the water earlier and found it tolerable."

She noted that his hair was still damp and realized he must have bathed while their meal was being prepared. "Can I go now?"

"Aye, as soon as Evan brings soap and a drying cloth."

As if on cue, Evan appeared with the necessary items.

"Direct me to the brook," Raven said, peering through the dark forest.

"I will take you." He grasped her elbow.

She dug her heels in. She did not relish being alone with Drake. He was too dangerous, too tempting, too male for her peace of mind. "I can find it myself; just point the way."

His mouth thinned into a determined

line. "I will take you. There are wild animals about. You may have need of my weapons."

Raven decided not to argue the point. She had learned something revealing about Drake these past few days. When he set his mind to something, he usually got what he wanted.

Guided by shafts of pale moonlight spilling through the lofty treetops, Raven stumbled beside Drake through the dark, threatening forest. She was thankful now for Drake's solid presence, aware that she never would have found the stream on her own. But Drake seemed to know exactly where he was headed as he led her around fallen stumps and clumps of underbrush that caught at her skirts. By the time they reached the stream, Raven was hopelessly lost. Now she knew why Drake had insisted on accompanying her.

They came out of the forest onto a grassy bank. Raven gave a gasp of pleasure at the sight that lay before her. It was pure enchantment. She stared in wonder at the million sparkling diamonds dancing upon the moonlit surface of the bubbling brook.

" 'Tis lovely, and so peaceful." Raven sighed. "Is it deep? I cannot swim."

Drake seated himself upon the grassy

bank. "The water will reach your waist, no more. 'Tis not dangerous. Bathe at your leisure, Raven. I will wait here for you."

Raven sent him a startled look. Did he expect her to undress before him? "Turn your back."

His arms crossed stubbornly over his chest. "I have seen you naked before."

He *had* seen her naked, but she did not want to think about that, or what had taken place in her bedchamber. Just thinking about it made her tremble.

"Nevertheless, you will turn your back, Drake of Windhurst. 'Tis best we both forget what occurred in my bedchamber on my wedding night."

With almost surly compliance, Drake handed her the soap and drying cloth and turned his back. Raven walked to the water's edge, and after a furtive glance over her shoulder to see if Drake was watching, she quickly undressed and tested the water with a slender foot. She gave a squeal of surprise and jerked her foot back.

"Is something wrong?"

"Nay! Do not turn around. The water is cold."

The urge to turn and watch Raven was so strong Drake had to force himself to think of other things. Then he heard a splash and his resolve melted away. He closed his eyes and imagined Raven standing in the water, her naked body gilded a pale gold. With his eyes still closed, he pictured her long chestnut hair floating around her, its rich color reflecting the moonlight. He felt his body stiffen in response to his fantasy and shifted to accommodate the hardening length of his sex.

A knight must despise weakness in himself, Drake reminded himself. His good intentions lasted until he opened his eyes and darted a furtive glance over his shoulder. His mouth went dry. Like Venus arising from her bath, Raven was as lovely as a goddess. Drake envied the droplets of water that clung to her breasts and ran in rivulets down her flat stomach. Passion rose swift and jarring within him as his imagination ran rampant. He wanted to lap the water from her nipples and delve below the water to taste that sweet place between her thighs.

Raven must have sensed his eyes on her, for she glanced over at him. He quickly turned his head away. He knew it was too dark for her to be sure that he was watching, and he felt no guilt when he turned back to watch her finish her bath.

His mouth went dry as she lifted her arms to soap her hair, her breasts thrusting upward in sharp relief. His erection throbbed painfully against his hose and he clapped a hand over his mouth to muffle his groan. He was completely turned around now, openly ogling Raven. When she wrung the water from her hair and waded toward the bank, he uncoiled himself like a cat and moved toward her like an animal stalking its prey. She looked up, saw him, and halted.

"Drake! You promised."

"Nay, I gave you no promise." He picked up the drying cloth she had dropped on the bank and held it out. "Come, the night air grows cold."

"Curse you!"

"Aye, curse me all you want, sweeting, but you have to admit there is a force pulling us toward one another."

She hugged her arms over her breasts, shivering in the cool air. "There is naught between us, Drake of Windhurst."

"We will discuss that later. Will you come out, or must I come in after you?"

Raven had no choice. The night air was raising goose bumps on her skin. She waded toward him. He held the drying cloth between his outstretched arms and she walked into it. His arms came around her. Her chilled flesh warmed quickly within the circle of his arms, and after a few minutes she felt his heat penetrating her through his tunic and the drying cloth. The scent of him was sharp and potent: wood smoke, ale, and aroused masculine flesh. The scent mingled with her recollection of shared passion to create a heady brew of seduction.

"You warm quickly, sweeting," he rasped into her ear. "Shall I make you burn? I can, you know."

Her reply was lost in the magic his lips were creating as he lowered his head and claimed her mouth. His mouth moved slowly over hers, taking, demanding, giving her no choice but the one he offered. He released his hold on the drying cloth and it fell to the ground. He ran his hands down her body, over the curve of her breasts, the indentation of her waist, the smooth roundness of her thighs and buttocks. He pressed her against him, his hips firm against hers, his leg moving relentlessly between her thighs. She gave a soft hiss of protest as he slowly lowered her to the ground.

Ignoring her protest, Drake whispered softly against her lips, "This is what we both want, Raven."

She stared into his determined gaze and felt resistance drain from her. This was not right, a voice inside her whispered. Stiffening her spine, she made one last attempt to defuse his passion.

"Nay! We cannot do this, Drake. It will only complicate matters."

He grinned at her. "I am willing to accept the consequences."

He touched her. His knees prodded her legs apart to allow him access to her treasure. Raven pressed her thighs together to stem the flow of desire building deep within her. She trembled from the force of it. She ached as she silently acknowledged her weakness where the Black Knight was concerned, and she renewed her vow to resist Drake's heady seduction with each breath she drew.

Raven lost the ability to think, much less speak, when she realized Drake had loosened his braies and hose and was positioning her for his entry.

Somewhere in her passion-dazed mind she heard him curse and lift his weight from her. "Someone is coming." He pulled her to her feet, wrapped the drying cloth around her, and shoved her toward her discarded clothing. "Get dressed. I'll hold them off."

"Who . . ."

"Drake? Lady Raven? Are you all right?"

Raven groaned. Sir John. She did not know whether to thank him or strangle him.

"John, stay where you are," Drake called back as he hastily retied his braies and hose and straightened his tunic. "Is aught amiss?"

"You and Lady Raven were gone so long I feared you had met with a mishap."

"Lady Raven was overlong at her bath," Drake replied. "Return to camp. We will join you directly."

"Is he gone?" Raven said in a hiss.

"Aye. Are you dressed?"

"Almost." A few moments later she stepped out from behind a tree, fully dressed, her long red hair hanging in wet hanks down her back.

Drake was unusually quiet as he tramped through the forest to their campsite, and Raven decided not to test his mood. She sincerely hoped Drake's silence meant that he was properly repentant for his attempted seduction. Nevertheless, she vowed to remain vigilant lest she succumb to the Black Knight's provocative wiles.

Raven sat close to the campfire, spreading her hair out to dry. She had no idea her simple gestures had garnered the undivided attention of every man present, including John and young Evan. Their admiring gazes were riveted upon the rhythmic stroking of Raven's arm as she ran a comb through her long tresses to remove the tangles. Lost in thought, Raven started violently when Drake jerked the comb from her hand. She gazed up at him in consternation.

"Enough." His voice was strangely harsh, and she had no idea what she had done to cause such a reaction. " 'Tis time to seek our beds. Evan has made a pallet for you beneath yon tree," he said, pointing to a pallet spread out beneath the lofty arms of an elm.

Raven sent him a look of haughty disdain and rose with all the dignity she could muster. "What have I done now?"

"Naught but beguile my men; even Sir John is besotted with you."

She gave a snort of laughter. "Surely not Sir John. He knows full well why I am here. Have you forgotten my wedding night, and how Sir John helped you cuckold Waldo?"

"That night is indelibly branded upon my mind and body," he said in a husky whisper. " 'Tis the reason you are with me now, my lady. Had I not gotten drunk and stolen your virginity, you would be in your husband's bed now instead of plaguing me."

"Plaguing you!" Raven sputtered indignantly. " 'Tis not *I* who wished to accompany you to Windhurst. *I* wanted to be taken to Scotland, if you recall."

He smiled at her. The smile did not reach his eyes. Obscured by shadows, they appeared murky, distant, and though she tried, Raven could not read his thoughts. It was obvious she was not welcome to delve into his mind, so she dropped her gaze.

"If *you* recall," Drake replied, "you have my protection, something you sought the moment I arrived at Chirk. Taking you to Scotland is not the best way to protect you. I know Waldo. He will punish you severely for daring to defy him. Waldo has always hated me, and now you have been added to his list of enemies. I may not like having you underfoot all the time but I do not take my vows lightly, my lady." The timber of his voice grew seductively low, his tone coaxing. "Were you to become my leman, our association would be a pleasure for both of us. Think about it." His words hung in the air like autumn smoke as he walked away.

Raven *did* think about it, and did not like it any better now than the first time he had suggested it. She sighed despondently. Becoming a man's leman was not what she had pictured for her life. Before sleep claimed her, she wondered if it would be a bad thing to become the Black Knight's mistress. She dismissed the thought as quickly as it formed. When Drake took a wife, as eventually he must, she would be tossed aside and abandoned like unwanted baggage. What would she do then? Return to Waldo? Never. Take up with another knight? Unlikely. Then the thought occurred to her that she could enter a nunnery and let God protect her. With that thought, she slid into exhausted slumber.

Too restless to sleep, Drake relieved the guard and paced the perimeter of the campsite himself. Raven was driving him mad. His body ached for her and his mind whirled with memories of Raven's naked body writhing beneath him. He knew she was not unaffected by him, for he had caught her staring at him when she thought he wasn't looking. Her gaze was admiring, though she tried to conceal her interest. It irked him that she was not amenable to his proposal. Most women would jump at the chance to become the Black Knight's mistress. How was he supposed to keep his hands off her? Wanting her when he knew he should not was making him witless.

He gazed toward the north, toward Chirk, and wondered what Waldo was doing now. Aware of his brother's vindictive nature, Drake knew Waldo was bent on revenge. Once Waldo learned that Raven had not fled to Scotland, he would raise an army and come to Windhurst to launch a siege.

Drake cursed violently. As soon as he reached Windhurst he intended to hire a stonemason and laborers to repair the walls and fortify the castle. Then he would send Sir John out to recruit mercenaries to join his own small elite army. But intuition told him all his plans for defending Windhurst would come too late. Drake had left Sir Richard at Chirk to report on Waldo. Richard was to disguise himself as a peasant and report to him the moment Waldo turned his sights toward Windhurst.

The men began stirring before daybreak. At first light Drake went to awaken Raven. He found her sprawled on her stomach, looking so fetching in sleep that he paused a moment to admire her. Aware of the path his mind was taking, he bridled his thoughts, squatted on his haunches, and gave her a gentle shake. Raven stirred but did not awaken. He shook her again. She moaned and opened her eyes.

" 'Tis time to rise, Raven. There is no time to break our fast. Evan is distributing leftovers from yestereve. We can eat in the saddle."

Raven sat up and stared at him, as if trying to remember where she was and why. Drake thought she looked adorably disheveled with her chestnut curls all awry about her head and her green eyes blurred with sleep.

"I need . . . a moment of privacy," she said, gazing longingly toward the thick underbrush surrounding their campsite. "I will not be long."

"I will stand guard," Drake offered, helping her to rise.

"Nay, thank you," Raven said crisply as she marched into the nearby fringe of trees.

Drake chuckled and walked away to make his own preparations for departure. For some reason he enjoyed baiting Raven. She was as prickly as a thistle, and he would give half his wealth to burrow beneath the thorns and pluck the flower she denied him.

They arrived at Windhurst five days later. Raven was exhausted. They had ridden hard and long, from daybreak until dusk on most days, and Raven hoped she would not have to mount a horse for a good long time.

Raven's first glimpse of Windhurst and the stark, windswept cliff upon which it had been built sent her heart plummeting to her feet. It was far more desolate than she had expected. Dusk and a swirling mist sat heavily upon the land. The castle looked forsaken and abandoned, a hulking mass standing sentinel above the wind-tossed sea and a strip of beach below. Angry purple clouds twisted above them. The sky was ominously dark, giving the keep an unfriendly, almost sinister look. The wind was raw, whipping her cloak around her. The roar of the surf crashing against the rocks below the cliff was nearly deafening.

The castle's outer wall lay in ruins, but by some miracle the curtain wall still stood, though in places it had crumbled down upon itself.

"Home," she heard Drake say with a kind of pride that puzzled Raven when she considered the bleak ruins before her.

Drake urged Zeus forward. He drew rein at the outer wall and stared at the dismal sight of collapsed stone and pulverized mortar. Raven followed close on his heels as he skirted the debris and entered the outer bailey. An exercise yard, overgrown now with weeds and gorse, looked as though it had not been used in decades.

Cold rain began to fall, adding to Raven's discomfort, and she pulled her hood over her head. Drake did not seem to notice the rain or the cold as he rode through the surprisingly intact barbican and entered the inner bailey. Again the sense of desolation and abandonment struck Raven as she glanced at the deserted courtyard that once had been teeming with life and energy. She spied a building whose thatched roof had fallen in and suspected it was the kitchen. Other buildings, probably the granary, barracks, and various domestic buildings, were all in desperate need of repair. The stables, mews, and smithy looked deserted and forlorn, tucked against the crumbling curtain wall.

Raven was somewhat cheered by the condition of the keep. Despite years of neglect, it stood proudly erect and almost wholly intact, its four towers starkly outlined against a depressing sky now lit by flashes of lightning.

Drake rode his destrier up to the stone steps and dismounted. He helped Raven to dismount and waited while someone went for torchlights.

"Windhurst will be grand again," Drake vowed, more to himself than to anyone in particular. Sir John handed him a torch. He grasped it in one hand and clasped Raven's elbow with the other. "Come, my lady. Shall we inspect my holdings together?"

Curious, Raven let him guide her up the stairs and into the keep. Two heavy, scarred doors studded with steel impeded their entry, and Drake stood back as two men stepped forward and shoved them open. The leather hinges squeaked in protest but gave beneath human perseverance. The noxious odor of rotted rushes and decayed food assailed Raven's senses, and she held her cloak against her nose.

"Aye, 'tis offensive," Drake agreed, "but naught that hard work cannot cure. Tomorrow I will engage servants and laborers to clean the keep. Bideford is a sizable village; everything we need to sustain us should be available there."

Raven held back as Drake examined

some of the rooms and alcoves off the hall. "Shall we see what the solar looks like?"

"I'll wait here," Raven hedged, not at all confident of what she'd find.

"Drake," Sir John called as he strode into the hall. "The barracks are not as bad as they first appeared. The men can make do until proper repairs are made. I found the armory and the smithy. They are mostly intact and will require only minor renovations."

"Raven and I are on our way to inspect the solar. Mayhap it is still habitable. Will you join us?"

"Nay. I thought to ride to the small village at the foot of the cliff. Mayhap they can provide food for our evening meal."

"Go then. While you are there, hire anyone willing to work for a good wage. Tell the villagers the lord of the castle is now in residence, and that I intend to restore the castle to its former grandeur. Anyone willing to work will be paid good wages."

Sir John took his leave. Drake and Raven walked single file up the winding stone stairs. They found a vacant room but naught that could be described as a solar. They returned to the hall and ascended another set of stairs leading to a second tower. At the top, Drake opened the heavy oak door and held the torch aloft. Raven peeked inside and gasped in surprise. The first room they entered appeared to be a sitting room, complete with hearth, settle, and other pieces of heavy oak furniture.

The room beyond revealed a sleeping chamber. The mattress on the bed, the heavy window coverings, and the bed draping were rotted and smelled foul. But most of the wooden furniture seemed to have survived neglect and abandonment with grace.

Drake went to the window and threw open the shutters, letting in the clean, tangy scent of salt air. " 'Tis not so bad," Drake allowed. "A good airing and new bedding will do wonders. These will be your chambers, Raven."

"Where will you sleep?" His provocative smile sent something deliciously wicked surging through her, and she regretted the question the moment it left her lips.

He glanced about the spacious room. "Right here, my lady. 'Tis sufficiently large for two people."

Her lips thinned. "I will not become your leman, Drake."

His smile deepened. "We shall see, Raven of Chirk."

Chapter Eight

A knight defends his lady's honor.

The fire blazed merrily in the huge hearth in the hall, fueled with wood salvaged from broken furniture. After their meal, Raven, Drake, and Sir John sat before the fire on benches someone had salvaged from one of the keep's cavernous rooms. Rain poured down in buckets, thunder rumbled across the sky, and wind howled through cracks in the wall, chilling Raven despite the roaring fire and her heavy cloak. Sir John had returned from the village earlier, drenched to the skin but in good spirits despite his bedraggled state.

The tiny village was nestled at the foot of the cliff upon which the keep stood. John reported that the villagers had been awaiting the new lord of the castle and welcomed him most heartily. They had loaned him a farm wagon, and each family had donated part of their own supper to feed the new lord and his men. During his short sojourn in the village, John managed to recruit several men and women willing, even eager, to serve the Black Knight. They promised to attend Lord Drake bright and early the next day.

" 'Tis time to retire," Drake said abruptly, interrupting Raven's thoughts. "The solar is not fit for occupancy, my lady. You will have to sleep elsewhere until the servants arrive from the village and give your chambers a thorough cleaning."

Raven's eyes snapped open and her nose crinkled in distaste. "I do not intend to sleep upon these filthy rushes. This bench will do for me."

"I think not. There is a better place. The rushes will be swept out and replaced with fresh ones tomorrow, and tonight Sir John and I will join the men in the barracks, but you will sleep in the hall."

"Nay!" Her voice was so vehement Drake looked at her askance. "I mean, I do not want to stay here alone," she said, sending him a sheepish look. " 'Tis . . . a frightening place."

"There is naught to fear," Drake promised.

"Stay with her," Sir John said, working hard to subdue his knowing smile. He rose. "Sleep well."

"I am sorry," Raven said, staring after

Sir John. "Do not stay on my account. I am sure you will be more comfortable in the barracks. The bench will suffice for me."

"That will not be necessary," Drake said. "I explored some of the alcoves off the hall and instructed Evan to clean the cobwebs from one of them. The alcoves were originally designed as private sleeping quarters for important guests. Each is quite roomy, with a wide sleeping ledge. Come, I will show you. It will not be so bad."

Raven followed uncertainly. Eerie shadows danced upon the smoke-blackened walls of the great hall, creating monsters of her own making, she was sure, but the thought of being secluded in a small alcove was not comforting.

Actually, the alcove was not as bad as she'd thought it would be, Raven decided after inspecting the rather spacious cubbyhole. It looked relatively clean, and no animals ran about. A pallet had been spread upon the ledge for her, and her bundle of clothes sat on a bench against the wall.

"Will this do?" Drake asked, casting a critical glance about the tiny room.

"Aye," Raven said. "Is there somewhere I can wash first?"

"The well is working, and Evan has

drawn water for you. 'Tis in the bucket beside the bench. The alcove originally had a hide curtain for privacy, but it has long since rotted. I will perform my own ablutions outside so you may have the privacy you require."

"My thanks," Raven said softly. "You do intend to return, do you not?"

He gave her a thoughtful look. "Aye. I will sleep on the bench before the hearth. I will not leave you alone."

Raven breathed a profound sigh of relief. Perhaps she would feel differently about this desolate, windswept castle in the light of day. Vaguely she wondered if it was haunted, then laughed at herself for being fanciful. There was no such thing as ghosts.

Drake turned and strode away. As soon as his footsteps subsided, she found the bucket of water and removed a soft cloth and clean shift from her bundle of belongings. She washed quickly, drying herself with her soiled shift and donning the clean one. Then she climbed onto the ledge and settled down on her pallet.

Raven shivered, chilled by the dampness seeping from the stone walls. Years of neglect had banished whatever charm the keep might have once possessed. Grateful for her fur-lined cloak, exhausted beyond belief, Raven rolled into a ball and fell immediately asleep.

Drake looked in on Raven when he returned a short time later and saw that she was sleeping soundly. He let his gaze wander over her, wondering if she knew how much he wanted her. Cursing, he turned away and stretched out on the bench before the fire. He must have fallen asleep immediately, for the next thing he knew he was lying on the floor amid the foul rushes, sporting a sizable lump on his head. He spit out an oath and tried to resettle himself on the bench. It was no use. Either the bench was too narrow or he was too large. It was a little of both, he suspected.

Had he not promised Raven he would stay with her, he would have joined his men in the barracks. They had done a creditable job of cleaning it, and he suspected it would be far more comfortable than the bench upon which he now lay. He glanced longingly at the alcove where Raven slept and decided that she would not be the only one to sleep in comfort this night. The ledge was large enough for two, and sharing it should present no problem.

Careful not to disturb her, he moved her close to the wall to make room for himself. Then he sat on the ledge, removed his clothing, lifted a corner of her cloak, and slid down beside her. Her warmth hit him like a fiery blast and he cuddled closer, soaking up her heat. His arm went around her and he pulled her into the cradle of his body. He smiled when she did not resist. Then it hit him: only a fine linen shift separated him from Raven's sweet body.

With great care he slid his hand upward to cup her breast. It nearly overflowed his hand and he squeezed gently. A soft, breathy sigh slipped past her lips and she arched her back, pushing her breast into his palm. Encouraged, Drake allowed his fingertips to stray to her nipple. Raven sighed again, and Drake's passion exploded. Tempted beyond endurance, he caressed the elegant line of her waist, the tempting rise of her hips, the sweet curve of her thigh.

When he reached the hem of her shift, he clutched it in his hand and slowly hitched it up to her waist. His hand paused on her bare stomach. A groan gathered in his throat and it became impossible to breathe. Throwing caution to the wind, he sifted his fingers through the nest of curls at the apex of her thighs and cupped her sex. The heat, the heady feminine scent of her, nearly unmanned him. The need to explore more intimately was a raw ache inside him. Heedless of his inner warning, he spread apart the petals of her sex and inserted a finger into her damp center. Her eyes flew open and she jerked violently upward.

"God's blood, Drake! What are you doing?"

"There is room enough for two on the ledge, and the bench was too narrow to accommodate me."

Raven glared at him. "Remove your hands from me, my lord. I did not give you leave to touch me."

"I cannot stop," Drake rasped as he pressed her down upon the pallet. Holding her in place with his sheer bulk, he moved his finger in and out of her wet passage. She gasped. He smiled. His finger moved again, and yet again. The tiniest movement of her hips was all the encouragement he needed as he inserted another finger beside the first.

"Drake, please, you cannot do this."

"Just watch me." Both fingers began to move in unison, in a slow, stretching motion that wrung a startled cry from her lips.

She surged upward. "Oh . . . Drake . . . Oh . . ."

"Fly for me, sweet Raven."

He lowered his head to her breasts, sucking her nipples through her shift as his fingers continued his loving torment below. With his free hand he released the tapes holding her shift together and spread the edges wide, revealing the rigid peaks of her breasts. He took one nipple into his mouth and sucked vigorously.

Raven was flying so high she feared she would never return to earth. Suddenly his mouth clamped down hard upon her nipple, alternately flaying her with his tongue and soothing her tenderly. When he stopped she wanted to cry out in protest. Then he raised his head and found her mouth, slanting it over hers, his tongue forcing entrance between her teeth.

His taste and scent made her breath catch and falter. She savored him on her tongue, absorbed him through her pores as he drew her further into his web of seduction. Her climax came swiftly and unexpectedly. The increasing urgency of his fingers working within her, combined with his soul-destroying kisses, released a violent reaction inside her. She shattered and cried out, clinging to Drake's shoulders as she tumbled headlong into an abyss of sensual pleasure. She felt overwhelmed, possessed, dominated.

Awareness returned slowly. Raven felt Drake's hips grinding against hers, felt the hard ridge of his sex prodding her stomach, and the realization of what she had just allowed to happen was like a dash of cold water. When he positioned her for his entry, she protested violently.

"Nay! You cannot come inside me."

He went very, very still. "You let me pleasure you. Do I not deserve the same consideration? I am burning for you, sweeting. No man has ever wanted a woman as I want you."

His voice was sexually charged. She felt herself softening, arching against him, but she steeled herself against the temptation of his wicked hands and hot mouth. It was obvious to her how the Black Knight earned his reputation with women. Who could resist him? Drake had been her first lover, so she had nothing to judge him by, but intuitively she knew she would never find another to match him.

There was a very substantial reason Raven did not want Drake to come inside her. She feared he would plant his seed in her. She was married to Waldo, and Drake could not marry her even if he wanted to. Her child, should there be one, would legally belong to Waldo, and she could not bear that.

His voice was ragged. "Raven . . . let me inside."

"I cannot, Drake, truly," Raven said on a sob.

With a groan, Drake shifted his weight off her. His muted curses hinted at his frustration, his discomfort, but she made herself deaf to them.

"Another time, Raven," Drake promised. "Soon," he added, in a voice ripe with promise.

Damn her, Drake thought as he turned away from her. Damn her for her beauty and for her stubbornness. And damn himself for not taking her when he wanted her so desperately.

Raven scooted as far as she could against the wall, unable to relax until she heard the even cadence of Drake's breathing. Even after he had fallen asleep she was still too keyed up to rest. She had been dreaming of pleasant things, sinful things, then she had awakened suddenly to find Drake's hands upon her. He had known exactly how to make her body fly, and like a puppet on a string, she had obliged him.

Why could she not hate him? He had more than earned her contempt, yet hatred for the Black Knight had found no lasting place in her heart.

With effort, Raven turned her thoughts from the man sleeping beside her. The echo of thunder rolling across the heavens and the sound of pounding rain finally lulled her to sleep.

The worst of the storm had passed when Raven awoke the following morning. The place beside her was empty, and for some reason that bothered her. She had awakened several times during the night and each time was comforted to find Drake curled around her, his warmth keeping the chill at bay.

The sound of voices outside in the hall lured Raven from bed. She rose and dressed hastily, eager to learn the cause of the commotion. Suddenly the doors of the hall were flung open, admitting a wide swath of light. A veritable army of men and women swept inside. Raven stepped from the alcove to greet them.

"We are from the village, milady," a spokesman for the group ventured. "Lord Drake instructed us in our duties before he left for Bidewell to hire a stonemason and laborers. 'Tis happy we are to see the lord of the castle in residence."

"Welcome," Raven said, smiling. "I am Lady Raven. As you can see, the hall has accumulated years of dirt and neglect. 'Tis the same wherever you look."

"Aye, we are well aware of the passage of time since our last lord occupied Windhurst. My name is Balder, milady."

"Since you know what needs to done, Balder, you may direct the others." She scanned the round peasant faces beaming at her and asked, "Is there a cook among your numbers?"

A plump matron of middle years stepped forward. "Aye, milady. I am Margot, the best cook in the village," she said with a hint of pride. She pulled a pretty young girl forward. "And this is Gilda, my daughter. Mayhap you can use her as your maid."

Raven did not know if Drake wanted her to have a maid, so she merely thanked Margot and said she would speak with Gilda later concerning her duties. "Meanwhile, Margot, please inspect the kitchen and let Balder know what is needed to set it to rights. Lord Drake will return soon with workers to make the necessary repairs."

Balder, apparently taking his position seriously, sent the servants about their assigned chores. They bobbed clumsily and scurried off. Balder followed close on their heels.

"Ah, there you are, Lady Raven."

Raven greeted Sir John with a smile. "Good morrow, Sir John."

"Good morrow, my lady. Lord Drake rode to Bideford before you awakened. I am to leave myself within the hour."

"And your errand?" Raven asked curiously.

"To recruit mercenaries and knights for Lord Drake's army."

"I understand," Raven replied, aware of Drake's need for more men. He expected Waldo to attack Windhurst soon, and his own small army was no match for the one Waldo would bring with him. She prayed Waldo would not come until Drake was ready for him.

"Aye. 'Tis no great task. Men consider it a privilege to fight under the Black Knight's banner. In less than a month I shall return with enough skilled warriors to meet the Black Knight's needs."

Drake returned from Bideford late that evening with a stonemason and an army of laborers. They came in two sturdy farm wagons he had purchased, one of them filled with tools, flour, and other staples; ale; and materials he thought might be of use to Raven.

The following days were busy ones for Raven. She was quite happy overseeing the refurbishing of the hall, solar, and sleeping chambers. Her own rooms pleased her greatly once all the soot and grime had been scrubbed away. Within two days of their arrival, furnishings and amenities began arriving on a daily basis. Bedsteads with rope springs and thick feather mattresses; pots, pans, and utensils for cooking and baking; a big brass tub for bathing; bed linens and everything else needed for their comfort.

Work began on the walls immediately. Carpenters set to work fashioning benches, tables, and chairs for the hall and sleeping chambers. Not a day passed without craftsmen arriving at the keep to offer their services or sell their wares.

At the end of two weeks a subtle change had begun to take place in the hall. Fresh, sweet rushes now covered the floors, banishing the foul odor that had sickened Raven. The walls had been whitewashed and hung with colorful tapestries. Newly hewn tables and benches gleamed with polish, and the hearth gave off sweet-smelling smoke. The kitchen had been hastily restored and was putting out simple but tasty meals under Margot's supervision. Raven was pleased with the progress and began to look upon Windhurst favorably.

Raven saw little of Drake during those hectic days. He slept in the north tower room, far removed from the solar, and was gone most of the day directing the laborers and training with his men in the tiltyard. Sometimes, when they were in the same room together, she felt his heated gaze on her and a strange prickling sensation crept up her neck. She was never, at any time, unaware of him, and knew he felt the same attraction that was constantly pulling them toward a collision course.

One bright morning Raven walked to the cliff's edge to watch the waves pounding against the shore. She loved the way plumes of white spray flew up from the rocks below, and the deafening sound the waves created. She had never seen the sea before, and it mesmerized her.

As the days passed Raven felt a subtle change in the servants' regard for her. She realized that her position in the keep and her relationship to Drake had never been clearly defined, and that some of the younger maids looked upon her as a rival for Drake's affection. Though Raven had accepted Gilda as her maidservant, the attractive girl made no secret of her desire for Drake.

One sunny morning Raven asked Gilda to gather the soiled bed linen from her chamber, wash it, and hang it out to dry. Gilda gave her a hostile glance, blatantly ignoring Raven's request.

"Gilda, did you hear me?" Raven repeated her request and was rewarded with an indifferent shrug.

Gilda gave Raven a condescending glare. "I do not have to obey you. You are not the lady of the castle. I take my orders from Lord Drake. You are neither his wife nor his whore."

Aghast, Raven stared at Gilda. "What did you say?"

"You heard me, *milady*. I know Lord Drake does not want you in his bed, for you sleep alone in the solar. I know not the manner of your relationship, but I assure you, *milady*, Lord Drake does *not* sleep alone."

She preened for Raven's benefit, thrusting out her impressive bosom. "His lordship is a lusty man," Gilda confided. She turned away, then whirled around to throw a final barb at Raven. "If you wish your laundry done, milady, do it yourself."

Raven had never been so humiliated, and she placed the blame on Drake. The lord of the castle had not officially placed her in charge of the household. She had taken it upon herself to see that the keep ran smoothly. She felt she could do no less, for she owed him much. Protecting her from Waldo was no easy task, and by so doing Drake placed his own life in jeopardy.

Her thoughts were so disturbing that she failed to see Drake enter the hall.

"What troubles you, my lady?"

Raven started violently. "Drake, you startled me."

" 'Tis no wonder. You were leagues away." His handsome brow furrowed. "What troubles you?"

Just then Gilda entered the hall, saw Drake, and sidled up to him, her breasts thrust out in flagrant invitation. "Ale, my lord?"

"Nay, Gilda, my thanks."

Gilda's long, dark lashes fluttered, her smoldering invitation anything but subtle. Hips swaying, she moved away, but not so far that she could not still see Drake.

"I do not appreciate being treated disrespectfully by your doxy," Raven said in a hiss. "I know I have no status in your household, but flaunting Gilda is beyond too much."

Drake's eyes widened and he turned his head to stare at Gilda. Gilda gave him a heated look and boldly tugged the neckline of her bodice down another notch.

"We must talk, Drake," Raven said, embarrassed by Gilda's blatant display.

"It never occurred to me that you would be treated with anything but the utmost courtesy," Drake said, scowling. "I will speak with the servants."

Raven saw Gilda watching them and turned away. "We cannot talk here. Privacy is impossible in the hall." She grasped his hand. "Come with me to the solar. No one will disturb us there."

Drake followed her up the narrow stone staircase without protest. Raven could feel Gilda's venomous gaze flaying her but she did not care. What she had to say to Drake was for his ears alone. She entered the solar, closed the heavy door, and leaned against it, staring accusingly at him.

"You are misinformed. I have taken no woman to my bed since arriving at Windhurst," he insisted.

Raven stiffened. "Gilda said —"

"She lies. Why would you believe Gilda?" He appeared puzzled, and Raven felt a pang of guilt.

"You are a man, Drake. I never expected you to live a celibate life."

He closed the space between them and framed her face in his big hands, making her sharply aware of his power and her fragility. "Nor do I intend to, Raven."

Then his mouth was on hers, hot and hard and demanding. Raven did not pull away, though she knew she should. She was a married woman — married to a man she feared and hated. Drake's tongue slid smoothly inside her mouth, stroking in and out repeatedly. A wet warmth gathered between her thighs, a forbidden heat. In a moment of clarity she realized she must stop this before it was too late, but instead she gripped his muscular arms and returned his kiss.

"What did you wish to talk about?" he whispered against her lips.

She clung to him. She could not think. "Drake."

His hands left her face and slid down her body, lightly caressing, soothing, coaxing. "What? Tell me."

"I . . . we . . ."

His hands circled around to her buttocks, gripping them, separating them, finding her feminine heat through her clothing. Suddenly light-headed, Raven shuddered, wanting him so very badly. His hands on her were arousing, exciting, driving her mad with need. He continued to caress her feminine folds through her clothes, until her knees began to buckle and she realized her will to resist the Black Knight had fled.

Desperately Raven clung to his shoulders until her breath came in choking gasps and she was trembling like a leaf.

Abruptly he tore his mouth from hers and stared at her, as if trying to read her thoughts. Then he smiled. She exhaled a strangled breath when he gripped her arms and propelled her toward her bedchamber. She stumbled. He swept her into his arms and carried her through the open door. Then he set her on her feet, slammed the door, and turned the key in the lock. He was still smiling as he crowded her backward toward the bed.

The husky timbre of his voice warned her that there was no turning back this time. " 'Tis time, sweet Raven. I gave you ample warning."

Sunlight streamed through the windows,

illuminating his dark face. His expression was ruthless and grimly determined, overwhelming in its intensity. Though she had resisted his masculine appeal thus far, she had always known this day would come. It mattered not that she was a married woman. The church did not consider a marriage legal until it was consummated, and Waldo had not bedded her. She had made certain of that.

"Do not think, Raven," Drake said, as if aware of her thoughts. "This was meant to be. Patience is a virtue I lack."

He drew his tunic over his head and tossed it aside. Then he loosened the ties on his hose, and his manhood burst free. She stared at him, at the incredible length and hardness of him. She had felt his male part inside her but had never seen it in the light of day. He was massive. She saw the veins along the sides throbbing and noted a tiny drop of fluid clinging to the purplish tip.

Her cheeks flamed as he pulled off his hose and tossed them beside his tunic. She caught her breath. He was magnificent. Tall, powerfully built, and virile, he was everything she knew he would be, everything she had dreamed about.

Abruptly his hands moved to the neat

braids she had plaited that morning and wound around her head. "I want your hair down when I make love to you."

She nodded and began pulling wooden pins out of her hair. When her braids hung down her back, Drake began to unravel them, spreading the silken strands out with his fingers until they fell in shimmering chestnut waves down her back.

Drake drew her hair aside and kissed her nape. "I love your hair," he murmured huskily. "When you were a child I thought it hideous. I must have been blind."

Raven recalled how Drake had teased her about the color of her hair, calling her Carrot Top and other unseemly names. But she had not cared, for she had loved Drake then, with the kind of love only a child was capable of giving.

"Take off your clothes." His voice sounded raw, urgent. "I want you, sweet Raven. Now. It will be different this time. There will be no pain, and I will take time to please you."

Raven swallowed a smile. Did he not know he had pleased her the first time despite the initial pain? Slowly, watching his expression change from appreciation to fierce need, she began to undress. When she moved too slowly to suit him, he grasped the neckline of her chemise.

"Nay. Patience, my lord. I cannot afford to lose a piece of clothing when I have so few."

"I will replace it with a dozen others." Then he tore it in half, tossing the pieces aside with a growl of impatience.

Raven quailed beneath his fierce perusal. She might have turned and run had he not gripped her arms and pulled her roughly against him. Breast to breast, hip to hip, his heat scorched her and left her wanting. When she felt his staff throbbing against her, she cried out her own need.

"I cannot wait!" Shocked by her outburst, she turned bright red.

"Ah, sweet Raven, how your impatience pleases me. We will go slowly, my lady. I want to learn all your secrets." Then he bore her backward onto the bed.

Raven's mind ceased functioning. His gaze was pure fire, flaying her everywhere it touched. He cupped her breast. His mouth found her nipple. He sucked it into his mouth, hard, wringing a cry from her. Her hands were on his shoulders, his back, his thighs. His hair-roughened skin affected her strongly, like an aphrodisiac. His touch, his taste, his scent, all combined to bring her the kind of greedy pleasure she had no right to claim. Not with this man, who was neither her betrothed nor her husband.

She trembled violently beneath the kisses raining down on her body. His mouth was hot, his tongue hard, firm, every flick sending unspeakable delight surging through her. She was losing control. She felt him sliding lower on her body and feared he would not stop until he reached . . .

"Drake!"

He knelt between her outstretched thighs and looked up at her when she screamed his name. His eyes flashed silver and he gave her a dazzling smile. Then he bent his head and stared at her intimate flesh as if she were a feast he could not wait to devour. She nearly lost control as his talented fingertips stroked up her inner thighs to the lips of her sex, spreading them for his pleasure.

Then he kissed her there.

Raven could not breathe, could not think. "Please." She did not know such things were permissible, much less wonderfully arousing.

He hesitated, looking up at her. "Shall I continue?"

"Nay . . . aye . . . I know not! 'Tis sinful."

"Aye," Drake agreed. "Deliciously sinful. Tell me, Raven, do you want me to stop?"

She could feel his hot breath against the tender folds of her womanhood and feared she would die if he stopped now. "Nay, do not stop. Take this to the end."

He lowered his head and slid his tongue over her wet, swollen flesh. She tried to embrace him and realized their fingers were entwined and her hands imprisoned at her sides. His tongue flicked over a place so sensitive it wrung a cry from her. Stunned, she arched violently upward. He freed her hands and they immediately fell to his shoulders, her nails biting into his flesh.

A joyous emotion bubbled up inside her. It was strong, so powerful it was like a volcano that soon must erupt. And then it did.

Chapter Nine

A knight fights with courage.

Drake rose up on his elbows and stared at Raven. Her face was flushed, her breath coming fast and harsh as she slowly descended from passion's towering heights. He'd never imagined he could experience pleasure from giving to another while denying himself, but Raven had just proved otherwise. He was still rigid and swollen, still wanting, but he felt her satisfaction as keenly as she did.

She opened her eyes; he smiled at her. She returned his smile, reaching up to caress his cheek. Drake grasped her hand and brought it to his mouth, kissing each finger.

"Is it permissible to enjoy what you just did to me?" she asked shyly.

Her naïveté was refreshing. "Anything we do in bed is permissible. As long as we both enjoy it."

She glanced down at his swollen staff and her eyes widened. "There was no pleasure in it for you."

"You are wrong, my love. I absorbed your pleasure and savored it as my own."

She grasped his hips and urged him down upon her. "Come inside me, Drake. Let me absorb your pleasure."

God's blood! He had never known such a woman existed. He spread her thighs and stared raptly at the swollen lips of her sex. He moaned and slid himself over her slick folds several times, until she shuddered and moved her hips restlessly beneath him. His eyes darkened with lust as he recalled how tightly she had cradled him the first time he had loved her. Then slowly, holding himself in rigid control, he pushed himself inside her.

Eyes closed, jaw set, he went deeper. Nothing had ever felt so right, so perfect. She was tight, so tight . . . so hot. The walls of her sex clasped him lovingly, as if God had fashioned her exclusively for him. He moved slowly so as not to hurt her, and was surprised when she grasped his buttocks, urging him deeper, harder. Her enthusiastic response, coming close on the heels of her previous climax, so shocked him that he went utterly still.

Her fingers dug into his flesh. "Nay! Do not stop!"

"Oh, sweet lady, never fear. I could not

stop were the earth to open up and swallow me."

He flexed his hips and drove deeply, wetly into her. Wanting, needing more, he lifted her legs and wrapped them around his waist. She thrashed beneath him, moaning his name. He felt her shudder, felt her sheath contract around him, felt tiny explosions erupting inside her. Then he lost the ability to think as he rocked forcefully against her, driving them both to completion. He threw back his head, opened his mouth, and roared, spilling his seed as a brilliant shower of fire and sparks ripped through him. His heart was pounding so loudly he did not hear Raven shout his name, or feel her nails digging into his shoulders.

Drake did not want to move. He wanted to stay inside her body until he grew hard enough to take her again. He rested his head against her breasts, her ragged breathing mingling with his. When he found the strength to move, he pulled out and flopped down beside her. Though his eyes were closed he felt her gaze upon him. He raised himself up on his elbows and kissed the tip of her nose.

"I want to love you again. And yet again. The rest of the day and all through the night."

Raven's mouth dropped open. "Is that possible?"

His eyes gleamed with promise. "Very possible." He grasped her hand and brought it to his loins, making her aware that his passion had been temporarily slaked, not satisfied. Her fingers closed around his erection, as if to test his readiness for herself.

"Can it not wait? I really do want to talk to you."

He sat up, drawing up one knee and resting his arms upon it. "Is this important?"

"I suppose I must consider myself your leman now."

Drake wondered where in God's name the conversation was going. He was not altogether certain he was going to like where it was headed. "Is that such a bad thing? We just proved we are compatible. God's blood, Raven, do you know how very much you please me?"

"You please me, too, Drake, but that will matter little to Waldo."

Drake's face hardened. "Must we talk about my brother?"

"He is my husband. He will come for me, you know. The castle is ill prepared for a siege, should it come to that." She took a gulp of air. "Mayhap I should return to Waldo and demand an annulment."

Drake grasped her shoulders, giving her a none-too-gentle shake. He could not believe what he was hearing. "Are you mad? He will kill you, and well you know it."

"He will kill *you* if he catches you. I dragged you into my affairs against your will. I do not want your death on my conscience."

"You did not drag me into this, Raven: I entered of my own free will. This is my penance for ruining you on your wedding night."

" 'Tis not the wedding night I would have chosen, but neither was bedding Waldo. Mayhap you did me a favor. You provided me with a way to escape a man I detest. I am not Waldo's wife," she said fiercely. "Our marriage was never consummated, and I will kill myself before I let him touch me."

Drake grasped her shoulders, dragging her against him. "I will not let him have you."

She gave him a puzzled look. "Why do you say that, Drake? You do not like me. When I begged for your help at Chirk, you denied me. I am naught but a penance you have imposed upon yourself."

He stared into her eyes; they were the color of the pastures surrounding Windhurst. "Perhaps I chose the wrong words. As for the past, it has no place now in our lives. What happened at Chirk when we were children no longer matters."

"It matters to me. Will you listen to me now, with an open mind? I swear upon the graves of my parents that I will speak naught but the truth."

"Aye, have your say," Drake said. If it would ease her mind, he was willing to listen, though in truth his memories of that time were vague. He had harbored a grudge against Raven all these years, not even realizing it no longer mattered. Except for the fact that Daria had died before her time, he would not think of it at all.

Raven sent him a look that spoke eloquently of her need to be exonerated in Drake's eyes. She took a deep breath and began.

"I loved my sister very much. At times she was fanciful and flighty, but mostly she was sweet and obedient. She may have fancied herself in love with you, but she would have never run off to elope. She wanted to be Waldo's countess."

"Are you saying Daria cared naught for me?" Drake asked harshly.

"Nay. I am merely telling you the truth. Daria did not like the careless way in which Waldo treated her, and she wanted to make him jealous so he would pay more attention to her. She was young, Drake; you cannot blame her. She was very fond of you, but she took her betrothal vows seriously."

"How did your father learn of our plans to elope if you did not tell him?"

"Daria confided in me, but I did not tell Father. She assured me she knew what she was doing, that becoming a countess was all she ever wanted. Wedding a penniless lad who claimed neither title nor land was not in her plans for her future. She took advantage of your love, Drake. I learned later that she told her maid about the elopement, aware that the girl would run to Father with the tale. I did not betray you, Drake, though I knew what you planned was folly."

Drake mulled over Raven's words and recognized them for the truth. Daria's fickleness hurt but no longer wounded. He had been young, and Daria was his first love. He had aimed high and been knocked down, but life had gone on and he had prospered. There was one thing he could not forget, however: Daria's early death.

"Think you Waldo is responsible for Daria's death?"

"I am sure of it!" Raven said fiercely. "She was strong and healthy when she left Chirk as Waldo's wife. She never complained of a stomach ailment. I do not know how or why, but I firmly believe Waldo is responsible for my sister's death. So many deaths." She sighed. "My parents. My betrothed. Waldo's mother, then his father. Daria's death followed soon afterward."

"How did Aric die?"

"He went with Waldo and Duff to fight in France. When Aric was slain at Crécy, Waldo asked Duff not to betroth me to another because he wanted me for himself. Were my parents still alive, they would not have agreed. As it was, years passed before a dispensation arrived from the pope allowing the marriage."

"If proof exists that Waldo hastened Daria's death, I will kill him. Daria may not have loved me as I loved her, but she did not deserve to die."

Her voice was pleading, disconsolate. " 'Tis important that you believe me, Drake. I let you make love to me. I could not live with myself knowing you hold me in so little regard."

Absently he stroked her hair, smoothing the tangled strands away from her compelling green eyes. He searched her face and was humbled by the desperate need for understanding he saw there.

"Aye, Raven, I believe you. I probably knew long ago that you were not capable of such deceit. Your heart was too loving. Mayhap I preferred to believe you had betrayed me and Daria rather than face the truth that Daria did not return my love and never planned to go through with the elopement. The truth would have been a bitter blow for a chivalrous lad with stars in his eyes and a heart filled with love."

She gave him a misty smile. "You do not know how happy that makes me."

Her words sent a jolt of renewed passion surging through him. He was instantly hard, desperately needy. He reached for her. His voice was husky, barely recognizable.

"Show me how happy you are, sweet Raven. Open yourself to me and let me share your happiness."

"Oh, aye, Drake, aye," she cried, flinging herself into his arms.

"Do you remember, long ago, when you asked me to kiss you?" he whispered against her lips. "What were you? Ten?

Twelve? Too young to know what you asked for."

"I remember very well. I loved you, Drake. I cared not about land or title. You had taken my girlish fancy and I claimed you as my own gallant knight."

"If I recall, I kissed your cheek."

She gave him a wistful smile. "It was not the kiss I wanted, but it made me very happy."

"I will make amends, sweet Raven. I will kiss you until you grow giddy and beg me to stop."

"Stop? Never! I have not changed much from that child who begged for your kiss."

Her lips parted and the tip of her tongue darted out to lick moisture onto them. Lust . . . pure, raging lust roared through him. He bore her backward onto the mattress and plundered her sweet mouth with his lips and tongue.

Writhing upon the bed, lost in a haze of sensual excitement, each sought pleasure from the other's body. Kissing and caressing wildly, they found fulfillment amid exploding stars and blinding light.

They remained secluded in their chamber until the evening meal was served. All eyes were upon them as they entered the hall together. It was not difficult for the casual observer to imagine what had taken place in the solar during the long afternoon. Raven's face was still flushed and her lips swollen from Drake's kisses.

During the repast Raven shared Drake's trencher and cup, adding more fodder for the rumor mill. After the meal, Drake escorted Raven to her chambers while the men returned to the barracks or bedded down in the hall.

"Tomorrow I will have the servants move my things to the solar," he said as he closed the door firmly behind him. "We will share this room for as long as you remain at Windhurst."

Raven shivered, as if a sudden chill had entered the room. "How long will that be, my lord?"

The confused look on Drake's face did not cheer her. They both knew she could not continue to live here forever. Drake's wife, when he decided to take one, would not want her underfoot.

"For as long as this arrangement pleases us," he teased. "Think you I will throw you upon Waldo's tender mercies? Nay, Raven. Waldo is not a forgiving man. He is cruel and sly and capable of things I suspect would surprise both of us. I do not wish to discuss Waldo tonight. I will help you undress."

The night was a repeat of the day. Drake could not seem to get enough of her, and Raven was as mad for him as he was for her. Their afternoon tryst had banished whatever shyness Raven might have felt. Now she explored his body as fully as he had explored hers earlier. She tasted the lust upon his sex and absorbed his scent into her pores. And when he stiffened and cried out that his restraint was gone and he was about to spew forth his seed, she flung herself astride him and rode him to completion.

The following morning Drake gathered the servants in the hall to inform them that Raven was the lady of the castle, that her orders were to be obeyed. All but a few of the younger women, who had their own agendas where Drake was concerned, smiled and bobbed their heads to Raven, satisfied that their lord had finally clarified Raven's place in his life. Instead of having no status in the household, she was now the respected leman of the Black Knight. An enviable position, most agreed, one that demanded their esteem, until their lord brought a wife to the keep.

Repairs to the walls and fortifications continued apace. Sir John's return was eagerly anticipated, as were the mercenaries to reinforce Drake's army. Drake was busy from prime till vespers, but the remaining hours belonged solely to Raven. The love she had harbored for Drake as a child was renewed and reinforced, emerging strong and steadfast. She refrained from voicing what was in her heart, however, because she was not free to ask for Drake's love in return.

She was still a married woman, living in sin with the man she loved.

A sennight passed. Raven tried to ignore impending danger, living only for the nights. Blissfully entwined in Drake's strong arms, she began to believe that no one could touch them in their safe haven. The walls around her dreamworld came tumbling down with the arrival of Drake's spy from Chirk.

Sir Richard rode into the cobbled courtyard on a raw day lashed by wind and rain. He was soaked to the skin and near collapse as he attempted to dismount. Fortunately Drake was standing nearby, for Richard fell from his destrier and into Drake's arms. Two sturdy knights came forward and carried Richard into the hall, placing him in a chair by the fire. A servant handed him a cup of ale and he downed it in one thirsty gulp.

Drake waited with surprising patience while Richard caught his breath and quenched his thirst.

"I have news," Richard said, panting between words. "I made myself inconspicuous at Chirk, posing as one of the villagers who passed through the gates daily to offer their services. No one recognized me as one of your knights." He paused and held out his cup for a refill. A servant hurried to comply.

"What news do you bring?" Drake said anxiously.

"Lord Waldo searched for his wife in Scotland and returned to Chirk in high temper." He cast a sidelong glance at Raven. "When I left he was recruiting men and making war machines for a siege on Windhurst. A knight from another camp told Lord Duff and Lord Waldo that he saw Lady Raven with the Black Knight. Waldo is convinced he will find her at Windhurst."

"How long do we have?" Drake asked.

"A fortnight, no more."

Drake began to pace. He glanced at Raven, saw her white face, and realized he would not give her up. Not now, maybe not ever.

Drake stroked his chin, his mind working furiously. "Our walls are still under construction, and the new fortifications are nowhere near completion. We have not the manpower yet to repel a siege such as Waldo and Duff intend to launch."

"What about Sir John?" Raven asked. "How soon do you expect him with reinforcements?"

Drake's expression turned grim. "We cannot wait for him. I am no coward, but the odds are against us. Fighting Waldo now will end in disaster. Windhurst cannot be defended in its present condition. The lives of my men are at stake. No man will die defending a pile of stone," he vowed fiercely. "I value life too highly."

"Sir Richard, if you are recovered now, return to the barracks and spread the word that we ride at daybreak. Every man is to ride in full armor and carry naught but necessities and a sack of oats for his mount."

"Aye, my lord," Richard said, striding briskly from the hall.

"What about Windhurst?" Raven asked. "Waldo will come and destroy all you have worked so hard to rebuild."

He grasped her arms. "It matters not,

Raven. 'Tis your safety that concerns me. I shudder to think what will happen should Waldo get his hands on you. I cannot protect you here. Windhurst is still vulnerable to attack, but I am not without a plan."

"Where will we go?" Raven asked, wringing her hands.

He pulled her into his arms, wondering if this was to be the last time he would hold her like this. He'd never imagined that taking Raven's virginity would result in his becoming Raven's champion and protector.

"I am taking you to my grandmother in Wales," he informed her. "You will be safe with Granny Nola."

Raven looked confused and frightened. "Wales? Isn't your grandmother's home close to Chirk and the border?"

"Aye, 'tis very close, but the only ones who knew of Granny are now dead. Granny lives in a small cottage in Builth Wells, no more than a day's ride from Chirk."

"Is that where your mother met your father?"

"Aye. Your father and mine were friends. Lord Nyle had a hunting box near the village. He and my father hunted there often. Granny said Mother was gathering berries in the woods when my father chanced upon her. When Lord Nyle returned to Chirk, Father was so smitten that he stayed and wooed my mother. They were married by the village priest within days of meeting."

"I do not understand. Everyone assumed you were born on the wrong side of the blanket."

"Granny said Basil's father, the old Earl of Eyre, was enraged over the marriage and sent men to burn down the church where the records were kept. The old earl had already chosen a wife for Basil and a wedding date was set. The banns had been posted and the dowry agreed upon. The old earl ordered Basil back to Eyre immediately, and his men-at-arms made sure his orders were obeyed. My father returned to Eyre and I never saw him until he came for me after Mother died."

"How did Lord Basil know your mother had died?"

"Lord Nyle kept him informed. I learned later that Nyle paid a villager to send word of my progress to him at regular intervals. He reported my mother's death, and in turn your father told mine. You know the rest."

"How do you know your grandmother is still alive?"

"Granny Nola is still hale and hearty. I visited her briefly before I attended the tourneys at Chirk. Only my most trusted knights know of the village and Granny's existence. You will be safe there."

"Will you remain at Builth Wells with me?"

He glanced away. "I cannot. After I escort you to Granny's home, I plan to ride out to intercept Waldo before he reaches Windhurst. All I own is within the keep. Before we leave, the valuables and gold I earned will be moved to a cave below the castle at the foot of the cliff, just above the high-water mark. Naught I possess will ever belong to Waldo." His expression softened. "And that includes you, sweet Raven."

Raven's dismay was obvious. "Waldo's forces outnumber yours. You cannot possibly hope to stop them with your small army."

"I am leaving Sir Richard behind in the village. He will know where to find me when Sir John arrives with the mercenaries."

He kissed the top of her head. "Go upstairs and pack, Raven, while I instruct the servants and workmen. When I return, I intend to make love to you all through the night."

Raven turned and walked away, sadness dulling her eyes. She had known this day would come, just as surely as she knew Waldo would never give her up. Drake's inadequate army stood little chance of defeating Waldo's and Duff's combined forces. She feared she was going to lose him before she'd really ever had him. The fear was so intense, she recoiled in pain. Something terrible was going to happen. She knew it. She could feel it in her bones, though she was no seer.

It was very late when Drake returned. She had already undressed down to her shift and was waiting for him on the bench before the fire. He was soaked to the skin, and she realized he must have been below the cliff, stowing his money chests. He seemed preoccupied as he tore off his wet clothing and dried himself with a soft cloth. Abruptly he threw the cloth aside and held out his arms to her. She walked into them and they closed around her.

"Everything is in readiness for our departure," he whispered against her hair. "The servants are to return to their homes in the village, but the stonemason and laborers will continue to work on the walls. Sir Richard has agreed to remain behind and wait for Sir John and the mercenaries.

When they arrive, Richard will take the mercenaries to join my men-at-arms, where they will await me in the forest near Chirk. I've instructed him to send Sir John to me at Builth Wells."

"If you expect Sir John soon, why not wait here for him?"

He stared at her, his expression unreadable. "I cannot take chances with your life. Once I know you are safe, I can concentrate on turning Waldo away from Windhurst."

"But . . ."

He placed a finger against her lips. "Nay, my mind is made up. This may be the last night we have together for a very long time; let us not waste it."

He tipped her face up for his kiss. She melted against him, trying not to think about tomorrow, or the tomorrows to follow. This man, the notorious Black Knight, might not love her as she loved him, but deep within her heart she knew he cared for her.

Drake removed Raven's shift and stared at her. Firelight gilded her flesh, turning it all gold and shimmery. Her breasts were perfect, just the right size to fill his hands. Her nipples were pink and prominent. He bent his head and licked them, each one in turn. Spellbound, he watched them tauten into rosy buds. Wordlessly she lifted her face, offering her lips.

His hands framed her face as he took her mouth. Then his hands drifted away, resting on her shoulders before sweeping down her back, over her hips, drawing her fully against him. He groaned against her mouth. He could wait no longer. He was already hard as a rock. Urgency drove him as Raven clung to him, her hands reaching for him. His manhood jerked in response as her fingers curled around him.

"God's blood, Raven, you are killing me!"

Grasping her buttocks, he lifted her. Her legs came around his waist, opening to him. She was wet and hot — so hot his loins were on fire where they meshed with hers. He could not think; he could only feel as he backed her up against a tapestry-covered wall and thrust himself inside her sweet passage. She cried out; he heard naught but the pounding of blood in his ears.

"Come to me now, sweet Raven," he rasped into her ear. "I can hold back no longer."

"I am with you," Raven said on a shuddering breath.

Her contractions triggered his own release.

Holding her gyrating hips in place, he embedded himself deeply and pumped his seed into her. When he had given her all he had, he could not bear to leave her, so he carried her to the bed with her legs gripping his waist and his manhood still buried inside her. Though he had climaxed scant moments ago, his erection had not softened.

He still wanted her.

He made love to her again, and yet again. The night ended as it must, however, albeit too soon for Raven. There were things she wanted to say that were left unsaid. She wanted to ask Drake if he cared for her. Sometimes he acted as though he did, yet . . . Drake, however, was a man who rarely expressed his emotions, and she was left in the dark as to the nature of his feelings for her. She knew he enjoyed making love to her, but men were men. They were all alike when it came to women. Making love did not necessarily mean a man liked or even loved the woman he made love to.

Those thoughts and more were still warring within her when sleep finally claimed her.

The following morning the servants gathered in the courtyard to bid the lord of the castle, his leman, and his knights fare-well. All the servants but Balder, who had refused to leave the castle, and Sir Richard, who remained behind to await Sir John and direct the work on the walls, were to return to their homes.

Drake's men carried enough food to last until the journey's end if they ate sparingly. They even brought along extra horses to replace those that could not maintain the rapid pace. Sir Richard stood nearby to receive final orders.

"Your orders will be relayed to Sir John when he arrives, my lord," he assured Drake.

"Very good, Richard. You know where you are to direct him, do you not?"

"Aye. Your army is to await you in the woods near Castle Chirk. Mayhap I will enter the keep dressed as a peasant to learn what I can about Waldo and Duff."

"Be careful," Drake warned.

"Aye. I was careful before. No one recognized me as one of your knights."

"Are you ready, my lady?" Drake asked as Raven rode up to join him.

"As ready as I will ever be," Raven replied. "I rather like Windhurst," she said wistfully. "But I am resigned. As long as I am married to Waldo, I will never have a home of my own."

She moved her horse close to Drake's destrier and touched his arm. "Mayhap I should return to Waldo and put a stop to further bloodshed. Or better yet, I could just disappear. Your life would be much simpler were I not around to complicate it."

Drake placed his hand over hers. "I am a knight, my lady. I have sworn to protect those weaker than myself. Besides, this blood feud between me and Waldo must come to a head one day. He has made attempts upon my life and I know not why. I will not rest until I learn what fuels his hatred. He considers me a threat to him, though I can think of naught he has to fear from me. He is our father's heir, not I."

Drake gave the signal and the small party left the courtyard. Raven followed, stretching her memory back to the time when they were all children growing up at Chirk. Even then Waldo had harbored animosity toward Drake. He had treated Drake with disdain and called him names, but that was as far as it had ever gone. Something must have happened in later years to turn Waldo's disregard for Drake into the kind of loathing that made a man want to kill his brother.

Did Drake's grandmother hold the key?

Chapter Ten

Love gives a knight courage.

Drake and Raven parted company with Drake's knights and men-at-arms before they crossed the Welsh border. The warriors remained in England, camped in the forest near Castle Chirk, where they were to await Drake's orders, while Drake and Raven continued on to Builth Wells. They had not encountered Waldo and his forces, for which Raven thanked God, and the weather had held, affording them a swift journey to their destination. They reached the Welsh border in less than a sennight and were within a day's ride of Granny Nola's cottage.

During their march to Wales there had been little opportunity for privacy, and Drake had not touched Raven in all that time, though she ached to feel his arms around her again. He had been preoccupied with strategy and often met long into the night with his men. They all slept out in the open, so when Drake joined her on the pallet Evan made up for them, they did naught but cuddle before falling into an exhausted sleep. Then they were up and on their way by dawn the next morning.

They rode now over hills and across moors ablaze with heather and crisscrossed with low stone fences that had withstood wind and rain and the ages with grace.

"Look," Drake said, pointing to a cluster of thatched cottages that clung precariously to a hillside. " 'Tis Builth Wells."

"Does your grandmother live in the village?" Raven asked curiously.

"Aye. Her cottage sits at the end of a crooked lane near the edge of town. I moved her there from the small shack we occupied when I was a child. I tried to bring her to England but she would not budge. She is probably standing now upon the doorstep, awaiting us."

His words puzzled Raven. "Did you send a messenger ahead to tell her of our arrival?"

Drake shook his head. "Granny Nola has ways of knowing things that few people comprehend. You will find out for yourself," he said cryptically.

They rode through the village. It was market day, and their appearance drew curious glances. Some of the villagers, apparently recognizing Drake, waved or called out a greeting. Drake waved back but did not stop as they turned down a narrow lane and continued to the end. The snug cottage was just as Drake described, its thatched roof rising against a backdrop of blue skies and scudding clouds. And just as Drake said, a small woman leaning heavily upon a cane stood on the doorstep, waiting to greet them. Raven cocked an eyebrow at Drake.

"I told you so," he said as he dismounted and lifted Raven from her palfrey. Hand in hand they approached the small, thin woman whose gray hair was rolled into a neat bun at her nape.

Suddenly the woman rushed forth to meet them, the cane merely a prop on her arm as her feet literally flew over the cobbled walk. There was nothing feeble about this woman, Raven thought as Granny Nola flew into Drake's open arms.

"I have been waiting for you," Granny said. "Danger lurks; you must take care." She turned her penetrating blue eyes upon Raven. Their intensity and clarity surprised Raven. One would not expect such stunning perception in a woman of Granny Nola's age.

"This is Raven of Chirk, Granny," Drake said, pulling Raven closer for his grandmother's inspection.

Granny smiled sweetly. "Raven, aye, I have been waiting for you," she said, as if confirming something she had always known.

Raven's eyes widened. "You have?" She sent Drake a confused look. "Have we met before, ma'am?"

"You may call me Granny Nola, or just Granny, if you prefer. And to answer your question, nay, we have not met, though I have known of you for many years. You are as beautiful as I knew you would be."

Raven was shocked but not alarmed. Sometime in the past Drake must have mentioned her to his grandmother. "Thank you, Granny, but I fear you exaggerate. I am not the beauty my mother was."

"Come inside. I have food waiting for you. You must be exhausted after your journey."

"Did I not tell you?" Drake whispered to Raven as they followed Granny into the cottage. "Granny Nola is unique."

Unique was not the word Raven would have used, but she certainly was different. She had heard about people who had the "sight" and wondered if Granny was one of those blessed with the gift.

The cottage was small by most standards, but scrupulously clean and neat. Delicious smells emanated from the hearth, where a pot hung over the coals. Raven made a slow perusal of the cottage and liked what she saw. The room into which Granny led them held a hearth hung with various cooking pots and utensils, benches, a table and chairs, and a settle decorated with colorful pillows. A door led to another room, which Raven assumed was a bedroom — probably the only bedroom.

"There is a loft beneath the roof," Granny said, as if reading Raven's mind. " 'Tis tidy and comfortable. I am sure you will find it adequate."

Raven flushed. "Thank you. It will be perfect."

"Sit down," Granny invited. " 'Tis lamb stew you smell. I will dish you up a bowl. There is fresh bread on the table and apple pie for dessert."

Drake smacked his lips. "You do know the way to a man's heart, Granny."

"How long can you stay?" Granny asked as she set the food on the table. "Your last visit was far too brief."

"I fear this visit will be no longer than the last. I am here now because I need a safe place to leave Raven. My men await me in the forest near Chirk. I intend to stop Waldo before he destroys Windhurst."

Granny's eyes grew murky with fear. "Raven is welcome, but there is danger in the air. Your half brother wants your death."

"Fear not, Granny," Drake soothed. "I can afford to fund an army. Sir John is out recruiting mercenaries now. When I meet Waldo, it will be on equal footing."

Granny gazed beyond Raven's shoulder at something only she could see. "My grandson fights for you, does he not, my lady? Are you not Waldo's wife?"

Raven exhaled sharply. Granny Nola was too knowledgeable, too canny. Did she blame Raven for bringing trouble upon her grandson?

"Raven hates Waldo," Drake said, plunging into the void, "and I do not blame her. Waldo is dangerous and cunning. He wants me dead, though I know not why. Raven suspects him of killing her sister, Waldo's first wife." His eyes darkened, fierce with determination. "I will not allow Waldo to have Raven."

Granny nodded sagely. "I know not what you did that required you to offer protection to Raven, but I know you, and you are an honorable man, Drake."

"I am a burden to Drake," Raven said. "I

offered to disappear, thus saving him from meeting Waldo in battle, but he would not hear of it. Mayhap you can convince him. I never intended to cause bloodshed when I asked for his help."

Granny's blue eyes dimmed. " 'Tis too late, dear," she said gently. "Waldo is plagued by demons so sinister and disturbing that naught can change his destiny. I know not what darkness drives him, except that it concerns Drake."

Raven's interest sharpened. "Does it concern Drake's mother and father?"

Granny's expression grew wistful. "Aye, Leta was a wonderful daughter. She fell in love with Basil of Eyre, Drake's father, and naught could dissuade her from marrying him. I knew 'twould be a disaster, but she would not listen."

"I knew it! Drake is no bastard!" Raven said with smug satisfaction.

Drake gave her an exasperated look. "I know it, Granny knows, and now you know. Unfortunately there is no proof that a wedding between Leta and Basil ever took place."

Granny's blue eyes gleamed as she leaned close and confided, "Proof exists, Drake. When the time is right, you will have your proof."

After those prophetic words, the conversation turned to mundane matters. Raven nodded off, and Granny suggested she turn in and get a good night's sleep.

"The privy is behind the house, dear, and the bed in the loft is freshly made. You will find water in the pitcher for a quick sponge bath, and tomorrow I'll have Drake fetch water for the tub so you can have a nice soak."

"Thank you," Raven said, rising. "I *am* tired, and a bath sounds wonderful. Will you still be here tomorrow, Drake?"

"I will stay until Sir John arrives, no longer. Shall I escort you to the privy?"

"Nay, I can find it."

"She is lovely," Granny said after Raven left the room.

"I ruined her," Drake admitted glumly.

"I was drunk, Granny. Waldo tried to poison me during the tourneys, and I thought that despoiling his bride was justified. I was wrong. When I first arrived at Chirk for the tourneys, Raven sought me out and pleaded with me to help her escape from Chirk before the wedding. She asked for my escort to her aunt's home in Edinburgh. She loathes Waldo and holds him responsible for her sister's death. I refused to help her."

"You helped her more than you will ever know," Granny predicted.

"I did her only harm. After I left her chamber I realized I could not abandon Raven to Waldo's wrath. I fully intended to return to the keep and rescue her." He gave a rueful laugh. "Raven was more resourceful than I gave her credit for. She bashed Waldo with a water jug and fled to my camp ere I could rescue her. She demanded my protection and I gave it. We left for Windhurst within the hour. She was angry when I refused to take her to Scotland, but I knew she would not be safe in her aunt's home, for that was the first place Waldo would look."

"Windhurst," Granny mused. "Did you not say the castle was naught but an ancient hulk?"

"I exaggerated. The keep itself has withstood years of neglect tolerably well, but the outer walls and fortifications have long since crumbled into rock and mortar. I undertook repairs immediately, but time ran out before the reconstruction was finished. I received word that Waldo was riding forth soon to attack Windhurst and claim his bride.

"I realized Windhurst could not withstand a siege, and until Sir John arrived with the mercenaries, my army was sorely undermanned. They await me now in the woods near Chirk. I hope Sir John will soon arrive with the mercenaries to join them. I intend to stop Waldo's forces before he reaches Windhurst and destroys what has been rebuilt."

"Raven will be safe here, grandson. That *is* what you want of me, is it not?"

"Aye. Waldo does not know you are alive, much less where to find you. Should I fail to return, you will be here for her. I intend to leave a purse of money for her should she need it. Waldo need never find her if she does not want him to."

"Is Raven your leman?" Granny asked, not mincing words.

"Granny, I —"

"Answer me, lad."

"Aye. The decision was a mutual one. I cannot marry her, you know that. She is already married."

"You love her," Granny said.

Startled, Drake quickly put Granny's supposition to rest. "Nay, I love no woman save you, Granny. Raven already has a husband. I cannot have her."

Granny clucked. "Silly boy."

Suddenly Granny seemed to wilt before his eyes. Her shoulders drooped and she appeared old and withered as she lifted herself from her chair with difficulty. "I am tired. We will talk tomorrow. You may sleep on the floor before the hearth. There are blankets in the chest beside the settle."

"You are disappointed in me," Drake said. It was more a statement than a question.

She touched his hair with a gnarled hand. "Nay, lad. Disappointment is not what I am feeling. I see frightening things, things I cannot speak of because they are not yet clear in my head." Her hand slid down to caress his cheek. "I fear for you, Drake. Blackness surrounds you, and blood." She sighed. "Go to bed, lad. I am an old woman. Mayhap I am being fanciful."

Leaning heavily on her cane, Granny Nola limped away. Drake stared after her. What did Granny see? he wondered. Granny might seem strange at times, but she had never told him anything that had not come true. Had she seen his death?

To his knowledge, Granny had never been fanciful. She had known about the intimate relationship between him and Raven. Was their affair that obvious? Was Granny disappointed in him for taking advantage of Raven?

His mind was still whirling with unanswered questions when Raven returned from the privy. "Where is Granny Nola?"

"She retired. I suggest you do the same." He rose and pulled on a rope, bringing the loft steps down. "Do you need help?"

"Nay, thank you." She put one foot on the bottom rung. For some reason Drake was loath to let her go. He had grown accustomed to sleeping beside her, knowing she was nearby even if he could not make love to her. Grasping her waist, he pulled her down and into his arms.

Raven gasped in surprise. "Drake! What are you doing?"

"I have missed you," he whispered into her ear.

"I have never left you," she replied.

"I will join you tonight in the loft. I must have you one last time before I go off to fight."

"Nay, you cannot."

He grinned at her. "I beg to differ."

"Your grandmother will not approve."

"She will never know."

"You know better than that."

He refused to accept defeat. He kissed her, hard, and gave her a little shove toward the ladder. "Go. I will come to you soon."

Hours later, Drake crept up the ladder

and was disappointed to find Raven sleeping soundly. She looked so peaceful he did not have the heart to awaken her. He placed a tender kiss on her forehead and crept back down the ladder to his own bed before the hearth.

The next morning Drake carried water in from the well for Raven's bath and waited outside while she had her soak. Raven was all too aware of Drake's imminent departure. Sir John could arrive momentarily, and Waldo could even now be on his way to destroy Windhurst.

Raven stepped from the tub and dried herself while Granny puttered around the hearth.

Suddenly, out of the blue, Granny said, "You love my grandson very much."

The drying cloth slipped from Raven's hands and she quickly retrieved it, wrapping it around herself. "I . . . what makes you think that?"

"I do not think, dear; I know."

Flustered, Raven began to dress. Were her feelings for Drake so transparent? "I am a burden to Drake. He will never love me."

"There will be great upheaval in your life," Granny predicted. "Your future remains murky."

Raven went still. Would she be forced to return to Waldo? Would he kill her? Her hands went to her stomach. Mayhap she was carrying Drake's child. What then?

"Drake is waiting outside," Granny said. "Mayhap you should join him. The moor is lovely this time of year." She glanced out the window to the heather-covered hills, and beyond. "Sir John comes." She turned away. "Soon my grandson will meet Waldo in battle."

Raven expelled a shaky breath. "What do you see, Granny? Will Drake survive?"

Granny stared at Raven. "I sense danger. There will be bloodshed, but I do not see Drake's death. Both you and Drake will face difficult times, but only God knows where it will all end. I cannot see beyond the blood, but I do know that Waldo holds the key to Drake's future."

"Tell me more!" Raven cried, frantic for a peek into the future.

Granny sighed. "I can tell you naught else. Go now, Drake waits for you."

Raven did not bother to braid her hair or don a cap after she had brushed her hair free of tangles. She waved to Granny and flew out the door to join Drake. This might be the last time they would be together in a very long time. She found him sitting on a stone fence, staring off into the distance. He must have sensed her presence, for he turned and watched her approach.

He is so handsome, Raven thought, admiring everything about him: the proud way he carried himself, his warrior's hard body, his passion, his adherence to the chivalric code. She had loved Drake when he was a lad, and she loved him still — loved him so much she would sacrifice everything for his sake.

"Did you enjoy your bath?" Drake asked when she joined him at the fence.

"Very much, thank you. Granny suggested that we stroll across the moor."

Drake looked startled. "Granny said that?"

"Aye. She said that Sir John will arrive soon, mayhap today."

"I have been expecting him. Come." He held out his hand to her. " 'Tis a fine day for a stroll."

Neither spoke as they walked hand in hand through the heather.

"What are you thinking?" Drake asked.

"About Chirk, and how happy and carefree we were."

Drake's expression hardened. "Mayhap you were happy and carefree, but Waldo and Duff made certain my days at Chirk were anything but pleasant."

Raven's heart went out to the forlorn child Drake had once been. "I'm sorry."

"Nay, do not pity me. I would not be the man I am today had I not been forced to fight for recognition. Let us speak of more pleasant things."

"The wildflowers are lovely," Raven remarked.

Drake stopped, plucked a posy, and presented it to her. She sniffed deeply, then held it beneath Drake's nose. "Very nice," Drake remarked. Suddenly his eyes darkened and he snatched the posy from her hand and tossed it to the ground.

"God's blood, Raven, I cannot pretend I do not want you. I think my wise old granny sent us here because she knew we needed to be alone."

He pulled her to the ground with him and pressed her down onto the fragrant heather. "I want to make love to you, sweet Raven. I want to take off all your clothes and fill my eyes with your beauty. I want to arouse you slowly, and when you are ready, I want to thrust myself into your tight, hot body and take you with me to paradise."

Raven swallowed convulsively. His words were intensely arousing, like a potent aphrodisiac, sending shimmering waves of heat coursing through her, and Raven burned for his touch. "I want that, too." She cast a furtive glance behind her. "What if someone comes along?"

"No one will come. Why do you think Granny sent us here?"

He raised her tunic and shift, but his hands were suddenly clumsy and fumbling. "Forgive me," he apologized. " 'Tis not like me to be so clumsy. I have never wanted a woman this much before and 'tis a frightening feeling."

Raven wanted to tell him she felt the same, but his hands on her body made coherent speech impossible. Yet somehow their clothing flew away. When they were both naked, Drake sat back on his heels and stared at her.

"I like making love in the daylight," he said as his heated gaze skimmed over her. "I never tire of looking at you. Do you know how you look now?" Raven shook her head. "Like a goddess dedicated to the sun. Your body is the color of pale ivory splashed with golden sunlight. Your hair is a combination of so many colors I cannot begin to describe it. Like rich, burnished chestnut woven with gold."

"You have a warrior's body," Raven said, smoothing her hands over the hard muscles of his back and buttocks. "Velvet on stone. I wish . . ."

"What do you wish, my love? Ask anything, for today is magical and all your wishes will be granted."

"Not this wish," Raven said wistfully.

"Tell me."

Tears gathered in her eyes. "Nay. My wish can never be. Just love me, Drake. We have today; let us not waste it."

Drake kissed her, plundering her mouth like a starving man. There was little finesse in his kiss; apparently he was too hungry for restraint. She sighed as he captured her head in his large hands, smoothing her hair as his hands continued down her back to her buttocks. Cupping the round mounds firmly, he pulled her against his turgid loins. Their heated gazes met a brief moment before he bent to taste her nipples. Drawing one ripe bud into his mouth, he sucked vigorously. She gasped in delight. Suddenly eager to touch him, she moved her hands between them, searching until she found him. Her fingers curled around him, sliding down his length with measured strokes.

His staff was full and hard. She felt it pulsing within her palm as if it had a life of its own. His groan echoed loudly over the enchanted moor, where no one existed but two star-crossed lovers seeking pleasure. Then she brought his staff to her entrance, spread her thighs, and wrapped her legs around his waist, opening herself to him. She felt herself stretching as he filled her, and she shifted to accommodate him, tilting her hips so she could take all of him. Then he began to move. The arousing friction, the bliss, were nearly unbearable. Raven rose up to meet his forceful strokes, clutching his shoulders, grinding her pelvis against him.

Raven climaxed first, crying out so loudly she did not hear Drake shout her name as he gave up his seed. Then he collapsed against her. Raven accepted his weight, holding him against her. She did not want to let him go for fear of losing him forever.

"That was too quick," Drake said as he slipped from his warm haven and rolled off her. "It has been too long."

They rested awhile, lying amid the heather, then made love again. With the sharp edge of their passion temporarily sated, they leisurely explored each other's bodies. Raven was not satisfied until she knew Drake's body as intimately as he knew hers. When he begged her to put an end to it, she mounted him and slid down over his erection. The perfect melding of their bodies flung them over the edge to bliss.

They had just finished dressing when Sir John appeared at the edge of the moor.

"Sir John is here," Drake said as he guided Raven across the moor to where the knight awaited them.

Raven paled. She felt as if an unseen hand were crushing her heart. Granny might not have sensed Drake's death, but she had implied that his danger was great. Her thoughts remained gloomy as they approached Sir John.

"I see my message reached you," Drake said, clasping John's arm.

"Aye. Sir Richard was waiting at Windhurst for me when I arrived with the mercenaries. I've brought you fifty strong warriors, all eager to swear fealty to the Black Knight."

"Did you see aught of Waldo?"

"Nay. I sent the mercenaries on to Chirk with Sir Richard. You will have an army of over one hundred warriors when they join the men already there. They but await your orders."

"You did well, John. We will ride as soon as you have eaten and rested."

Raven paled. "So soon?"

Drake's expression softened. "I cannot allow Waldo to reach Windhurst. He will destroy everything I own with his war machines if I do not intercept him. Thanks to John, our armies are now evenly matched. Fear not, Raven. I will return."

Granny was waiting on the porch for them. Her lined face was creased with worry, and she leaned heavily upon her cane.

"I have food ready," she said. "Come and eat."

Sir John removed his armor and joined Drake at the table. Raven and Granny set food and drink before them and they ate in silence. When they had eaten their fill, Granny packed the remains in a cloth sack for them to take along. Then Raven helped both John and Drake don their armor.

"Walk outside with me," Drake said as he guided Raven out the back door to the lean-to where his horse was stabled.

Raven could not stop her trembling as she followed Drake. Was this to be their final farewell? Would she ever see him again? She watched fearfully as he saddled Zeus. Then he removed his helm and drew her into his arms.

"Promise me you will remain here no matter what."

Raven could not bear looking into those silver eyes, so compelling in their intensity. He was asking something she could not grant.

"Nay," she whispered shakily. "Circumstances might arise that may require me to leave."

"Heed me well, Raven. Waldo will not treat you gently should you fall into his hands. No matter what happens to me, you must remain with Granny."

She gave him a tearful smile. "I cannot give you that promise, Drake."

"Bloody hell," Drake rasped as he bent his head for a farewell kiss.

Chapter Eleven

A brave knight defies death.

Drake and Sir John found the Black Knight's men with little difficulty. Over one hundred strong, his army was hidden in the forest near Chirk. Sir Richard hurried over to greet them as they dismounted.

"What news have you, Richard?" Drake asked.

"Lord Waldo and Lord Duff rode forth from Chirk two days ago. I was in the bailey when they left. They have combined their armies and lead nearly two hundred men."

"God's blood!" Drake cursed. "I had not expected them to have so great a force. What of war machines?"

"Aye, they have war machines and crossbows. What are your orders, my lord?"

"We may not have the numbers but we have surprise on our side," Drake said. "Waldo does not expect a rear attack. The war machines will slow them down, allowing us to overtake them. John, mobilize the men; we ride immediately."

An hour later Drake's army rode in hot pursuit of Waldo and Duff. They rested briefly during the darkest hours of night and continued on at daybreak. Dusk was rolling over the land the following day when Drake rode to the top of a hill and spied Waldo's forces camped in a valley beside a stream. He rode back to inform his men and to devise a battle plan with his knights.

Drake decided they should attack shortly before dawn, when the enemy was most vulnerable. The attack would come from several directions at once. The warriors were immediately informed of the plan and split up into three separate groups. Drake was to lead one group, Sir John a second, and Sir Richard the third. The moment the other two men spied Drake leading his men down the hillside, they were to swoop down upon the sleeping camp from their positions. They parted then, each taking a third of the men and leaving Drake behind with the remaining third.

Drake inspected his weapons and armor, gave Evan last-minute instructions, and lay down on the ground to rest, rolling up in his cloak for warmth. Thoughts of Raven intruded upon his sleep. Leaving her had been difficult. No woman had ever captured his fancy like Raven of Chirk. Dimly he wondered if the day they had made love in the heather would be the last he would see of Raven. He could die in battle tomorrow. Would she miss him? Lord, he hoped so. If he died, would Waldo find her and punish her? The answer offered him no comfort.

He could not die, he told himself. He had to live for Raven's sake. And for his own sake. He could not die before proving that there had been a legal marriage between his mother and father. If Granny could be believed, and she had no reason to lie, the vast estates and wealth Waldo claimed should belong to Drake; Waldo was the bastard. That thought was so comforting Drake managed to sleep a few hours before Evan awakened him.

It was time.

Drake donned his armor over a quilted gambeson and bent forward as Evan pulled a black tunic with a red dragon emblazoned on the front over his breastplate. Then he mounted Zeus. Gravely, Evan handed Drake his helm, shield, and weapons. Drake donned his helm and grasped his sword in one hand and his shield in the other. When shades of mauve streaked across the horizon, Drake raised his sword high and led his men down the hillside to the enemy's camp.

Glancing right and left, Drake saw that Sir John and Sir Richard were attacking from their own positions. Then one of Waldo's guards heard the clamor of approaching riders and cried the warning. There was a mad scramble for weapons and armor as Drake's men rode through the camp, hacking and slashing at will.

The battle was fiercely engaged. It registered in Drake's mind that Waldo's army was reported to outnumber his two to one, but he estimated their numbers at no more than one hundred. He saw naught of Duff and that worried him. But Drake had scant time to wonder about that now. Waldo's men had quickly rallied, fighting off the initial attack and launching one of their own. Drake's men fought valiantly for the Black Knight, their battle cries ringing over the valley.

Drake searched for Waldo amid the warriors fighting in the early morning dawn and spotted him crossing swords with Sir John. Both men were afoot, having abandoned their mounts to engage in hand-to-hand combat. Drake fought his way to Sir John's side. If anyone was going to dispatch Waldo, it should be the Black

Knight. He dismounted and shoved Sir John aside.

"I will take it from here, John," he rasped.

"I will protect your back," John replied, stepping behind Drake with his sword raised in defense of his liege lord.

Waldo deftly evaded Drake's slashing sword, and the battle was engaged. All around them the fighting continued. Men were slain. Blood flowed freely. The sound of clashing weapons was deafening.

"Where did you come from? Where is my wife?" Waldo said, panting as he hacked viciously at Drake.

"Where you will never find her," Drake answered, deflecting Waldo's sword with his shield.

"You raped her and kidnapped her," Waldo charged.

"Do you think so?"

"Bastard! You have more lives than a cat. You should have died years ago."

Thrust and parry. Slash and hack. Small wounds resulted when vulnerable places in their armor were breached.

"Your past efforts to do away with me did not succeed," Drake rasped. " 'Tis time for retribution."

"Did you enjoy my wife?" Waldo

taunted. "Ironic, is it not, that the son of a whore made a whore of the wife of our father's legitimate son? Raven will suffer when I find her."

Both men were tiring, weighted down by their heavy armor and weapons. Advancing mercilessly, Drake had maneuvered Waldo into the stream, and he could smell victory. Then disaster struck. One hundred reinforcements poured onto the battlefield. Drake no longer had to wonder about Duff, for he rode at the head of his army, his warriors turning the tide of battle in Waldo's favor. Drake cursed himself for a fool. He should have known Waldo would split his army to reduce the chances of a surprise attack from whatever enemy they might encounter along the way. And the precaution had paid off. Drake's men, brave though they might be, were being driven back by the combined forces of Waldo and Duff.

"Save yourself, John," Drake called as he drove Waldo into the water. "Flee to the woods with the men."

"Nay. I will not leave you," John replied as he deftly dispatched a warrior coming to Waldo's defense.

Suddenly Drake dove beneath Waldo's defense and slipped his sword into the unprotected place where his helm and breast-plate met. He would have driven the sword home had not John called out a warning. From the corner of his eye Drake saw six mounted warriors, swords drawn and at the ready, riding straight for him. They formed a tight circle around Drake and John, looking to Waldo for orders.

"All is lost, Sir Bastard," Waldo taunted. "Throw down your sword or you both die."

"We will die whether or not we drop our weapons," Drake returned. "I can kill you easily; just one thrust will end your miserable life."

"Do it, Drake," John urged.

"If you do not wish to save your own life, think about your faithful friend," Waldo said. "Surrender and Sir John shall go free."

"Nay, kill the bastard," John cried. "Think not of me."

Drake could not do it. It was one thing to kill Waldo, but he did not want John's death on his conscience. Slowly he removed his sword point from Waldo's neck.

Waldo strode from the water, grasped Drake's weapon, and flung it to the ground. "You are mine, Sir Bastard."

"Kill me now and be done with it," Drake goaded him.

"In good time, Sir Bastard. I need you alive, at least until Raven is back where she belongs."

"You will never find Raven."

Waldo sent Drake a look that said otherwise. "Mayhap not, but I wager Sir John knows where to find her."

"Even if I did, I would not tell you," John said with a sneer.

"No need," Waldo said.

Drake frowned. Waldo's complacency worried him. He knew his brother had something fiendish in mind for him and Raven, and a shiver of apprehension slid down his spine. "Hurt Raven and you will regret it," he said with a snarl.

"My plans for Raven are none of your concern, Sir Bastard. As for yourself, mayhap you will find Chirk's dungeon to your liking." He turned to Sir John. "And you, Sir John, will carry a message to my wife."

Drake went very, very still. "Damn you! It will not work, Waldo. Raven will not fly to my defense because you order her to. She knows better."

Waldo smiled. "We shall see, *brother*." He returned his attention to John. "You are to tell my *wife* that she should present herself at Chirk within a fortnight if she wishes her lover to live. Should she fail to heed my warning, Drake will die in the most horrible way imaginable."

"Do not do it, John," Drake pleaded. "I will not live no matter what Raven does. I have known for a long time that Waldo wants me dead."

"You will not be followed, Sir John, if that is what you fear," Waldo continued. "But I expect you to return with Raven within a fortnight, else your friend's life is forfeit. No one will condemn me for slaying the man who stole my wife on our wedding night."

"How do I know you will not kill him ere I leave?" John charged.

"You have my word as a knight," Waldo said. "I swear the Black Knight will not die unless you return without Raven. But heed me well: he will be kept alive a fortnight, no longer."

John sent Drake a pleading look, as if begging for his understanding. "I am sorry, Drake, but 'tis Raven's choice to make. Only she can decide whether to obey Waldo and return to Chirk or . . . or . . ."

"Or to sacrifice Drake's life for her freedom," Waldo interjected. He laughed. "I think I know Raven. She is too tenderhearted for her own good. She will return to Chirk," he said with certainty.

Drake thought so, too, and despaired. The thought of Raven subjected to Waldo's cruelty made his skin crawl. Yet he knew with grim certainty that Raven would risk her own life to save his. Unfortunately her capitulation to Waldo's demands would not save him. His life would end the moment Raven returned to Chirk. And if he was not killed as he expected, his heart would surely stop, knowing that Raven was at Waldo's mercy, abused both mentally and physically by her husband's sick nature.

Drake said naught as Sir John mounted his destrier and rode off. The knight glanced back several times to make sure no one was following. Then he gave Drake a farewell salute and kneed his mount into a full gallop.

"Disarm my brother," Waldo ordered when John had disappeared over a hill. Two warriors hurried to comply, quickly divesting Drake of his armor and weapons.

Standing before Waldo in hose, gambeson, and tunic, Drake glared menacingly at his brother. When Waldo blanched and took a backward step, Drake summoned a smile despite his dire circumstances.

"You do well to fear me, brother," he said in a hiss. "You cannot keep me in your puny dungeon."

"We shall see how brave you are after you have walked the distance to Chirk behind my horse," Waldo said with a sneer. "Bind the bastard's hands," Waldo ordered, "and give me the rope. I will set the pace and we shall see if the courageous Black Knight can keep up."

His men complied with alacrity. Then Waldo mounted his destrier and held out his hand for the long tether. He dug his heels into his destrier's flanks and Drake was jerked forward. He stumbled, righted himself, then concentrated on placing one foot before the other. The pace was brutal, the terrain rough. His face set in hard lines, Waldo ignored his brother's pain. He did not even slacken the pace when Drake stumbled over a rock and was dragged several yards before regaining his feet.

The grueling ordeal drained Drake's mind of everything but the struggle for survival. He had to live. For Raven's sake he must not let Waldo defeat him. He had always considered himself invincible. Knights who lived by war and combat held the belief that they were indestructible, and he was no different.

He tried to concentrate on the dungeon instead of on his pain, recalling that he had explored those dark regions as a child. But as he stumbled along behind Waldo's horse, his thoughts turned to Raven. He saw her sweet face in front of him. He remembered her naked in his arms, her long chestnut curls twisted around him as she writhed beneath him, her face flushed with passion. Every image he had of her evoked a memory to treasure.

A memory to love.

Though Drake was tiring, he steadfastly refused to succumb to misery and exhaustion. Somewhere he found the strength to keep his legs moving.

Raven sat on a stone fence, staring into the distance, her heart sorely troubled. Drake been gone a sennight and might have already engaged Waldo in battle. She did not doubt Drake's courage, or question his battle skills, for she knew Drake's experience would stand him in good stead. What truly concerned her were the unfavorable odds. She was dishearteningly aware that Duff would join his own men with Waldo's, creating an army twice the size of Drake's. Not even Drake's enormous courage could overcome his lack of manpower.

Raven heaved a despondent sigh. She had to believe that Drake had defeated Waldo until word arrived announcing otherwise.

"Do not despair, Raven."

Raven started violently. "Granny, you startled me."

"You were lost in thought, my dear."

"Was my despair so obvious?"

"Only to me, Raven." Granny touched Raven's arm. "Fear not; Drake lives."

Raven's heart leaped with renewed hope. "Are you sure?"

Granny's bright eyes seemed to glow with inner knowledge as she stared at the distant hills. "Aye. Drake lives but he is in grave danger. You must prepare yourself."

Raven's heart, so hopeful scant moments before, was suddenly devoured by fear. "Prepare for what?"

"I know not," Granny lamented. "I sense extreme tribulation and hardship in the near future. For your child's sake, you must persevere. Your survival will depend upon your cunning."

Raven stopped thinking when Granny said she must persevere for her child's sake. Her hands flew to her stomach. Was it possible? It was far too early to tell, for her courses weren't due yet. Smiling dreamily, she recalled the day she and

Drake had lain in the heather and made love. He had left shortly afterward, and she would not know if his seed grew in her for at least another week.

"A child?" She searched Granny's face. If the Black Knight's child grew within her, she would treasure it forever. "Will I give Drake a son?"

Granny smiled. "Only God knows that. I see naught but what He allows me to see."

"What about Drake? Can you tell me more? Has he defeated Waldo?"

Granny shook her head. "My grandson suffers." Her gnarled hands fluttered to her heart. "I feel it here." Her small frame seemed to diminish before Raven's eyes, and she staggered backward. "Soon you will be forced to make a decision, one only you can make. No one can help you."

Raven leaped down from the wall and rushed to Granny's aid. "Are you all right? Let me help you into the house."

"Aye. There is naught we can do now but wait."

Sir John arrived the following day. He had ridden straight from the battle and was exhausted. Raven saw him and held her breath, waiting for Drake to appear. When he did not, her heart plummeted. With a wail of despair, she ran out to meet him. He slid from the saddle and collapsed into her arms. Raven offered a supporting arm and helped him into the house. With the utmost restraint, she refrained from asking the question uppermost in her mind as she helped Sir John out of his armor and fetched him a drink of water. Granny hovered nearby, looking small and frail and extremely upset.

Unable to stand the suspense a moment longer, Raven blurted out, "Drake? Is he . . ."

John's eyes met hers, then slid away. "He was alive the last I saw him."

"Then why are you here?"

"I will start at the beginning," John said. "We found Waldo and attacked at dawn. Things were going well until Duff showed up with his men. We had no idea Duff had chosen a separate campsite. When he arrived, we were sadly outnumbered. I fought at Drake's back. He had his blade at Waldo's neck when Duff showed up."

"How did you escape?"

"A great many of our men escaped. Waldo was interested only in Drake. He let me go to deliver a message to you."

A soft "ah" escaped Granny's lips.

Raven girded herself for bad tidings. She

knew it would not be pleasant. Nothing Waldo did was ever pleasant.

"Tell me, Sir John. What does Waldo demand of me?"

"First, I must tell you I am here against Drake's wishes. He does not want you to sacrifice yourself for him. I disobeyed his wishes because I believe the choice should be yours to make."

"Go on," Raven demanded. She would do as her heart directed, no matter what Drake wanted.

"Waldo demands that you present yourself at Castle Chirk within a fortnight."

"And if I do not?" Raven knew the consequences would be dire.

"He will kill Drake. I am sorry to put you in this position, Lady Raven, but 'tis your decision to make."

The decision was not a difficult one for Raven. She faced Sir John squarely, her expression determined. "Aye, Sir John, the decision is mine, and I have made it."

John seemed startled. "So soon? I beg you to think this over very carefully, my lady. Should you return to Waldo, you will be placing your life in serious jeopardy."

Raven's small chin went up. "Are you saying I should let Drake die?"

"Nay, my lady. I am only cautioning you

against making a rash decision."

Raven's lips thinned. "How soon can we leave?"

"Give Sir John a day or two to rest, Raven," Granny advised. "He has ridden hard to reach you with Waldo's message. Chirk is but a two-day journey, and Waldo has allowed you a fortnight."

"You do not know Waldo as I do, Granny. He could change his mind and kill Drake." She winced. "Or torture him."

"He gave his word," Sir John injected.

"He will not kill Drake," Granny said with conviction. "Not yet, anyway," she added cryptically.

Raven took little comfort from Granny's words. For all she knew the old woman predicted things she only wished would come true. She could trust no one but herself in this, and her decision had already been made. She loved Drake and would do anything to preserve his life. She knew Waldo would punish her, but she doubted he would kill her. His first wife had died under mysterious circumstances, and the king might question the sudden death of a second wife.

"Give me this day and night to rest, Raven," Sir John said. "I am as anxious to reach Chirk as you are. Be ready to leave at daybreak."

The dank, foul-smelling dungeon was just as he remembered. Drake lay unmoving on the putrid pile of rotting straw and tried to recall how many days had passed since Waldo had thrown him into the dark chamber beneath the castle.

Every bone in his body ached. Fortunately he could not recall much of the forced march to Chirk. When his feet had refused to keep pace with Waldo's mount, he had been dragged along behind. His gambeson had saved him from serious injury, but his exposed skin had been scraped raw and at least two of his ribs had been broken during that harrowing journey. He had been given neither food nor water, until Waldo, fearing he would die before Raven appeared, had allowed him small amounts of nourishment.

Had he been given time to heal, he would not be so weak. But Waldo had ordered a beating. There were times during the beating that Drake had wished for death, but the thought of leaving Raven to Waldo's mercy had instilled in him the will to live. If they would just leave him alone long enough, he knew he would remember something of grave importance about the dungeon, something his fuzzy mind refused to grasp in his present condition.

With painful effort Drake lifted his head and stared through swollen eyes at the winding staircase and the locked door at the top. He had been here before; he was certain of it. And he remembered . . . He remembered . . . His head dropped to his chest. He could remember nothing; the pain pounding within his head robbed him of coherent thought. He closed his eyes and uttered a prayer for Raven's safety. Would she throw caution to the wind and come to Chirk against his wishes? Knowing Raven, she would do the opposite of what he wanted her to do.

Suddenly a light appeared at the top of the stairs, and Drake heard shuffling footsteps and voices. He forced his eyes open and saw two men.

"Are you alive, Sir Bastard?" a harsh voice grated from the top landing.

Squinting toward the light, Drake saw his brother standing at the top of the stairs.

"I am alive, no thanks to you, brother." Drake hated the weakness in his voice but could not help it.

"My man brings food and water," Waldo said. "Enjoy it, for 'tis all you will get. When your whore arrives, you will have outlived your usefulness. Why waste good food on a corpse?"

Had Drake the strength he would have launched himself up the stairs at Waldo for disparaging Raven. It took all the strength he could muster just to form a coherent reply. "You do not deserve a woman like Raven. Blame me for what happened, not her, for she is blameless."

The guard placed a bucket of water and a trencher of food beside Drake. Drake thought he was hearing things when the man whispered as he backed away, "I will bring food and drink when I can, my lord." Stunned and not knowing what to think, Drake watched warily as the guard ascended the stairs.

"Enjoy your meal, Sir Bastard," Waldo taunted.

"Wait! Do not remove the torchlight. How do you expect me to eat what I cannot see? I am no animal."

Waldo laughed, an eerie sound that drifted down to Drake on a chill breeze. "Look at you. You say you are no animal, but your best friend would not recognize you now, crouching like an animal in that dank straw. Very well. Never let it be said that Waldo of Eyre is a man without a heart. I will leave the torchlight here in the sconce. Think not about escape, for the door will be guarded at all times. Pray for your sins while you await death, Sir Bastard."

The heavy door banged shut but the light remained, much to Drake's relief. Though only a dim glow reached him, the torchlight provided sufficient light to afford him his first clear look at his surroundings. He rolled over on his side to reach for the trencher of food and sucked in his breath as pain shuddered through him. When the pain subsided, he pulled the trencher toward him, suddenly ravenous, and wolfed down the contents. He even consumed the trencher, which was made of bread so stale he nearly choked on it. Then he dipped his hand into the water and drank deeply.

Replete for the first time in days, he fell asleep. He wanted to be rested should the guards return to administer another beating. Mayhap when he awakened his mind would be clear enough to recall what he had been trying to remember.

Raven stared through the mist at the castle where she was born and had grown into womanhood. She and Sir John had halted at the edge of the forest that lay beyond the outer walls. The portcullis stood open and the drawbridge had been lowered over the moat. Though the castle appeared tranquil and inviting, Raven felt a deep foreboding inside her.

"I will go in alone," Raven said. "You can be of more use to us outside than imprisoned within."

"I cannot let you go alone, my lady."

"This is my home, Sir John. Duff has not always been a good brother but I cannot believe he will allow Waldo to hurt me. Besides, I will refuse to cross the drawbridge unless Waldo can prove that Drake still lives. Remain here and be ready to ride if I turn away. I will not enter if Waldo cannot show me Drake."

"Be wary, my lady. I trust Waldo not."

"Nor do I, Sir John, nor do I."

Raven guided her palfrey from the cover of trees and halted at the end of the drawbridge, close enough to be seen by the watchmen on the parapet. Almost immediately a watchman heralded her arrival. In an amazingly short time Waldo appeared on the parapet.

"So you came," Waldo called out.

"Aye, I came," Raven shouted in reply. "Where is Drake?"

"Come inside and I will show him to you."

"Nay. I do not trust you. Show me Drake first. How do I know you have not slain him?"

"My own brother? You wound me sorely, wife. I have kept my word. The Black Knight still lives."

"I do not envy you if you have taken Drake's life," Raven shouted. "The king thinks highly of his champion. You will be punished for what you have done to him."

Waldo's laughter drifted over her like an ominous cloud. "The king's champion abducted my wife and deprived me of my wedding night. Think you Edward will condone that kind of behavior from his own knight?"

"Show me Drake," Raven demanded. Dread shivered through her. Was there some reason Waldo refused to bring Drake forth? Did her love still live?

"Very well," Waldo roared, clearly angered by her refusal to surrender herself unconditionally. He turned to speak to one of his men, and Raven felt a modicum of satisfaction at having won the first round. "It will take a while to bring him up here."

"Do not try to trick me, Waldo. And do not send your men from the castle to seize me, for I can outrun them and disappear forever."

Ready to turn her horse and bolt should the situation demand it, Raven waited impatiently for Drake to appear on the parapet.

Three whole days had passed since his last beating, allowing Drake to regain some of his former strength. The friendly knight had managed to sneak food and water to him just once, but Drake was grateful for whatever the man provided. He had even wrapped his broken ribs and provided salve for his injuries. He had also told Drake that there were men among Waldo's army who respected the Black Knight and did not like what Waldo was doing to him.

Unfortunately, fear of Waldo's wrath prevented them or any of Chirk's servants from helping him escape. But now that Drake's mind was functioning again, he began to recall something very important from his childhood days at Chirk, something that gave him hope.

Drake's thoughts scattered as he felt a draft coming from the open door at the top of the stairs. Someone was descending the stairs. It was two men-at-arms wearing Eyre colors. He sensed danger and braced himself.

"You are wanted above," one of the men

said in a growl. Pain exploded through him as he was seized and dragged up the stone stairs. Light exploded before his eyes, momentarily blinding him after living in the dark for so long. Holding his ribs, he fought to catch his breath as the guards pulled him up along a flight of stairs winding to the parapets.

"Where are you taking me?" Drake said with a gasp.

"Our liege lord commands your presence on the parapet," the guards informed him.

The parapet! Waldo must have decided to fling him over the parapet to his death. Then another thought occurred. If Waldo no longer needed him alive, did that mean that Raven had refused to return to Chirk? Though it meant his death, Drake was comforted by the knowledge that Raven was still with Granny, where her husband could not hurt her.

He learned how wrong he was when he reached the parapet and saw Raven seated on her white mare just beyond the moat.

Chapter Twelve

A knight holds pain in contempt.

Drake was seized by terror such as he had never known before. Raven looked so small and utterly vulnerable, and his fear for her escalated. "What is Raven doing here?"

"She is here at my command," Waldo said. "But she demands to see you before entering the keep. She did not trust me to keep you alive. Foolish girl. She fancies herself your savior."

He slanted Drake an assessing look. "You look better than I expected." His words held a wealth of contempt and the barest hint of awe. "Some believe you are indestructible, but every man has his breaking point. I do not understand. You look not like a man who should be half-dead from lack of water and food."

"Mayhap I am indestructible," Drake replied.

"No man is invincible," Waldo said with a sneer. He nodded toward one of the guards. "Bring him forward so his whore can see him."

Drake was dragged forcibly to the crenel, where he could be seen from below. Raven shaded her eyes against the sun and stared up at him. Throwing caution to the wind, he cupped his mouth and called out, "Flee, Raven! Waldo means you harm. Keep yourself safe for my sake."

"Bastard!" Waldo said in a hiss, pushing him aside. Drake fell to his knees but quickly recovered.

"Now that you have seen your lover," Waldo called down to Raven, "you may enter the keep. No harm will come to you."

Duff appeared on the parapet beside Waldo, frowning when he saw Raven standing below. " 'Tis Raven."

Drake felt hope stir within him when Duff appeared. Though Duff had never shown much gumption, he was, after all, Raven's brother and should protect her. "Waldo means your sister harm," Drake warned. "Do not let him hurt her."

"Stay out of this, Duff," Waldo advised. "Your sister is my wife; let me handle her however I see fit."

"You promised you would not harm Raven," Duff said, surprising Drake. Duff had never been vocal about anything, preferring instead to follow Waldo's lead. Drake had always thought Duff a spiritless fellow.

"I have no intention of hurting Raven," Waldo lied smoothly. "She will be punished, of course. She made a cuckold of me. 'Tis my right to demand redress. But let me assure you she will live to bear my heir."

Duff looked dubious but offered no further argument. Drake was quick to pursue his small victory. "I would watch Waldo were I you, Duff. Raven is your only sister. As I recall, your other sister died under mysterious circumstances while married to Waldo. Has he explained to your satisfaction how a healthy woman could sicken and die so quickly?"

Duff's thoughtful expression cheered Drake. He prayed the seed of doubt he had planted would take root, and that it would save Raven from serious harm.

"Weakness does not become a knight," Waldo chided Duff. "Show yourself to Raven. Convince her to enter the keep."

Duff walked to the crenel and stared down at Raven. "Sister!" he called loudly. "I promise you will be safe. You must return to your husband. In time he will forgive you."

"Very good," Waldo said, nodding approval.

Drake dragged himself to the crenel and peered down at Raven. "Do not believe them, Raven. Flee!"

Waldo forcibly removed Drake and flung him away, where he was immediately seized by the guards and prevented from interfering.

The moment Raven saw Drake, she knew he had suffered excessively on her account. Though she could not see every bruise and injury from so great a distance, she knew from the sound of his voice and the way he held himself that he had been tortured. It took tremendous strength to remain calm, to keep herself from rushing into the keep and begging for his life. Despite Drake's warning, she was not going to flee.

She gained scant comfort when Duff promised that she would not be harmed, for Duff was not now nor had he ever been her champion. Aware of Waldo's sly nature, she had a request of her own to make.

"Bring Drake down to the portcullis. I refuse to enter until I speak to him."

"Bitch," Waldo muttered beneath his breath. "Very well," he shouted. "Your lover will greet you at the portcullis."

Raven did not realize she was holding her breath until she felt herself grow dizzy from lack of air. She released it in a great whoosh and sucked in another breath as she guided her mount over the drawbridge. She passed the barbican and drew rein just short of the portcullis, her heart pounding as she waited for Drake to appear.

She gasped aloud when she saw him supported between two guards. She wanted to cry. He looked terrible. Disregarding her own safety, she crossed the moat and rode through the portcullis. She brought her palfrey to a skidding halt, slid from the saddle, and rushed to Drake's side.

"What have you done to him?" she cried, sending Waldo a scathing look.

"You should not have come," Drake said in a croak.

Tears sprang to Raven's eyes. Drake was in worse shape than she had imagined. His face was battered, his eyes and mouth dreadfully swollen. His hose was in shreds and his gambeson torn beyond repair. She wanted to take him in her arms but did not dare.

"You have seen your Black Knight, or what is left of him," Waldo taunted. "Are you ready to become my wife now?"

Raven heard Drake groan and felt his pain as if it were her own, but she kept herself focused on her purpose.

"Release Drake first," she demanded.

"Not yet," Waldo said with a snarl. "His release depends upon your willingness to submit to my will. I will have an heir from you, Raven."

"Nay!" Drake cried. "Make no promises. Waldo cannot be trusted."

Drake's impassioned plea nearly destroyed Raven's resolve, but she squared her narrow shoulders and followed her heart. "I will give you an heir, Waldo, after you set Drake free. You have no right to hold him prisoner. Until you release him, I vow no child of yours will grow in my belly. If you think I jest, *husband,* you should know that women have ways of preventing conception."

Raven had a vague idea of some of the things women could do to prevent conception but had no real knowledge of them. She prayed her bluff would convince Waldo of her determination to see Drake set free.

"Drake will remain my prisoner until you conceive my child," Waldo proclaimed. "Then, if I am in a good mood, mayhap I will release him."

Aware that Waldo was rarely in a good mood, Raven tried another tactic. "Drake is the king's champion. Edward will not be pleased with your treatment of Drake. 'Tis the king's right to mete out punishment if punishment is due."

"I fear Raven is right in that," Duff contended. "The Black Knight is the king's champion. The charges against Drake should be presented to Edward so he can resolve them however he sees fit."

Waldo's face swelled with rage. "Are you turning against me, Duff?"

"Nay, I but speak the truth."

"The truth is that Drake of Windhurst deflowered my bride and abducted her on my wedding night."

"Nay!" Raven denied. "I went willingly. Duff knew I was never keen on our marriage. I would have accompanied the devil to escape you. You killed my sister."

Waldo raised his arm to backhand Raven. Duff grasped Waldo's arm with surprising strength, stopping the blow before it fell.

"You said you would not harm Raven," Duff reminded him. "Having to bear your child should be punishment enough for her. We both know she despises you. Injuring her will solve naught."

No one was more stunned by Duff's defense than Raven herself. It was not like Duff to defy Waldo. Cheered by Duff's words, she decided it was time Waldo was reminded that there could be consequences from her association with Drake. His reaction might be brutal, and she prepared herself both mentally and physically for Waldo's wrath.

"Mayhap I carry Drake's child."

Waldo *did* strike her then, his blow knocking her off her feet. She lay on the ground, staring up into his glowering features, wondering if he would kill her.

"Hit her again and you will suffer a slow death," Drake promised as he struggled to free himself.

Waldo paid him little heed; his rage was centered on Raven now. "Bitch!" he roared. "Are you carrying my brother's bastard?"

Raven held her head high, refusing to be crushed by the likes of Waldo. She shrugged. "Mayhap."

"How long before you know?" Waldo's face was so red Raven feared he would burst.

"I am not sure. Two weeks," she said, stretching the truth. "Three at the most. 'Tis difficult to predict."

"Guards!" Waldo bellowed. "Take my *wife* to the solar and lock her in." Raven was hemmed in by two burly guards. "My dear *wife* will wait upon me in her chamber until I see solid proof that she is not breeding."

He turned to Drake. "You had better pray, Sir Bastard, that your whore is not carrying your child. Meanwhile, you will enjoy Chirk's dungeon until such time as Raven becomes my wife in more than name only. Knowing that your life is in my hands will make her more amenable to my attentions."

He waved his hand and the guards started to drag Drake back to the dungeon. "Wait," he cried, refusing to budge. "What will happen to Raven should she be carrying my child?"

Waldo gave him a nasty grin. "Then, dear *brother,* you and Raven will meet in hell."

Enraged, Drake broke free and reached for Waldo, but the guards dragged him back. Waldo nodded to one of the guards, who promptly brought the hilt of his sword down upon Drake's skull, rendering him unconscious. Raven screamed and had to be forcibly restrained as his limp body was hauled away.

Raven paced her chamber, fear for Drake a cancer eating at her soul. Her coming to Chirk had done nothing to help Drake. All she had accomplished was to place her own life in danger. She did not know for certain that she was carrying Drake's child, but Granny had seemed to think a babe was already growing inside her.

She walked to the window embrasure and stared out across the heather-covered hills. Wales and safety lay just beyond the border, but it might as well be a hundred leagues away. She sank down onto the wide ledge and pondered her meager options. First, if her courses did not arrive in a reasonable length of time, Drake would die, and so would she and her child. She could not, would not, allow that to happen. Drake's child must be protected at whatever cost.

Raven heard the metallic scrape of a key and looked expectantly toward the door. A maidservant Raven did not recognize entered the chamber. She carried a trencher and a cup.

"I am Lark," the girl said, staring at Raven with ill-concealed contempt. "I am to attend you."

"Where is Thelma? She has served me in the past."

Lark shrugged. "I know not. There is no maidservant named Thelma employed here."

"What about Sir Melvin? He is my brother's steward."

"That I do know," Lark said. "Sir Melvin retired and resides with his daughter in the village. Sir Edgar is the new steward. Are you hungry? I have brought you food." She placed the trencher and cup on the table beside the hearth with so little care that some of the ale spilled out.

At least Waldo does not intend to starve me, Raven thought. Dimly she wondered why Thelma had been dismissed. It seemed odd that the servants she once knew so well were no longer here to offer help.

She watched Lark as she moved about the room, suddenly realizing that she had called Waldo by his given name, not Lord Waldo, or milord. It did not take Raven long to guess at the role the buxom Lark played in Waldo's life. "You are new here, are you not?" Raven quizzed. The maid was comely as well as shapely, and showed a marked lack of respect.

"I belong to Waldo," Lark said with a sniff. "He takes me wherever he goes."

"You are his leman," Raven said.

"Does that bother you? Waldo is a virile man, with a virile man's needs. Since you are so reluctant to serve him in bed, I have taken your place." Her cold blue eyes gleamed with a mixture of malice and curiosity. "You are the Black Knight's leman. 'Tis rumored that he is a magnificent lover."

Raven turned away in disgust. "If my *husband* sent you to spy on me, or to ask impertinent questions, tell him I have naught to say. My thoughts are my own to savor."

"Savor them, my lady," Lark said disdainfully. "While you are locked away, and your lover suffers below in the dungeon, 'tis I who will sport with Waldo in bed."

"You have my blessing," Raven said with a careless wave of her hand. "I never wanted to be Waldo's wife. Drake is twice the man Waldo will ever be. Leave me; I prefer my own company."

Lark headed toward the door. "I will return to examine your clothing before you retire tonight. I am to inform Waldo when your courses arrive. Or when they do not," she added meaningfully.

Still groggy from the blow to his head, Drake regained his senses after he had been returned to the dungeon. Despite his ferocious headache, his mind was beginning to clear. Raven was in Waldo's custody and he wanted to curse, to scream, to pummel someone, anyone. He could not bear the thought of Raven submitting to Waldo and suffering his hands upon her, his body melding with hers.

Despite his blinding headache, Drake's mind was clearer now than it had been when he'd first arrived at Chirk. Dimly he wondered when Waldo would order more beatings, and how he would endure them. His thoughts delved inward, searching for a piece of information that had dangled out of his reach until now. Something about the dungeon. Focusing his disjointed thoughts on the small, damp chamber he vaguely recalled from his childhood, he let his gaze wander over the stone walls of his prison, fighting the overwhelming fear that this filthy hole would become his tomb.

Then, in the midst of his gloomy thoughts, the information that had eluded him was suddenly within his grasp. He recalled something so vital that he threw his head back and laughed aloud at his inability to remember it before. Long ago, when he had first arrived at Chirk, Waldo had dared him to spend an entire night in the dungeon. Though he was frightened, he had done it to prove that he did not lack courage.

That night, torchlight in hand, he had descended the stone stairs into the black depths of the unknown. He was as scared as any boy could be, but determined to prove to himself that he was not a coward. He had found the tunnel accidentally. During his lonely hours in the dungeon, he noticed a huge stone that did not match the others and decided to investigate. Even as a youngster his strength was considerable, and when he pushed on the stone it slid open, revealing the gaping entrance to a tunnel. The passage was narrow and dank and festooned with cobwebs, and he had been too frightened to explore it.

Pleased with the thought that he knew something no one else knew, he pushed the stone back into place and returned to his bed the following morn, telling no one of his discovery. Curiosity and the knowledge that he knew something that Waldo did not sent him back to the dungeon on three separate occasions. During those clandestine visits he had explored the tunnel and each of the three side tunnels that branched off the main one. The longest angled downward and ended in the woods beyond the moat. Another led to the garrison on the first floor of the keep. And the third and last led to the solar. Though Drake had been too frightened to enter the solar, he learned that the entry was hidden behind a large tapestry hung on the west wall of the sleeping-chamber wall.

Drake had no idea if the tunnel had ever been put to use, but he supposed its purpose was to provide a ready escape for the family should they need one. After he had explored to his heart's content, he had never returned, and even forgot about the tunnel. Drake wondered if he could find the entrance again and if it would still open after all these years. Of one thing he was certain, however: neither Duff nor Waldo seemed to know about the tunnel. Had Waldo known, he would have had Drake shackled.

Drake spent the following days searching for the tunnel. He had to find it soon, for he was growing weaker from lack of water and food. Waldo had doubled the guard stationed at the dungeon's entrance, making it difficult for the friendly knight to get food and water to Drake.

He had all but given up hope when he found the entrance, or what he hoped was the entrance. It had been many years since he had explored the dungeon, and he feared his memory might be faulty.

Time held no meaning for Drake. Hours could have elapsed as he pushed and prodded the stone, or mayhap days, since he saw no daylight. No more food or water had been forthcoming, so he could not even judge each new day by the guard's arrival. His stomach rumbled and his tongue was thick, but he ignored his discomfort. He had been hungry and thirsty before. He was on the verge of abandoning all hope when the stone he had been pressing on moved. Not much, but enough to encourage him.

Excited, he wanted to rush ahead with the plan he had devised, but exhaustion had weakened him. He had no idea if he could escape the hell Waldo had cast him into, but he was going to give it his best try. Succeed or die, those were his choices.

Drake crept back to the bed of foul straw and tried to rest before attempting his escape, but his active mind refused to give him peace. So he resorted to prayer instead. It had been a long time since he had turned to God, but God and His commandments played a vital role in a knight's life. The knight's oath required that he attend daily Mass whenever possible. Drake remembered how devout his mother had been despite adversity, and even recalled childhood prayers he had been taught. And so he prayed, and when he finished, his thoughts turned to the only thing that mattered to him now.

Raven.

She had become more important to him than he had imagined any woman could ever be. Had Waldo taken her yet? he wondered. Had he punished her for running away? For taking a lover? Drake quickly offered another prayer, begging God to give Duff the strength to protect his sister.

Drake finally found sleep, but was rudely awakened a short time later by the sound of footsteps descending the stairs. He bolted upright, wondering what perverse punishment Waldo had in store for him now. He relaxed somewhat when he recognized the friendly knight who had provided him with food and drink.

"I can stay only a moment, my lord," the man said in a whisper. "I have been removed from guard duty and ordered back to the ranks. Lord Waldo suspects something, for he has replaced all your guards with men he trusts implicitly. There will be no more food. I fear Lord Waldo means for this dungeon to become your tomb."

"I suspected as much," Drake said grimly. "I am grateful for your help."

"If you should live, my lord, I am Sir Hugh of Blackstone. Were I given the choice, I would gladly claim you as my liege. And I know of others in Lord Waldo's service who feel the same."

"My thanks, Sir Hugh. If I get out of this alive, I will remember you and your acts of kindness."

From beneath his mantle, Sir Hugh pulled out a cloth sack and a small jug and handed them to Drake. "Here, 'tis all I could bring. Take it; 'tis unlikely you will see more. And," he confided, "Lord Waldo ordered another beating for you. I know not when, but soon. I am sorry."

Drake accepted Hugh's offering. With any luck he would not be here to receive the beating. Digging into the sack Sir Hugh had thrust into his hand, he inspected the contents. He smiled when he saw a succulent roasted pigeon and a hunk of bread. He tore into the bird immediately, eating half of it and a portion of the bread and drinking half the water in the jug. Then he rewrapped the remains, intending to eat them later. Still beset by hunger pangs but determined to ignore his rumbling stomach, he lay down and fell into an uneasy sleep.

★ ★ ★

Raven paced her chamber like a caged animal. Many days had sped by without her seeing anyone but Lark. She had filled her idle hours on her knees, praying for Drake. She had asked Lark about him but the spiteful girl would reveal nothing of his condition. Raven's frequent requests to speak with Waldo had been denied. She had been fed and even allowed to bathe, but was granted no other favors. She knew not whether to pray for her courses to arrive or to wish them away. Should they arrive, Waldo would claim his husbandly rights. On the other hand, should she fail to bleed, she could expect a swift death. She touched her stomach, certain now that a child did indeed grow there, and she feared for its life.

For the sake of her child she had to live. That tiny seed growing inside her must survive, even if it meant allowing Waldo into her bed. Should she be forced to bed him, mayhap Waldo would believe the babe was his. She almost laughed aloud at that irony. Drake's child would inherit Eyre one day. What a delicious thought.

Raven sighed, searching her mind for an answer to her dilemma. When one arrived, she liked it not, but her choices were severely limited. If she wanted to live to bear

Drake's child, she had to become a wife to Waldo in every sense of the word. She shuddered, no more accepting of the union than she had been when Waldo first proposed it.

Grim resolve took charge. Aware that Lark would arrive soon to inspect her underclothing, she found the small knife she used to cut her meat, lifted her shift, and made a small cut in her upper thigh. When it began to bleed freely, she rubbed the blood in strategic places on her undertunic. When the number of stains satisfied her, she undressed and draped the undertunic on a chair. Then she donned a clean shift and climbed into bed, pulling the covers up to her neck.

Anxiety rode her as she waited for Lark to appear. Would her ruse work? If it did not, all was lost. Raven did not have long to wait. A short time later she heard the key turn in the lock. Then the door opened and Lark entered the chamber.

"Abed already?" Lark asked. "Are you unwell, my lady?"

"Would you care?" Raven returned.

Lark gave a cheerless laugh. "Nay, not really. But fear not; I will not linger. Waldo is awaiting me in his bed, and I am eager to join him."

Raven pretended a painful grimace. "I need some clean cloths."

Lark's eyes narrowed suspiciously. "Have your courses arrived?"

"Aye, I do not feel well. My stomach cramps so. Mayhap you could ask the cook to prepare a soothing draft for me."

Hands on hips, Lark moved closer to the bed. "I do not believe you."

Raven motioned wanly toward her stained undertunic. "See for yourself."

Lark glanced in the direction Raven pointed and saw the stained undertunic. Obviously still not satisfied, she plucked the stained garment from the chair and inspected it closely. "I will take this to Waldo and bring you some cloths," she said sourly. She headed toward the door, dangling the garment between her thumb and forefinger. Suddenly she whirled, her face mottled with hatred. "Do not think you have seen the last of me. You will not be able to satisfy Waldo as I do. Once he gets you with child, he will be mine again."

"I sincerely hope so," Raven said meaningfully. She intended to make Waldo's life as miserable as humanly possible. When he finally bedded her, she would make the experience as thoroughly unpleasant as she knew how.

The next day Waldo visited her in her bedchamber. She had been forced to cut herself again to provide the doubting Lark with further proof that she was bleeding; she was perfectly willing to continue doing so as often as necessary. She was not, however, prepared for Waldo's visit, nor was she comforted by his eager smile.

"Lark tells me your courses have finally arrived, and that you were ill yesterday. Is that true?"

"Your leman told you the truth."

Her retort seemed to please him. "Are you jealous?"

Raven gave him an incredulous look. "Jealous? Nay, you flatter yourself. Your leman is welcome to you."

"When can I come to you?"

Never, Raven wanted to say. Bowing to the inevitable, she answered, "Five days."

"Three. 'Tis long enough for any woman." He stared at her, his face set in harsh lines. "I have not forgotten that you bashed me on the head and made a cuckold of me, nor have I forgiven you. Duff has suddenly found a spine and refuses to allow me to punish you in his home, but when we return to Eyre, your brother will not be there to protect you."

"Release Drake now," Raven insisted.

"Mayhap I will if you please me. I am not a gentle lover. I do not expect you to complain to Duff should I hurt you. Heed me well, Raven — you will not be treated with the consideration I would give a faithful wife. But I vow you will learn to like my cock better than my brother's."

Raven blanched, stunned by his crude remark. "How do you expect me to conceive your child if you treat me roughly?" she challenged.

"I will endeavor to control myself until my son is born. Then I will have no further need of you."

"Mayhap I will give you a daughter."

"Nay! You would not dare. But if you do, I will not leave your bed until you conceive again. I will have from you what your sister failed to give me."

"You and Daria were married less than six months," Raven argued.

"Time enough to conceive a child. Do not defy me, wife. You will do your duty by me or suffer the consequences. I will never forget that my brother had you first, so you would be wise to submit willingly and tread lightly."

Without warning, he grasped her shoulders and dragged her against him. When

300

she refused to look at him, he seized her chin between his thumb and forefinger and forced her head up. Then his mouth slammed down on hers. His kiss was meant to show his strength, his absolute power over her, and it succeeded. His mouth ground down on hers and his thick tongue forced her lips open. Raven gagged as his tongue thrust repeatedly in and out of her mouth at the same time his loins pumped furiously against her.

He released her so suddenly that Raven had to cling to his shoulders for support. She cringed away from his knowing grin.

"What a hot little bitch you are. I suppose I have my brother to thank for that."

Before she could form a reply, he shoved her away. She stumbled against the bed, then righted herself quickly, fearing he would do more than kiss her. She nearly collapsed in relief when Waldo sent her a searing look and stomped out of the chamber.

Three days. She had three days before Waldo would claim her. He expected her to submit willingly to him, and for her child's sake she must accept his hateful kisses and suffer his vile member inside her body. A strangled cry ripped from her throat and she collapsed on the bed, weeping for Drake, for herself, and for their unborn child.

Chapter Thirteen

A knight embraces the concept of good conquering evil.

Drake crept up the staircase and snatched the torchlight from its holder. He quickly retraced his steps to the dungeon and made his way to the stone blocking the tunnel entrance. He studied the stone door from every angle. When he was a lad he had found the strength to push the stone aside. He hoped he was not too weakened to open it now. He delved into his memory and recalled that when he had shoved the stone a certain way it had pivoted inward. Desperate to remove Raven and himself from Waldo's clutches, Drake set his shoulder to the stone and pushed with all his strength.

Beads of sweat popped out on his forehead as he strained and pushed, but he made little headway. The stone pivoted inward a few inches, but the opening was still too small to let him pass through. Driven by determination, Drake took a deep breath and put his shoulder to the stone. Miraculously the door pivoted another few inches. Would it be enough?

Sucking in a breath, Drake angled his body into the opening. He squeezed through to the other side with only a few bloody scrapes. Drake paused, aware that if his escape was to succeed, he had to close the stone door from the inside, making it look as if he had disappeared into thin air. Should the entrance be left open for Waldo to discover, his brother would be hard on his heels. Holding the torchlight aloft, Drake examined the stone and decided that it could be pivoted back into place by pushing in the opposite direction. The mechanism was unique, Drake discovered, and he credited the master stonemason who had designed the castle for creating such an ingenious device.

Drake mustered his strength and shoved and pushed until the heavy stone slowly but surely pivoted back into place. Exhausted but elated, he followed the narrow tunnel to where it forked into three separate tunnels. Ahead of him, steps carved from stone angled upward to form one tunnel. A second tunnel curved to the right and the third angled to the left. Pushing aside cobwebs and ignoring small furry animals scattering before him, Drake paused a moment to catch his breath. Disaster would follow should he take the wrong tunnel and barge into the garrison, and he was not ready yet to follow the tunnel that led to freedom. Not without Raven.

Drake closed his eyes and tried to recall his forays through the tunnels all those years ago when he was a lad trying to prove his courage. Suddenly it all became clear. The stone stairs ahead of him would take him to the solar. He set his foot on the bottom step and slowly ascended.

Raven stared out the window, her mood as bleak as the darkness that claimed her mind. One more day was all that remained before Waldo came to claim her body. She knew it was a sin to wish for another's death, but she sincerely hoped he would choke on his meat tonight. She had finished her evening meal and suffered through a visit from Lark, but sleep eluded her.

A strange tension was building inside her. She had been on edge all day, as if something extraordinary was going to happen, and she wanted to be prepared. She had not undressed, nor had she brushed out her braids. She could only sit and wait for only God knew what. The silence was oppressive. No sounds from the hall below filtered through the thick stone walls to the solar.

Raven let out a sigh. She was a prisoner in her own home. She felt so helpless . . . so utterly defeated. The one thing she was certain of was the babe growing inside her. Signs had begun to appear. Her breasts were very tender, and though she had not vomited, her stomach was queasy in the mornings and she could not eat the food Lark brought to break her fast. The illness usually passed within a few hours and her appetite was restored.

Raven's mind drifted to the child she would bear Drake. She smiled wistfully, picturing a tiny replica of Drake, or a small image of herself. She was so engrossed in her mental wanderings that she paid scant heed to the scraping sounds coming from behind the tapestry-draped west wall. Then suddenly she became aware of another presence in the chamber. She whirled and glanced toward the door. It was still closed. She almost laughed aloud at the notion that the castle was haunted. Then the candle flickered, as if stirred by a breeze. No breeze came through the windows, and Raven wondered if she were imagining things.

The hair prickled on the back of her neck and the breath caught in her throat as she slowly turned and saw him. Flesh and blood, no ghost. Though his flesh was bruised and battered, he was the most glorious sight Raven had ever seen.

She could not move; she could only stand there and gape at him. "Drake . . . How . . . ?"

He stared at her a long moment before reaching for her hand. "You shall see how very shortly. Come, we must leave immediately."

"But Drake —"

"Hurry, my love; we have little time. Once they learn I am not in the dungeon, the keep will be swarming with men. We have but a few hours' head start before the search spreads beyond the castle walls."

Suddenly Raven found her tongue. "Drake, oh, thank God you are all right. I have been beside myself with worry." She launched herself into his arms.

He held her close. "Thinking about what Waldo was doing to you drove me nearly insane," he said, hugging her as if he never wanted to let her go. He gave her a quick kiss, then gently set her away from him as he searched her face. "Are you well? Has Waldo hurt you?"

"I am fine. For once in his life Duff stood up to Waldo and would not let him hurt me. But . . . I fear I would not have been able to hold Waldo off much longer. He is . . . anxious to consummate our marriage."

"Over my dead body," Drake said with a snarl. "We must leave immediately. Bring a cloak and whatever else you can carry in your pockets."

Raven grabbed her cloak from a hook on the wall, stuffed a comb and brush in her pocket, and proclaimed herself ready. She had no idea how they were going to leave the heavily guarded keep without being caught, but she trusted Drake implicitly. By some miracle he had escaped the dungeon, and she wondered what other miracles he could perform. Clutching his hand tightly, she followed close on his heels, puzzled when he halted before a dusty old tapestry that had covered the wall for as long as she could remember.

Raven had no idea what Drake found so interesting about the tapestry. But knowing Drake as she did, she was not unduly surprised by anything he did. She *was* shocked, though, when Drake pulled aside the tapestry, revealing a narrow wooden door she had never known existed. The door was ajar, and she watched with bated breath as he widened the opening, motioned her through, and quickly followed. The door scraped once in protest when Drake pushed it shut, and she remembered hearing that same sound earlier and ignoring it.

"I brought the torchlight from the dungeon," Drake said as he removed the light from the iron ring he had found in the wall. "Do not let go of my hand; I will guide you."

"How did you know about the tunnel? Do you know where you are going?" Raven asked, eyeing with misgiving the cobwebs blocking their path.

"I explored these tunnels as a young lad and had nearly forgotten about them. My mind was not clear when I arrived at Chirk, but when I regained my senses I recalled exploring the dungeon years earlier and finding the tunnel. I did not tell the other lads about it because I wanted to savor something only I knew about. When I left, I thought no more about these tunnels. I wanted to forget Chirk and everything associated with it."

Raven shuddered when something skittered across her feet. "Where are we going?"

"There is a side tunnel leading off the main tunnel. If memory serves, it travels beneath the moat to a wooded hillside beyond."

His explanation offered Raven little comfort. She had lived at Chirk all of her life and never knew a tunnel existed. By now it could have collapsed, or might end nowhere. "What if the tunnel no longer exists as you knew it? Many years have passed since you last explored it."

"I will think of something," Drake promised. He stopped suddenly and she bumped into him. "The tunnel to freedom lies just ahead. I wish we had horses waiting for us, but 'twas not possible. I know not how long we have before Waldo sends out his men to search the forest and surrounding area."

"Where are we going?"

"First I will take you to Granny's house; then I will return to Windhurst. I must see to my holdings."

"Think you Waldo will come to Windhurst?" Raven asked breathlessly. The tunnel had grown increasingly dank and foul, making breathing difficult. She thought they must be under the moat now, for water seeped from the walls and puddled on the dirt floor. The hem of her tunic and the soles of her leather shoes were soaked. She gathered her cloak more closely around her, grateful for its warmth. Except for his tattered gambeson, Drake had no protection against the chill.

Drake did not respond to Raven's question, for they both knew Waldo would come. Besides, Drake was far too intent upon guiding them safely out of the tunnel. He was on uncertain ground now. The air was damp and thin and he feared the torch would go out, plunging them into darkness. He grasped Raven's hand tightly.

"Be careful," he admonished. " 'Tis slippery."

"How much farther?"

" 'Tis difficult to recall after so many years, but I believe the escape route is a long one. It travels beneath both the inner and outer bailey and the moat."

Drake halted abruptly. Raven slammed into him. "What is it?"

He raised the torchlight, groaning in dismay when he saw an obstruction blocking the tunnel. Over the years, water had eroded the walls and roof of the portion of tunnel that ran beneath the moat, and a pile of dirt and stones now blocked the narrow path.

" 'Tis blocked," Drake said, trying not to sound as grim as he felt.

"Can we not dig through it?"

"I know not," Drake said uncertainly. He examined the debris carefully from every angle and was heartened to see that the tunnel was only partially blocked. "We are in luck," he crowed. "Look." He stared intently at the pile of dirt and rock blocking their path. "See?" he cried excitedly, pointing toward a space near the ceiling. "If I clear away some of the dirt, mayhap we can climb through to the other side."

"What if the tunnel is blocked farther along?"

He pulled her close and kissed her hard. "It will not be blocked," he whispered against her lips. "We have to believe that. And if it is, we will return to the keep and I will think of some other way. Do you trust me?"

Despite her fear, she would trust him with her life. "Aye, I trust you. I will help you dig."

"Nay. Hold the torchlight for me." He handed her the light and began clawing at the dirt near the top of the pile. Inch by painful inch the opening grew, until Drake cleared a space large enough to scrape through.

" 'Tis done," Drake said as he stood aside for Raven to see. "I will go first and explore a bit. Hand me the torch when I am safely on the other side. If the tunnel ahead is safe, I will return for you."

She murmured a protest and he pulled her against him. "You said you trusted me, Raven. I am asking you to trust me one more time. I *will* come back for you."

"I believe you, Drake. Hurry, please." She shivered. "I do not like it here."

Drake touched his lips to hers in tender farewell, then scooted up the pile of debris and crawled through the space he had made. He dropped to the other side and found his footing on solid ground.

"Push the torch through the opening," he called to Raven. "Careful; 'tis the only light we have."

Stretching to her toes, Raven passed the torch through to him.

"I am going to scout ahead now, Raven. Do not move."

"I . . . I will stay right here," Raven promised.

Drake knew she was frightened and found one more thing to admire in her. Among her other fine qualities, she had the courage of a lion. There were so many things to love about Raven that Drake was momentarily stunned by his newfound discovery.

Did he love Raven?

The notion had entered his head before, but he had always found reasons to disregard his feelings. This time he did not search for excuses; he merely accepted the inevitable. He loved a married woman, one who could not legally share his life . . . unless Waldo were dead.

Drake pushed on through the tunnel and, finding no more obstructions, he retraced his steps to where Raven was waiting.

"Drake! Thank God. I saw the light through the opening."

"Aye, I am here. 'Tis safe for us to go on. Can you climb through on your own?" He smiled when he saw her head appear in the opening and reached for her. "Give me your hand."

Drake grasped her hand, taking surprising comfort from the small, soft hand clinging to his. With little effort, he pulled her through to the other side. She clambered to her feet, refusing to release his hand.

"The way is clear up ahead," Drake said.

They continued on. The tunnel narrowed, but they were able to squeeze through. The air was somewhat better now, not as damp or humid. The walls no longer seeped water and the puddles beneath their feet were gone.

"We must be on the other side of the moat," Drake said. " 'Tis not far now."

Drake had no idea what to expect at the end of the tunnel. Obviously no one had used this tunnel since he had explored it years earlier, and mayhap it had never been used. To his knowledge, Castle Chirk had never been under attack. King Henry I, the savage conqueror of Wales, had ordered Chirk built during his reign to guard the borderlands against invasion by Welshmen. At that time he created the earldom of Chirk. That made the castle over one hundred years old.

"I smell fresh air!" Raven cried excitedly.

Drake had begun to notice the subtle changes himself. The stale air was interspersed with drafts of cool, fresh air. "We should find the exit soon," he said, encouraged by the signs pointing to the end of their ordeal.

Moments later they stumbled into a cave. A shaft of moonlight speared through the opening, and relief nearly overwhelmed Drake.

"I know not what we will find outside," Drake warned. "Wait here; I will go first."

" 'Tis dark outside," Raven whispered. He sensed her fear and wished he could tell her the exit would lead to freedom, but he could not.

"The dark works in our favor," Drake said as he drew her against him. Her arms circled his neck, and she pressed herself against him, hugging him tightly.

"I would rather be in this dark hole with you than in Waldo's bed," she whispered against his mouth.

"Raven, I —"

She placed a finger against his lips. "Nay, 'tis the wrong time to express feelings. I am another man's wife, and one day we must part. Let me take what comfort I can from you in the time we have left. When you take a wife, I will disappear from your life."

Drake felt her pain and knew not how to ease it.

"I will do everything within my power to protect you," he promised.

"Do not make rash promises," Raven whispered. "I belong to another. Naught will change that. I do not want you to suffer on my behalf. I will do what I must to keep you safe, even if it means returning to Waldo."

"You will *not* return to Waldo," Drake said fiercely. "I will go to the king myself and plead your cause."

"Could he dissolve a marriage?"

"Your marriage was never consummated," Drake reminded her. "Anything is possible if you desire it enough."

"Then I shall wish it with all my heart and soul," Raven said fervently.

Drake felt as if the shield he had placed around his heart had been breached. Since that disastrous day when his plans to elope with Daria had been thwarted, the shield had remained firmly in place — until Raven entered his life. He wished he could give Raven her heart's desire, but he could not, not yet. He had no solution to Raven's problems so he kissed her instead, trying to convey without words that he would not abandon her to Waldo. Then he released her and handed her the torch.

"You keep this. If the cave exits where I think it does, moonlight will guide me."

"Be careful," Raven called after him.

The exit was so small Drake had to drop to his hands and knees and crawl through. He emerged from the cave and gave a whoop of pure joy when he looked up and saw the moon and stars beaming down upon him. He gulped down several deep breaths of fresh air before returning his attention to the cave. He saw that its exit was precisely where he'd thought it would be: on a hillside surrounded by trees and gorse.

"You can come out now," he called softly to Raven. "Leave the torch; we do not want to announce our presence. It will burn itself out in time."

A few minutes later Raven's head popped out of the exit and Drake knelt to help her through. She was shaking. He held her for a moment, loath to let her go but aware of the danger that existed for both of them.

"Think you Waldo will find the tunnel?" Raven asked.

"Eventually," Drake answered truthfully. "A thorough search of the keep will reveal the door behind the tapestry in your bedchamber. We had the advantage of knowing which tunnel to follow; they do not. Nevertheless, we must hurry. We are afoot; Waldo's men will be mounted."

"How long do you think we have?"

"It will take time to search every nook and cranny of the castle and outbuildings. My guess is that we have a day or two before they extend their search to the forest." He offered her his hand. "Come, I will lead the way."

"I do not want to go to Wales," Raven said, aware of Drake's plans to take her to Granny Nola's house. "Take me to Windhurst with you."

"Nay, 'tis likely the first place Waldo will look for you. Michaelmas approaches, and with it winter. For the first time in my life I will pray for an early snow."

"We must go directly to Windhurst," Raven insisted. "There is no time to waste."

"Nay, you will not be safe there."

"I care not," she said stubbornly. "Be practical, Drake. We are afoot. Had we coin we could purchase horses in a village, but we have naught but the clothing on our backs."

Drake gave her a mischievous grin. "I planned to steal horses."

"We are wasting time. I am going to Windhurst and that is final."

Drake stared at her in consternation. Raven had grown from a pesky, impertinent child to a feisty, courageous woman. He wished he had known her during her formative years so he would have insight into what had molded her into the kind of woman she was today.

He gave a defeated sigh. "Very well, but 'tis against my better judgment."

Moonlight guided them as they made their way through the silent forest. Drake did not want to frighten Raven, but he feared their lack of horses would hinder them. He had not been joshing when he'd said he intended to steal horses. They had far to travel, and he knew Raven was exhausted, for he was nearly dead on his feet himself.

Suddenly Drake stopped, pressing Raven's hand in warning. "Did you hear that?"

"Nay, I heard naught."

"Listen."

Drake remained perfectly still and so did Raven as they listened to the night sounds around them. A horse snorted and Drake stiffened.

"Do you hear it now?"

"Aye. What does it mean?"

"Someone is camped nearby."

"Poachers?"

"Mayhap." But he did not think so. "Stay here while I take a look."

Drake crept through the thick gorse toward the sound he had heard. He stumbled upon the camp without warning, for no campfire had been built to give the campsite away. Drake saw a man lying on the ground, wrapped in a blanket, his head upon his saddle. He searched the site for others and relaxed somewhat when he saw no one but the one man. Catlike, he circled the campsite, tense, waiting. Was the man friend or foe?

Moving stealthily, he crept from tree to tree, stopping short when he spied a pair of horses hobbled close to the campsite. Two horses. That puzzled Drake, for he had seen only one man. One horse lifted its head and swished its tail. Drake was speechless when he recognized his own Zeus. And the second horse belonged to Sir John. Zeus snorted a greeting.

Suddenly a shadow fell across his path and Drake reached for a weapon that did not exist.

"I thought you would never get here, my lord."

"John!"

"Aye. What took you so long?"

"How did you know it was I?"

"Zeus. Your horse sensed your presence before I did. I pretended sleep until I realized 'twas you snooping around my campsite."

"Were you so certain I would appear, then?"

John smiled. "Aye, I never doubted it."

"Where did you find Zeus?"

"One of your men found him after Waldo dragged you away. Most of our warriors survived the battle. When I returned from Builth Wells, I found them camped in the forest. They were waiting until they learned your fate."

"Where are they now?"

"I sent them back to Windhurst with the wounded. I knew you would escape, Drake. No dungeon in the world is strong enough to hold the Black Knight."

"Your faith humbles me, John, but for a time I truly believed I would breathe my last in Chirk's dungeon."

"How did you escape? I can hardly wait to hear."

"Later, John," Drake said. "Raven will be frantic with worry if I do not return for her soon."

John looked stunned. "Lady Raven is with you? God's blood! 'Tis incredible. Get her, by all means. Meanwhile, I will break camp and saddle the horses. You and Raven can share Zeus's back."

Drake clasped John's shoulder. "Thank you, my friend. You have quite possibly saved both my life and Raven's."

Raven was consumed by fear as she waited for Drake to return. She imagined all kinds of danger he could have walked into and wished he had taken her with him. He had been gone far too long, and though she knew he had warned her not to roam, she wanted to be of help if he were in trouble. Throwing caution to the wind, Raven started after Drake.

She had not gone very far when she heard the murmur of voices and paused to listen. Following the sounds, she moved cautiously forward. Then she saw them, standing in a patch of moonlight beside a pair of horses, speaking in low tones. One of the men was Drake. The other was . . . Sir John! She gave a cry of pleasure and rushed out to join them.

They must have heard her, for they were immediately on guard. Drake recognized her first.

"Raven! I told you to wait for me."

"I was worried and wanted to help if you were in trouble."

"Did you think to defend the Black Knight with naught but your teeth and nails?" Sir John asked, laughing softly.

Raven did not laugh. If need be, she would indeed fight tooth and nail on Drake's behalf. "Why are you still here, Sir John?"

"I could not leave until I learned Drake's

fate. And I wanted to be here to help him when he escaped. After I left you at Chirk, I found the remnants of our men hiding in the forest. They, too, were awaiting word of Drake's fate. I sent them on to Windhurst and remained behind. You see, I never doubted Drake's ability to escape."

"We must leave immediately," Drake said. He searched Raven's face. "You are exhausted. You can sleep in the saddle. Zeus is fully up to carrying our combined weight."

John had already saddled both horses. "I hope you are not hungry, for I have little to offer you," he said. "We can purchase food in the first village we pass."

"I have no coin," Drake said.

John smiled. "Fear not, my friend. I have enough coin for our needs."

"I would ask a favor of you, John," Drake said. "You have shown your loyalty to me time and again, but I would ask one more thing of you."

"Name it, Drake."

"Ride to Builth Wells and inform Granny Nola that Raven and I are safe and well for the moment. She will be worried about us, and you are the only one I trust with her location."

"Of course I will go," John said. "I will

meet you at Windhurst. But first you must take the coins remaining in my purse. I will not need them." He removed his purse from his belt and handed it to Drake.

"Save some for yourself, John," Drake said, accepting only part of the money.

Drake mounted Zeus and John lifted Raven into the saddle. Raven placed her arms around Drake's waist and held fast. Then his arms came around her, holding her firmly against him as he gripped the reins and kneed Zeus forward.

Chapter Fourteen

A knight's word is his honor.

They rode throughout the night with no sign of pursuit. Raven slept in the saddle, curled against Drake. They had left the forest behind and rode over moors carpeted with heather and alongside cliffs where the sound of water dashing against rocks reverberated like thunder. Raven stirred in Drake's arms. A few moments later she awakened, confused and disoriented.

"Where are we?" she asked, gazing up at Drake. Deep grooves of exhaustion lined his face, and she wondered how he had kept himself in the saddle this long.

"Far enough from Chirk to stop and rest," he answered. "A village lies a short distance inland, and a stream just beyond. I passed them on my first trip to Windhurst. We can visit the village to purchase food, then rest a few hours beside the stream. The spot I have in mind is secluded and will conceal us from travelers. Zeus can drink his fill and rest while we refresh ourselves."

"Can I bathe?" Raven asked eagerly. "My skin crawls. I am filthy from creeping around in the tunnel."

"The water will be cold."

"It matters not."

Drake grinned. "I am of the same mind. I am eager to wash the stench of the dungeon from my skin." He reined Zeus away from the cliffs.

A short time later they reached the village. It was market day. The narrow streets were filled with people and vendors hawking their wares. They bought two meat pies, wolfed them down, then purchased more pies, cheese, bread, and ale, enough to last until they reached Windhurst if they ate sparingly. Sufficient coin remained to buy a dappled mare for Raven, a mantle for Drake, and a change of clothing for each of them. The vendor took one look at their dirty faces and added a cake of soap to their purchases.

After Drake tied the sack of provisions and the skin of ale to his saddle, he lifted Raven atop her mare and led them both away from the village. They found the stream with little difficulty. Drake seemed to know exactly where he was going as he guided Zeus and the mare to a bend in the stream where a canopy of trees hid them from passersby.

"I camped here once," Drake explained as he dismounted and lifted Raven down from her mare. " 'Tis a quiet spot. We can build a campfire without fear of being seen. There are few travelers in this part of Wessex."

"Think you Waldo knows we are missing by now?" Raven asked.

"Aye. Doubtless you were missed this morning when food was brought to break your fast. 'Tis unlikely my own absence will be discovered until the guards visit the dungeon to administer the beating Waldo ordered. When Waldo puts two and two together, the entire castle will be in an uproar. He will spend a day or two searching the keep and surrounding buildings before he sends men out to scour the forest. Then it will be another sennight, mayhap longer, before Waldo figures out how we escaped."

Raven found a grassy spot beside the stream and sat down. Drake unsaddled the horses and led them to the water. After they had drunk their fill, Drake hobbled them where they could nibble on sweet grass and dropped down beside Raven.

"Are you ready for your bath?"

Raven removed her slippers and stockings and dangled a toe into the water. " 'Tis cold."

"Too cold?"

"Nay." She stood and removed her clothing except for a thin shift. "I am too filthy to quibble about cold water. Besides, the sun is warm enough."

Drake could not look away. Her beauty was mesmerizing despite the layers of dirt upon her face. He thought her more graceful than a willow as she waded fearlessly into the cold water. The stream was shallow. She reached the center and sat down on the sandy bottom, flinching when the water crept up to her breasts.

"You forgot the soap," Drake called. "Do not move. I will bring it to you."

He found the soap in the same package with their clean clothing. Then he retrieved the blankets from his saddle and returned to the stream. He stripped quickly and unwound the bandage from his broken ribs, his hungry gaze riveted on Raven.

"God's blood! It *is* cold," he cried as he waded toward her.

She laughed. Drake could not recall when he had heard a more provocative sound. Of late, he and Raven had found little to laugh about. He wished fervently that he could change all that and was surprised that making Raven happy should be so important to him.

"Stand up," he said, grasping her hand and pulling her to her feet. "I have the most profound urge to wash every part of that delectable little body."

" 'Tis unseemly for the Black Knight to act as maid," she teased.

"The Black Knight does as he pleases," Drake responded as he grasped her shift, pulled it over her head, and tossed it upon the bank.

"I have missed you," Raven whispered as she walked into his outstretched arms.

Her hands roamed freely over his shoulders, his back, his taut buttocks. His flesh felt warm and alive beneath her fingertips. His manhood stirred restlessly against her stomach and a moan slipped past her lips. She loved this special man with all her heart and soul and despaired that she could not announce it to the world, or even to Drake. She had not the right to love the Black Knight when she belonged to another.

Suddenly she went still. Her fingers had encountered raised places on his back and shoulders that should not have been there. "Turn around, Drake."

He looked at her askance. "Why?"

"Your back . . ."

" 'Tis not important."

"It is to me. Turn around."

Reluctantly he presented his back. A cry of dismay slipped past her lips as she gazed at the raw ridges crisscrossing his flesh.

"He beat you!" she cried. "Waldo beat you. And look at your face." She hadn't mentioned it before, but she could no longer contain her anger at what had been done to him by her husband. Then she noted other injuries that had escaped her notice before.

"Your eyes and lips are swollen and your skin is covered with bruises. Did I not see you unwind a bandage from your middle before you entered the water? What else did Waldo do to you?"

"Everything will heal," Drake insisted.

"You had broken ribs?"

"God's blood, Raven, I said 'tis naught. A cracked rib or two will not kill me. The bruises on my face are from a beating; so are the welts on my back. Now you know everything."

"I hate him!" Raven sobbed. "He is a monster. 'Tis my fault he hurt you."

"Forget Waldo, sweeting. Let me wash you before we both freeze to death."

Cupping the cake of soap in his palm, he made a rich lather and spread it over Raven's body. The water was cold, but Drake's hands quickly warmed her flesh as they skimmed over every inch of her, from her forehead to the tips of her toes. She was trembling with desire by the time he had rinsed the soap off her and asked her to dunk her head so he could soap her hair.

"I can do it."

"Nay, let me."

Her breathing quickened and she closed her eyes as his hands moved gently through her hair. Then he helped her to sit so she could dip her head into the water to remove the soap.

"Your turn," Raven said, taking the soap from his hand. "Turn around so I can scrub your back." When he hesitated, she said, "I promise not to hurt you."

"Pain is not what I am feeling right now," Drake said in a voice made husky with need. He grasped her hand and brought it to his groin. "I want you, Raven. It has been too long. I need to be inside you, to feel your heat surrounding me."

Her hand closed around him. He was hard as rock; his erection rose high and proud from the dark hair between his legs.

She shivered, but not from cold. She wanted to experience the ecstasy of his loving again before he was taken from her.

"I want you, too," Raven said. "But first I will bathe you." She ran the soap over his chest and was moving toward his loins when he grasped her hand.

"Nay. I will do it myself. 'Tis cold. Dry yourself in the sun. I will join you when I am finished."

Reluctantly Raven surrendered the soap and waded to the grassy bank. She found the blankets Drake had brought and used one to dry herself. Then she sat down in a patch of sunshine and watched Drake bathe. Her hungry gaze roamed over his body, and she thought that he had lost weight. His body was whipcord lean, his muscles and tendons more prominent beneath his flesh than she recalled. She agonized over the bruises and scars and thanked God that Drake was a strong man with a warrior's honed body.

Drake finished his bath and joined Raven. "I will build a fire so you can sit before it and dry your hair."

"Are you not cold?" Raven asked as he draped his blanket over her shoulders.

"Nay, I am used to the cold."

It did not take long for Drake to gather

dry wood for the fire, and soon a cheery blaze was burning in the firepit. Raven retrieved her comb and brush from the pocket of her soiled tunic and moved closer to the fire. She spread out her hair and lazily drew the brush through her long chestnut locks.

Drake sat down behind her, drawing her into the vee of his legs. Then he took the brush from her hand and slowly ran it through the tangles.

"You have beautiful hair," he whispered against her ear. "Like fine silk."

"You are very good at this," Raven remarked.

" 'Tis not all I am good at."

His voice was raw with sensuality, somewhat husky, and, oh, so arousing. He shoved her hair to one side and kissed her nape. Raven trembled with anticipation. Impatiently he pushed aside the blankets covering her and trailed fiery kisses down her spine, down to the crease separating the twin cheeks of her buttocks. He nipped her there, then licked his way back to her nape.

"Your skin is as smooth as cream and tastes delicious." His arms came around her, molding her against him. He touched her full breasts and rubbed his fingers over her nipples until they were achingly erect. His hands slid lower, over her rib cage, lower still, pressing against her throbbing womanhood.

She felt his rampant arousal pushing against her bottom and tried to turn in his arms. But Drake would not let her; he held her securely in place and spread her legs apart. When his talented fingers found the slick folds of her sex, Raven went limp.

"I love the way you weep for me," Drake murmured against her hair. "I want to pleasure you first with my hands, then with my mouth. When you are screaming your pleasure, I am going to thrust myself inside you and take us both to paradise."

His words bathed her insides with hot liquid, flooding his fingers with damp heat. His fingers penetrated her and she moaned. While one hand tantalized from below, the other teased her nipples. Her heart pounded, her blood congealed in her veins. The movement of his talented hands, so intensely arousing, sent her hurtling over the edge. She screamed his name and collapsed against him.

Drake let her rest a few minutes; then he laid her down upon the blankets. Raven stared up at him, her green eyes glazed with passion. She had no idea what Drake was going to do next but she did not want to stop him. He seemed in no hurry as he stretched out beside her and devoted long, tender minutes to her mouth, kissing and licking and exploring with his tongue.

"I dreamed of loving you like this while I lay in the dungeon," Drake rasped against her lips. "I feared I would never hold you in my arms again, that the dungeon would become my tomb."

"I knew you would not die," Raven replied. "'Tis not like you to give up. I prayed for your life, and God answered my prayer."

Drake paused for a long, thoughtful moment, then said, "I have no right to claim you, sweeting. But if I could —" His sentence ended abruptly but his meaning dangled between them.

Raven placed a finger against his lips. "Please, make no declarations. It would be wrong. 'Tis enough right now that we are together. Our fate is in God's hands."

Though Raven knew not how God would punish her, she did know that neither God nor the church condoned adultery.

"Aye," Drake agreed. "We are together now." His grim reply did little to comfort Raven. He had to know that one day they must part.

He kissed her mouth, then worked his way down her body to that place where her heat was centered. His eyes darkened as he spread her thighs and gazed at her. Raven gave a startled gasp when he thrust his face into the vee between her legs and kissed her there. Using his thumbs, he separated the folds of her pouting nether lips and wet her with his tongue.

She moaned, gripping his head and panting as he alternately sucked at the hard nub of her femininity and laved it tenderly. Hovering on the brink of forever, Raven wondered if she could pleasure Drake as he was pleasuring her, and if he would allow it. Deciding there was no time like the present to find out, she pushed him down on his back and straddled him. He seemed startled but did not protest.

" 'Tis my turn," she said in a throaty whisper.

She took her time exploring his body, kissing and nipping and sucking all the places she hoped would drive him wild. Then she gripped his manhood, stared into his eyes, and brought him to her lips. She opened her mouth.

A guttural cry was wrenched from Drake as he flexed his hips and sent his hard, thick length against the back of her throat.

She knew not how it happened, but suddenly she was stretched beneath him and he was embedded deep inside her. Her legs clamped around his waist as he drove into her, again and again. She bucked against him, no longer cold but burning hot. Her body was scalded by his; her senses swamped by love for the Black Knight. Then her thoughts were blown away as strong contractions racked her body. She heard Drake shout her name as he joined her in midflight, soaring with her to that special place where lovers dwell.

Castle Chirk

"She is gone!" Lark screamed at the top of her lungs as she left the solar and flew down the steps.

Everyone in the hall stared at her as if she had just lost her mind.

"Who is gone, woman?" Waldo roared, rising from his bench as Lark ran through the hall, wild-eyed with fright. "Can a man not break his fast in peace?"

"*She* is gone! You know. Lady Raven."

Waldo grasped Lark's shoulders and shook her none too gently. "Calm down. You must be mistaken. There is no way

Raven could escape from her chamber. Go upstairs and look again."

"She is gone, I tell you!" Lark insisted, nervously twisting a corner of her tunic. "I have searched everywhere. The chamber is empty."

Waldo shoved Lark aside and took the steps two at a time. The guard still stood outside the door, looking perplexed and anxious. Waldo flung open the door and charged into the chamber. At the first sight it appeared unoccupied, but of course he knew it could not be. Dropping to his knees, he looked under the bed; she was not there. He checked the chest sitting against the wall, scattering clothing about with blatant disregard for the fragile silks and satins. He searched behind the bed hangings and drapery, his anger palpable.

"Raven could not have disappeared into thin air," he argued. His face darkened with rage, and Lark cautiously backed away from him.

"Summon the guard," Waldo commanded.

Lark turned and fled. The guard who had been standing outside the door entered the room, quaking in his boots. Waldo's vile temper was to be feared, and most of his men knew better than to cross him.

Waldo glared at the man, his expression hard, unrelenting. "Blake of York, what do you know of this?"

"I remained at my post the entire night, my lord," Blake insisted. "If Lady Raven is not in her chambers, then she left by some other exit. She could not have gone through this door."

"Aye, she flew out the window," Waldo barked sarcastically. "You are one of my most trustworthy men. How could this happen?"

"I did not fail you," Blake said. "Lady Raven did not leave by this door."

Waldo spit out a curse. He did not believe Blake. Raven could not have gone out the window, for the drop would have killed her. A vicious sneer curved his lips as a plausible explanation occurred to him. "Admit it, Blake. My wanton wife seduced you into letting her go. I hope you enjoyed her, for you shall die for your betrayal."

"My lord! 'Tis not so. I betrayed you not."

Suddenly two men-at-arms burst into the chamber, their faces etched with fear. Waldo's scowl deepened. He knew immediately he would not like the tidings the men carried.

"Lord Waldo," one of the men blurted

out. "The Black Knight has escaped!"

"Nay!" Waldo roared. "It cannot be!"

Waldo rushed from the solar and raced down two flights of stairs, his men-at-arms close on his heels. He slid to a halt before the open door of the dungeon.

" 'Tis dark. What happened to the torchlight?" Waldo asked, staring pointedly at the empty sconce.

" 'Twas missing when we arrived to administer the beating you ordered," the guard revealed. "He must have taken it with him, for we did not find it in the dungeon."

"How thoroughly did you search?" Waldo asked.

"There are no hiding places in the dungeon, my lord," the man answered.

Unwilling to believe two people could disappear simultaneously from separate locked chambers, Waldo started down the stairs to search the dungeon himself. "Hand me a torchlight."

Moments later someone placed a torch in his hand and he descended the stairs, rage pounding through his body until he feared he would explode with it. He kicked at the foul straw that had been Drake's bed and inspected every corner of the dungeon twice.

"The guards on duty yestereve are to be confined to the barracks," Waldo barked. "I will get to the bottom of this." He pounded up the stairs, ordering out the entire garrison to search for the missing prisoners.

Duff, who had gone out with the huntsmen early that morning, returned to utter chaos. "What has happened?" he asked when Waldo entered the hall.

"They are gone," Waldo said in a hiss. "Fear not; I will find them."

"Who?"

"Your whore of a sister and my bastard brother."

Duff stiffened. "You go too far, Waldo. Remember, Raven is my sister. How did they escape?"

"Raven flew out the window and Drake walked through walls," Waldo said sarcastically. "Personally, I believe there is a more mundane answer. The guards on duty yestereve are confined to the barracks until I can launch an investigation. As I speak, the keep and outbuildings are being thoroughly searched. No stone will be left unturned."

"The gates were closed yestereve and the drawbridge up," Duff said. "They could not have left the castle proper. What do you plan to do to them when you find them?"

Waldo's expression hardened. "My *brother* will die. 'Tis the fate I intended for him all along. As for Raven, I will have an heir from her. After that . . ." He shrugged.

"I will not allow you to hurt Raven," Duff warned. "Mayhap I was wrong to force her to marry you. I should have heeded her pleas and found someone more to her liking."

" 'Tis too late," Waldo pointed out. "Raven is my wife. I will take her to Eyre and do with her as I please."

"Like you did with Daria?" Duff charged. "I know not what happened to Daria, but should you harm Raven, I swear I will ask the king to launch an inquiry into Daria's death."

"You make me laugh, Duff," Waldo said with a snort. "You are a spineless worm and we both know it. Order your men out to search the inner and outer baileys."

Duff sent Waldo an insolent stare and walked away, muttering beneath his breath. "Mayhap the worm will turn, Waldo of Eyre."

Waldo was not satisfied until every inch of the keep, the outbuildings, and both the inner and outer baileys were thoroughly searched. Three days later Waldo ordered his men into the forest, the village, and neighboring towns. The escape of his prisoners was nothing short of miraculous, but Waldo did not believe in miracles. Someone had helped them, but not even torture had loosened the guards' tongues. The men on duty that night continued to proclaim their innocence.

Waldo was livid. Careful questioning of the castle servants and villagers had produced nothing but blank stares. He should have known no help would be forthcoming there. Raven had been the lady of the castle far too long for them to betray her.

Chapter Fifteen

A knight always obeys his king.

The sky was gray and heavy with clouds the day Drake and Raven reached Windhurst. The ocean churning below the cliffs appeared black and ominous. The wind howled, buffeting them ruthlessly as they approached the barbican. Drake's heart swelled with pride when he saw that the outer walls had been fully restored during his absence; they would be a solid buffer against enemy attack. A guard stepped from the barbican as if to challenge the intruders. Then he recognized Drake and gave a welcoming cry.

Drake rode through the gate into the outer bailey. Several men were engaged in mock combat on the training field and did not see them as they passed by.

"I cannot believe your workers repaired the walls so quickly," Raven remarked when she noted the newly reconstructed curtain wall. They reached the portcullis and it opened to admit them.

"They have more than earned the bonus

I promised," Drake said, delighted with the miracle his workers had wrought during his absence.

They reached the keep and drew rein. Evan rushed forward to greet them. "Lord Drake! Lady Raven. Thank God you are both safe. Had we not heard something soon, Sir Richard was going to take your army to Chirk and demand your release."

Drake dismounted and lifted Raven from her dappled palfrey. Knights and warriors, having been alerted to Drake's arrival, hurried forward to greet him. Balder must have heard the commotion, for he rushed from the keep, saw Drake, and stumbled down the stairs, a broad smile wreathing his face.

"My lord, my lady, welcome home. I called the servants back when Sir Richard arrived. Everything is in readiness for you. A hot meal will be forthcoming directly."

Drake was touched by the welcome he received from his people, and his heart swelled with pride. Such loyalty was rare, and he knew not if he deserved it. Placing a protective arm around Raven's shoulders, he led her out of the pounding rain and up the stairs to the keep.

The hall was warm and inviting, redolent with delicious cooking aromas. A fire burned in the hearth, spreading warmth throughout the hall. Drake guided Raven to a bench and seated her before the fire. Someone handed him a cup of ale and he pressed it into Raven's hand.

"Drink," he said. "It will warm you."

Warriors and knights alike followed them inside, helping themselves to pitchers of ale placed on the tables for their consumption. They all crowded around Drake, waiting for him to regale them with his adventure.

"Is Sir John not with you?" Sir Richard asked. "He remained near Chirk to await word of your fate. He intended to camp in the forest with Zeus until you either showed up or . . ." His words trailed off. He cleared his throat. "I see you found Zeus, but what of Sir John?"

"Fear not. Raven and I stumbled upon Sir John's campsite shortly after we escaped from Chirk. I sent him on an errand."

"Tell us how you escaped from Chirk," a knight called out. "Spare us no details, my lord," he added. It was obvious the knight was not alone in wondering how and where their lord had encountered Lady Raven.

"I am weary," Drake hedged. "I will relate the details after my lady and I have

346

supped. I know you are all anxious to hear what happened after my brother dragged me off to Chirk."

"The adventure will doubtless add luster to the Black Knight's fame," Richard pointed out. "Soon every jongleur in the kingdom will sing of the Black Knight's newest exploits."

Drake heaved a sigh. He hoped the tale would not reach the king, for he knew not how Edward would react when he learned his champion had taken another knight's wife as his leman. He shoved those thoughts aside; he would worry about the king if and when the problem arose. He offered his hand to Raven.

"You should rest. I set a grueling pace and forced you to follow." He searched her face, suddenly aware of her paleness and the dark smudges marring the delicate skin beneath her eyes.

Raven placed her hand in his and followed him up the winding staircase to the solar. He ushered her inside and closed the door behind them.

"I mean it, Raven," he said sternly. "You are sorely in need of rest. I will have a tub carried up so you can bathe. Take your time. Nap, if you can. Mayhap you would like your meal sent up."

"Aye, that would be nice. I feel as if I could sleep for a sennight."

He took her into his arms and gazed intently into her face; he liked not what he saw. "Are you ill? I should have been more careful of you. I am accustomed to riding hard, but I should have taken a woman's weaker constitution into consideration. Forgive me."

"There is naught to forgive. If not for you I would belong to Waldo now, in every way," she added meaningfully.

He grimaced and gave her a quick kiss. Then he released her and set about building a fire in the hearth. "I will return after I bathe, eat, and regale my men with the tale of our escape." He kissed her again and left the chamber.

Raven indeed felt drained. The swift journey to Windhurst had taken its toll. She had forced herself to struggle through the inevitable morning sickness so that Drake would not recognize her symptoms.

No matter how desperately she wanted to tell him about the baby, she had maintained her silence. Telling Drake would serve no purpose and would only complicate the situation and make things more difficult.

Raven had already decided she must

leave Windhurst before Waldo arrived. Drake had suffered enough on her account. If she was not here when Waldo arrived, and he *would* arrive, there would be no need for an armed confrontation.

Raven had thought about this a long time and decided to flee to the safety she knew her aunt would provide. Edinburgh was a long way to travel alone, but she had no other choice. She would live quietly in her aunt's home and raise her child. Drake need never know he had become a father, for in all likelihood she would never see him again.

That terrible thought brought tears to her eyes. Surely living without the man she loved would be a fitting penance for the grave sin she had committed. But had she really committed a sin? Her conscience told her she had done no wrong. Being intimate with the man she loved could not be a sin when it brought such happiness. Mayhap Drake did not share her love, but her heart told her he cared for her.

Surely no man would risk so much for a woman unless he was emotionally involved. A niggling voice inside her warned that the only thing Drake felt was guilt. He had, after all, stolen her virginity on her wedding night in a most unchivalrous manner. Then there was lust, which they both felt in abundance. But Raven knew her lust was motivated by love. Unfortunately she could not say the same for Drake.

Raven's bath arrived then and her thoughts turned to mundane matters, such as soaking away all the dirt and dust that had accumulated during their journey to Windhurst. A shy young maid stayed to help her.

"I am Lora, my lady. Lord Drake asked me to attend you."

"What happened to Gilda?" Raven asked.

"Gilda married the blacksmith's son and already carries his child."

Raven searched Lora's plain features and saw no guile, no cunning, unlike the conniving Gilda. "I welcome your assistance, Lora," she said with a smile.

Raven finished her bath and stepped into the large linen drying cloth Lora held out for her. She stifled a yawn. The bath had made her drowsy.

"Would you like to rest, my lady?" Lora asked. She moved to the bed and pulled back the covers.

"A nap sounds wonderful," Raven said, unable to resist the lure of the turned-down bed.

She dropped the sodden drying cloth and climbed naked into bed. Lora pulled the covers up to her neck and quietly left the chamber. Raven was asleep before Lora closed the door behind her.

She had no idea how long she slept, but when she awakened she felt a warm body curled around her. She must have been so exhausted that she had not awakened when Drake crawled into bed. The fire in the hearth had been rekindled, she noted, for the chamber was warmed by a soft golden glow. She perched on one elbow and looked at him, startled to see him watching her with glittering eyes.

"I wondered when you were going to awaken. I cannot sleep when I am hard as a rock." He pushed his loins against her, demonstrating the strength of his need. "You were sleeping so soundly I did not want to disturb you. Are you hungry?"

"Aye, a little."

Drake shoved back the covers and climbed naked from bed. "I brought a tray up for you. 'Tis beside the hearth, keeping warm. You must have been completely worn out. I am sorry I drove you so hard."

" 'Tis no fault of yours. We both knew the danger in dawdling. Set the tray on the table," she instructed, attempting to rise.

"Nay. Stay where you are. I will fetch the tray."

Raven pulled herself up and propped a pillow behind her back, watching him. His naked warrior's body fascinated her. Though he was leaner than when she first saw him, the corded muscles rippling beneath the skin of his massive shoulders and chest were long, powerfully developed, and granite hard. His buttocks were high and taut, and his muscular legs were covered with fine dark hairs.

Raven's eyes widened when he turned and carried the tray to her. His staff was hard and turgid, rising upward from a nest of black. She quickly averted her gaze as he placed the tray on her lap and perched on the bed beside her. Her mouth watered when he whisked the cloth away, revealing a feast fit for a king. There were meat pies bursting with succulent pieces of venison, slices of suckling pig, bread, an assortment of late vegetables, fruits, and cheeses. Though Raven could not begin to consume everything on the tray, she made quite a dent in it.

Replete, she shoved the tray aside. "How many people did you expect to feed?"

"You have not eaten enough to keep a bird alive these past days," Drake pointed out as he removed the tray. "A steady diet of good, nourishing food is what you need. It has not escaped my notice that you are looking peaked of late. I know I asked you before, but I must ask again. Are you ill?"

Raven refused to meet Drake's eyes. Lying did not come easily to her. "Nay, I am not ill. Give me a few days to rest and recuperate from the arduous journey and you will see a difference."

He lifted her chin, forcing her to look at him. "Are you certain? There is naught you wish to tell me?"

Raven went still. Did he suspect? Nay, she decided. He could not possibly know. Her stomach was still as flat as it had ever been. Were it not for her sore breasts and queasy stomach, she would not suspect herself.

"There is naught wrong with me, Drake. Do not worry about me; you have more important things to occupy your mind."

"No one is more important than you, Raven." He sounded so sincere that Raven wanted to cry. "Everything that has happened to you thus far is my fault. Had I not stolen your virginity your life would be far different today. I owe you my protection."

Now Raven really *did* want to cry. She

did not want Drake's pity. He owed her nothing. Nor did she want to be told she was with Drake because his honor demanded that he protect her. Her hand went to her heart; she felt as if she had suffered a mortal blow. She carefully considered an answer but failed to come up with one that did not bare her soul to him. When she left, as she eventually must, he would not miss her, she decided. In fact, he would probably be relieved to be rid of the responsibility.

Raven did not stop to consider that Drake could have taken her to Scotland if he truly wanted to be rid of her. Or that he could have left her at Chirk instead of risking his life to rescue her. Nor did she remember that Drake had taken her to Granny Nola's house to keep her safe. All Raven recalled were words that omitted love. Words that only reinforced Drake's commitment to protect those weaker than himself.

When Drake reached out to make love to her, she went willingly into his arms. When the time came, she wanted to leave with enough memories to last a lifetime. And so she surrendered to his kisses, savored the feeling his hands and mouth aroused in her, and clung to him, crying his name when he brought her to completion.

Drake pulled himself free of Raven's tight passage and sank down beside her. Something was wrong but he could not put his finger on it. Raven had been as passionate as she had ever been, but afterward he had made the mistake of looking into her eyes. They were distant, as if she had withdrawn into herself, something she had never done before, not even that first time.

Was she beginning to regret all they had shared? Did she want to return to Waldo? That thought was not worth considering. Instead, he pulled her into the curve of his body and cast aside the thought of a future without Raven of Chirk in it.

Castle Chirk

A fortnight passed before Waldo decided he had missed some vital piece of the puzzle. He had pondered long and hard upon methods one might use to escape from locked chambers and always came to the same conclusion: an escape route existed somewhere within the castle walls. Somehow, some way, Drake had found it. It was the only plausible answer.

After the exhaustive search ended, Waldo took Duff aside to discuss the mystery. "You know the castle better than I, Duff. How could Raven and Drake have escaped?"

"Only an idiot would believe they had walked through walls or flew out of windows. I know not how they left, for the gates were closed and the drawbridge was raised," Duff claimed. "I have questioned the servants but they knew naught of it."

"I have given this considerable thought," Waldo confided. "Did you ever hear your father speak of a tunnel within the walls of the keep?"

Duff's brow furrowed, then suddenly lifted. "Now that you mention it, I dimly recall Father mentioning a secret escape route, but it never seemed important enough to question him about it," Duff mused. "Chirk has never been under siege. However, I do remember one instance when I overheard Father telling our old steward, Sir Clement, to make sure the tunnel was kept in good repair. Unfortunately the steward is dead now."

"Did you ever try to find the tunnel?" Waldo asked, growing excited.

"Nay. It did not seem important at the time. I'd forgotten all about it until you brought it up just now."

"I knew it!" Waldo exclaimed. "I knew

there had to be a secret way out of the keep. People do not fly, nor do they disappear into thin air. I will order another search of every chamber."

His men's failure to find the tunnel did not discourage Waldo. He simply ordered them back into the chambers with orders to keep searching until they found the escape route. It was Waldo himself who discovered the door behind the tapestry in the solar, and he roundly cursed himself for not finding it sooner. Weeks had been wasted while they searched for something that lay beneath their noses.

Flushed with success, Waldo, Duff, and two men-at-arms entered the narrow passage. At length they found the place where Drake had dug through the cave-in. After a slight hesitation, Waldo climbed through the opening, motioning for the others to follow. Eventually they entered the cave and found themselves in the forest beyond the castle walls.

"I never knew," Duff said, clearly stunned by their discovery. "I wonder how Drake knew?"

"I should have thought of it before," Waldo groused. "I recall now that I taunted Drake into spending time alone in the dungeon when we were young lads. He wanted to prove his courage. Mayhap he found the tunnel then."

"What are you going to do now?"

"Attack Windhurst, kill Drake, and bring my wife home where she belongs," Waldo said with a snarl. "Are you with me?"

"I refuse to take part in this vendetta, Waldo," Duff said. "I always knew you hated Drake. As a lad I joined in your pranks because he was a bastard and beneath us in rank. But Drake has done naught to us. He has distinguished himself in battle and was dubbed by the king on the battlefield. If you want justice, take the matter before the king, but do not kill Drake."

"The king! Bah. He is too fond of Drake for my liking!" Waldo roared. "Drake abducted my wife, relieved her of her virginity, and made me look like a fool."

"It was wrong of Drake to take Raven," Duff agreed. He searched Waldo's face. "But mayhap he had good reason."

Waldo searched Duff's face, wondering how much he knew. "What reason could a man have for stealing another's wife?"

"I will ride with you to Windhurst," Duff said, "but my men-at-arms will remain at Chirk. Mayhap I can negotiate a peaceful solution to this feud."

"Bah, I do not want a peaceful solution. I want Drake's head and Raven's body. Naught else will satisfy me," Waldo said gruffly. "Join me or not, 'tis your choice."

Three days later Waldo, Duff, and Waldo's army clattered over the drawbridge and turned south toward Wessex. After years of groveling at Waldo's feet and being his toady, Duff had come to the conclusion that Waldo was a cruel tyrant and possibly a little bit insane. Belatedly he realized he had not always been a good brother to Raven, that he never should have forced her to wed Waldo. That was why he had agreed to travel to Windhurst with Waldo. He wanted to make amends and prevent bloodshed.

Windhurst Castle

Raven awakened in Drake's arms and cuddled closer. It was still very early, not yet prime, but she had much to do today. For weeks she had been preparing for her departure. Drake had been generous with his coin, urging her to purchase whatever she desired from peddlers visiting the keep, and she had hoarded a portion of the money instead of spending it foolishly. If she were frugal, the money would see her safely to Edinburgh before the first snow-fall.

The days had been exceptionally fine of late, prompting Raven to put her plan to leave into motion. Her figure was beginning to ripen. Though Drake appeared not to have noticed, her waist was thickening and her breasts were larger. If she did not leave before he guessed her secret, she knew he would not let her leave at all. That meant a battle between Drake and Waldo was inevitable.

After they had made love the night before, Drake had informed her that he would be joining the huntsmen today. Meat for the larder was needed, and he hoped to bag a fine buck or a wild boar. The game not used for immediate consumption was to be salted and stored for the winter ahead. Drake would be gone for most of the day, and Raven had decided to take advantage of his absence. She would find no better time to leave. Edging away from Drake, she eased out of bed.

Drake awakened and reached for her. "You seem eager to leave our bed this morn, sweeting. Have you something special planned today?"

Raven blanched. Did he know? "Nay. I thought to make candles today. 'Tis a long, tedious process and I wanted to get an early start."

"And I must rise and join my huntsmen," Drake said. "I would prefer to remain in bed and make love to you, but duty calls. Sir Richard remains behind. Ask him if you need anything," Drake continued as he rose naked from the bed and struck a light to a candle. "The watchmen patrolling the parapets have been instructed to keep their eyes peeled for visitors. I have a feeling that Waldo will arrive soon, but this time the castle is prepared for a siege."

"Can a confrontation be avoided?" Raven asked hopefully. "I want no bloodshed on my account."

"This feud has gone beyond you," Drake explained as he pulled on his clothes. "Waldo wants me dead, whether or not he gets you back. Waldo's hatred for me started long ago and has deepened over the years. I know not what motivates him, but one day I intend to find out.

"Kiss me good-bye, sweeting. Tonight we will feast on fresh venison."

He bent down to brush a kiss across her lips, but Raven was not satisfied with a fleeting kiss when it might very well be the last she and Drake would ever share.

Throwing her arms around his neck, she pulled him down and kissed him hungrily, with all the fervor in her slender body. When the kiss ended he reared back and stared at her, his expression thoughtful.

"Mayhap I should climb back in bed and satisfy your hunger, sweeting."

"Tonight," she said, smiling up at him despite the gnawing ache devouring her insides. She knew leaving would anger Drake, but she had to do it in order to prevent carnage.

"Tonight, then," Drake agreed.

Raven waited until the door closed behind him before leaping out of bed and dressing in her warmest clothing. She pulled on a flannel undershift with long, tight sleeves and topped it with a woolen tunic. Then she donned heavy knit hose and her sturdiest leather shoes. When she was dressed, she spread out her mantle and piled the items she intended to take with her upon it. Then she folded it all into a neat bundle and placed it under her bed.

Raven had but one thing left to do and she dreaded it. She had mulled this over for a long time and had decided to write a note for Drake to find. She would simply tell him that she felt it was time to part and beg him not to follow. She would advise him to let Waldo know immediately that she was no longer under his protection. She might even hint in her note that she intended to return to her husband.

Her mind made up, Raven sought out Balder and asked for parchment, quill, and ink, explaining that she needed to make out a list of personal needs. The steward provided the items Raven requested without comment, and Raven returned to the solar to compose her note. She labored over it a long time, and when she finished she folded the parchment in half, wrote Drake's name on the front, and left it on the pillow, where he was sure to find it. After her note was written, Raven carried her belongings from the solar and hid them in the stables. Had anyone asked, she was prepared to say she was taking soiled clothing to the laundry shed. But no one questioned her.

Raven planned to sneak out while everyone had gathered in the hall for the midday meal. That morning she had supervised the making of candles so as not to arouse suspicion. Now, as the men ate and drank and talked, she crept down the stairs and slipped out the door the servants used to bring food to the hall from the kitchen.

She hurried to the stables, hoping to saddle her dappled mare before anyone saw her.

Unfortunately fate worked against her. Just as she reached the stables, the watchman on the parapet blew the warning horn. Raven knew what it meant immediately. Riders were approaching the keep. Men scrambled from the hall, still chewing their dinner as they ran for their weapons. Raven groaned in dismay. Too late. She had delayed leaving too long. Now Waldo was here and a siege was inevitable. Her thoughts flew to Drake, who was outside the walls, and her knees buckled in fear. She clung to the wall until her heart stopped pounding; then she returned to the keep.

The bailey was alive with activity. Men bearing weapons climbed up ladders to the walkways constructed along the walls while others rushed to guard the portcullis. Raven entered the hall and ran up the stairs to the solar, where she could look out over the battlements. She nearly collapsed in relief when she saw Drake and his huntsmen ride through the portcullis. The iron gate was lowered the moment the huntsmen passed through. Drake conferred briefly with Sir Richard, then entered the keep.

Raven wanted to go down to meet him but was forestalled when he burst into the solar.

"Did you hear?" Drake asked. He appeared distracted and Raven could not blame him. Waldo was a formidable enemy.

"Think you 'tis Waldo?"

"Aye. I must arm myself. Do not leave the solar until we know Waldo's intentions."

Raven's reply never left her lips. Someone was banging on the door most insistently.

"My lord! 'Tis Evan. The king's pennant has been sighted. A herald just arrived to inform us of the king's imminent arrival. What are your orders, my lord?"

"Wait for me in the hall, Evan. I will be down directly," Drake called through the door.

"The king!" Raven exclaimed. "Whatever could he want?"

"We will soon find out," Drake said grimly. "Mayhap Waldo sought the king's intervention and Edward means to punish me."

"Sweet Virgin," Raven said with a gasp. Had she not approached Drake that first time at Chirk, none of this would be happening. Surely the king would not punish the Black Knight, would he? Running from Waldo on her wedding night had been as much her doing as Drake's.

Drake glanced down at his bloodstained tunic and grimaced. "I cannot greet the king like this, with the blood from my kill splattered all over me. There is so little time. Balder is waiting in the hall for instructions."

"I will speak to Balder," Raven said.

"Tell him that rooms must be prepared for our guests, and that a feast fit for royalty is to be prepared for tonight's repast. I know not how many travel in Edward's entourage, but the number will be considerable."

"I will speak to the cook myself," Raven said. "Do not fret; all will be well." She turned to leave.

"Raven, wait," Drake said, grasping her arm. "Do not tarry belowstairs. I know not what the king wants. 'Tis best you remain out of sight when he arrives. I will endeavor to speak to him privately before I present you."

Raven nodded in perfect agreement. It would be best for Drake to sound out the king before making her presence known. "I will not be gone long," she threw over her shoulder as she hurried out the door.

Drake removed his tunic and poured water from a jug into a bowl. He was stripped to his braies when Evan entered without knocking.

"Lady Raven sent me to help you dress, my lord," the squire said. "Tell me what you want from your chest."

"My best black hose and velvet doublet," Drake said without hesitation. "And my short black mantle."

While Drake washed, Evan spread Drake's finery out on the bed. "Thank you, Evan. Go now and fetch my sword from the armory."

Drake sat on the bed to don his hose and boots after Evan hurried off to do his bidding. His keen eyes immediately spotted the note bearing his name propped up on the pillow. He stared at it with deep foreboding, then reached for it, flipped it open, and read the flowery script. When he finished, he read it again, then crushed it in his hand.

"The little bitch," he said between his teeth. She wanted to leave him. She wanted to return to Waldo and had forbidden him to follow her. How long had she been contemplating this betrayal? Her lying lips and tempting body had blinded him to her true feelings where he was concerned. Rage swelled and surged within him. He had protected Raven with his life, had suffered excruciating pain for her, and she had not the decency to tell him in person that she wanted to leave. Instead she left a coldly worded note for him to find. Had not the king arrived, he knew Raven would have left before he returned with the huntsmen. The sweetness of her kisses and her passionate lovemaking had been but a sham.

Drake knew that Waldo's wealth and lands far surpassed his own. Had Raven decided she was unwilling to give that up for a small, isolated keep atop a windswept cliff?

Drake cursed himself for a fool. His experience with Daria should have taught him that the women of Chirk could not be trusted with his heart. The breath caught in his throat. Had he given Raven his heart? The answer stunned him. The Black Knight had indeed entrusted Raven of Chirk with his heart. Thank God he had never told her how he felt.

He rose abruptly, clenching the note in his fist. Then he strode to the hearth and tossed it into the fire. He watched dispassionately as the edges caught the flame and turned to ash. His mood dark and dangerous, he donned his doublet and threw his mantle over his shoulders.

Scant moments later Evan returned with the sword, his eyes shining with excitement. "The king approaches the barbican, my lord."

Drake took his sword from the young man's hand and secured it to his belt. "Have you seen Lady Raven?" He could barely say her name without snarling.

"Aye, she was with Balder in the hall a moment ago."

"I am here," Raven said, striding briskly into the chamber. "Balder is carrying out your orders even as we speak."

Drake gave a curt nod, too incensed to speak.

Raven slanted him a puzzled look. "Is aught wrong?"

"Get dressed. We will greet the king together."

"But . . . I do not understand. You said I should remain in the solar until you had spoken privately with Edward."

"I changed my mind. Hurry."

Raven ran to her chest and pulled out a new tunic and undershift she had made herself from a bolt of silk recently purchased from a peddler. She donned them quickly, belted the tunic with a richly embroidered kirtle, and placed a veil on her head, topping it with a gold circlet.

"I am ready, Drake."

Drake gave her a careless glance, then grasped her elbow and guided her out the door.

Suddenly Raven recalled the note she had left for Drake. She could not afford to have him find it now. She dug in her heels. "Wait, I forgot something."

"Nay, you did not," Drake rasped.

His fingers dug painfully into the soft flesh of her upper arm and she cried out in pain. "You are hurting me. What is wrong with you? Why are you angry?"

"Wrong?" Drake said with sneer. "What could be wrong? When Waldo arrives, I will personally escort you to him. If he does not come, I will send you to him."

"What are you talking about?" He knew! Oh, God, he had found the note. Recalling her words, she knew they must have sounded cold and impersonal, but she had planned it that way so he would not come after her. She had tried, in the only way she knew, to prevent a brutal confrontation between Waldo and Drake.

"You read the note," Raven whispered. Never had he looked upon her with such contempt.

"Aye," he said in a hiss. "What kind of woman are you?" Derision dripped from every word. "You lacked the decency to tell me to my face that you wanted to return to your husband. You are the one who begged for my protection, if you recall. You lived under my roof, ate the food I provided, made love with me as if you enjoyed it. I do not understand you, lady. Did you suddenly decide a bastard was not good enough for you?"

Stunned, Raven could not believe her note had roused such animosity in Drake. She had thought he would be glad to be rid of her. Didn't he know she would do anything to protect him from Waldo? How could she have been so misguided as to think he would understand?

"You do not understand, Drake," she cried, distraught. "I hoped my leaving would prevent bloodshed."

"I do not wish to discuss it, Raven," Drake bit out as he propelled her toward the stairs. "The king awaits below."

Raven stumbled down the stairs, her eyes wide with fright. She did not know this angry man. They reached the hall just in time to greet the king as he and his entourage swept through the door into the hall.

Raven hung back as Drake rushed forward and knelt before the king. "Sire, your visit does me great honor."

King Edward III was a large, rawboned man with even features and a ready smile. He enjoyed excellent relations with his barons, for he had married several of his eleven children into baronial families. Edward and his much-admired son, the Black Prince, were very successful in war and respected by their subjects.

"Rise, Drake of Windhurst," the king said. "I had to see for myself the wonders you have wrought at Windhurst. But 'tis not the only reason I have traveled these many leagues. Nay, Drake, I bring you a gift."

"A gift, sire? You have already given me more than I ever dared hope for."

"You have earned all this and more," Edward said expansively. "Now I bring you a wife."

Raven's legs wobbled beneath her and she dropped down upon the nearest bench. A wife! Drake was to marry a woman the king had chosen for him. Raven had known this day would arrive and felt as if her world had just spun out of control. Drake hated her, and now he was going to take a wife.

"A wife, sire?" Drake repeated. "I . . . I

had not thought to marry so soon."

"A man needs a wife," Edward said heartily. "Your keep will benefit from a woman's soft touch, not to mention the heirs you will get from this marriage."

"Aye, sire," Drake said uneasily.

At the king's nod, a young woman stepped forward. Head bowed submissively, the girl glanced shyly at Drake from beneath lowered lids. She was richly dressed in velvet. Her waist was cinched in gold and her headdress was an elaborate affair that made Raven's simple veil and circlet look plain by comparison.

"Greet Lord Drake, Willa," Edward said fondly.

Willa raised her head, gave Drake a wobbly smile, then quickly lowered it again. Raven was quick to note the girl's dark beauty. Her hair was as black as a raven's wing and her flawless, creamy complexion and tawny eyes put Raven's own beauty to shame, or so Raven thought. Willa executed a perfect curtsy and Raven wondered how Drake could resist such an innocent beauty.

"Willa is my ward," Edward said. "When I considered husbands for her, I thought immediately of you. The betrothal shall take place tomorrow, with the wedding to follow the day after. I brought my own confessor to perform the ceremony."

Blackness closed in all around Raven. Her head spun and so did the hall. She had to get away before she embarrassed herself. With the king's words still ringing in her ears, she rose on shaky legs, intending to escape to her chamber where she did not have to look upon Drake's bride, but it was not to be. For the first time in her life, Raven fainted.

Chapter Sixteen

A knight fights for what is his.

Raven awakened to see Drake's face hovering scant inches above hers. His expression was fierce, his mood apparently as black as his scowl. She was surprised to find herself stretched out on a bench and tried to rise.

"Rest a moment more, my lady."

Raven shifted her gaze to Edward, who was regarding her with concern. Then she remembered. Drake was going to marry Lady Willa and she had fainted.

"I am sorry, Your Majesty," Raven apologized. "I know not what happened. I am fine now."

The king offered his hand and she rose to a sitting position. "Do I know you, my lady?"

"My pardon, sire," Drake said, indicating Raven with a careless nod. "My leman, Lady Raven of Chirk."

"Drake!" Raven was so close to swooning again she had to close her eyes to stop the room from spinning.

The king stared at Raven, then said in an aside to Drake, "You are being intentionally cruel, Lord Drake. We will speak of this later."

He returned his attention to Raven. "I heard you had wed Waldo of Eyre, Lady Raven."

Raven bit her lip to keep it from trembling.

"My lady?" the king prompted.

"Aye, I am Waldo's wife. In name only," she added. "The marriage was never consummated."

"If I recall correctly," Edward mused, "Waldo did not ask my permission to wed. Was he not married to your sister? She died, did she not? Wedding a sister-in-law smacks of incest," he said sourly.

The king's words brought his priest shuffling forward to whisper something in Edward's ear.

"Oh, aye, I remember now, Father. Lord Waldo received a dispensation from the pope to wed his dead wife's sister. I cannot argue with the pope, but I like it not. Where is your husband, Lady Raven?"

"Probably on his way to Windhurst to claim his wife," Drake said. His curt reply put a swift end to the king's questions.

"I understand none of this," Edward said

with a hint of annoyance. "I am too fatigued after the long journey to listen to a lengthy explanation. Later, after the evening meal and the betrothal, we will meet in private, Lord Drake. I suspect the tale will entertain me well past matins. Have chambers been prepared for me and my party?"

Balder stepped forward and bowed. "If you will follow me, Your Majesty, I will show you to your chambers. The south tower has been made ready for you and your entourage. Your men-at-arms will find beds in the garrison, and Lady Willa and her maid have rooms in the solar. I pray the arrangements are acceptable."

"I do not find your hospitality lacking, Lord Drake," the king said graciously.

"If you need anything, sire," Drake added, "you have but to ask."

"I will show Lady Willa and her maid to their chamber," Raven offered.

She saw Drake's body tense. His anger, she knew, was directed at her. His announcement proclaiming her his leman had left her shaken and now she felt numb. She realized how much her callous note had hurt him, but it did not compare with what he had just done to her. He had labeled her his whore before the king.

Lady Willa hesitated, as if unsure whether she should accompany Raven. She cast a shy glance at Drake, but Drake appeared unaware of Willa's delicate sensibilities. After a long pause, she followed Raven to the solar.

"How long have you been Lord Drake's leman?" Willa asked as they ascended the winding staircase. Raven thought her question intrusive and decided not to answer.

"I would never become a man's whore," Willa continued with a sniff of disdain. "After Lord Drake and I are married, you must find another protector."

"How old are you, Lady Willa?" Raven asked.

"Fifteen. King Edward says 'tis a good age to marry."

Raven sighed. "You are so young and innocent. You know naught of life. Lord Drake devours innocents like you."

Willa's eyes grew round. "Whatever do you mean?"

"Pay no heed to my rambling," Raven replied. "I am not myself today." She paused before an empty chamber. "I hope you will be comfortable here. If you need anything, please have your maid inform one of the servants."

"Where is *your* chamber?" Willa asked.

"At the far end of the hallway. Your trunks will be delivered to your chamber shortly. If you wish to bathe, send your maid to the kitchen to request a tub." She turned to leave.

"Lady Raven."

Raven paused, looking over her shoulder at Willa. "Aye?"

"Where does Lord Drake sleep?"

"Wherever he pleases," Raven answered as she forced her trembling limbs to move down the hallway.

Raven did not collapse until she was inside her chamber. She grasped the door for support and unsuccessfully tried to erase from her mind the image of Willa and Drake intimately entwined. She pictured him kissing Willa, loving her with his hands and mouth, and finally claiming her in the most basic way known to man. She pushed herself away from the door and threw herself down on the bed. She lay there a long time, staring up at the ceiling.

Drake conferred briefly with Balder, then spoke to Sir Richard about accommodations for the king's knights. Assured that everything was as it should be, he sat at the table and called for ale. A servant appeared almost immediately with a flagon and placed it on the table before Drake. Drake filled his mug and drank deeply, his mind reeling with the surprising turn of events. The need to hurt Raven had driven him to introduce her as his leman, and he already regretted his harsh words. The arrival of the young woman who was to become his bride had stunned him, and he was still reeling.

Though Lady Willa was beautiful, she did not appeal to him sexually. She seemed vapid and passionless, unlike Raven, whose spirit and fire scalded him on occasion. Aye, Willa would run his household and bear his children without complaint, and remain unobtrusively in the background. Unfortunately he expected more than obedience from a wife. He wanted a partner, a lover, a woman whose hot blood matched his own. A woman who would welcome her husband in her bed.

He wanted . . . Raven.

He could not like Lady Willa. She reminded him of a pouting, immature child who probably would faint dead away on her wedding night.

Drake finished the ale and called for more. Try though he might, he could not get drunk. He relived in his mind the moment Raven had fainted and how frightened for her he had been. Raven was a strong woman, not prone to fainting spells. She was going to leave him. She had planned to travel alone along hazardous roads in dangerous times, and that took courage.

The more he thought about the coldly worded note Raven had written, the angrier he became. Though his rage was tempered somewhat by his concern for her health, it was not entirely assuaged. The need to see Raven, to rail at her for her dishonesty, drove him to his feet. He took the stairs two at a time, his mood so foul the servants scattered in his wake. He barged into Raven's chamber without knocking and slammed the door behind him.

He found Raven lying on the bed, staring at the ceiling, and the urge to tear off her clothing and thrust himself into her was so strong he nearly exploded with it.

Raven jerked upright, her startled gaze challenging him. "What are you doing here?"

He strode to the bed and regarded her silently, hands on hips, his expression fierce. "Are you ill?"

"Nay. I am well."

He did not believe her. "Why did you faint?"

Their gazes met and collided. She answered with a question of her own. "Why did you introduce me as your leman?"

"Answer my question."

"Answer mine."

"Very well. I introduced you as my leman because that is exactly what you are," Drake pointed out.

"Oh, how cruel. How arrogant," Raven raged.

"I but follow your example, my lady," he said with a snarl. "You planned to leave me. The callous note you penned was left by a coward. Think you I would stop you from returning to your husband if that was your desire? Why, Raven? Why did you decide to leave me? I would have protected you with my life."

"I wanted to prevent bloodshed," Raven whispered.

"The truth, Raven," Drake said harshly. "I want the truth. Does my being a bastard bother you? Is that why you wished to return to Waldo?"

"Nay! I never intended to return to Waldo. I worded my note to make it sound that way."

"I said I wanted the truth, my lady. No more lies."

" 'Tis you I want, Drake. It has always been you."

Drake's eyes narrowed. "Then prove it."

He came down on the bed, covering her with his body. His head lowered and his mouth slammed down over hers. He kissed her hard, slanting his mouth over hers until her lips opened beneath his probing tongue. He ravaged her mouth savagely, wanting to punish her for making him care. No woman had ever gotten to him like Raven, nor disappointed him so thoroughly. He wanted to shake her, to yell at her, to tell her he had been willing to die for her. What more could a woman ask of a man?

His mouth slid away from hers and he stared into her eyes. "I am going to make love to you, Raven. You know you want it. 'Tis always like that between us."

A sob escaped her throat but he closed his ears to it. He knew his words hurt her, but no more than she had hurt him. Bursting with impatience, he began tearing away her clothing until he had stripped her bare.

"This is how I want you," he said through bared teeth. "Naked, with your legs spread wide."

He disrobed with incredible speed, rendering himself as naked as she. Urgency gripped him, and in his need he forgot patience, forgot tenderness. He pulled her beneath him, drawing a rosy nipple into his mouth while his fingers teased her other breast and his hips bucked against hers, his erection seeking that warm place between her legs.

Dazed, Raven stiffened as incredible sensations radiated from her breasts to that wet place where Drake's sex was demanding entrance. He was wild, unpredictable. She did not want his anger; she wanted his love.

"Nay! Not like this."

He raised his head and stared at her. Lost in the depths of his silver gaze, she could no more resist him than she could stop breathing, nor did she try.

Surrendering to him, she tangled her hands in his hair, clutched at his neck, his shoulders, moaning his name as his mouth ravished her tender breasts. His heartbeat, a loud, heavy thud, reverberated through her. She stifled a cry with the back of her hand when his mouth slid down her body, lapping greedily at her navel on his downward path to sweeter territory. Then he found her. Her hips arched upward as he buried his face between her legs, alternately licking and sucking the moist folds of her sex.

She fought to regain her wits and won, albeit briefly, as she grasped his hair, trying to pull him away. This was not right. She was losing control. Drake wanted to punish her, to prove his mastery over her. Unfortunately he was succeeding. Her entire body vibrated with need as his mouth drew on her and his fingers slid inside her.

"Drake!"

Drake raised his head and smiled at her. "Do you want me to put my cock inside you now, Raven?"

That was *exactly* what she wanted. If he did not fill that aching void inside her soon she would go quite mad.

"Aye! Nay! Oh, please."

His smile turned feral as he spread her legs and thrust hard and deep, filling her.

"Put your legs around me," he commanded.

She did, and he slid even deeper. Then he began to move. No slow, gentle loving, this, but a fierce mating, with her legs wrapped around him and his hips rising and falling in savage rhythm. She was lost, hopelessly lost, possessed by the man she loved — a man who belonged to another, just as she was not his to claim. But in her heart she knew she would be forever his. And she had his child inside her to prove it.

The pressure built deep inside where he was touching her soul. Then she exploded. She screamed, her mind shutting down as her climax swept over her. She clung to him as his body convulsed and his hot seed filled her.

Seconds later he collapsed on top of her. She accepted his weight without complaint, frighteningly aware that they could never be together like this again. Knowing Drake, he would obey his king and marry Lady Willa. Alone and bereft, Raven would be forced to pick up the broken pieces of her life and flee to her aunt's home. She would never return to Waldo, she vowed, and she would protect her child with her life.

Raven opened her eyes and was startled to see Drake regarding her with a strange light in his eyes. "You look at me as if you hate me."

"I do not hate you," he said as he pulled himself out of her and rolled away.

His voice was so devoid of feeling that she could not stop herself from reaching out and touching his shoulder. He stiffened, then turned and leered at her. "Ready for more, are you?" She recoiled, hurt by his cruel words.

"What I want is the truth," she said angrily. "Tell me. Am I naught to you but your whore?"

He rose abruptly. "I think of you not at all."

Lies. All lies, Drake's inner voice whispered. Lady Willa could never take Raven's place, neither in his bed nor in his heart. Raven had breached the wall around his heart and now he had to do what he must to repair it.

"I refuse to believe you care so little for me."

"I could say the same about you," he tossed back as he yanked on his hose with more force than was necessary.

"Nay! How can I explain when you refuse to listen?"

" 'Tis too late for us, Raven. The truth no longer matters. The king demands that I wed Lady Willa and I must obey."

Raven acknowledged Drake's words with a broken sigh. "I will leave before the wedding."

Drake wanted to ask where she would go but refrained from doing so. Raven was no longer his to protect. "Ask Balder for money to see you through your journey. When you decide upon your destination, an escort will be provided for you."

He strode to the door, his hand poised

on the knob. Was this it, then? he wondered. A loving so fierce he would remember it the rest of his days, then this cold leavetaking? He glanced over his shoulder at Raven. She had pulled a sheet over her nakedness and was staring at him as if she expected more from him. Silent tears coursed down her cheeks, and her full, pink lips were trembling.

"God's blood!" Drake cried, striding back to the bed. "What do you want from me, lady? I am sworn to obey my king. I know I dishonored you, Raven, but afterward I swore to protect you with my life. I made myself vulnerable for you. Do you know what your note did to me? It nearly destroyed me. Though she does not appeal to me, I must marry Lady Willa. But after the bedding, I intend to leave Windhurst and seek my pleasure elsewhere. No one will ever engage my heart again."

Having said more than he'd meant to say, Drake stormed from the chamber, and ran headlong into Lady Willa.

"Lord Drake!" Her eyes widened in fear when she saw his fierce expression, and she backed away from him. "I . . . I thought this was the ladies' solar. I did not expect to find you here." She gazed pointedly at the door from which Drake had just exited. "Is that not Lady Raven's chamber?"

Drake was in no mood for bantering. "So it is, my lady."

"When is Lady Raven leaving Windhurst?"

His mood was growing darker by the minute. "When it pleases her."

"Forgive me, my lord, I did not mean to anger you."

"Nay, forgive me, my lady. I fear I have distressed you."

She gave him a wobbly smile. "You are forgiven, my lord." She covered her mouth and tittered nervously. The sound grated on Drake's nerves.

"I look forward to the banquet tonight. Mayhap we can get to know one another better," she added.

Drake inclined his head and offered his arm. "May I escort you to the hall?"

"Nay, I was looking for the . . . the . . ." Her face turned a bright shade of red.

Drake was saved from directing her to the garderobe when her maid came puffing down the hall. "I have found it, my lady. Follow me."

"Until tonight." Willa simpered as she curtsied and hurried after the maid.

"God save me from simpering innocents," Drake muttered beneath his breath. Whatever had the king been thinking? Any fool could see he and Willa would not suit. He hurried away in search of Balder. Tonight's banquet must be perfect. He wanted the king in a good mood.

Raven would have preferred to eat in her chamber tonight but decided that hiding away was cowardly. Donning her best silk gown, undertunic, and a new headdress she had recently purchased from a peddler, she gathered her courage and went down to the hall. Everyone was already seated when she arrived, and she slid into an empty place as far away from the high table as she could get.

Margot and her kitchen helpers had outdone themselves, Raven thought as dish after sumptuous dish was served. In honor of the king, the table gleamed with silver: knives, spoons, salt dishes, and cups. Each place was set with a thick trencher of day-old bread, which served as a plate for roasted meats.

Servants circulated about the hall, carrying trays of bread and other delicacies. Then the best wine Drake had to offer was decanted into ewers and poured into each guest's silver cup.

The soup course was served; then came jellied eels, boar's head, venison, peacocks, suckling pigs, and a variety of birds. The vegetables consisted of peas and green beans. The meal concluded with fruit tarts, nuts, and cheese.

Raven barely touched her food. Her appetite had fled the moment she saw Lady Willa leaning toward Drake to whisper into his ear. Lowering her eyes to her trencher, she felt her stomach heave. Pretending indifference toward the man she loved was the most difficult thing she had ever done.

Drake had seen Raven enter the hall and had lost his train of thought. Some might think Lady Willa more classically beautiful, but Drake found her pale and lifeless compared to Raven's vibrant beauty and spirit. He stared across the room at Raven, suddenly puzzled by something about her he had noticed of late: a special inner glow. He regarded her with an intensity that soon drew the king's disfavor. He returned his gaze to his trencher, thinking that Raven belonged at the high table, beside him. He wanted to escort her to his side but knew that flaunting his leman before his bride-to-be would anger the king.

Drake returned his attention to the food

on his trencher. Everything was delicious, but he had little appetite. He glanced at Edward and was pleased to note that he appeared to be enjoying the repast. Beside him, Willa picked at her food with ladylike delicacy.

"Is the food not to your liking, Lady Willa?" Drake asked.

Willa dropped her knife and blinked up at him, her eyes clouded with fear. "Did I frighten you, my lady?" Drake asked, surprised by her response to his simple question.

Willa dropped her gaze to her lap. "Forgive me, my lord. I was raised in a convent and male voices sometimes startle me."

Drake groaned. Convent raised. The first time Willa saw him naked she would probably swoon. "Why were you raised in a convent, my lady?"

"I am a great heiress, my lord. I became a ward of the king when my parents died of fever. I was seven years old when Edward placed me with the nuns to protect my fortune from those who would wed me to possess it."

"Have the nuns instructed you in your wifely duties?" Drake asked.

Her eyes remained respectfully downcast. "I know what I must do, my lord. I . . ."

She shuddered and dared a glance at him from beneath long, feathery lashes. "I pray you will not be too demanding. Once a child is conceived it would be sinful to continue . . . relations, until another child is desired," she said primly.

Aghast, Drake stared at her. This was impossible. "Feeling as you do, you should have no complaints if I take a mistress," he said, testing the waters.

Willa's eyes widened as they rose to search his face. " 'Tis against God's laws. You would be committing adultery. I will not have it, my lord." She sounded like a spoiled child, demanding that their marriage be conducted according to her rules.

"What will you have me do, my lady? You just said I would be welcome in your bed only when we wish to conceive a child. I fear you are misinformed about a man's needs. You are young, my lady. The king was wrong to bring you here. We will not suit."

Drake turned back to his food, blatantly ignoring Willa's gasp of dismay. He had no idea that King Edward, who sat on his right, was watching the interchange.

Edward leaned toward Drake and whispered, "Does Lady Willa displease you?"

"Lady Willa is far too young and innocent for me," Drake said, choosing his words carefully. "We will not suit."

"Nonsense," the king blustered. "She is just what you need to settle you down. Granted, she is young, but most men relish the chance to mold an innocent girl's passion to suit their needs." He leaned closer. "Lady Willa is immensely rich as well as beautiful. She brings several estates with the marriage."

Wealth did not interest him. "Is there naught I can do to change your mind, sire?"

Edward frowned, his gaze roaming the hall, finally settling on Raven. " 'Tis Lady Raven, is it not? She is the reason you are unwilling to take a wife. We must talk privately, Drake. I am anxious to learn how the lady came to be your leman. I know Waldo of Eyre. He would not let his wife go without a fight."

"Aye, we do need to talk," Drake agreed. "Mayhap we should postpone the betrothal and wedding."

"Nay. Father Bernard is prepared to conduct the betrothal ceremony after the entertainment you have planned for me. There *will* be entertainment, will there not?"

"Aye," Drake said sourly. He was at his

wit's end. He did not want Lady Willa. The marriage would make them both miserable. "Balder has summoned entertainers from the village. There is even a jongleur among them skilled in storytelling."

Edward's eyes lit up. "Ah, I do love a good story. As to the marriage, I predict it will be good for both of you."

Drake thought otherwise but remained silent. Angering the king was not a good idea. He signaled to Balder and immediately a troop of acrobats tumbled into the hall. Drake sat stoically through the performance, remaining unamused even when the jester came afterward with his comical antics. Then the jongleur regaled the guests with tales of Drake's courage. The jongleur was still singing Drake's praises when a guard rushed into the hall.

He proceeded directly to the high table and bowed before the king. Then he turned to Drake. "Sir John and an unidentified rider approach the barbican, my lord."

"Raise the portcullis," Drake ordered. "Bid Sir John come to the hall. I am most anxious to see him."

"Has Sir John been gone long, Drake?" Edward asked.

"Aye. I expected him back long before this and feared something had happened to him. My mind is greatly relieved to see him arrived back safe and sound."

The jongleur finished his song, bowed to the king, and left the hall scant seconds before Sir John, accompanied by a frail old man dressed in brown robes, arrived.

"Sir John," Drake said in greeting. "Bring your guest forward. 'Tis good to see you, friend. Greet your king, then tell me who you have brought with you."

Sir John executed a courtly bow. "Your Majesty, 'tis good to see you again. I was surprised to see your banner hanging from the parapet. What brings you to Windhurst?"

" 'Tis good to see you, too, Sir John. You and Drake are two of my staunchest supporters. I will never forget how bravely you defended England. My visit here is not without purpose. I bring Lord Drake a bride. Greet Lady Willa."

John looked at Drake askance, then directed his gaze to the lovely young girl sitting beside Drake. If he wondered what had happened to Raven, he kept it to himself. "Well met," he said, making a sweeping bow in Lady Willa's direction.

"Who is your guest?" Drake asked.

"Someone you will be most happy to meet," John said. "Drake of Windhurst, this is Father Ambrose, the priest who married your mother and father."

Drake leaped to his feet, clutching the edge of the table so hard his knuckles turned white. "Father Ambrose! Tell me true. Did you marry Sir Basil and Leta ap Howell?"

The white-haired priest stepped forward and paid his respects to his king. Then he turned his myopic gaze on Drake. "Aye, my lord, 'tis true. Your mother and father were legally married in the Welsh village of Builth Wells. The village lies near the border and not far from Castle Chirk. I entered the marriage in the parish records myself."

The king leaned forward. "Why did you not step forward before now with this information?"

"Shortly after I performed the ceremony, the church was destroyed by fire. I fled for my life when friends told me Lord Basil's father wanted no living witness to his son's marriage to a Welsh commoner. He succeeded in burning down the church, but I saved the record book. I carried it with me when I fled the burning church."

"Father Ambrose has brought the pages

from the book with their names inscribed, sire," Sir John said.

The king rubbed his smooth-shaven chin, apparently pondering everything he had just heard. "Continue with your story, Father Ambrose. Where have you been these many years?"

"I fled to north Wales, Your Majesty. I found a village in need of a priest and settled down to serve my new flock."

"Where did you find the good father, Sir John?" the king asked.

"Lord Drake dispatched me to Builth Wells to deliver a message to his grandmother. When I arrived, she informed me that she had finally located Father Ambrose, the man who could verify Drake's legitimate birth. He had just recently returned to a monastery near Builth Wells to live out his remaining years. The village priest informed Drake's grandmother of Father Ambrose's whereabouts. Nola has been searching for the priest for many years, in hopes of proving Drake's legitimacy."

" 'Tis true," Father Ambrose confirmed. "I had no idea Nola was looking for me or I would have returned and shown her the proof she required. Unfortunately, I knew naught about a controversy concerning a child whose birth occurred after I fled. But I am here now to proclaim before God and my king that Drake of Windhurst is not a bastard. If Basil of Eyre married another woman without dissolving his marriage to Leta ap Howell, then any progeny of that marriage is illegitimate."

"This changes a great many things," Edward declared. "I have much to think about. And of course I will want to examine the records before I declare Lord Drake the true Earl of Eyre and Waldo the bastard. Until this is settled to my satisfaction, the betrothal must be postponed."

A smile curved Drake's lips as his gaze searched the hall for Raven. He found her amid a sea of faces. Their gazes met and clung. Then she rose somewhat unsteadily and fled.

Chapter Seventeen

*A knight realizes that with love
anything is possible.*

Drake frowned. He wanted to rush after
Raven, but the king placed a hand on his
shoulder, reminding him that there were important matters pertaining to his new status
to discuss.

Edward's hand tightened. "You can go to
her later." He unrolled the page removed
from the church record book and perused
it briefly. "Sit with me before the hearth,
where we can speak privately."

"Aye, sire," Drake said, following Edward to the far end of the hall.

Balder appeared with a flagon of ale and
two cups. He set them on a small table
near Drake's elbow. Drake waved him away
and poured wine into the cups himself. He
handed one to the king and cradled the
other between his palms. He stared absently into the dancing flames while the
king studied the page from the church records.

After a moment of introspection, Edward said, "It appears a grave injustice has been done to you, Lord Drake. I knew the old Earl of Eyre, Basil's father. He was a proud man, albeit a conniving one. Apparently he was prepared to go to any lengths to see his son married to a woman equal to him in rank and lineage."

"I never doubted the legality of my mother's marriage to my father," Drake said. "My grandmother told me to bide my time, that proof would turn up one day, and she was right."

Edward handed the parchment to Drake. Drake perused it carefully. "It appears legitimate."

"Aye. I would have believed it had there been naught to back up the priest's claim. Priests do not lie." He drummed his fingers on the arm of the chair, as if considering the steps he must take to right the wrong that had been done to Drake.

"From this day forward you are to be known as Lord Drake, Earl of Eyre and Windhurst. All the lands and wealth contained in both estates are yours to claim," Edward proclaimed.

"What of Waldo, sire?" Drake asked.

"He deserves naught, but because he fought bravely at Crécy, he will not be punished. Let it be known that henceforth he will be simply Sir Waldo, and that you are his liege lord. As his overlord, you can require him to swear fealty to you."

After years of being called a bastard, Drake found his new circumstances overwhelming. However, the thought of what Waldo would do when he found out brought him quickly back to reality.

"Waldo will not willingly accept your decision," Drake warned.

Edward smiled complacently. "I know Waldo is a difficult man to deal with, but I am his king and he must obey me."

Drake did not agree with the king's assessment of Waldo's reaction but refrained from voicing his opinion.

"Now that your new status as Basil's heir is established," Edward continued, "let us speak of your marriage to Lady Willa. Your combined estates will make you one of the wealthiest men in all of England."

Drake cleared his throat. "About Lady Willa, sire. She fears me. 'Tis in her eyes every time she looks at me. I beg you to reconsider. Find the lady a husband more to her liking."

Edward's scowl deepened. "Mayhap 'tis time we spoke of Lady Raven. She is the reason you do not wish to marry Lady

Willa, is she not? How did Waldo's wife come to be your leman?"

Drake sighed. There was no help for it; he had to tell the truth. One did not lie to one's king. "Your good opinion of me will likely change when you learn what I did."

"Let me be the judge of that. Pray continue, Lord Drake."

"Very well, sire. Several months ago I entered a tourney at Chirk. At the time I did not know the tourney was held to celebrate the marriage between Raven of Chirk and Waldo. I fostered at Chirk and left when I was a lad of seventeen. If you recall, you were good enough to accept me into your service and offer me a chance to fight with you and the Black Prince in France."

Edward eyed Drake fondly. "I remember well. You saved the Black Prince's life, not once but twice, and I dubbed you on the battlefield. Later I made you an earl and gave you Windhurst. You have not disappointed me. Windhurst is everything I dreamed it would be in the hands of the right man. Finish your story, Lord Drake."

"Aye. The tourney was a success. I was declared champion and won the purse. Raven recognized me as the lad she knew from her youth and sought me out. She asked me to help her escape a marriage she found repugnant. She wanted to flee to Scotland. I refused, of course."

Drake went on to explain why he had disliked Raven at first. "I know now that Raven said naught to her father about my intention to elope with Daria, but it took a long time to accept that Daria was not meant to be mine."

"Why did Lady Raven want to flee Waldo?"

"She holds Waldo responsible for Daria's sudden death."

Edward digested that piece of information, then said, "Go on, Lord Drake."

"I steadfastly refused to help Raven, though she entreated me many times during my stay at Chirk." Then he confided that Waldo had tried to kill him with poisoned wine.

He paused and took a large swallow of ale, knowing the king would not think well of him after he heard the rest of the tale.

"The wedding took place after the tourney," he continued. "I attended the wedding feast with the other guests and drank too much. My mood turned dark and morbid. I wanted to punish Waldo for all the injustices my mother and I had suffered over the years."

He took another large swallow of ale and

refilled his cup. "After Lady Raven retired to the wedding chamber, I waited for Waldo to join her. Instead he continued to drink and exchange crude remarks about Raven with his knights until finally he passed out. And this on his wedding night! 'Twas then I decided to take something from Waldo that he valued: his wife's virginity. My befuddled mind found logic in the dishonorable act I contemplated."

The king appeared bemused. "The devil you say! Your audacity stuns me."

Drake's honor demanded that he absolve Raven of all guilt. "I took Lady Raven by force, sire."

"You violated her?" Edward thundered.

"Nay, sire, Drake did not violate me. I was willing."

Drake jumped to his feet, dribbling ale on his tunic. "Raven! What are you doing here? This is a private conversation."

"Not when the subject concerns me. I returned to the hall to speak with the king."

"Pull up a bench and sit down, my lady," Edward invited. "I will hear you out. Did Lord Drake violate you or did he not?"

" 'Twas not rape, Your Majesty. I fought Drake at first, but his seduction won me over and I submitted willingly. He took my virginity, aye, but 'twas not a brutal act. Waldo would have torn away my innocence with callous disregard for my pain or feelings; Drake was a caring, tender lover."

She studied her fingers. "Though Drake and I had not met since our parting many years ago, I have always loved him."

Drake started violently. Raven had never spoken of love before, and he could scarcely credit it.

"Did Drake tell you I fled to his camp that night and demanded that he take me with him?"

"I deeply regretted what I had done to Raven, sire," Drake interjected. "When Raven appeared in my camp that night, demanding escort to Scotland, honor demanded that I offer my protection for as long as she needed it. But I did not take her to Scotland. I knew that Waldo would follow her, demand her return, and punish her. Her aunt could not protect her as well as I could, so I brought her with me to Windhurst."

"And you made her your leman," Edward charged.

"Aye, sire."

" 'Twas a mutual decision," Raven insisted. "Did Drake tell you Waldo imprisoned him in Chirk's dungeon? That he was

406

tortured and starved? When Waldo brought his army to Windhurst, Drake knew the castle could not withstand a siege, so he took me to Wales for safekeeping. Drake was captured when he rode to meet Waldo in battle. Unfortunately his army lacked the numbers necessary to defeat Waldo."

"I knew this tale would keep me entertained well past prime," Edward said, motioning for Raven to continue.

"After Waldo took Drake prisoner, he sent Sir John to tell me that Drake would die if I did not present myself at Castle Chirk within a fortnight. I could not bear the thought of Drake dying on my account, so I obeyed Waldo's command. When I arrived at Chirk, I was immediately locked in my chamber to await Waldo's pleasure. His anger was fearsome."

"This is getting more complicated by the minute," Edward said, sitting forward in his chair so he would not miss a word. "How did you escape?"

Drake took up the story, explaining about the tunnel and their subsequent flight to Windhurst.

"So now you are waiting for Waldo to come with his army to claim his wife," Edward mused.

"Aye, sire."

"And you, Lady Raven. Are you prepared to return to your husband?"

"I beg your pardon, sire, but I do not consider Waldo my husband. Though a ceremony was held, the marriage was never consummated. I throw myself on your mercy, sire. Pray, do not send me back to Waldo."

"What kind of game are you playing, my lady?" Drake asked coolly. "I thought you wished to leave me?"

" 'Twas only a ruse. I knew Waldo would come to Windhurst, and I wanted no more bloodshed on my account. You have suffered enough, Drake, and I wanted you safe. I feared I was becoming a burden and wished to make your life easier."

"I wronged you," Drake returned shortly, "and vowed to protect you with my life."

"I wanted your love," Raven whispered. As if realizing what she had just admitted, she lowered her eyes. "Forgive me, sire. My tongue grows overbold."

"Look at me, Raven," Drake said, forgetting the king, forgetting all but the thumping of his heart. When she raised her tear-swollen face, he took her hand and knelt before her. "Tell me what you want from me."

"Must I repeat what you already know?" she cried.

"I know naught. We have never spoken of our feelings."

"How could we speak of feelings when I was not free? And now you are not free. You will wed Lady Willa, and if I am fortunate, I will be allowed to go to Scotland to live out my days in peace."

Edward sat back, listening and watching with rapt attention.

"Tell me one thing, Raven," Drake said, pinning her with his intent gaze.

"If I can."

"Are you carrying my child?"

"God's blood! Even I want to know the answer to that question, Lady Raven," Edward said, leaning closer so as not to miss her reply.

Raven's face drained of all color. "How did you know?"

Drake gave a satisfied smile. "You have not been yourself of late. You never faint. If you recall, I inquired about your health several times during the past weeks. I was willing to let you return to Waldo if that was your wish, until . . ." He sent Edward a sheepish grin and stumbled on. "Until we made love today. Afterward, little things I noticed about you began to make sense. Your waist is larger and your breasts are more tender. I can recall many times in the past weeks when the sight of food turned you green, especially in the mornings. I was a fool not to realize it sooner."

"I agree," Edward said. "As the father of eleven children, I would have noticed the signs immediately. One problem remains, however. Raven is another man's wife. Should she return to her husband, the child will legally belong to him."

Drake leaped to his feet. "Over my dead body!"

"Mayhap I will sleep on this and find a solution to your liking," Edward said, yawning. "I bid you both good night."

He rose and swept from the room, leaving Raven and Drake to hash out their differences.

"Come," Drake said, extending his hand. " 'Tis late; we should seek our bed."

Raven placed her hand in his and followed him up the stairs. She expected him to leave her at her door, but he did no such thing. He opened the door and followed her inside. Lora had left a squat candle burning, and a muted glow suffused the chamber.

Raven wrung her hands, suddenly at a loss for words. What could she say? Drake knew her note had been a sham, and now he knew she had deliberately kept the knowledge of his child from him.

"I prefer to sleep alone," she said as Drake lowered himself to the bench before the hearth and removed his boots.

"And I prefer to sleep with you," Drake replied. "Go to bed, Raven; you look exhausted. We will merely talk tonight, and try to clear the air between us."

Too tired to argue, Raven removed her dress and undertunic, poured water into a bowl, and washed her hands and face. While Drake pulled his tunic over his head and removed his hose, she slipped into bed. When Drake climbed in beside her, the only thing between their bodies was her thin chemise.

She stiffened when he pulled her roughly against him. "Tell me about our child. How long have you known?"

"I knew at Chirk, when my courses failed to arrive. I cut myself and bloodied the bedding and my clothing to convince Waldo's leman that my courses had begun. Waldo refused to touch me until he knew for sure I was not increasing. If Waldo knew I was expecting your child, he would have slain me. As much as I hated the thought of Waldo touching me intimately, I could not sacrifice your child."

"You would have taken Waldo into

your bed and foisted my child off on my brother," Drake charged.

"I had no choice. I prayed for a miracle but was prepared to do whatever was necessary to spare our child. Fortunately God did not demand so great a sacrifice. He answered my prayers and sent you to me."

"Why did you not tell me? Why did you want to leave Windhurst when you knew I would protect you and our child with my life? Your note left me teetering on the edge of sanity. I was prepared to hand you over to Waldo the moment he showed up at the gate."

" 'Twas as I told the king. I did not want you to sacrifice your life for me. I was going to flee to Scotland and place myself in my aunt's care. Never," she stressed, "would I have returned to Waldo."

"I doubt even the Scottish king could keep Waldo from claiming you. No law protects wayward wives from their husband's wrath. Now Waldo's vendetta is against both of us."

"You are to wed Lady Willa," Raven accused. "Your bride-to-be made it abundantly clear that I was not welcome in her home. That still holds true. The king said naught to indicate he would change his mind about the betrothal. I have no place in your life, Drake."

"Did you mean what you said, Raven?"

Raven frowned, trying to recall what she had said. "About what?"

"You said you loved me."

"How can you doubt my love?" Raven cried. "I have loved you since I was a child. You were my hero, my knight in shining armor. I was jealous of your attention to Daria."

"You were a child, hardly capable of strong feelings. I am speaking of now, Raven."

"Heed me well, Drake of Windhurst! I am a woman now, with a woman's feelings and a woman's needs. You are the man I love, the man I have always loved."

"I dishonored you," Drake reminded her.

"Nay, you did not. You made love to me. You gave me pleasure, and a wedding night I will never forget. You have been sufficiently punished for that night, and suffered a great deal. Though we can never be together as man and wife, remember me with kindness and know that I will protect your child with my life."

"Whether or not we marry, you are now and will always be mine. I will not abandon you, Raven. Not even the king can demand that of me. If all else fails, we will flee to France, or Italy. It matters not, as long as we are together."

"You would give up Windhurst and Eyre for me?"

"I would give up my life for you. Have I not proven my willingness to die for you?"

"You did what your honor demanded," Raven returned, convinced that he did not love her.

"The devil take my honor!" Drake said in a hiss. "I did not ask to fall in love. I had plans to make Windhurst the finest castle in Wessex. In time I would have had to marry, of course, but only to sire heirs. I even knew the type of wife I would choose. She would be young, virtuous, and submissive. She would never question my authority, or rail at me should I stray. I wanted not a wife who would challenge me with her intelligence. I wanted a woman I would not have to care about."

"You just described Lady Willa," Raven whispered.

"Then I found you," Drake continued as if Raven hadn't spoken. "A woman with all the attributes I considered unattractive in a wife."

"You liked me not."

"Not true. I liked you too well."

"You refused to help me flee, however much I begged."

" 'Tis silly to enumerate our many mistakes when we both want the same thing."

Raven's breath caught in her throat. "What is that, Drake?"

"We want to be together."

" 'Tis all I ever wanted. Unfortunately God and the king have conspired against us."

"You love me, Raven, and . . ."

"And?" Raven asked hopefully.

"And I love you. I have thought of naught else since we made love earlier today. I could not have gone through with the betrothal tonight had there been one. I was willing to defy my king for you. Sir John arrived with Father Ambrose before I could make my intentions known."

Raven stopped listening after Drake said he loved her. "You love me?"

"I was willing to die for you. Why would you doubt my love?"

She snuggled closer, drawing upon his strength, fearing she would need it before this was all settled. She fell asleep in his arms, contented for now that he loved her.

Raven stirred and pulled the pillow over her head. How could she sleep when someone on the ramparts was blowing a horn? The racket was most distracting. She realized something was amiss when Drake leaped from bed and reached for his hose.

"What is it?"

"Do you not hear it? The horn is a warning that visitors are approaching the gate. By now the garrison is stirring and every man is racing to his post. I must go."

"Be careful," Raven called. "It could be Waldo."

Drake hurried to the battlements to await the intruders. Sir Richard and Sir John were already there.

"Can you see the pennant?" Drake asked.

"Not yet," Sir John replied. "Wait! I see it now. 'Tis the rampant falcon of Eyre."

Suddenly the king appeared beside him, peering out over the rampart at the approaching army. "Who comes, Lord Drake?"

"Waldo of Eyre, sire."

"Think you he plans to attack Windhurst?"

"Aye, sire. I have been expecting him."

"When they see my pennant hanging from the parapet, they will not attack," Edward said with conviction. "Invite Waldo inside when he arrives. 'Tis time he learns he is no longer the Earl of Eyre. I suspect this will be a challenging day for all of us."

He turned to leave.

"Sire," Drake said. "A word with you, please."

"What is it, Lord Drake? I have not yet broken my fast."

"I know not what you have decided about Raven and me, but I will not abandon her. I . . . I love her and she loves me. She carries my child, sire. I beg you, give Lady Willa to a man who will appreciate her good qualities. I need not her wealth."

"We will speak of this later," Edward said curtly. Drake feared the king's surliness did not bode well for him and wisely did not press the issue.

"Go down and greet your guest," Edward commanded. "Invite him to the hall. I look forward with relish to this day."

One of Waldo's knights had been sent to scout ahead; the man returned in a high state of excitement to report his findings.

"Lord Waldo, the king's herald hangs from Windhurst's battlements!"

" 'Tis not possible," Waldo said, stunned. "Why would Edward visit Windhurst?"

Duff rode up beside him. "Is aught amiss?"

"If Sir Justin can be believed, the king is at Windhurst," Waldo said sourly.

" 'Tis true, my lord," Sir Justin claimed.

"You cannot attack Windhurst if the king is in residence," Duff warned.

"Nay, I cannot," Waldo answered. "God's blood! What am I to do now?"

"I am sure you will think of something," Duff said dryly.

A glimmer of a smile lifted the corners of Waldo's lips. "Aye, you are right, Duff. I know exactly what I will do. Raven is my wife. Not even the king can prevent me from claiming her. I will simply march up to the gates and demand entry. Once I am inside, I will name Drake as Raven's abductor and accuse him of making her his whore. The king will have no choice but to punish Sir Bastard."

"Have you forgotten Raven? 'Tis likely she will repudiate your accusation and claim she was not abducted."

Waldo's face hardened. "She will not dare dispute my words. Not if she knows what is good for her."

Duff remained silent. He knew his sister well. If she truly cared for Drake, as he believed she did, she would speak up in Drake's defense. Duff himself was becoming more and more disenchanted with

Waldo. Over the years Waldo had done many things of which Duff did not approve.

Then Windhurst came into view and Duff's thoughts scattered.

" 'Tis true," Waldo said angrily. "The king's herald does indeed fly from the ramparts."

Drake left the battlements, mentally preparing himself to meet Waldo. He had already sent word that Waldo was to be allowed into the outer bailey, and he intended to be at the portcullis himself to welcome his brother. He walked through the hall and down the steps to the inner bailey. Work had come to a standstill as his men scrambled for their arms. Of course they would not need them with the king in residence, but being prepared was always a good policy. He reached the portcullis and waited for Waldo to approach.

He did not have long to wait. Waldo detached himself from his knights and approached the iron portcullis guarding the entrance to the inner bailey. Duff appeared at his side. Somehow Drake was not surprised to see Duff.

"We meet again, Sir Bastard," Waldo taunted.

The salutation grated on Drake and he clamped his teeth together lest he tell Waldo exactly who the bastard was in the family. That honor belonged to the king. He merely smiled and said, "Indeed."

"I want my wife," Waldo informed him. "Open the portcullis."

"Welcome to my demesne," Drake said with a flourish. "I assume you come in peace." The portcullis grated open, allowing Waldo and Duff to enter. When Waldo's army rode forward to follow their leader, the portcullis lowered with a bang, barring their entrance.

"My men go where I go," Waldo said gruffly.

"Nay, the keep is filled to overflowing. The king's guard is garrisoned within the walls. Your men can camp on the moors beyond the walls. Fear not; no harm will come to you. The king does not condone fighting between his subjects."

"How is my sister?" Duff asked anxiously.

Drake's brows arched sharply upward. "Do you actually care?"

"Aye. Raven is all the family I have left. I have made some grave mistakes in my life; one of them was giving Raven to Waldo. I hope she will forgive me."

"Bah! You speak nonsense." Waldo snorted. "Raven is mine and there is naught anyone can do to change that. Not even the king can deny a man access to his lawful wife. 'Tis good that Edward is here. Mayhap he will find what you did so dishonorable that he will banish you from his kingdom."

"Mayhap," Drake agreed. He did indeed fear that the king would return Raven to Waldo. If Edward decided in Waldo's favor, Drake would be forced to do more than strenuously object. Two people who loved one another belonged together.

The king was breaking his fast at the high table when Drake entered the hall, followed closely by Waldo and Duff. All three men dropped to one knee and waited for Edward to acknowledge them.

"Rise," Edward said. "Come, break your fast with me. You will not find Lord Drake's hospitality lacking."

They seated themselves at the high table. Immediately servants carried in trays of food and pitchers of ale. Silence reigned while the men ate, and Drake wondered how long Waldo's patience would hold.

To Waldo's credit, he said nothing until the king pushed his empty trencher away and belched.

"Sire, I have traveled a long way to retrieve my wife from Drake's custody. Did he tell you he raped her and carried her off?" Waldo asked around a mouthful of food. " 'Tis a sad tale, sire, but true, nonetheless."

Drake continued to slowly chew and swallow his food. "Raven is not your wife."

"God's blood, man, of course she is my wife. Bring her forth immediately."

When Drake made no move to comply, Waldo said, "Does His Majesty know you made Raven your whore? That I am willing to take her back after she has been defiled should speak well for my good character. Once Raven is returned to my protection, she will be properly chastised."

The king cleared his throat. "Lord Drake, would you please summon Sir John, Father Ambrose, and my own confessor? Methinks 'tis time for Sir Waldo to learn of his new rank. And," he added, "Lady Raven should be present, since this also concerns her."

Drake rose, spoke briefly to Balder, who was hovering nearby, then rejoined the others.

Waldo blanched. "What is this all about, sire? I am here to claim my wayward wife, not to make trouble. And what is this new rank of which you speak? I have been Lord Waldo since my father died and made me an earl."

The king's answer was forestalled when Raven entered the hall. Drake rose to meet her. He kissed her hand and seated her beside him at the high table.

"I hope your clothes are packed," Waldo said angrily by way of greeting. "We leave for Eyre before the day is out."

Raven glanced at Drake, her eyes revealing her fear. Drake clasped her shoulder to reassure her. "Naught has been decided," he said.

Waldo's eyes narrowed. "What are you talking about? There is naught to decide. Raven belongs to me." He turned to the king. "What say you, sire? The Earls of Eyre have always been forthright in their loyalty to the Crown. I demand respect."

"The Earl of Eyre does indeed have our respect," Edward assured him.

"Believe naught that my bastard brother told you. I demand what is rightfully mine."

"I have a great fondness for the present Earl of Eyre," Edward replied. Waldo's chest puffed out and he gave Drake a condescending look.

"Sir Waldo, please acknowledge the new

Earl of Eyre. Rise, Lord Drake."

Drake rose. He had waited a long time for this moment. Pride swelled within him. Finally his mother had been vindicated. The title mattered not, nor the wealth. What mattered was the acknowledgment of his legitimacy.

Chapter Eighteen

A knight knows his enemy.

Waldo leaped to his feet, his face mottled with rage. "What did Drake tell you, sire? 'Tis a lie, all of it. I am the rightful Earl of Eyre. Naught he says can change that."

"Careful," Edward warned. "I do not pass judgment on the word of one man. There is proof that Leta ap Howell and Lord Basil of Eyre were legally wed. That would make Drake of Windhurst Basil's oldest son and legal heir, while you . . ." His words trailed off, but the full impact of what he meant was not lost on Waldo.

"Show me your proof," Waldo demanded, "and I will discredit it."

"Ah, here come Father Ambrose and Sir John now," the king said.

"Who, pray tell, is Father Ambrose?"

"Father Ambrose married my mother and father," Drake answered. "The marriage was legal, but Basil's marriage to your mother was not. Given our closeness in age, and the haste with which your parents were married, no formal annulment or divorce could have possibly been granted in so short a time. Basil's father ordered the church burned to destroy the records. You are the bastard, Waldo, not I."

"The priest is lying!" Waldo said angrily. "He was paid to bear false witness."

Father Ambrose stepped forward. "I do not lie, my son. I performed the marriage in good faith and recorded it in the record book myself. I brought sufficient proof to verify my claim."

"The church burned years ago," Waldo replied smugly. "You are an imposter."

"Enough!" Edward thundered. "The proof is overwhelming, and my decision has already been made. All that is required of you now is to swear fealty to your liege."

"Swear fealty to Drake!" Waldo exploded. "Nay! Never." His dark gaze settled on Raven, and a smile that did not reach his eyes stretched his lips. "You have stripped me of my title and wealth, but you cannot take my wife. 'Tis my God-given right to take Raven with me when I leave this cursed place."

Drake's expression turned feral and his lips drew back in a snarl. "Over my dead body!"

"That can be easily arranged," Waldo said smoothly.

"Aye, you would like that, *brother*. Until now I could never figure out why you wished me dead. You feared the truth would come out."

"You do not know the half of it," Waldo muttered beneath his breath. More loudly, he said, "Your Majesty, only God can take a man's wife from him."

"There is no true marriage," Raven claimed, jumping into the fray. "An unconsummated marriage is not legal."

" 'Tis your word against mine that our marriage was never consummated," Waldo maintained.

"And we all know you are a liar," Raven charged. "How long have you known Drake was the true heir of Eyre?"

"I owe you no answers, *wife*."

"Mayhap not," Edward injected, "but I am your king, and you owe me an answer. How long have you known Drake was Basil's heir?"

Drake was afraid Waldo would lie, but apparently his brother feared the king too much. "I have known since I was old enough to question Father about his decision to foster Drake at Chirk. Had Drake been a bastard, Father would not have cared about his welfare." He returned his regard to Raven. "Come, wife, 'tis time to leave."

Raven turned to the king, her eyes pleading. "Your Majesty, I beg you, do not send me away with Waldo. I could not live with a man I hold responsible for my sister's death."

"What say you to that, Sir Waldo?" Edward asked.

"My wife knows not what she is saying, sire. Daria died of a stomach ailment. I challenge anyone to prove otherwise."

"I cannot make a judgment without first weighing everything I have heard today," Edward said, tapping a finger against his chin. " 'Tis not a simple matter. Mayhap Father Ambrose and Father Bernard will lend me their wisdom. Together we will decide whether a legal marriage exists."

"The marriage is legal," Waldo persisted. "I will not allow Drake to have Raven. I have waited too long for her."

"Drake is not the issue," Edward advised. "I already have a bride in mind for Lord Drake." He sent Drake a benevolent look.

"When can I expect your answer?" Waldo asked curtly.

"I will confer with the priests and give

you my answer when a decision is reached. Meanwhile, you and Lord Duff can either return to your campsite outside the gates or remain within the keep."

"I will stay," Duff said. "I have not always been a good brother to Raven and I would like to make amends."

"I will stay also," Waldo replied.

"Very well," Edward said, "so be it. I am sure Lord Drake will find adequate quarters for you within the keep."

Drake motioned to Balder and the steward hurried forward. "My steward will show you to your rooms."

"Follow me, my lords," Balder said, bowing to Waldo and Duff.

Moments later the king swept from the room and shortly afterward the hall cleared, leaving Drake and Raven alone.

"I am worried," Raven said, clutching Drake's hand. "What if the king decides that I should remain Waldo's wife and you should wed Lady Willa?"

"Come, we cannot talk here," Drake said, urging her toward the stairs. Neither spoke again until they entered Raven's chamber and Drake closed the door behind them.

Drake opened his arms and Raven launched herself into them. "I hate him,

Drake, I truly do. I shall die if I have to remain his wife. Where will he take me to live? Eyre is no longer his home."

"I believe Waldo's mother left him a small estate near York. He will not be penniless. Do not concern yourself. I vow he will never have you. No matter what Edward decides, you are mine."

His hand caressed her belly. "My child," he said possessively.

"Aye, yours," Raven acknowledged.

Then he sealed his vow with a kiss. When the kiss ended he released her and stepped away. "Duty awaits, my love. Try not to worry. I trust the king to make the right decision."

Drake hated to leave Raven, but running the castle was complex and time-consuming, especially with the king in residence. When he reached the hall he found the captain of his guards waiting to speak with him.

"My lord, Sir Waldo's captain of the guards wishes a word with you. He awaits you at the portcullis."

"Do you know what he wants?" Drake asked, puzzled by this new turn of events.

"Nay, but he was quite adamant about speaking to you in person."

"Very well," Drake said, hurrying off.

The scene that greeted him beyond the

portcullis stunned him. Ranged behind their captain, whom Drake recognized immediately as Sir Hugh, the man whose gifts of food and water had kept him alive in Chirk's dungeon, was Waldo's army. The portcullis was raised and Drake stepped through.

"What is this all about, Sir Hugh?"

" 'Tis simple, Lord Drake," Sir Hugh explained. "We wish to swear fealty to the Black Knight, the new lord of Eyre." As if on cue, every man knelt before their new lord.

Drake looked out over the sea of eager faces and a lump rose in his throat. It had never occurred to him that one day he would command the kind of respect these men now accorded him.

"How did you know?"

"Word spread like wildfire. It reached us a short time ago. I speak on behalf of everyone present. We offer our fealty to you, Lord Drake of Eyre and Windhurst." He fell to his knee and held out his hand, palm upward. Drake placed his foot in it.

"Rise," Drake commanded. "I accept your fealty."

"What are your orders, my lord?" Sir Hugh asked, rising.

"Stay tonight for the feast. On the

morrow, take the army to Eyre to protect my demesne from predators. Tell the steward to expect me soon to inspect my estate, and inform the bailiff that I intend to go over the books with him upon my arrival."

"What is this?"

Waldo appeared at Drake's elbow, his anger palpable. "I came to address my men. Why are you giving them orders? You have no right to command them."

"They are no longer yours," Drake said. "I am the new lord of Eyre. Every man present has sworn fealty to me."

"Every man?" Waldo asked, clearly stunned.

"Aye, every man. I have ordered them back to Eyre. Windhurst cannot support so great a force."

"Wait!" Waldo shouted to Sir Hugh. "I command you to stay."

"We serve the Black Knight now," Sir Hugh replied. "Lord Drake is a worthy lord; we will serve him well. We are no longer yours to command."

Having had his say, Sir Hugh saluted Drake and led the men back to their campsite.

"You will pay for this, Drake," Waldo said in a hiss. "You think you have it all now, but there is still Raven. Naught can change the fact that she is my wife." His voice vibrated with menace. "The only way you will have her is dead. Think about that, Sir Bastard."

Then he whirled and marched away. Had Drake seen Waldo's menacing expression he would have slain Waldo on the spot, for Waldo's eyes revealed his intention to exact retribution on the two people he hated the most.

The hall was crowded for the midday meal. The king looked harried when he and the priests appeared, and Raven wondered if Edward had reached a decision yet. She sat beside Drake at the high table, trying to remain calm despite her anxiety. She felt Waldo's evil glare upon her and refused to look at him. He had not been invited to sit at the high table and she was grateful, but his malevolent gaze rested on her far too often for her peace of mind.

Raven chewed thoughtfully on a succulent piece of roasted venison that Drake had put on her trencher and turned her attention to Duff and Lady Willa. Seated side by side, they seemed to have found common ground as they chatted comfortably with one another. Unlike Drake, whom Willa feared, Duff seemed to have captured her fancy. Raven had to admit that Duff was a handsome and unassuming sort of fellow, except when Waldo goaded him into doing things that went against his nature.

Raven had been surprised when Duff sought her out and begged for forgiveness. He expressed regret for forcing her into a marriage she abhorred and vowed that he would do nothing to hurt her again. They had made a tenuous peace, and Duff had told her she was welcome to return to Chirk, that he would keep her safe if she chose to seek his protection from Waldo.

Raven suspected Duff would become an entirely different person without Waldo's evil influence; it seemed Lady Willa had already discovered Duff's good qualities. She smiled as an idea suddenly occurred to her. Duff had no betrothed, nor to her knowledge did he have a mistress. He was two years older than she and should have taken a wife long ago. When she saw Lady Willa blush at Duff's outrageous compliments, Raven's spirits rose.

"What are you smiling about?" Drake asked, leaning close to whisper in her ear.

"Look at Duff and Lady Willa," Raven answered. "They seem quite taken with one another."

Drake glanced at the pair and grinned. "Think you Lady Willa likes Duff better than me?"

"I hope so. Mayhap I will ask her whom she prefers. I believe the king wishes her to be happy, and Duff needs a wife."

His gaze caressed her. "I always knew you were clever."

After the meal the king cloistered himself with the priests again and Drake left to train with his knights. Waldo slunk off on his own to sulk, and Duff joined Drake.

Raven cornered Lady Willa before she left the hall. "May I have a word with you, Lady Willa?"

For a moment she thought Willa would refuse and was relieved when the lady grudgingly acquiesced. "Very well, Lady Raven. What is it you wish to discuss?"

Raven led her toward a deserted spot near the hearth. "My brother appears quite taken with you."

"Your brother is a gentleman. He does not frighten me like . . ."

"Like the Black Knight," Raven said, completing the sentence. "Why do you wish to marry Drake if you dislike him?"

"I must obey the king," Willa said. "But I did not know the Black Knight would be so . . . so frighteningly male. So virile." She gave a delicate shudder. "I had hoped for someone like . . . Lord Duff. But I will obey my king and endeavor to make Lord Drake a good wife. Do you intend to leave with your brother? This marriage may not be to my liking, but I will not allow my husband to keep a leman."

"Mayhap this marriage is not to Drake's liking, either," Raven suggested. "He will not give me up, you know. If you prefer Duff, as I believe you do, you should make your preference known to the king. Duff is as good a catch as Drake. Better in some ways, for he does not keep a mistress. His lineage is impeccable, and he is wealthy."

"Lord Drake is wealthier now that he is an earl," Willa mused thoughtfully. "The match would be a good one."

"Are you prepared to deal with Drake's enormous capacity for bed sport?" Raven asked. "He is a sensual, masterful lover."

Willa blanched. "I have already informed him that once I am increasing he will no longer be welcome in my bed. And that we will only do *that* again should he desire more than one child."

Raven nearly laughed in Willa's face. "I can imagine what he said to that."

"Is he so insatiable then?" Willa asked, clearly shaken. Raven hoped Willa was having second thoughts about marrying Drake.

"Aye, but 'tis not a bad thing."

Willa grimaced. "I would not like it."

"Then I suggest you set your sights elsewhere. Mayhap on Lord Duff. He is the kind of man who will honor your wishes. Mind you, Duff was not always a good brother. Lord Waldo led him astray. But Duff has apologized to me, and I truly believe he intends to change his life. You are exactly the kind of woman he needs to keep him from following unscrupulous men like Waldo."

"Do you really think so?" Willa asked hopefully. "Lord Duff *does* seem to like me. And he strikes me as a man who would not be overly demanding."

"Think on it, Lady Willa," Raven encouraged. "Then make your decision wisely."

"You want the Black Knight," Willa said.

"Aye, I want him, my lady." She splayed her hands over her stomach. "And so does our child."

She smiled and whirled away, leaving a speechless Willa in her wake. She had no idea Waldo had been lurking in the shadows, not close enough to hear their words but near enough to see that Raven had said something to shock Lady Willa.

"What did my wife tell you?" Waldo asked as he sidled up to Willa.

Willa started violently. "Oh, you frightened me."

"What did my wife tell you that was so shocking?" Waldo persisted.

"I do not think your wife likes you overmuch." Willa sniffed.

Waldo gave a snort of laughter. "Tell me something I do not know. Nevertheless, Raven is mine. If she were out of your life, mayhap Drake would pay you more heed."

"Nay, he would not. Drake is right. We would not suit. Besides, Lord Duff looks upon me with favor. Mayhap I can persuade the king to give me to Duff instead of to Drake."

So much for enlisting Lady Willa's help, Waldo thought as he strode away. There had to be some way to get Raven alone; all he had to do was find it. He was convinced that the only way to hurt Drake was through Raven. Somehow, before he left Windhurst, he would have his revenge upon Drake and Raven.

The servants paid Waldo scant heed as he left the hall. He made directly for the stables. No one was about this time of day, so he saddled his own horse. Chickens and geese scattered as he rode through the inner bailey. Drake caught up with him at the portcullis.

"Where are you going?"

"I feel in need of exercise. Am I a prisoner at Windhurst? Have I not the right to come and go as I please?"

"I will instruct the gatekeeper to allow you to pass freely," Drake replied. " 'Tis not my intention to keep you at Windhurst any longer than necessary."

Sawing on Zeus's reins, Drake rode off. Waldo smiled slyly and continued through the raised portcullis. He wandered aimlessly along the cliffs before he realized the possibilities they offered. He found a place where his horse could easily negotiate the steep path and reined the destrier down the cliff to the rock-strewn beach below. He saw the cave by accident as he absently scanned the cliffs. The opening was above high-tide level and he dismounted to explore it. To reach it, he had to climb over rocks embedded in the cliff's face. To his surprise he found an unlit torchlight lying on the ground outside the cave, and he realized he was not the first person to enter the cave.

He struck a light to the dry branches and it caught immediately. Guided by the light, he wandered deeper into the cavern and saw signs of recent activity. Smiling with satisfaction, he doused the torch and left it where he had found it. Then he climbed down to the beach, where his horse awaited him. When he returned to the castle, his mind whirled with nefarious plans involving Drake and Raven.

The king was in a jovial mood during the meal and entertainment Drake had arranged that night. The portcullis had been left open so that the men camped outside the walls could attend the feast and come and go at will. The hall was crowded. Edward said nothing of his decision concerning Raven's fate, nor did he mention his private conversation with Lady Willa earlier that day, but he did have a twinkle in his eye that Raven was hard put to identify. She fidgeted nervously throughout the oppressively long meal.

Drake's solid presence beside her failed to cheer her as it usually did. For some reason she could not dispel a deep sense of foreboding.

After the jongleur had spun his last tale, the king rose and motioned for silence. "I propose a toast," he said, raising his cup to

Drake. "To Lord Drake, Earl of Windhurst and Eyre." A loud cry of "Hear, hear!" echoed throughout the hall. The king drank deeply, then turned to Raven. "And to the new lady of Windhurst and Eyre!"

At the back of the hall, Waldo cast down his cup and spit out an oath. A stunned silence ensued as all eyes turned to Waldo.

"Come forward, Sir Waldo," Edward commanded.

Waldo charged forward, his chin jutting out pugnaciously. He stopped before the high table, glaring at the king, at Drake, and especially at Raven.

"You cannot do this, sire," Waldo railed. "My marriage to Lady Raven is legal and binding."

" 'Twas not consummated," Edward returned. "My decision is made. Since my presence is no longer needed, I intend to leave tomorrow. My daughter is expecting a child and I promised to return to London in time for the birth. I had not intended to remain at Windhurst so long."

"Are the priests in agreement?" Waldo challenged. "Are they willing to set aside a legal marriage?"

"They agree with me. The marriage was not consummated; no legal marriage exists. 'Tis within my power as king of the realm to annul the marriage, and I have done so."

"But the pope —"

"It matters not what the pope decreed; the marriage still smacks of incest to me. Besides, you did not ask my permission to marry."

"What about Lady Willa? Was she not intended for Drake?"

"Aye, but neither party was willing. It appears that Lady Willa prefers another." He blessed Lady Willa with a fond smile. "Lord Duff has asked permission to wed her."

"Lord Duff!" Waldo sputtered. "That spineless toady!"

Edward dismissed Waldo with an angry chop of his hand. "Be gone; you offend me! The decision was mine to make and I made it."

His face mottled with rage, Waldo gave the king an insolent bow and strode away.

"The feast tonight is a true celebration," Edward announced grandly. "Will Father Ambrose and Father Bernard please come forward?" The two priests rose from a bench close to the high table and approached the dais.

"Before I leave Windhurst, it would please me to see Lord Drake wed to Lady Raven and Lord Duff wed to Lady Willa."

Duff, looking properly smitten, and Willa, shyly accepting the king's edict, were escorted by the king's own squires to the center of the hall. The ceremony uniting Duff and Lady Willa was short but moving. Afterward the entire assembly offered rousing cheers to the newlyweds. Raven was the first to congratulate her brother and his new wife, thrilled that Duff had finally escaped Waldo's evil influence and become his own man. Duff had done many things she found hard to forgive, but in time she hoped the family would be reunited.

Then it was Drake and Raven's turn. Though this was the happiest day of her life, Raven could not shake her persistent feeling of dread. She blamed it on her pregnancy, for she had heard that expectant mothers were often fanciful and weepy. Yet the fact remained that while Waldo lived, she would never know peace.

"What is it, sweeting?" Drake asked as they waited for the ceremony to begin. "Are you having second thoughts?"

"Nay!" Raven denied, aghast that Drake would even think such a thing. "Being your wife is all I have ever wanted."

Moments later Raven's wish became reality. She was Drake's wife. Her child would bear his name and know a father's love. She savored Drake's kiss and clung to him, tears blurring her eyes as they received a standing ovation from all those present. Then, disregarding ceremony, Drake swept her into his arms and carried her up the stairs to their chamber. Once inside, he slammed the door shut with his foot and sat her down on the edge of the bed.

Then he knelt at her feet, peeled back her skirts, and removed her shoes and stockings. "Tonight is ours to savor," he said, kissing his way up her bare leg to her inner thigh. "I am going to love you so thoroughly, no one will ever question the legality of our marriage."

"Our marriage was consummated long before the priest spoke the words over us," Raven quipped.

His mouth paused on a tender spot above her knee. "I will always regret the way I took you that first time."

"Do not. I regret naught."

That dark feeling came over her again and she shivered. Drake sat back on his haunches and stared at her. "Something is wrong. Tell me."

Raven bit her bottom lip, aware that her explanation had no basis in fact. She shook her head. "I cannot. 'Tis naught but a feeling."

" 'Tis Waldo," Drake said harshly.

"Aye," she admitted. "He frightens me. He will always be there, waiting to hurt you."

"I can handle Waldo. He has no power. Though not penniless, he no longer claims Eyre's wealth or manpower."

"What will he do?"

"Return to his small demesne near York. I suspect he'll hide there to lick his wounds. Forget him, my love. I have. I will never let him hurt you again." He kissed her nose. "Smile. 'Tis our wedding night. I want to undress you slowly, to kiss you until you lose your fears, and to make love to you until you beg me to stop."

The breath caught in Raven's throat. "I want that, too. I want to feast my eyes upon your warrior's body, to return your kisses until we are both breathless, and to feel your hardness moving inside me. Oh, Drake, thank God for the king. Without him we would not be husband and wife."

"We will pray for his long life," Drake allowed. "But not tonight. Stand up, my love. You are wearing far too much clothing for my liking."

He stripped her slowly, kissing and

stroking each part of her body as he bared it. When she finally stood before him, gloriously naked, she was shaking so violently she could scarcely breathe. She admired his warrior's body as he stripped himself as naked as she. They faced one another as God had made them, bare, without artifice or pretense.

Suddenly shy, Raven tried to hide her growing girth with her hands, but Drake would not allow it. He smiled and pulled her hands away, then bent to kiss her stomach. "Nay, do not hide yourself from me. 'Tis my child growing inside you. You have never looked more beautiful to me than you do now."

He bore her down upon the bed, covering her with his body. She hooked her arms around his neck, bringing his face down to hers. They kissed fervently, their kisses increasing in length until both were gasping for breath. Their tongues tangled and dueled, as if they could not get enough of one another. His caresses were tender, patient, arousing her slowly, with great gentleness despite his raging need. He caught her nipple between his thumb and forefinger and licked the hardened nub. She shifted restlessly and moaned.

After a long time he abandoned her nipples and slid his mouth over her flushed skin, lapping a trail of fire down her belly and lower, until his hot mouth claimed a spot so sweet the pleasure was nearly unbearable. She arched upward into his wet caress as his fingers opened her and his mouth sought even greater intimacy.

On fire, trembling with need, Raven pulled on his hair to claim his attention. "Come inside me, please!"

He smiled and moved over her, his face inches from hers, and with one quick, smooth thrust, he was deep inside her. She surged against him, taking him, all of him, wanting more. They strained together, seeking, hungry mouths joined, their passion ignited, driving them to even greater heights.

Fulfillment, absorbing, all-consuming, burst upon them simultaneously. Rapture flowed, crested, flinging them over the edge of forever, then ebbed, floating them in a sea of sublime ecstasy. Blissfully satisfied and totally spent, they clung to one another, vowing without words their everlasting love.

Drake eased beside her and placed a tender kiss upon her lips. She snuggled close and laid her head on his shoulder.

"You belong to the Black Knight now,"

Drake said, pulling her possessively against him. "Naught but death will part us."

Though she was happy and sated, Raven's mind refused to relinquish the fear that had been plaguing her since the day Waldo had appeared at Windhurst. Drake had just told her that only death would part them. Were the words a harbinger of doom? Were they more prophetic than either of them realized?

She knew Waldo, knew how he thought, and he was not going to give her up without a fight. Though the king had ruled in Drake's favor, she feared they had not heard the last of Waldo.

There was something, something she could not put her finger on, that warned her Waldo's evil was driven by fear. Fear of what? What horrible thing in his past drove him? Was it Daria? He had denied killing her sister, but she did not believe him. It suddenly occurred to Raven that the darkness she felt around her was not her own. It was Waldo's. His past held something so sordid and contemptible that evil emanated from him in waves. Was she the only one who perceived the corruptness of Waldo's soul, the only one who worried about it?

Then Drake reached for her again and

she went willingly into his arms, losing herself in his lovemaking.

Afterward, sleep came, but it was not an easy sleep, for a villain bent on mayhem lurked in the darkness.

Chapter Nineteen

*A knight's vow to protect his lady
is not given lightly.*

The persistent clanging of a bell dragged Drake from a deep sleep. He shook himself awake and pulled on his hose. Since he had no knowledge of the nature of the catastrophe, he grasped his sword and headed for the door. It was then he noticed the orange light flickering against the windows and realized the calamity was worse than he'd thought.

Fire.

He ran to the door; Raven's voice stopped him. "Is aught amiss, Drake?"

His answer was forestalled by a frantic hammering on the door. "Drake, 'tis Sir John. There is fire below in the inner bailey. The smithy is already ablaze and the kitchen is threatened."

Drake's heart thundered wildly. Fire! "Organize a bucket brigade," he called through the door. "I will be down directly."

"Wait for me," Raven cried, throwing back the covers.

"Nay, do not bestir yourself, my love," Drake said as he donned his leather hauberk. "Remain in the keep, where you will be safe." When Raven objected, he said, "Promise me."

"Very well," Raven reluctantly agreed. "Be careful."

Drake kissed her lightly on the mouth and made a hasty exit. Raven did not lie abed long. She rose and dressed in haste, wanting to be ready should she be needed below. She moved to the window. The bright red glow against the inky black sky was stunning . . . and frightening.

She could not see the smithy from her window; it was situated around the corner of the keep, separated from the kitchen by a storeroom. All the buildings had thatched roofs, and Raven feared a spark would ignite the roof of the shed and quickly spread the blaze to the kitchen. Should the wind pick up, all the buildings in the inner bailey could go up in flames.

Raven was so worried about the spreading fire that she did not hear the chamber door open, nor was she aware of a presence behind her. She was aware of nothing until she felt a hard hand clamp over her mouth and a brawny arm anchor her against a solid body.

"Well, dear *wife,* I finally find you alone," a voice whispered into her ear.

Waldo! Sheer panic seized her. She kicked backward, but her soft slipper did nothing but earn her a vicious shake.

"Try that again and I will kill you," Waldo said in a growl.

Suddenly her mouth was free and she opened it to scream. The scream died in her throat when she felt a knife pressed against her stomach, where her child grew.

"What do you want?"

"Is that not obvious?" Waldo said against her ear.

He released his hold on her waist and tore the cords from the drapery. "Put your arms behind you."

Fearing for her unborn child, she did as he directed. He quickly bound her arms behind her and dragged her to the bed, roughly pushing her down. Fearing that he would take her sexually, she vowed, "I will scream if you touch me."

"Scream all you want," he said with a snarl. "No one will hear you. Everyone is in the bailey battling the fires, and these walls are thick. Besides, I have other plans for you," he said as he knelt and bound her ankles. "You are Drake's weakness. Losing you will hurt him more than anything I could do to him, including a quick death. Killing is too easy, too painless. Nay, I have something else in mind. Something that will make you suffer as much as Drake when he cannot find you. Your death is likely to be slow, but all the better."

Despair settled over Raven. Waldo was right. She could scream at the top of her lungs and no one would hear her. She had to keep her wits about her until she learned what Waldo planned for her.

"What are you going to do?"

"You'll find out soon enough. Where is your cloak?"

He spied it hanging on a hook. He removed it, along with a silk scarf he found lying nearby. Raven had scant time to wonder what he was going to do with the scarf, for he grasped her chin and stuffed the scarf into her mouth.

"Now I won't have to listen to your carping," he said, hauling her to her feet and settling the cloak around her shoulders.

He ignored Raven's muffled cries as he pulled the hood over her head and tossed her over his shoulder like a sack of grain. Raven could see little except his heels as he opened the door and peered into the corridor.

"Deserted," Waldo crowed as he descended the narrow stone staircase. His shoulder dug into her stomach, and she emitted a silent groan as she bounced against him. She tried to kick him but he held her legs securely.

The hall was deserted. Dismay turned to panic when Raven realized that everyone, including the servants, was in the bailey fighting the fire. Waldo quickly traversed the hall and opened the door. When Raven felt a blast of cold air, true fear gripped her. Waldo was going to carry her away without anyone being the wiser. Raven raised her head and saw people rushing between the pump and the burning buildings, too intent upon the fire to notice them.

When Waldo veered away from the burning buildings, Raven realized he was heading for the stables. Abruptly it occurred to her that the fire had not been an accident. Whoever had started it knew precisely what he was doing and exactly where to set the fire in order to conceal his movements.

Waldo.

Once inside the stables, Raven saw that Waldo's horse was already saddled. He tossed Raven upon the destrier's broad back and mounted behind her. With a flick of the wrist he guided the horse out of the stable and toward the portcullis, which was still raised to allow the men camped outside the walls free access to the keep. To Raven's horror, the gate-keeper had abandoned his post to fight the fire, just like everyone else in the castle.

When they rode through the barbican unchallenged, Raven's heart sank. It appeared that Waldo would have his revenge after all. Drake would never see their child. She would not live to give birth. They rode along the cliffs now, the howling wind tearing at her cloak. She heard the sea crashing against the rocks below and wondered what Waldo had in mind when he guided his destrier down a steep incline leading to the beach. Did he intend to drown her?

The thunderous sound increased as they neared the narrow strip of beach at the bottom of the cliff. Sea spray dampened her face and plastered her hair against her cheeks.

"We are almost there," Waldo said above the roar of the crashing surf.

Where? Where? Raven cried in silent supplication. When Waldo drew rein, Raven feared she had been right. Waldo did indeed intend to drown her.

Waldo dismounted and pulled Raven down with him. Then he tossed her over his shoulder and ascended a rocky path that led sharply upward. He was panting when he finally let her drop to the ground. To Raven's horror, she found herself in a place so dark she felt as if she had been thrust into the deepest pit of hell.

A light flared. Waldo appeared before her, holding a torchlight and looking so smug she wanted to smash the smile off his face.

"As you can see," Waldo pointed out, "we are in a cave. You will die of hunger and thirst before anyone finds you. Mayhap you will never be found."

Raven's muffled curses seemed to delight Waldo, for he threw back his head and laughed. "Think you Drake will look for you here?" he taunted. Then he squatted before her and pulled the gag from her mouth. "No one can hear you above the pounding surf. What think you of my cunning now, Raven of Chirk?"

Raven sucked in a ragged breath, gathered what little saliva she had in her mouth, and spit at Waldo. Livid with rage, he dashed the glob of spittle from his face and backhanded her. She rolled with the blow and scooted away from him. "You are the devil incarnate!"

"Aye, and well you know it."

"Why? Why are you doing this?"

"Because I hate Drake, of course. I learned that the only way to hurt him was through you, and planned my revenge accordingly. The fire was a brilliant stroke, was it not?"

" 'Twas the work of the devil."

He rose and glared down at her. "Enjoy your solitude, *wife*. 'Tis all you will enjoy until death claims you."

"Wait! Do not leave me like this. I am carrying Drake's child. Would you kill an innocent babe to spite its parents?"

"A child!" he crowed gleefully. "Even better. Does Drake know?" Raven nodded. "I had not expected such a bonus. Revenge," he said, gloating, "how sweet it is."

Appalled, Raven stared at him. She had never known such evil existed in the world. She believed now more than ever that he had murdered Daria.

"Before you leave me to my ignominious death, tell me the truth," Raven challenged. "Did you kill Daria?"

Waldo pondered her question a moment before answering. "Since it seems important that you know, and you will not live to tell anyone, I see no harm in telling you. Aye, I killed Daria."

Raven lashed out in fury. "Monster! Why? What did she do to deserve death?"

"She knew too much. I could not trust her to keep her mouth shut."

"About what? Naught could be that important."

"You think not? Then let me tell you precisely why I killed Daria. My mother died shortly after I brought Daria to Eyre as my bride. Before Mother died she made a deathbed confession. She told Basil she had been carrying another man's child when they wed. I was that child. 'Twas why her father insisted on a hasty marriage. He was told naught of Basil's marriage to Leta. The old earl forced Basil to marry my mother while Basil still had a living wife."

"You are not Basil's son?" Raven gasped.

"Nay, and when he found out, he vowed to make Drake his legal heir. I could not let that happen."

"So you killed him," Raven guessed. "He did not die in a hunting accident."

"I *arranged* for his death to keep from being disinherited. I paid the huntsman who accompanied Basil that day to kill him and make it look as though he were slain by a poacher. Unfortunately Daria heard me talking to the huntsman and put two and two together. 'Twas obvious I could not let her live."

"What I see is a diabolical man with no conscience. You killed two people in order to keep your secret; then you tried to kill Drake so he would not discover his legitimate birth and take Eyre from you."

"Aye. But there is more to it than that. I wanted you, Raven. It was always you. But your father betrothed you to Aric and Basil betrothed me to Daria before I could claim you."

"Aric's death must have made you very happy."

He laughed. "Think you I left Aric's death to chance? He died a hero's death on the battlefield. In the heat of battle no one saw me deliver the killing blow."

Raven recoiled in horror. "Sweet Virgin! You killed Aric!"

"Aye, I was determined to have you, Raven. I went through hell to get you, waited years for a dispensation from the pope. Then you chose another. Now no one will have you. You wrote your death warrant the day you fornicated with the Black Knight." He turned to leave.

"Nay! Do not leave me here to die."

"Farewell, Raven. Losing you will hurt Drake more than any torture I could devise. Think on that while you are slowly dying of thirst and hunger."

Then he was gone, plunging the cave into total darkness. Raven screamed once and began to sob.

Waldo made his way back to the castle. He rode past the barbican without being challenged, pleased with his night's work. Everyone was fighting the fire, including the gatekeeper. The portcullis was raised, and he proceeded through to the inner bailey. He saw at a glance that the fires had been extinguished for the most part, and that the men were now combing the ashes for embers that could reignite. He smiled. The fire he'd started had served him well. He had created the diversion he needed, and Drake had lost at least three buildings to the blaze.

Waldo dismounted and led his horse into the stables. He quickly unsaddled the animal and rubbed him down. Then he crept back to the keep. The hall was deserted, and he went directly to his chamber to pack his meager belongings. Dawn was just breaking through the clouds when he returned to the hall. The newly returned servants paid him scant heed as they prepared food for the hungry horde who would soon converge upon them.

Waldo strode from the hall in search of Drake. He wanted to make sure Drake saw him leave alone, so that no suspicion fell upon him when Raven's disappearance was discovered.

Drake saw Waldo approaching, noted that his clothing was neither soot-stained nor rumpled, and guessed that he had remained safely in the keep while everyone else had lent a hand to extinguish the flames.

"Fare-thee-well, Drake," Waldo said, gazing with satisfaction at the destruction he had wrought. "Should we meet again, it will be too soon for me."

Drake harbored the same thought. "Where were you when we needed you? Did you not hear the fire bell?"

"Aye, I heard it, but why should I help someone I despise?"

"Lord Drake, there you are."

The king, dressed for travel, joined them. "I am no longer needed here. 'Tis time my men and I left you in peace. The buildings can easily be rebuilt, and no lives were lost. Thank God the flames were contained in time."

"I am most grateful for everything you have done for me, sire. Will you not linger long enough to break your fast with us?"

"Nay, I cannot, but your servants were kind enough to provide food for our sojourn today."

"Whatever I have is yours, sire," Drake said graciously.

"I, too, leave Windhurst this morn, sire," Waldo informed him.

"Then I bid you good-bye," Edward said, sending him off with a careless wave of his hand.

It was obvious to Drake that Edward held Waldo in contempt, which Drake understood and applauded.

"You are well rid of him," Edward said as Waldo walked smartly toward the stables.

"I pray he never darkens my door again," Drake said fervently.

The king and his contingent took their leave. Duff had already expressed his intention to leave today as well, and Drake could not fault him for wanting to be alone with his bride. Drake was grateful that for once Raven had obeyed him and remained in her chamber.

The fires had been thoroughly extinguished now, and men were gathering in the hall to eat. Tomorrow he would summon workers from the village to rebuild the three buildings that had been lost to the flames. And later, after he had cleaned up and eaten, he intended to investigate the cause of the fire.

Before returning to the solar, Drake stopped at the well and washed away all traces of soot and ashes from his skin so as not to offend Raven with his stench. He entered the hall and went directly to the solar to tell her about the fire, and to reassure her that whatever was lost could be easily replaced.

The door to Raven's chamber was ajar and he pushed it open, calling her name. He expected her to fly into his arms, and frowned when she did not.

"Raven, where are you, love?"

Thinking she had visited the garderobe, he decided to change his clothing, convinced she would return by the time he was dressed. When Raven failed to appear, he feared she might be ill. He hurried to the garderobe and found it empty. Tamping down his panic, Drake told himself there was nothing to worry about. Most likely he would find Raven in the bailey with the women, who were setting up a makeshift kitchen until a new one could be built.

A shiver of dread slid down Drake's spine when he did not find Raven in the bailey. He immediately ordered men forth to comb the keep. Drake questioned Duff and Lady Willa when they appeared in the hall, but they had not seen Raven since the night before.

"Where is Waldo?" Duff asked. "I trust him not."

"Nor do I," Drake agreed. "Waldo left Windhurst early this morn. I spoke to him myself before he left. He was alone."

One by one Drake's men returned, each reporting negative results. Raven was not in the keep. Drake extended the search to the outer and inner baileys and all of the buildings therein. He did not order a search of the area outside the castle walls, for he knew Raven would not venture beyond the walls alone.

"What do you think happened?" Duff asked worriedly when they met in the hall after the futile search.

"Waldo. It has to be," Drake replied. He had thought this out thoroughly and there was no other answer.

"Did you not say Waldo was alone when he left?" Duff asked.

"Aye, but I cannot help wondering. He was not in the bailey helping to fight the fire. The hall was deserted; the fire had claimed everyone's attention. I believe now that the fire was deliberately set to create a diversion. Waldo is not above using devious methods to work his evil."

"Aye," Duff agreed. "Waldo was ever a sly fellow. There is a blackness in his soul. I have seen glimpses of what he is capable of and liked it not." His brow furrowed. "Why would he abduct Raven? He would not . . . Nay, he would not hurt Raven, would he?"

Drake rose abruptly. His voice was harsh with fear. "What think you?"

"Waldo is corrupt and capable of great evil," Duff said slowly.

Drake was through talking. It was time for action. As if reading his mind, Sir John appeared at his side.

"The men await your orders, Drake."

"Choose six men to accompany me; we will leave within the hour. Waldo has several hours' head start; we must ride hard to catch him."

Sir John left immediately to do Drake's bidding.

"I will come with you," Duff offered.

"Nay, stay here with Lady Willa. Should Raven return to the keep, send word with a messenger."

"You know not where to find Waldo," Duff said worriedly.

"I can only assume he is headed for his estate near York," Drake said.

"Waldo's mind is devious. He will not go where you expect him to go."

Drake's hard features and thinned lips promised dire consequences for the man who dared to threaten his wife and unborn child. "I will find him."

Waldo rode as if the devil were on his tail. Drake was not stupid. In time he would figure out who was responsible for Raven's disappearance and come after him with blood in his eye. Fortunately time was on his side. He had several hours' head start and hoped to confuse Drake by riding away from York, not toward it. Instead of riding north, he rode south, to Exeter, where he intended to book passage to Brittany or Bayeux. Once the king got wind of what he had done, Waldo gravely doubted he would be welcome in England.

Eight armed men, including Drake, Sir John, and Sir Richard, rode from Windhurst within the hour. They headed north, in the direction of York. They rode hard for two hours before Drake sawed on

Zeus's reins and leaped from the saddle. Transfixed by something no one else was aware of, he turned his face toward the south, listening, his ears attuned to voices only he could hear. Pulled by some unseen force, he stared toward the southern coast. He knew his men were confused by his strange behavior but he cared not; Raven's life was at stake. Should he be wrong about Waldo's destination, Raven could die.

"What is it, Drake?" Sir John asked as he reined in beside Drake.

"Waldo does not travel north," Drake said with certainty.

"Think you he went to Londontown?" John wondered.

"Nay, not Londontown."

"Where then?"

There was a roaring in his ears. He heard a voice. Granny Nola? *Seek your prey south.*

Drake went still, very still. "Drake, is aught amiss?" Sir John cried. "Are you ill?"

Drake seemed to come to himself. "Nay, not ill. Waldo rides south."

"South? But . . ."

"Trust me, John."

"Think you Waldo has Lady Raven with him?"

Drake sighed. "I know not." The roaring

began again. Then the voice. The answer was very clear, very distinct. "Nay, my lady is not with Waldo. But he knows where to find her."

His expression would have frightened the devil as Drake remounted and spurred his destrier toward the southern coast.

Waldo stopped to rest his horse. He knew he was close to the coast, for he heard the sound of surf and smelled tangy, salt-laden air. He smiled. He was nearly to Exeter. Soon he would be on a boat sailing to France, where no one could touch him. His one regret was that he had never lain with Raven. He could have taken her before leaving her in the cave, but time was against him. He wanted to be several hours south of Windhurst before Raven's disappearance was discovered.

Exhilarated by his success, he gave a shout of laughter. The wind caught it and sent it echoing across the moors. How good it felt to defeat the Black Knight, the king's darling. He had done his utmost to prevent Drake from learning he was the legitimate son and heir to Eyre and all its wealth, and had failed. Now he had deprived Drake of something he wanted badly. Something Drake would never have.

In time, when everyone had forgotten about him, he would return to York and take charge of his estate. His bailiff had been collecting his rents for years, and when he eventually returned, he would have all the coin he needed.

Waldo set his spurs to his destrier. Exeter and France awaited him. He entered a wooded area on the outskirts of Exeter and found a well-trodden path leading through the forest toward the city. Soon, he thought, soon I will be safe from Drake and the king.

Certain that he had won, Waldo became incautious, forgetting that forests were often havens for thieves and all manner of ruffians. Thinking himself safe, he was taken by surprise when two men dropped down from the tree under which he was riding and pulled him from his mount. Before he could reach for his dagger, the pair of thieves were joined by another, and he found a blade pressed against his neck.

"Your valuables," a barrel-necked thief ordered.

Waldo was loath to part with the sack of gold he carried on his person. The coins were meant to last him a long time. "I have naught of value."

Apparently the thieves did not believe him, for he was forced to his feet and searched.

" 'Tis just as I thought," the second thief groused when he found the heavy sack.

"How much?" a third thief asked, crowding close.

The second thief opened the drawstring and emptied the contents into his hand. There were so many coins they overflowed his palm. "Enough to split four ways," he crowed gleefully. He shoved the pouch into his belt and sent a furtive glance over his shoulder. " 'Tis best we leave."

"What about *him?*" Barrel-neck asked.

"Kill him or leave him; it matters not."

Barrel-neck removed his blade from Waldo's throat and started to rise. Determined to retrieve his money despite the consequences, Waldo tugged his dagger from his belt and slashed upward, opening a fatal wound on Barrel-neck's throat. The man made a gurgling sound and died instantly. Waldo pulled his sword free and attacked the remaining two thieves, who were armed with only crude daggers.

Unfortunately Waldo had not listened carefully enough to the thieves when they talked of dividing the gold four ways. Thus far only three men had shown themselves.

But as Waldo charged the surviving two men, the fourth thief, unseen before now, crept up behind Waldo and plunged a blade into his back. Then all three thieves melted into the forest, leaving Waldo barely alive, his blood spilling onto the ground.

Dusk was moments away. Drake and his men had ridden hard all day. As the hours passed, Drake's hopes for finding Raven alive plummeted. What if he were wrong and Waldo had ridden north? The thought persisted that Waldo had already slain Raven, and his heart bled. How could he live the rest of his life without Raven? He would never know what his child looked like. Whether it was a son or daughter. *God's blood!* When he caught Waldo, and he would, he would slit the bastard from gullet to groin once he had the information he sought.

"My lord, Exeter lies just beyond the forest," Sir Richard said. "I have been here before. There is a path leading through the forest to the city."

"Find the path, Richard," Drake said with grim determination. "If Waldo is in Exeter, we will find him. He cannot be far ahead of us, nor would he have had time to find passage to France."

Scant light remained as Sir Richard led the group through the forest. Fear rode Drake. What if Waldo had ridden north to York, or gone to Scotland, or some other unlikely place?

Suddenly a horse appeared in the path and Drake sawed on the reins. Zeus reared once, pawing the air, then settled down. Drake leaped from the saddle and grasped the destrier's trailing reins. He recognized Waldo's mount instantly. It was the one he had ridden forth from Windhurst.

Drake stumbled over Waldo before he saw him. He was lying facedown in a pool of blood. Drake turned him over and spit out a curse. "God's blood!"

Sir John came up beside him. "Who is it?"

"Waldo."

"Is he dead?"

Drake knelt and placed an ear to Waldo's heart. "He breathes, but barely."

Waldo groaned and opened his eyes. All Drake's attention was focused on the dying man, willing him to breathe. "Waldo, can you hear me?"

Silence.

"Waldo! Damn you! Answer me. Where is Raven? What have you done with her?"

Waldo made an attempt to speak. His

voice was barely above a whisper. "Drake? How . . . did you know . . . where to find me?"

"A hunch. What happened?"

"Thieves. I killed one." A long time passed before he said, "Am I dying?"

Drake's voice held no pity. "Aye." He grasped Waldo's tunic and pulled up his head. "Where is Raven? Do you wish to die with a woman's death on your conscience? Raven carries my child."

A parody of a smile twisted Waldo's bloodless lips. "You will never find her."

"Is she dead?"

"Nay . . . not yet . . ." He coughed, staining his lips with blood and spittle.

"Damn you! Where is she?"

Drake heard the death rattle in Waldo's throat and pressed harder for answers. "Clear your conscience, Waldo. Tell me where to find Raven."

Waldo said but one word before death claimed him. "Water."

"Bastard!" Drake shouted as Waldo drew his last breath. "May you burn in hell for all eternity!"

"He asked for water," Sir John said.

Drake stared into Waldo's sightless eyes and wished him alive so he could kill him himself. *Water.* With his dying breath the bastard had asked for water.

He rose abruptly. "Sir John, tie Waldo's body to his destrier's back. We will take him with us to Windhurst."

"There is another dead man, Drake. What should I do with him?"

"Leave him for the scavengers."

Chapter Twenty

A knight is a sworn enemy of all evil.

Duff ran out to meet Drake when he rode into the inner bailey. He saw the horse with a body draped over it and skidded to a halt.

"Is that Waldo?"

Nodding absently, Drake dismounted. He had more important things on his mind than a dead man.

"Is he dead?"

"Aye."

"Did you kill him?"

"I wish to God it had been me. Thieves got to him first. It happened in the forest outside Exeter."

"Exeter! I thought you were riding north."

"We did ride north, for a time. Something, a premonition mayhap, told me 'twas the wrong direction. It suddenly made sense that Waldo would try to leave England."

"God's blood, Drake! Did Waldo tell you where to find Raven before he died?"

Drake's fists clenched at his sides, his anger palpable. "I will tell you what I know as soon as I quench my thirst. I am parched." Though Drake could not speak of it aloud, his greatest fear was that Waldo had raped Raven and left her somewhere to die.

They entered the keep together and took seats at the high table, where Lady Willa awaited them. The midday meal was in progress, and someone placed a tankard of ale and a trencher of meat and cheese before him. He ate and drank, heedless of what he put into his mouth as long as it filled his belly and quenched his thirst.

"Did Waldo tell you naught?" Duff exclaimed. "Is Raven dead?"

"I know not. Ere Waldo died he said but one word. He asked for water. I begged him to tell me what he had done with Raven and all he said was water." He pounded his fist on the table. "Waldo must be laughing all the way to hell. He has finally succeeded in destroying me."

Duff's brows furrowed as he pondered Drake's words. "Something is awry, Drake. I know Waldo, and he would not ask for water. Ale, mayhap, but never water. To my knowledge, Waldo never touched water."

Drake stared at Duff. It was not unusual

476

for a dying man to ask for water, though at the time he'd thought it an odd request, coming from Waldo. But anger and grief had held sway over him. Now that Duff had spoken, however, his mind began functioning again. If Waldo wasn't asking for water then . . . His mind raced. His heart thudded. Windhurst was built on a cliff overlooking the sea. There was water nearby. Lots of it.

"Waldo could not have taken Raven very far," Drake observed, growing excited. Why had he not thought of it before?

Abruptly another thought occurred, a thought so disturbing he could not put it into words. As if reading his mind, Duff spoke the words for him.

"Do you suppose Waldo threw Raven into the sea?"

Drake closed his eyes against the pain Duff's statement conjured. Then he remembered Waldo's words. A shudder of relief speared through him.

"Nay. Raven lives. We will find her near water."

Sir John, who had joined them at the high table, heard the conversation and leaped to his feet. " 'Tis high tide now, but as soon as the tide ebbs, every man in the garrison will be on the beach below the cliffs. Fear not, my lord; we will find your lady."

"See that each man has a horn," Drake directed. "The man who finds her is to give two blasts upon the horn."

"Aye," Sir John said, hurrying off.

"I pray you find Lady Raven well," Lady Willa said. "We were at odds with each other at first, but my marriage to Duff changed all that. I was hoping we could make peace and become friends. Eyre is not so far from Chirk that we cannot visit often."

"We will find her, Lady Willa," Drake said, grimly determined. What he could not promise was the condition in which he would find her. There was no telling what Waldo had done to her.

Raven stirred and groaned. By her reckoning she had passed two nights in the cave. She was thirsty and hungry. The hunger she could manage, but the thirst was nearly unbearable. She had tried to lick moisture from the walls of the cave but the foul taste gagged her. Presently it was neither thirst nor hunger that plagued her. Her limbs were numb and the pain was fierce, and she was cold.

Throughout the empty hours, Raven's

thoughts had returned time and again to Drake. His image danced before her eyes, strong, powerful, his honed warrior's body invincible. His loving left her aching for more, always more, and he had never disappointed her. She loved him so much it hurt. He was arrogant and demanding and unpredictable at times, but those qualities were part of what made him so appealing. Even now, with pain, hunger, and thirst plaguing her, she was able to close her eyes and recall the strength in his arms. And his face. No man should be as handsome as the Black Knight.

Her thoughts fractured when she noticed daylight streaming through the mouth of the cave. Another new day without hope of rescue, she thought despondently.

During the previous night and day Raven had given her dire circumstances much thought. If she did not want this cave to become her tomb, she had to get outside.

Using the wall behind her to steady herself, she pushed herself to her feet, inch by painful inch, until she was standing on her bound feet. Pain shot up her legs and she nearly collapsed, but her iron will refused to let her fall. When the pain subsided to a bearable level, she shoved herself away from the wall and hopped to the mouth of the cave. The light blinded her. She blinked twice, then stared down at the churning sea below her.

The tide was in, and the narrow strip of beach had disappeared. Raven lowered herself to the ground, watching the water lap at the rocks below, wondering how she was going to negotiate the steep incline without full use of her arms and legs. Until the tide ebbed, attempting such a feat was not to be undertaken.

Raven glanced upward, her despair tangible when she realized she would not be visible to anyone standing at the top of the cliff looking down. There was no other solution. She had to reach the beach. Fear rode her. Hindered by her bound limbs, she was in danger of falling and hurting the babe she carried. What a dilemma.

A jagged edge of rock embedded in the cliff face jabbed into Raven's bottom, and she shifted to find a more comfortable position. Unfortunately, the cliff's face offered no comfortable spot; the entire cliff was studded with sharp-edged rocks. She sighed and stared at the pounding waves, wondering when the tide would turn and what she would do when it did.

She moved her legs to ease the pain and

a sharp rock punctured her flesh. Thoughtfully, she stared at the wound, then turned her gaze to the rock with a keen sense of purpose. Had her mind not been befuddled from lack of food and water, the answer to her dilemma would have occurred to her sooner. A rock sharp enough to pierce her flesh would surely cut through silken cords. Driven by desperation, Raven searched for a sharp rock nearby, found one, and scooted over to it, wincing when sharp stones dug into her tender bottom.

Excitement thrummed through her as she backed up to the rock and lifted her wrists to the sharp edge. Her first attempt to saw through the silken ropes was unsuccessful. Her cloak kept getting in the way. Though it pained her to do so because it was so very cold, she struggled out of the garment and pushed it aside with her feet. It rolled down the slope, fell into the water, and flowed out to sea on the receding tide. Paying it little heed, she began the painstaking process of sawing through the cords binding her wrists.

Hours passed, or so it seemed, before Raven felt a slight loosening. Heartened, she renewed her efforts. The tide ebbed and the sliver of beach reappeared. The sky clouded over and a cold mist settled over the cliffs, chilling Raven to the bone. Then, miraculously, her bonds snapped and her arms were free. The pain that followed was so sharp and debilitating, Raven nearly passed out. Tears rolled down her cheeks when she tried to undo the knots binding her ankles. Her hands were as useless as two chunks of meat, and her fingers simply refused to work.

Determination furrowed her brow as she pushed herself to her feet and stared down at the windswept strip of sand below. Grimly she realized that reaching the beach without mishap would take a small miracle. Dragging in a steadying breath, Raven hopped, and hopped again. Each time she gained a little more ground. Though it was not a lengthy distance, the incline was steep and packed with obstacles. For Raven, with limited use of her hands and feet, the descent was perilous indeed.

Raven stopped to catch her breath and steady herself against a large rock. So far so good, she thought as she executed another hop. Then her luck ran out. Her bound feet landed on loose stones and slid out from beneath her. She collided with the ground hard, skidding and sliding down the slope on her bottom. She hit the wet sand on the beach below, unable to catch her breath, every bone in her body violently jarred. Then she knew no more.

Drake had already explored several caves along the beach and had almost given up on finding Raven when he saw a body sprawled in the sand a short distance ahead of him. His heart raced; fear propelled him forward. Instinct told him it was Raven. It had to be.

Stumbling across the sand, he dropped to his knees beside her, softly calling her name. When she did not answer, he gathered her inert body in his arms and hugged her close. She was so very cold, as cold as death, and he feared he had reached her too late. An anguished cry erupted from his throat as he rocked her against him. Tears slid down his cheeks as he lifted his face to the misty rain and asked God to spare her life. Then, miraculously, a soft sigh slipped past her lips.

Daring to hope again, he brushed hanks of wet hair from her pale face and stared at her. Her skin was transparent, her eyelids shadowed with purple, and her lips bloodless. Her wet clothing was plastered to her body, but she lived. He pulled off his mantle and wrapped it around her. When he noticed that her legs were bound with cords, he swore and slit them with his dagger. Then he tugged the horn from his belt and blew two short blasts.

Carefully lifting Raven into his arms, he started down the beach. Soon he was joined by more than a score of men. Sir John took off his mantle and placed it over Raven for added warmth.

"Is she . . ."

"She is alive," Drake rasped. "Though nearly frozen to death. Send someone ahead to the keep. I want a hot tub prepared and plenty of beef broth and warm ale available as soon as I arrive. And," he added grimly, "send someone to the village for the midwife." Though he did not speak the words aloud, he feared for the life of his child.

"I will go myself," John said, sprinting off.

"Would you like me to carry her?" Sir Richard offered.

"Nay. I will carry her myself." If Raven recovered with no ill effects, and God willing she would, Drake silently vowed to take better care of her.

Raven stirred and he held her closer, tighter, willing his warmth into her. He took the path leading to the top of the cliff, negotiating it with ease; Raven's slight weight was as nothing to him. His men followed, their faces grave, concern etched upon their brows.

Drake reached the top, where grooms were waiting with their horses. Drake reluctantly handed Raven to Sir Richard while he mounted; then he took her up in front of him and kneed his destrier forward. Raven lay so still Drake feared for her life. Her lips were blue, her face pale, her chest barely rose and fell with each breath. Were he able to breathe his own life into her, he would do so gladly.

Duff and Willa met him at the door. "How is she?" Duff asked worriedly. "She looks so pale."

"God willing, she will live," Drake replied as he brushed past his brother-in-law.

The servants were prepared for Drake's arrival. They waited with warmed blankets, broth, and ale. Brusquely Drake ordered everything carried to the solar. A warm tub was waiting before a roaring fire in their bedchamber. When Lora lingered behind to help, Drake ordered her out. Raven was his and he would take care of her.

Once everyone had withdrawn, Drake placed Raven on the bed and with great care removed her sodden clothing. He cursed over each and every bruise marring her lovely body and fervently wished he could resurrect Waldo from his grave and make him suffer as Raven had suffered. When he had rid Raven of her clothing, he carried her to the tub and lowered her gently into the water. Raven's eyes flew open, her eyes widened, and she screamed.

Frightened, Drake froze, wondering what he had done to hurt her. "What is it, sweeting? Tell me where you hurt."

Raven stared at him, her mouth working wordlessly as she tried to leave the tub. Drake held her down with a firm hand.

"Do you want something to drink?"

Raven nodded. Drake filled a cup with ale and held it to her lips so she could drink. She sipped a few drops and shook her head, as if too tired to swallow.

"Where does it hurt?" he asked as he set the cup aside. "Is it the babe?"

Her face paled and her hands flew to her stomach. Noting her badly bruised wrists for the first time, Drake roared in outrage. Carefully he grasped her hands, lifting them so he could inspect them more closely. Raven inhaled sharply.

"What did that bastard do to you?"

"He tied my hands behind me, bound

my ankles, and left me in the cave to die," she rasped weakly. "I feared you would not find me. Did Waldo tell you where to look?"

"Waldo is dead," he said flatly. "May he burn in hell."

"Amen," Raven said. Her eyes fluttered shut.

"Is the warm water doing you any good?"

"I am not so cold anymore."

"How long were you lying on the beach?"

She shrugged. "I know not. I managed to cut through the cords binding my wrists, but my hands were too numb to remove the cords from my ankles. I started hopping down the slope and lost my footing. 'Tis all I remember until I woke up in your arms." Her hand splayed over her stomach. "How fares my babe?" she asked worriedly.

"Is there pain?"

She shook her head.

"Then he is still firmly entrenched. I sent to the village for the midwife."

Raven sighed. "I will not lose your child, Drake. I swear it."

Raven's words were so resolute that Drake did not doubt her for a minute.

"Your flesh is no longer chilled. 'Tis off to bed with you now," he said, reaching for one of the blankets warming beside the hearth. "Can you stand?"

"Nay. My feet are numb."

"Put your arms around my neck and hold tight," Drake said. In one smooth motion, Drake lifted her out of the water and wrapped her in the blanket. Then he carried her to the bed and tucked her beneath a fur robe. When he had made her comfortable, he sat at the edge of the bed, staring at her. He did not know how to broach the subject, but he knew he must for his own peace of mind. Not that it would make any difference. Nothing Waldo could do to Raven would soil her in his eyes.

"Sweeting," Drake began, "you need not distress yourself with details, but I want to know everything that Waldo did and said to you. But first you must take some broth. You have not eaten in three days."

He fetched the broth and painstakingly spooned the rich liquid into her mouth. When she signaled that she had eaten her fill, he set the bowl aside and kissed her forehead. "Do you wish to sleep?"

"Nay. I want to tell you . . . everything. 'Tis important you know."

"Only if you feel up to it."

"Waldo is not your half brother."

Stunned, Drake stared at her. "What makes you say that?"

"He told me himself. He believed I would die in the cave, and spoke freely of the evil things he had done."

She told him everything Waldo had related to her. When she revealed that Waldo had killed Daria, Basil, and Aric, a sickness came over Drake. He had always known Waldo was possessed of demons, but he had had no idea how truly evil he was.

"The man was insane," Drake said, stunned by the tale of evil intrigues Raven had just spun. "It all makes sense now. During our youth, Waldo hated me because he knew I was Basil's rightful heir, but when he found out he was not Basil's son, his fury drove him to commit murder in order to keep his embarrassing secret from becoming public knowledge. Thank God the world is rid of him."

"Did you kill him?"

"Nay, though I wish it had been me. Thieves got to him first. He was slain in the forest near Exeter. We brought him back to Windhurst for burial. Balder saw to it. I did not wish to know where he was buried."

A knock on the door announced the midwife, and Drake ushered her inside the chamber. She was young and robust and seemed to know exactly what she was about. She ordered Drake from the chamber so she could examine Raven and closed the door in his face.

Drake was joined by Duff, who questioned him closely about Raven's condition. Only when Duff was assured that Raven would recover did he return to the hall, leaving Drake to pace and worry until the midwife reappeared. "Are my wife and child well?" he asked gruffly.

"Lady Raven still carries the babe. 'Tis a good sign. Your wife is a determined woman. Keep her abed for a fortnight. The rest is in God's hands. Send for me if she feels pain."

Cheered by her words, Drake nodded, anxious to return to Raven. "See my steward. He will pay you for your services."

Drake returned to the bedchamber and perched on the edge of the bed. A sleepy-eyed Raven smiled up at him. "Our child fares well," she said. "Did the midwife tell you?"

"Aye. She said you are a strong woman. But I never doubted that."

Raven's lids fluttered. Drake rose, aware

that she needed sleep more than she needed to talk right now.

"Nay, do not leave me," Raven whispered, reaching for him. "Lie down beside me. I need to know you are here. Talk to me until I go to sleep."

Drake eagerly complied. The bed ropes creaked as he gathered her in his arms. Holding Raven was something he intended to do a lot of in the future. Then he began to speak in low, soothing tones.

"You are the bravest woman I know. We might never have found you in time if you had not left the cave and sawed through your bonds. 'Tis a miracle you were not hurt badly when you fell. Most women would have accepted their fate and awaited death. But not you, my courageous wife. You defied fate. I care not what Waldo did to you. You are back with me where you belong; naught else matters."

"Waldo touched me not except to bind my limbs," Raven murmured, half-asleep.

Though his feelings for Raven would not have changed if Waldo had raped her, he knew instinctively that it would have mattered to Raven, and that he would have felt her pain as keenly as she.

"I love you, wife," he whispered against her ear.

491

"I love you, husband," she murmured drowsily.

A fortnight later Raven negotiated the stairs without Drake's help and entered the hall. She halted abruptly, embarrassed when the folk assembled there rose to their feet and saluted her with their cups. She blushed as she proceeded to the high table, where her husband awaited her.

"You look radiant," he said as he seated her next to him. "Are you sure you are well enough to join us tonight?"

Her hands spanned her stomach. "I am well; my babe rides comfortably within me, and I am bored lying abed all day."

His eyes darkened with desire, and he touched her cheek. "What say you we retire early tonight? I have missed you."

Raven met his gaze; her breasts tautened and her limbs grew languid. "Just as I have missed you, husband."

Drake grinned. "Who would have known that coltish, mischievous child who begged me for a kiss would become my wife?"

"Mayhap Granny Nola knew," Raven teased as she chewed a succulent piece of roasted pork he had placed on her trencher. "I hope your grandmother arrives soon. Are you certain Sir John can convince her to come live with us?"

"Sir John is a persuasive fellow. I am certain he will charm her into accompanying him to Windhurst."

"Think you we can find wives for Sir John and Sir Richard? 'Tis long past time they married."

"Once we settle in at Eyre you can play matchmaker to your heart's content."

"I will miss Windhurst, but I am not sorry to leave." She shuddered. "There are too many bad memories here. Besides, Eyre lands march along with Chirk's and the castles are within a day's ride. I want to become friends with Willa and visit Chirk from time to time."

The meal finally ended. Drake bade everyone good night. Then to Raven's surprise and delight, he scooped her into his arms and carried her up the stairs. The moment the chamber door closed behind them, Drake placed her on the bed and followed her down. Their clothing flew in every direction, driven by love, by need, by eagerness to renew their vows of everlasting love.

With tender care the Black Knight filled her, pressed deeply, rocked against her, completed her . . . claiming her for all eternity, body, soul, and senses.

Epilogue

A knight believes that love conquers all.

Eyre Castle, three years later

Seated in a comfortable chair, Granny Nola dozed before the hearth, tuckered out after helping bring Raven's twins into the world. The midwife had just finished cleaning Raven when Drake stormed into the bedchamber. Three-year-old Dillon trailed behind him. Drake stopped just short of the bed, looking askance at the midwife.

"You may see your wife now, my lord. Try not to tire her, for she has put in a full day's work. Birthing twins is no easy task."

"I will not tire her," Drake promised.

The midwife quietly left the room and closed the door behind her. Drake knelt beside the bed, enveloping Raven's small hand in his. He bent to kiss her forehead. Raven opened her eyes and smiled up at him.

"The babes are small," she said.

494

"Can I see them, Mama?" Dillon asked excitedly. "Do I have brothers or sisters?"

"One of each," Raven said, smiling fondly at her robust son. He was a miniature of Drake, possessing the same admirable qualities that had made her fall in love with his father. "They are resting in the cradle, quite eager to meet their big brother."

"You outdid yourself this time, my love," Drake said. "Two babes, I cannot believe it. Thank you."

"I have the daughter I wanted, and you have another son to follow in your footsteps. Will you name them?"

"Shall we call the girl Leta, for my mother?"

"Aye, and mayhap the boy Nyle, for my father."

"I am anxious to make their acquaintance, but first I wanted to make sure their mother was well."

Drake brushed a kiss across her lips. Raven was asleep before he lifted his head. He stared at her a moment, his heart overflowing with love. Then he strode over to the cradle to inspect his children. Leta, her tiny arms stretched above her head, slept contentedly, while Nyle sucked vigorously upon his fist. Awed by his twin babes,

Drake gazed at the tiny scraps of humanity that were part of both him and Raven and prayed for their survival. They were so very small.

"They are too little for me to play with," Dillon complained, clearly disappointed with his new siblings.

"They will grow, God willing," Drake said, placing a hand on his son's dark head.

"May I go play at swords with Trent in the tilt field?" Dillon asked, already bored with the babes. "I hope Trent stays for a long time. I like playing with him."

Trent was Duff and Lady Willa's sturdy son, several months younger than Dillon. They had come to Eyre to await the birth. Drake hoped the cousins would become close friends, recalling how lonely his own childhood had been.

"Run along," Drake said absently as Dillon skipped away.

He was still gazing rapturously at the newest additions to his family when Granny Nola awakened and joined him.

"They are strong," Granny said, as if reading his mind. "They will survive."

Drake gave her a startled glance. "You know this? Children so often die without reason."

Granny sent him a reassuring smile. "Not these children. I know this. Just as I knew you should ride south to catch Waldo." She patted Drake lovingly on the shoulder and quietly left the chamber.

More than a little in awe of Granny's mysterious power, Drake turned back to the cradle. He observed his sleeping babes a few minutes longer before returning to Raven's bedside. She was sound asleep. He bent and kissed her lips.

"Thank you, my love, for my children. We have suffered adverse times to get where we are today, but we have survived and prospered. I promise that you and our children will always come first in my heart."

About the Author

Connie Mason is the bestselling author of more than 30 historical romances and novellas. Her tales of passion and adventure are set in exotic as well as American locales. Connie was named Storyteller of the Year in 1990 by *Romantic Times*, and was awarded a Career Achievement award in the Western category by *Romantic Times* in 1994. Connie makes her home in Clermont, Florida, with her husband, Jerry.

In addition to writing and traveling, Connie enjoys telling anyone who will listen about her three children and nine grandchildren, and sharing memories of her years living abroad in Europe and Asia as the wife of a career serviceman. In her spare time, Connie enjoys reading, dancing, playing bridge, and freshwater fishing with her husband.

LOUISVILLE PUBLIC LIBRARY
Louisville, OH 44641

Fine on overdue books will be charged at the
rate of five or ten cents per day. A borrower must
pay for damage to a book and for replacing a
lost book.

DEMCO